"You call yoursel————————————is voice was hoarse. A cool glass touched his lips, and he took a sip of water. The pressure of her palm on his chest felt like an anchor, binding him to reality and the world. "I think you're an angel."

She laughed. "You have so got the wrong girl, Duncan Sharp."

Her eyes were so dark they drew him in and covered him as softly and surely as the sheet she adjusted. "I don't think I'm that far off the mark. Angel."

"Stop that," she told him, then let her fingers trail across his forehead. A rich, relaxing energy swept across his body, and once more he drifted away.

The next time he woke, she was gently bathing his face, his forehead, now his cheeks and chin and mouth. The connection between them was a real thing, a bright thing, and he wondered if he could touch it if he tried.

"Rest," she said, and her voice made him want to hear more. His body reacted to her nearness, getting warmer and warmer until he had to sit up and find a way to touch *her*.

"Rest," she said again as he yanked against the cuffs on his wrists.

Her fingertips tingled along his jaw, and that wave of relaxing peace claimed him again.

Angel, his mind whispered.

That had to be what she was.

Or maybe, just maybe, she was a witch.

ALSO BY ANNA WINDSOR

Bound by Shadow
Bound by Flame
Bound by Light

CAPTIVE SPIRIT

A NOVEL OF THE
DARK CRESCENT SISTERHOOD

ANNA
WINDSOR

BALLANTINE BOOKS • NEW YORK

A Ballantine Books Mass Market Original

Copyright © 2010 by Anna Windsor
Excerpt from *Captive Soul* copyright © 2010 by Anna Windsor

Published in the United States by Ballantine Books, an imprint of The Random House Publishing Group, a division of Random House, Inc., New York.

BALLANTINE and colophon are trademarks of Random House, Inc.

This book contains an excerpt from the forthcoming book *Captive Soul* by Anna Windsor. This excerpt has been set for this edition only and may not reflect the final content of the forthcoming edition.

ISBN 978-0-345-51389-2

Printed in the United States of America

www.ballantinebooks.com

9 8 7 6 5 4 3 2 1

For my new friends at WSH—
I'm really not working there just to research a book!

Not till we are lost, in other words not till we have lost the world, do we begin to find ourselves.
—HENRY DAVID THOREAU

❨ prologue ❩

August, two years after the fall of the Legion

Bela Argos stood in her battle leathers on an ancient marble platform in the thick woods surrounding Motherhouse Russia, because she'd been summoned.

She stood in silence, watching her own breath curl outward in frosty plumes, chilled even in the milder spring weather, because she'd been trained.

She stood with her shoulders back, her chin out, her head high, because she had no choice.

She was a warrior of the Dark Crescent Sisterhood, a Sibyl sworn to protect the weak from the supernaturally strong, and she bore the mark of mortar, pestle, and broom in a triangle on her right forearm to prove it. If she'd rather tear out her own hair than be in this ceremonial clearing, on display with forty-two other earth Sibyls who shared her particular strain of pain and humiliation . . . well, that was just too fucking bad, wasn't it?

The huge clearing, easily the size of the fighting grounds in an old Roman stadium, had been picked clean of leaves and limbs, and even the tiny stones left behind by melting snow and ice. The big stone pillar at the center, the one with all the names carved into its endless gray reaches, had been polished until it gleamed in the morning sunlight.

On Bela's far left stood fire Sibyls and green-robed Mothers from Motherhouse Ireland, letting off steady streams of smoke. The area in the center had been packed with earth Sibyls and Mothers in brown robes from Bela's own Motherhouse. The big space on her right had been filled with exactly one water Sibyl from Motherhouse Kérkira in the Ionian Sea—a lone woman named Andy Myles, dressed in an obnoxious canary yellow robe—surrounded by the soft blue robes of air Sibyl Mothers from Motherhouse Greece. These Mothers and the Sibyls they'd brought with them gave off a steady flow of warm, gentle wind Bela assumed was meant to be comforting.

Bela wished they'd stop with the hot air. She'd rather just hurt from the cold right now, because that felt honest and right. Her dark hair whipped in the breeze, stinging her eyes until the tears didn't flow just because her heart kept trying to chew itself to pieces.

Mother Yana, the oldest of the Russian Mothers, made her way forward below the platform, walking with the aid of a gnarled wooden staff. She took a position near the gray stone pillar and raised her staff for silence, even though no one was talking.

"Ve fought the Legion cult for more than a century," she announced in her ancient but powerful voice. "Two years ago, in a battle that stretched from New York City to the slopes of Mount Olympus itself, by the grace of the Dark Goddess, ve defeated that evil forever. Ve lost many warriors. Today, ve honor the dead of Motherhouse Greece and Motherhouse Ireland, as in their years to hold remembrance they honor the dead of Motherhouse Russia."

Bela closed her eyes.

She didn't want to hear the rest of the speech, not any of it—because some of the dead had been hers.

Sibyls always worked in triads. Earth Sibyls functioned as mortars, responsible for choosing their fighting group, protecting it, and holding it together. Fire Sibyls, the pestles, handled communications, and air Sibyls, the brooms, fought at a distance, kept perspective, and cleaned up all the messes. In the old days, water Sibyls had handled emotional flow and concentrated on healing—but seeing as there was only one fully trained water elemental in the world right now, they weren't currently a part of fighting groups, and they hadn't been a part of the war with the Legion until its very end. Though Andy Myles had faced a devastating personal loss during the fighting, Motherhouse Russia, Motherhouse Ireland, and Motherhouse Greece had accounted for all the Sibyl deaths.

And Bela had suffered two of them.

The earth Sibyls with her on the marble platform had lost one or both of their triad sisters, too. Bela knew the Mothers intended to honor their pain by setting them apart from all the other Sibyls like this, but it sucked. It was horrible, and on most of the faces around her Bela saw the same shame she felt on her own. Motherhouse Greece and Motherhouse Ireland did the same thing for their Sibyls who had known losses in battle, when it was their turn to host the yearly remembrance of the dead—but that was different. Fire Sibyls and air Sibyls weren't responsible for their fighting groups. They weren't mortars.

Mortars who had cracked and let the life's blood of their triad run out on the ground.

Mother Yana moved around the gray stone pillar, traveling past centuries of wars and battles and losses, until she came to the area dedicated to the war with the Legion. She focused her rheumy eyes on a spot halfway between top and bottom and started reading names.

Bela's back got so tight she thought the bone would snap. It wouldn't take long to get to the first one she dreaded—and here it came.

"Devin Allard, Motherhouse Greece."

Bela's hands shook, because she could still feel Devin's cold, still body in her arms. Devin had been killed by a demon in a battle at Fordham University. Bela hadn't been able to do anything to save her, but she'd tried. She'd tried so hard.

A few of the earth Sibyls beside Bela and behind her started to cry as their most dreaded names reeled past in the litany. Sometimes Bela saw the others flinch or twitch—just as she did when her second name got read.

"Nori Kelly, Motherhouse Ireland."

Nori had been murdered a few months before Devin died, snatched away from Bela's triad in the middle of patrol, broken like a doll, and left like trash in a dumpster by demons following the commands of a Legion-sponsored psychopath.

I never got to hold her and say goodbye. There wasn't enough left.

The name reading and the memorial prayer to the Dark Goddess seemed to last a century, and when the nightmare finally ended, it seemed to take another century to get everyone off the marble platform. Bela almost shoved the two women in front of her to make them hurry. She wanted off the platform and out of the clearing. She wanted to be back in her dark, quiet room deep in underground chambers beneath Motherhouse Russia. If she had her way, she'd stay there forever.

When she finally got to the bottom of the platform steps, somebody caught her by the elbow.

Bela turned around too fast, ready to curse the ass who had touched her—but she stopped in mid-snarl.

Riana Dumain Lowell, the mortar of the North Manhattan Triad, kept a tight hold on her arm.

Riana had her dark hair pulled back away from the shoulders of her battle leathers. Her dark eyes bored into Bela, hard but sympathetic—loving, but a little pissed off. During the war, Riana had been Bela's good friend, and sometimes one of her better enemies. "Where are you going?" she asked, her calm voice sounding overcontrolled, even for her.

Bela glanced toward the spires of Motherhouse Russia, visible above the distant trees. "Home."

Riana laughed, and from somewhere in the woods, the wolves that made themselves companions to the Mothers started to howl. "Motherhouse Russia was never your home. You belong in New York City. Come back with us."

Us . . .

Riana's gesture took in redheaded, fire-breathing Cynda Flynn Lowell and blond, gentle Merilee Alexander Lowell, her fire Sibyl and her air Sibyl. The three women had married brothers and shared the same last name now. They were all together, all happy, and all alive.

Screw every one of you.

"I'm not going back to New York." Bela pulled herself free from Riana, trying not to choke on the hot rush of envy and anger blasting up from her toes. "I've got nothing there."

Riana shook her head and let Bela get about one step away before she said, "Over the years, I've thought a lot of things about you, Bela Argos, but I never took you for a pussy crybaby."

Bela swung around, the ground shaking underneath her feet. She got in Riana's face then, so close she could almost taste the mint from Riana's last piece of chewing gum. "Please, give me an excuse to kick your ass. I'd probably feel better if I got to kill something."

Riana didn't give an inch. Instead, she held up a silver key on a string. "I'm not giving you an excuse, but I am giving you this. It's the key to my brownstone. Sixty-fourth and Fifth, on Central Park. You remember the spot, right?"

What the hell?

Bela blinked and eased back a fraction.

Riana couldn't be serious. The brownstone? That was one of the best properties in Manhattan, in Bela's opinion.

"Take it." Riana dropped the key.

Bela caught it on reflex. Her mouth opened to ask why, but the cold metal of the key captured all of her attention.

"My triad moved into our husbands' townhouse." Riana sounded sad now, but also relieved. "We just couldn't stay in the brownstone anymore. The bad memories wouldn't go away."

Bela stared at the key. During the last battle with the Legion, Riana and Cynda, both nine months pregnant, had been kidnapped and locked in the basement of the brownstone. They'd had to give birth down there, alone and terrified, and they and their babies—now healthy, adorable kids, as far as Bela had been hearing—had almost died before Merilee rescued them.

It made sense to Bela that they wouldn't want to keep living in the brownstone, just as she didn't want to keep living in New York City.

Riana's sigh sounded like an air Sibyl's whispered wind. "It's a really good house, Bela. Don't let it go to waste."

"But I'm not ready." Bela looked up and tried to hold the key out to Riana, but Riana was already walking away, back toward her very alive triad, then out of the clearing and into the woods, leaving Bela alone with the key, the cold, and the distant howl of Motherhouse Russia's wolves.

"I'm not ready," she said again, but the clearing was almost empty now, except for the marble platform and the gray stone pillar, with its endless observance of the dead and the gone and the not coming back again.

Okay, okay, said the voices of two of those dead, Nori and Devin, echoing quietly in the back of Bela's mind, as they had since the day they died. *But you gotta admit she's right, as usual. It* is *a really good house.*

(1)

July, three years after the fall of the Legion

Fire.

Bela coughed against the sulfurous wind in her face before she even broke free of the transportation channel.

I have to be crazy, coming here *first.*

The saner part of her mind urged her to turn around and run right back to the earthy, orderly comfort of Motherhouse Russia, but she'd be damned if she'd let a bunch of fire-spitting Irish bitches send her home with her tail between her legs.

Bela lunged through the final barrier of elemental power separating her from her destination. She barely managed to keep her balance as she stumbled out of the ancient channel of energy onto the large, round platform in the communications chamber deep within Motherhouse Ireland. Her right hand gripped the hilt of her sword before she could see or hear or get her bearings. Her battle leathers felt a size too tight as they reacted to the heat in the big stone chamber, and her heart thumped like ritual drums during a Solstice celebration. She jerked in a ragged breath as her chest expanded in opposition to the crushing pressure of moving through space and time so quickly. The ancient channels of transportation and communication that crisscrossed the earth were effective—but a real bitch for people without lungs the size of Rhode Island.

As Bela's vision cleared, she caught a last glimpse of the place she had just departed—Motherhouse Russia.

Home.

Or a great place to hide.

Screw it.

The familiar images of brown-robed Russian adepts lingered in the projective mirror, the special piece of elementally treated glass sealing the channel from which Bela had just emerged, but faded as the glass once more grew solid. Smoke swirled through the surface, gradually obscuring everything Bela associated with peace and safety.

She was all alone now.

Bela's jaw clenched as fire billowed around her.

In hell.

The hot blast of energy singed her from all sides, flowing down from the huge castle above her. It took all of her elemental earth talents to keep the scalding power from sizzling her into ash and tooth enamel.

Did *everything* with fire Sibyls have to be so confrontational?

If she had more status in her Motherhouse, if she had managed to make herself somebody's favorite, one of the Russian Mothers might have stood with her this night and lent her support as she took this step toward reclaiming a useful life. But Bela had never been the endearing type. She was nobody's favorite, and being alone, well, that was just fine and normal, wasn't it?

Refusing to choke on the smoke and stench of singed hair—her own—Bela wiped sweat off her forehead with her palm and faced the frowning fire adept who had managed the transport. The redhead's arms were still raised and smoking, and her feet moved in the dance necessary to close the ancient channels that allowed Bela's instant travel from Russia to Ireland. Four more green-robed adepts stood in the chamber around the platform, finishing the chant. Tiny jets of fire blasted from their fingers, feeding the gray-white cloud that hung over the high-ceilinged space.

"It's late," growled a sixth woman, this one standing

toward the back of the stone room. She wore green robes, too, but her hood had been shoved back to reveal her frail features and the ropes of gray hair lying across both shoulders. Her face was a collection of wrinkles, but her green eyes burned with a timeless, ferocious light. Her gnarled hands looked deadly, never mind the Irish hand-and-a-half sword belted at her waist, or the tip of the gigantic Chinese great sword visible above one shoulder.

Shit.

None of the Russian Mothers will give me the time of day, but this *bitch shows up to welcome me to Ireland?*

Bela didn't bother to fake a smile. She had grown up hard on the streets of New York City despite the weekday respite of training at her Motherhouse, but she had never bothered with learning to con or hustle. Her fists usually persuaded people to see things her way.

Forcing herself not to draw her weapon on women who were supposed to be her fellow warriors, Bela stepped to the side of the adept who had brought her through the channels. To the small figure in the back of the room, she gave a half bow from the waist. "Mother Keara. Thanks for showing up to say hello."

The old woman snorted, and a halo of sparks burst over her gray head. "I'm not makin' a social call. What the livin' hell do you think you're doin', coming here this time of night?"

Bela climbed down from the big round platform and pushed her way through the glaring, smoking adepts. Willpower alone kept her expression flat and her eyes calm despite the roar of blood through her veins. There were few times in life that an earth Sibyl could show weakness, and showing up unannounced, unaccompanied, and uninvited to choose a fire Sibyl for her fighting group was definitely not one of them.

"I don't owe you an explanation for my timing." Bela came to a stop in front of Mother Keara, doing her best to keep fear and irritation out of her tone as she gazed down at the tiny icon of fire power. "I can choose my fighting partners when the energy feels right to me."

The old woman's green eyes narrowed until Bela was certain Mother Keara couldn't see anything but the zipper on Bela's leather bodysuit.

"Yer last triad fared poorly." Mother Keara let fire flash along her skin to punctuate her statement. "What makes you think I'll waste another fire adept on yer questionable skills?"

Pain hotter than any flame lanced Bela's very soul. She swayed on her feet but somehow managed not to close her eyes or let loose with a heart-deep scream.

Unfair words. Bald and awful. But true. Even after three years, the loss still cut so brutally Bela thought she'd die from the sharpness. A Sibyl without her triad was orphaned by the universe itself, severed from the spirit of life and fighting and battle. Months spent in meditation and retraining at Motherhouse Russia melted into nothing, and all Bela could think about was the first time she'd come here searching for a good fighting match.

Nori's smile had been so bright, and her fiery power had surged through Bela, joining Bela's earth energy so completely. Bela ached at the memory as if she were bleeding to death inside—and she almost wished she could will herself to do just that, here, now, to atone for whatever shortcomings had led to the deaths of her original triad sisters.

What kind of mortar loses her pestle and broom?

And what kind of monster uses that pain to gain advantage in an argument?

Bela glared at Mother Keara, who glared right back.

Even though Bela had expected a challenge, her rehearsed defenses caught like dry bread in her throat.

I fought for Nori and Devin. . . .

I'll tear off my own arms before I lose another triad sister. . . .

Lame.

Completely inadequate.

Mother Keara was honest. Merciless, but telling the truth. How could Bela argue with that? But Mother or no, mean was mean, and Bela wasn't about to be out-nastied by some sawed-off flamethrower. She squeezed both hands into fists. "A lot of triads lost Sibyls when we kicked the Legion's ass. You suffer through those damned remembrances just like I do—so why are you being such a bitch?"

Fire crackled in the air over Mother Keara's head and singed Bela's cheeks, but Bela didn't move an inch. So much for her eyebrows. Who needed eyebrows anyway? They'd grow back fast enough.

Without breaking eye contact with Bela, Mother Keara gestured to the adepts in the stone chamber. The younger women immediately broke ranks and filed out of the arched wooden doorway, trailing smoke behind them as they returned to the upper reaches of the castle.

The door once more swung shut, and an unusual chill grabbed the quiet space.

Mother Keara's smoke faded to a light fog. She faced Bela with a calculation and coolness Bela never expected from any fire Sibyl, even a Mother. "Yer air Sibyl, Devin, went down in battle. For that, I won't be faultin' you. But Nori was murdered. You let her down."

The ground beneath Bela's feet trembled as a burst of her own dangerous elemental energy escaped. She couldn't hold back the quake of earth power and she didn't want to, even if she tore open a canyon beneath Motherhouse Ireland and the whole damned castle crashed all the way to the planet's molten core.

Feeling like she could breathe fire herself, Bela leaned down until her face was only inches from Mother Keara's wrinkled cheeks and angry green eyes. "You think I don't live with Nori's death every second of my life, old woman?

You think I don't miss Devin, too—that I don't know my triad is dead because of me?"

Mother Keara's lips pulled back in a snarl, and Bela matched it. She met Mother Keara's explosion of fire energy with a crushing wave of earth energy. Growling like the Russian gray wolves that roamed the halls and forests of Motherhouse Russia, they locked in combat, earth to fire, fire to earth, energy broiling between them, shaking the air itself.

Bela's fingers twitched above her sword hilt. She wanted to draw the serrated blade and beat the stone wall over Mother Keara's head until sparks flew, until the stones broke open and turned to dust.

I'm an earth Sibyl.

All the months in silence, trying to relearn control despite the pain and grief and loss—did that effort matter?

Damnit!

She couldn't turn loose her temper—it was wrong. Dangerous. But that's exactly what she was doing. If Mother Keara's energy hadn't been battling Bela's earth power, Bela really would be tearing a hole the size of New York in the ground beneath them.

"You're weak." Mother Keara's eyes gleamed like green fire as her words knifed through the radiating elemental energy. "Draw yer sword. Give me the pleasure of riddin' the world of an unworthy Sibyl."

Bela kept a wall of earth power plastered against the orange sheet of flames spilling off Mother Keara. Her hand moved outside her own bidding, ripping her serrated blade free of its leather guard and raising the blade so close to Mother Keara's nose she might have drawn blood.

Control.

What was that?

Who cared anyway?

Motherhouse Ireland started to shake with the earth beneath it.

Three years of trying to move on from her losses, and not a day of it mattered. She'd never get over them. Mother Keara was right. To hell with this. She had no chance of beating a Mother in a sword fight—especially not *this* Mother—but Bela really, really didn't give a shit.

"For Nori, then," Bela said through her teeth, hearing her Bronx accent surge over the neutral inflection her mother had taught her. "She never liked your scrawny ass anyway."

Mother Keara stepped back, drew her hand-and-a-half sword in a fluid movement so fast Bela wondered if she imagined it—and the old woman started to laugh.

At the same second, a blazing wall of heat slammed into Bela, singed off a half inch of her hair, and smashed her against the chamber's rock wall. Her sword went clattering across the stone floor. Pain exploded through her shoulders and back. She tried to swear but only wheezed as the blow bashed all the air out of her lungs. The communications chamber faded from view, and bright lights flashed in the corners of her eyes.

She couldn't hear a thing but laughter.

She couldn't do a thing but wait for Mother Keara's sword to take her head or the old woman's fire to burn her into nothingness.

A moment of agony, and all the hurting would be over.

Heat bore down on her. Her leathers had to be melting. Any second her skin would dissolve.

"You want to kill me." Mother Keara's words slid into Bela's ear as if she were standing over her, bending down, whispering into her very consciousness. The tip of a sword pressed into Bela's chest through a hole in her jumpsuit, hot metal branding the skin between her ribs. "But you didn't even shield against my fire, because you'd rather die than live another minute without yer triad."

"Yes!" Tears streamed down Bela's cheeks. She struck

out blindly with her fist, hitting nothing but air. "So kill me, you hateful old bitch!"

The heat torturing her entire body evaporated like steam on a griddle. Gone. Along with the fiery kiss of metal on her flesh. Cold air rushed over Bela, jarring her back to full awareness.

In the next instant, Mother Keara had sheathed her sword, grabbed the front of Bela's leather bodysuit—which was intact despite a few smoldering holes—and lifted her to her feet like she weighed nothing at all.

"You underestimate yer own heart, child." Mother Keara's green eyes remained bright, but now Bela saw nothing but kindness and approval in the stern gaze. "Did yer own Mothers never teach you how strong you are?"

When Bela just stood there mute and trembling from the force of her remnant fury and despair, Mother Keara sighed. "They get distracted. As do we all, I suppose. You weren't Motherhouse-born, were you?"

Bela shook her head. "My mother was Russian, born and raised in the Motherhouse, but my father was from New York City. We were living in the Bronx when my talent manifested."

"So you boarded during the week, yes?"

Bela nodded. "Then I worked with my triad in the Bronx until—"

Until I lost everything.

Mother Keara seemed to ignore the catch in Bela's voice. "We have our share of boarders." The old woman glanced upward toward the castle. "They don't get as much attention as those born to our care or given over to us completely."

Bela chose not to comment. That was an old anger and, relatively speaking, a small one in her life now.

Her silence drew a second sigh from Mother Keara. "I miss Nori, too. I miss all the fire Sibyls who lost their lives fightin' those Legion bastards." The old woman seemed to grow smaller as she spoke, and Bela actually had an urge to piss her off just to ease her obvious pain. "Our numbers are still low, but we have a few adepts ready for consideration. I'll arrange for quarters and provisions. You can begin attendin' battle trainin' tomorrow and—"

"No, thanks." The words burst out of Bela's mouth before she had a chance to consider them.

Damn, damn, damn!

Was she out of her stupid mind?

She had known this would be the hardest part of what she came here to do, and she had just blurted it out instead of working her way up to it.

A thin column of smoke rose from Mother Keara's shoulders. The chamber heated up again as the old woman once more grew wary—and looked freshly angry. "You're not plannin' to live with us until you determine which girl makes the best match with yer energies?"

Bela swallowed despite her dry throat. When she trusted herself not to sound like an idiot, she said, "I know which fire Sibyl I want."

This time it was Mother Keara who remained silent.

Even though Bela's earth energy had gone still as she calmed down, an earthquake rattled in her belly.

Knock it off. Bela realized the voice in her head sounded like a blend of her dead fighting sisters. *You've seen more battles than some of the Mothers.*

Mother Keara was staring at her like she might be judging the temperature necessary to roast her for breakfast.

Suck it up! screamed the ghost voices of Nori and Devin.

"I claim the only fire Sibyl here who knows as much pain as I do," Bela shouted, just to be louder than her hallucinations. "I claim Camille Fitzgerald."

Thicker smoke rolled off Mother Keara, a startled wave of it, and Bela knew she had shocked the old woman. It took Mother Keara a full minute to recover enough to growl, "No. She's not stable. And she's not reliable in battle."

"I don't care." Bela's anger came flowing back, and the ground shook for a few seconds until she got herself under enough control to add, "Camille lost her triad just like I did, to murder and in battle. We'll have grief as a starting point, and we can help each other heal."

Mother Keara kept up her intense scrutiny, but she obviously hadn't considered that reality until Bela brought it up.

Point for me. Bela was still shaking, but she almost gave a victory shout—way too prematurely.

After a time, Mother Keara said, "Camille's been locked away here since she lost her triad. No visitors, no datin', no socializin'—just trainin', and too much work inside her own head." Her tone grew more reflective. "Much as you were doin' at Motherhouse Russia . . . but Camille might refuse you."

Bela folded her arms. "She's a Sibyl. Some part of her heart wants to fight, just like mine. Stop dicking with me and let me talk to her. If she says no, I'll back off—for a little while."

Another few seconds of silence passed between them, during which Mother Keara's fire energy built, and built, and built. Her stare burned into Bela, and Bela could almost taste flames and soot.

Could death by fire be slow and torturous?

Probably.

Would a Mother really bake a fully trained Sibyl on the spot, just for being a disrespectful asshole?

Possibly.

Bela kept her arms folded and her eyes narrowed. No way was she backing down.

You're nuts, whispered the ghosts in her head.

Without warning, Mother Keara's fire energy ebbed. "You have a problem with rules. I can see that. If you never do what you're told, if you never take the calm, easy roads through the world, it's no wonder those old hens in Russia don't give you the time of day." She let out a breath laced with smoke and sparks. "I suppose next you'll be going to Greece and asking Dionysia Allard to be yer air Sibyl. She'd as soon blow you to Athens as look at you, since you let her sister die."

Bela didn't flinch, at least not on the outside. "You think I'm scared of a little wind? Damn straight I'm going after Dio, because I owe Devin that much. It's the only amends I'll ever be able to make, if I can convince Dio to fight—and I'm not stopping there." She held out her right forearm and jabbed a finger at the subtle, wavy lines connecting the tattoos of mortar, pestle, and broom—the lines that signified the recent reemergence of the fourth and perhaps most dangerous type of Sibyl, those who controlled the powerful element of water. "I'm going to Kérkira to get Andy Myles. We'll be the first fighting quad in twelve centuries."

The expression on Mother Keara's face shifted from intrigue to ridicule to stunned vacancy. Bela expected the old woman to argue, but she stayed quiet instead.

That was probably bad.

The silence got longer and wider. It lasted so long that Bela wanted to sing or scream or throw a punch—anything to smash the motionless, heavy quiet.

At last, Mother Keara averted her eyes and seemed to be studying a point on the wall over Bela's left shoulder.

"You are strong, child," the old woman said, as if to affirm her previous judgment. "That I won't be denyin', to you or to myself." She brought her green eyes back to Bela's, and her voice dropped to a rough whisper. "But now I'm speakin' a darker truth. You are also insane."

(2)

Duncan Sharp gripped his Glock and edged toward a darkened brick corner of the Tobacco Warehouse in DUMBO—Down Under the Manhattan Bridge Overpass. Over his head, vehicles whizzed across the old suspension bridge connecting lower Manhattan with Brooklyn. The bass rumble of suspended subway cars blocked the rush of blood in his ears. The smoke-gray twilight weighed against his shoulders and face, cool and heavy at the same time. The East River slapped at its banks, but from Duncan's vantage point at the edge of the shell of the warehouse, his world went dead quiet.

His focus narrowed to the few yards of shore and concrete and brick making up this edge of Empire–Fulton Ferry State Park.

I'm coming for you, John.

Duncan's back scraped against rough, aged brick as he inched toward the building's edge. Three intact walls. One concrete floor.

No place to hide, John.

Duncan had tossed his jacket near Central Park. His overshirt had been pitched on one of the Manhattan Bridge's pedestrian walkways. His badge hung around his neck, resting against his sweat-soaked T-shirt. His jeans were just as wet, and his heart was still punching his ribs. It had been one hell of a chase, on foot, across parts of two boroughs, but it would end here, now.

Taking down a buddy was the worst thing any cop ever

faced, but Duncan Sharp had been a homicide detective for four years, a street cop before that, and a soldier for the eight years prior to hiring on with the NYPD. He could do this. He *would* do this. No request for backup. No courtesy call to the Eighty-fourth Precinct or the park police. If John Cole died tonight, it would be Duncan's bullet that killed him.

It was the least he could do for the son of a bitch who had been his best friend since he was seven years old.

For one long gut-kicking moment, Duncan remembered being a grubby scrub-kneed kid in rural Georgia, playing hide-and-seek with John Cole in his grandfather's endless cornfields. Fun. Innocence. Freedom.

All gone now, wasn't it?

Here in New York City, the time for games was long gone. Five women had been murdered, a bloody trail almost six years in the making. Duncan had found John Cole's latest squeeze, the heiress Katrina Alsace Drake, in pieces in her penthouse apartment. And he had found Cole beating it out the window and down the fire escape holding on to some weird, curved dagger. No way Duncan could risk a shot into the crowded streets, so he had kept visual contact and humped it across miles of city streets—and the bridge.

To the psychotic bastard he had last spoken to on the slopes of the Hindu Kush near Kabul, Duncan said, "Can't hide, sinner."

It was a line from an old gospel song, from the music that formed the soundtrack of their childhood, before the Army at eighteen years old, and the war, and everything that had gone so unbelievably wrong in Afghanistan.

"I'm not being chased, Duncan." Cole's desperate voice echoed through the warehouse shell. The sound of it made Duncan's insides tighten. "I haven't been running from you. Damn it, don't you get it? I'm doing the chasing—of the creatures who slaughtered Katrina. Get out of here before they use you against me."

"Bullshit." Duncan reached the corner and tensed for action. "Hit the concrete, hands over your head."

Cole spoke again, closer now, maybe on the other side of the bricks from Duncan. "I can give you contacts at the Pentagon. They'll explain. Water slows them down, but not for long. Get out of here."

Duncan swore to himself and tightened his grip on the Glock.

Fuck. He didn't want to do this.

"Don't make me shoot you, John."

Please.

Duncan pivoted and swept around the corner of the building weapon first, moving from grass to the warehouse's concrete floor—and came face-to-face with John Cole.

Cole eyed Duncan, then the gun.

He got down on one knee, arms over his head. "Christ, Duncan. You never stop, do you?"

Cole still had hold of that curved dagger. Duncan thought it might be Roman. It looked old as hell, but lights from the Manhattan skyline played off the polished blade.

No blood.

Must have wiped it off while he was running.

"They smell you by now." Cole sounded defeated. "They'll be here in seconds. One of us won't make it out of here."

Duncan ignored the delusional crap. Cole was still as buff as he had been in their Army days, but minus the black suit and white collar. The former priest was wearing torn fatigues.

No bloodstains that I can make out . . .

A chain with what looked like an ancient Afghan dinar hung around Cole's corded neck. He had long black hair now, loose at his shoulders. Duncan couldn't see the man's laughing green eyes in the growing darkness, eyes that had broken the hearts of dozens of nurses and officers and barmaids from Fort Benning to Bagram, but he was willing to bet they had a lunatic gleam.

"Drop the knife and get on the ground." Duncan kept the Glock trained on Cole's head.

Cole didn't move. "If you run now, I can hold them off. You have no idea what's happening here."

Duncan had a little bit of a clue. If he wasn't way lucky, Cole's "friends" at the federal level would interfere after the arrest, like they had been interfering in the investigations all summer. Sealing Cole's records, refusing to provide information on his whereabouts, stopping just short of ordering the NYPD to quit trying to track and apprehend a dangerous serial killer.

Whatever Cole had gotten into that last day in the mountains of Afghanistan, it was major. And apparently the government would just as soon no one knew about it—or about John Cole—at all.

But Cole was a murderer, and he had to be stopped.

"Drop the weapon," Duncan growled, this time through his teeth. "Now."

A sound like foot-long nails scraping down a chalkboard echoed through the three-sided warehouse ruins.

Duncan felt the grating noise in his bones. His nostrils flared. His skin prickled.

What in the living . . . ?

Claws on brick?

Claws . . . ripping into brick?

Was that even possible?

Every aspect of his consciousness tried to tear away from Cole and look to his right, toward the East River, but he didn't dare take his eyes off the suspect he had chased through half of Manhattan.

Cole kept his hands and that knife over his head, but

faster than a blink, he was on his feet and facing away from Duncan, staring toward the riverside warehouse wall.

The air was getting colder. Duncan's breath fogged in front of his face—in August, for God's sake. A nasty smell, something like ammonia and dung, made him cough.

The spine-curling rake of claws on brick came again.

This was weird shit.

Duncan didn't do weird shit. He didn't believe in weird shit, he didn't accept weird shit—this needed to stop. Whatever was clawing the brick, he'd shoot it along with John Cole if he had to.

A feral howl, utterly out of place in New York City, drove Duncan to wheel toward the wall.

His skin was *crawling* now.

"What the hell was that?" Duncan asked Cole, more reflex than anything else.

"Last chance, Duncan." The former priest gazed into the darkness, bringing his dagger down to the ready position. All of the worry and anxiety had left him. What remained, Duncan knew, was the raw, toneless voice of a soldier about to die in a firefight.

"*Run!*" Cole shouted. Then he leaped between Duncan and the far side of the warehouse.

Brick shattered as the riverside wall exploded inward.

Cole's body shielded Duncan from the worst of it, but Duncan turned his head and took a load of rock shrapnel in the temple. Too-bright light flared through his vision, and his head hurt like a bastard—then stopped.

Not good.

Am I dead?

But he was still standing, and his dulled eyesight took in Cole, who hit the ground hard, not five feet from him. Flecks of stone stung Duncan's forehead, and a cloud of dust rained across the whole space.

Blood and sweat blurred Duncan's vision even worse, but

he steadied himself, turned back to the wall in a shooting stance—and wondered if the blast had knocked him out.

Because he had to be hallucinating.

Cole was prone on the debris-strewn concrete, his knife a few feet away from him. The skyline of Manhattan still rose in the background, split by the big suspension bridge. The world looked completely normal—except for the three human-sized cats slowly creeping toward him from the ruined wall.

Giant tigers, a white one, a black one, and a golden one. Except they're walking like men.

His heart just . . . stopped thumping. The blood thundering in his ears went silent, and his whole body turned polar cold.

The things coming toward him—how far? Thirty yards? Twenty?

They had as much skin as fur, human-like faces, wicked claws, and fangs. Their striped fur glowed in the rising light of the moon, and the stench of ammonia made Duncan's eyes water.

From the concrete, a bloodied, groaning Cole was getting up, grabbing for his knife, urging Duncan over and over again to run.

"Get out . . . not here for you . . . Duncan, go . . ."

The words didn't compute at all. Nothing in Duncan's mind was working very well, but he sighted the creatures and squeezed off nine rounds. Triple-tap for each beast, chest level, right in the hearts.

The tiger-things flinched but kept coming. Fifteen yards. Fourteen. Thirteen.

Holy God.

Duncan fired again and again, barely processing the sound of his own gunfire. A raking, maddening tickle started in his brain, like something was rifling through his thoughts and memories. Images flashed from his childhood, from his life as a cop, from his military service. No order. No logic. He shook his head, still holding his Glock even though some part of him knew the magazine was empty.

I'm unconscious.

This isn't happening.

Tiger-men who reacted to bullets like they were spit-wads—that shit didn't exist in his universe.

Nothing happened, except that the black tiger-thing closest to Duncan . . . changed.

Took on a more human form. The light from its fur—no, skin now—let Duncan see the man's black hair and black eyes. His high cheekbones and darker complexion. For a few seconds, the thing actually looked familiar.

Then it looked too familiar.

Cropped brown hair. Fashion-plate suit. Big smile. The thing had turned into Calvin, one of the Brent brothers, one of the few men Duncan called friends in his adult life. But Cal Brent was a desk jockey now. His brother Saul was in narcotics—and now the tiger-thing shifted into Saul, long hair, earring, T-shirt, torn jeans, and all.

Right in front of him. Raising his tattooed hand . . . only the hand had tiger claws.

The Saul-thing swung its fist, claws out.

The blow staggered Duncan and sliced the flesh on his left side, neck to chest. He heard Cole swearing. There was a scuffle, and the tiger-man backed off. Duncan felt somebody grabbing him, pulling him upright. Duncan's mind swam laps around his skull, but he couldn't make sense out of any of this. The cut on his left side burned like somebody had a torch to his neck and shoulder.

A bloodied, dirty hand jerked at his arm, and Duncan swung the muzzle of his useless weapon into John Cole's face.

The green eyes of his first—and for so long, his only—friend pierced Duncan's brain fog. He lowered his weapon.

John's eyes were dull with grief and narrow with fear. "I

can't let you die," he said as he gazed at the cuts on Duncan's left side. "Not you. Anybody but you. *Fuck*, Duncan! Why couldn't you listen, just once in your life?"

Time was moving funny, and the world seemed sideways and unreal to Duncan now. He was hearing John on two levels, as a grown man and a fugitive, and as the little boy he had known way, way too long ago. Was John seeing Duncan as a cop now, or a kid in a cornfield?

"I'm sorry, but you'll have to find some way to heal yourself and keep this fight going." John's tone turned grim as he pressed the hilt of that Roman knife into Duncan's free hand. "Use this if you have to cut them to get out of here."

"John—" Duncan started, but Cole kept talking.

"And keep this around your neck at all times—*forever*, you understand? Get in touch with Jack Blackmore through the Pentagon. He'll tell you what you need to know." John pulled the chain and coin over his head, thrust it out, and dropped it over Duncan's head. As Duncan felt the coin bounce against his chest and dangling badge, John gave him a huge, sudden shove.

Caught off guard, Duncan sailed backward.

His Glock clattered against the concrete as he crashed shoulder-first onto the rough warehouse floor. Bone cracked. Fresh bolts of pain stole his awareness, and his breath left in a rush. It was all he could do to kick his legs enough to get to a sitting position and reorient himself. The knife was still clutched in his good hand. That had to be worth something.

The tiger-things ringed John, and none of them looked like Cal or Saul Brent anymore. They looked like cover models for a bodybuilding magazine, if you didn't count the paws and claws part. And they were laughing.

Then they were growling.

They roared and fell on John, tearing and snarling and ripping and howling, howling so loud Duncan thought the sounds would bash his ears off his head.

He raised the knife and lurched toward the bloody, awful scene, shouting even though his throat was trying to close. His badge and that damned coin necklace seemed to weigh four thousand pounds. Closer. Almost there.

"Off him," he managed. "Get. Off!"

Fighting a weird repelling force, kind of like a magnet shoving away the wrong charge, Duncan sliced at the nearest tiger-thing with the knife.

Missed.

He jammed the knife into his belt and used his freed hand to jerk the big cat away from John. The one with darker fur. The one who had made itself look like the Brent brothers. It spun on Duncan and let out a roar, but its hateful yellow cat eyes fixed on the chain and necklace. It looked like it wanted to rip out Duncan's throat, but it didn't so much as raise a clawed hand to take action.

Duncan lifted his good arm. His face was on fire. His head throbbed. His busted arm felt like it had swords sticking through the bone. He couldn't see shit. Could barely hear anything except the gut-sickening sounds of animals in a feeding frenzy. With what little strength he still had, Duncan punched the tiger-thing right in its blood-streaked nose.

The repelling force shoved him backward. He hit the concrete, and that's when the real hallucinations started.

As he rolled to his back, a bunch of women dressed in black leather bodysuits leaped over him.

The women had swords.

And daggers.

And something that looked like a dart gun.

One of them was on fire.

Then everything was on fire in Duncan's mind.

I'm history.

He thought the visions in leather were fighting off the cat-things. Lots of shouting. Lots of swearing. The stink of burned hair—or was it fur?

"I think I got one."

"Shit, then get this one!"

"At the river, Andy! The big one's getting away."

"Move, Camille!"

"Sorry. Sorry."

The earth shook. Wind howled over Duncan's head.

The sounds and burning and shaking and all the weird shit was moving away from him. He rolled over and puked, then used his good arm to drag himself toward John Cole.

It took seconds. Then minutes.

Outside the warehouse, water splashed like some freak-ass tidal wave had just come down the East River.

Duncan reached Cole.

He turned his head and puked again.

The man was torn wide open. Guts everywhere. Limbs chewed. Not breathing. Eyes staring—yet blinking. Somehow blinking.

"John?" Duncan's question came out hoarse, nothing but a whisper.

The brutalized, dying man managed to look Duncan right in the face.

Everything faded away. The strange crap in Afghanistan. The years of no contact. The murders. All of it. In that instant, nothing in the universe mattered more to Duncan than helping his friend.

He held his bad arm against his badge and that necklace and used his good hand to press against one of the wounds on John's neck. "Don't die. Hey. You hear me?"

John made no response. Of course he didn't. How could he? Logic warred with reality in Duncan's brain, and his consciousness starting swirling and lurching.

Then John blinked. Once. Twice.

He was still alive.

"Don't you die." Duncan's messed-up perceptions heard the voice of a little boy from Georgia, a younger version of himself, calling out to this torn husk of a human being on the warehouse floor. Blood spread around them in a black, hot pool. Oozing. Not pumping. All the works were shutting down.

Everything inside Duncan balled up like a fist as he focused his will and belief in miracles in that total way only little boys could achieve. "Damnit, John, *stay with me.*"

Sorry, John mouthed.

Then his eyes widened, and he went still.

The necklace under Duncan's bad arm tingled.

A blast of lightning hit him full force in the forehead, and he crashed backward. More pain. Agony now. His neck. His arm. His back. His heart.

John's knife vibrated, then seemed to melt away from his belt.

Energy.

Too much—

What the hell was that?

But it didn't matter.

Whatever was happening, maybe it would kill him, and maybe it should, because John Cole was dead. His friend was ripped open and bloodless, and those green eyes were empty now, forever.

"John!"

Did he yell that name?

Duncan couldn't be sure.

He wished he could tear apart the warehouse with his bare hands, find those tiger-things, and start on them next.

Rakshasa.

The word blared through Duncan's mind like somebody shouted it through a megaphone.

Rakshasa. The Unrighteous. That's what they are, Duncan. Murdering, evil demons called Rakshasa.

A megaphone in his brain . . . speaking in the voice of John Cole?

You asked me to stay. Here I am.

A thunderstorm broke across Duncan's awareness. Lots

of crashing and raining and blue-white flares of hurt and misery. He shoved his good hand against the side of his head and managed to roll away from John's corpse.

Sounds and voices rose from every direction.

Duncan couldn't tell what was happening inside his body and what was happening in the world. The world that had gone completely insane.

He rolled into something solid and lost the little bit of air he had left.

Legs.

Legs clad in leather.

"Did we kill any of them?"

"I don't think so, but we cut the hell out of one of them."

"Good."

As Duncan once more collapsed on his back, a woman said, "Damn, Bela, he's got head and neck wounds and a broken arm—and look at how those cuts are swelling on his neck—they go all the way to his chest!"

Okay, that sounded halfway normal. When Duncan heard the woman who'd just spoken talking on her phone or radio or whatever, he had no doubt she was an officer. The inflection, the jargon, the way she reported their position—definitely law enforcement.

He turned his head to his left even though his neck nearly cracked from the effort.

An officer in a black leather bodysuit complete with face mask, talking on a pink cell phone and carrying some kind of dart gun?

The woman standing next to the cop, the one with the big honking scimitar sword, had her face mask off, and she was on fire. Like, everywhere. And the long-haired blonde beside her was holding a bunch of evil-looking three-clawed throwing knives and had wind-devils coming out of her head.

I've got a helluva concussion. I'm hallucinating hot women with kick-ass weapons. I even thought my dead best friend was talking to me. At least the tiger-things are gone.

Fingers pressed against his neck, gentle and warm.

Duncan's attention turned to the woman touching him.

In the ever-brightening moonlight, he saw long dark hair falling in loose waves, a shade that reminded him of night itself, like her black, black eyes.

"Pulse is stable," she said in a voice so sexy it made him blink. "We need to get him back to the brownstone."

Need'a get'im back to thah brownstone.

Oh, yeah. Now *that* was an accent. He was good at accents, and this one was something interesting—like a mix of Bronx and European, getting more Bronx as she got worked up. Very exotic. Like the tilt of her eyes and her perfect, regal features.

A Slavic goddess, tall and athletic, sword belted at her waist, breasts pushing against her tightly zipped leather bodysuit.

Now, this was one hallucination he could get behind. Duncan let the image of the beautiful woman chase back his grief, his aches and pains, and the strangeness of everything in the warehouse. He let her fill his eyes, his senses.

Somehow through all the blood and singed hair, he caught an earthy, comforting almond scent. He wanted to lift his hand and touch her face just to see if she was real, but one of his arms was broken, and the arm that sort of worked was pinned under his side.

The woman's graceful fingers drifted to the burning wounds on his neck, shoulder, and chest, and she stared at him so intently he thought she might bend down and brush her lips against his face.

Duncan's entire body tensed with anticipation. Those lips would be cool and wet. He thought he might crumble to dust from the pain if he moved to kiss her back, though it might be worth it to taste her, to feel this woman against him a single time.

The goddess vision lowered her face closer, closer, until her soft, sweet breath played off his skin. She stared at him so deeply, so completely, that he had to believe she was seeing everything about him, understanding all that could be understood.

Her beautiful lips parted, and that sexy voice said, "He's infected. We'll have to call the Mothers."

Damn, Duncan, said the voice of dead John Cole, directly in the center of Duncan's brain. *I see you still know how to impress the ladies.*

The entryway of the converted Garment District warehouse was dark and quiet as Strada held his youngest true brother in his arms. His chest crushed with disbelief at the torn tissue, at Aarif's dark blood flowing across his fur. A pool of the liquid spread across the hardwood floor, radiating heat and light to Strada's acute senses. Aarif's life-force smelled of ammonia and earth, of all that was rich and natural, and it tore at Strada's essence to see one of his pride so wounded.

"Why do you grieve?" From the doorway that led to the larger office space beyond the entryway, Tarek's deep voice echoed against the high ceilings. "Let him pass so the healing can begin."

The converted former warehouse had been fitted out with ultramodern décor and designed to resemble a top-level human business operation. When Strada glanced up at the true brother nearest to his own age, he thought how odd Tarek looked in tiger form, still gripping his sword in one pawed hand, against a tableau of brick walls, Renaissance prints, computers, desks, and leather chair. The desert expanse they had known for millennia seemed incredibly distant now, lost to them forever.

"Death should never be rushed," Strada said. "Even now. Especially now."

Tarek's black eyes were little more than shadows against the dark golden fur of his face. He chose to stay in tiger form most of the time, even though Strada had instructed all of the Eldest to remain in the shape of their new human allies as much as possible, to give them every advantage in remaining anonymous. They had to learn the new speech, the new ways, the new world, if they were to continue to rise—but Tarek preferred more brutish methods.

"Death is inconsequential," Tarek growled at Strada. "It is temporary! Cease Aarif's suffering and allow him to come back to us."

"They wounded him," Strada snarled back, rocking Aarif and watching as the stain of blood coated his brother's thick black fur. "Those women struck blows against us. They cut Aarif as if he had no more strength than a kitten. Each death teaches us something. I will not deny Aarif his experience, his growth."

As if to deny the reality that humans had bested one of the Eldest in a hand-to-hand battle, that a mere four warriors—*female* warriors—had done harm to them, Tarek grumbled, "Aarif will learn, whether his death takes minutes or hours."

Strada bared his teeth even though he couldn't muster much volume in human form. "Honor your brother's suffering. Aarif is in pain."

Tarek roared so loudly that three warehouse windows cracked. He sprang forward and rammed the point of his blade directly into Aarif's barely beating heart. "Now he is not!"

Blood sprayed, then abruptly stopped as Aarif quivered and went still in Strada's grip.

Shock at such rank disobedience held Strada in place for the blink of a human eye. Then rage boiled through his veins, stretching muscles and tendons and bones. His heart pounded with the force of his fury, filling him with a blast of power so great his mind seemed to split as he howled. Fur erupted across his skin, white and shimmering even in the darkness, scalding him with pain as it moved. He flung Aarif's body to the wooden floor and launched himself at Tarek, slashing before he even stopped moving.

Tarek leaped backward.

Too slow.

And not far enough.

Strada slit Tarek's tiger throat in five places, the razor tips of his claws far more deadly than swinging swords.

The punch of claw through skin satisfied him so deeply he forgot his pain.

Tarek's black eyes bulged. His challenge roar strangled away in his damaged throat. He gurgled as he pawed at his face and neck, but Strada hit him again and again, flaying his flesh as Strada roared his fury at Tarek's insolence.

Throughout the five-story warehouse, the Eldest would be calming the Created, keeping them on task, training their ever-increasing numbers to carry out contracts they received. Expensive contracts, negotiated through their intermediary.

They would clean up the gore from Aarif's death, and Tarek's, too. Looking at the remnants of death and pain would be a lesson in strength and power, and on remaining ready for all possibilities.

White-hot battle frenzy consumed Strada. His own blood roared through his veins even as he spilled Tarek's. "You *will* learn respect," he shouted in the ancient language, and then in English, for any of the Created that might be listening. "No one stands against me, Tarek!"

Tarek was a brutal fighter, always thinking he was ready to challenge for pride leadership—but Tarek couldn't match the most powerful and skilled of the Eldest. Sooner or later he would understand that. Strada absorbed a fresh, blistering rush of heat as he hammered his advantage, feeding off the glorious power of his age and knowledge and strength.

"Suffer Aarif's pain." Strada shredded Tarek's arms even as the younger Rakshasa tried to cover his mutilated head. His flesh was soft, all too easy to destroy. "Know the humiliation our brother felt at the hands of those—those *females.*"

Tarek stumbled backward between the desks and chairs, his dark blood flecking monitors and papers and keyboards. Strada advanced, striking harder with each blow. His growls echoed against the brick walls, and the sound pleased him. Pieces of Tarek's ears, hands, and chest rained on the once-spotless floor, chunks of fur and skin. The coward tried to shift to fire form, but Strada easily used his energy to block Tarek's attempt.

"Fall," he instructed his brother. "Die now, fool, and get it over with."

Near the back of the room, by the single door that separated Strada's private office and the elevator to the upstairs quarters of the warehouse, Tarek collapsed with a weak, pitiful mewl. Strada kicked him, his energy flowing even stronger now, racing through his very being like a mad, ceaseless storm. Tarek's ribs cracked under this fresh assault, then his arms, and finally, most satisfying of all, his spine.

The delicious snapping of bone fed Strada as surely as blood and flesh from a kill. He laughed, kicking Tarek's limp body once more. He watched as the corpse struck his office door, leaving a dark red streak as it bounced off the wood and once more fell limp on the floor. With a trumpeting snarl of triumph, Strada left the ingrate on the floor. At least his blood wouldn't make a permanent stain on the expensive flooring.

By the time he reached the warehouse's entryway, Aarif had already been reborn. He was sitting up in tiger form, massaging the newly knit black fur stretching across his healing chest. "Brother," he whispered as he came back to himself completely, then immediately and obediently shifted to human form, to obey Strada's standing instructions.

Strada shifted to human form with him, impressed by how well Aarif managed the subtleties of pulling together elements to create human clothing appropriate to his age and youthful appearance as well as his station in the life they were creating for themselves. Slacks, a white shirt. Even well-made leather shoes. Aarif looked American, perhaps with Hispanic heritage. He might have stepped out of a photograph taken at an East Coast preparatory school—which was fitting, given the number of such photos they had studied.

Strada's natural human form was a complement to Aarif's. An older brother, perhaps, or a father who'd had his first child very young. The blood coating Strada's fur after his punishment of Tarek shifted away with his tiger form, leaving his gray silk business suit untouched by anything unpleasant. Strada knew he was impeccable, and he took pride in Aarif's perfection as well.

"Welcome back to us," he told Aarif, opening his arms.

Aarif took a step toward him, then halted and hung his head, obviously shamed. "I was defeated in battle."

Strada's smile felt as natural as his suit in human form. "We were surprised, little brother. Do not let it trouble you. Learn from your pain and death, and we will all move forward."

But Aarif was troubled nonetheless, which was one of the reasons Strada approved of his youngest true brother. Aarif managed to raise his head, and his chin quivered only once before his face became a mask of determination and anger.

"It will not happen again." Aarif's voice grew louder with each word, a tiger-form roar laced behind each syllable. "I give you my word, *culla*."

Culla.

Leader. The head of the pride.

Strada's smile widened. He enjoyed how this one never forgot who ruled him, or how to speak to his betters. "I have no doubt."

Tarek slunk into the entryway, his rapid rebirth a testament to how many times he had died in the past. He was in human form, his business clothing poorly formed and mismatched, but Strada acknowledged that his most stubborn true brother had at least chosen to make a proper effort to follow standing orders. He did not hug Tarek to welcome him back to the pride. Tarek's averted gaze and submissive posture were sufficient for now, despite the obvious anger rippling through his muscled human body.

"Fetch Griffen again, and have him bring the Created," Strada instructed. "The office must be cleaned before the start of business tomorrow. We are a security firm, not a slaughterhouse."

Tarek quickly reversed course, out of the entryway, back through the office space, and toward the elevator to the upstairs quarters, which was located at the rear of the large square room. His posture communicated even more rage at his continued humiliation. Their human intermediary and all of the Created that Griffen supervised would know whose blood and fur they were scouring from the floor, walls, and furniture. And they would know even more clearly who had won the battle between Tarek and Strada.

Strada was the first and strongest. He was the most powerful of the Rakshasa, and he had been since the universe chose to create him. It never hurt to remind Eldest and Created alike. If Tarek didn't enjoy being the stooge of the lesson, perhaps next time he would choose not to challenge his *culla*.

Minutes later, perhaps only moments, activity filled the staircase and elevator, and Tarek, Griffen, and the Created swept quietly into the office space, cleaning supplies at the ready. Many different colors of fur and scents tickled Strada's awareness as Griffen set the Created straight to work, and with a definite sense of pride he watched the numbers in the room swell.

Where there had been five Created, now there were dozens, too many, even, to answer his call. They were still in full possession of their reason and ability to follow commands, so conversion methods were definitely improving.

Hundreds of years in limbo, with nothing but his own thoughts for company, had given Strada plenty of time to consider what might have gone wrong in the sharing of Rakshasa and human blood.

Even if these Created were still smaller than true Rakshasa, and unable to assume full human form, they were far superior to the mindless golems he had created centuries ago to fight their wars in the desert. The two nearest to him had paws, while others had pointed ears atop their heads, or patches of fur marking their skin. A few flickered back and forth between flame form and fully shaped bodies, giving them the appearance of human candles. But they were sane, sentient, and capable of learning.

Tarek broke away from the laboring crew and came to stand beside Aarif. He remained, respectfully and atypically, in his human form. Strada was impressed by his obedience, even if he knew it wouldn't last.

"These Created do better every day." Aarif's angular face softened as he grinned. "I hope our true brothers across the globe are faring as well."

Strada felt his own human-form face ease once more into a pleased expression. When they had been released from that cursed desert temple in the Valley of the Gods, Strada had divided his small family of thirty Rakshasa into groups of two and three and sent them forth.

By now, small armies of his kind would be surging through major cities on all seven modern continents. Strada was learning to use devices like computers, though electronic equipment often didn't wish to cooperate with his kind, with their powerful energy. Still, he could use the contraptions to see that their coffers were filling. Working hard for his promised reward of immortality, Griffen had taught Strada much about banks and accounts, about how digital signals now filled air once populated by only the psychic workings of gods like the Rakshasa.

Humans were just as clever now as they had been in ancient times. Perhaps even more so—and perhaps that was why they were having more success establishing Created who didn't go mad and require immediate extermination.

As the Created finished rendering the office space presentable once more, Griffen separated himself from the ranks and strode toward Strada, Aarif, and Tarek. His blond hair seemed to gleam in the unnatural bulb lighting, and his blue eyes were bright with the intelligence and elemental ability that had drawn Strada to him when the Rakshasa arrived in New York City. Tonight, Griffen wore jeans and a shirt he'd called a "polo" when he brought Strada his own collection of such garments.

"*Culla,* I think they're close to ready," Griffen said, gesturing back to the Created, who were polishing chairs, desks, and the floors. Griffen's movements were fluid and exact, like the trained warrior Strada knew him to be.

"And your . . . men?" Strada had almost said *pride,* but corrected himself.

Griffen's gaze sharpened with his cool smile, and the twinned-serpent tattoo on his forearm seemed to writhe and pulse. "The Coven is more than prepared."

A heat rushed through Strada, anticipation mingled with his never-ceasing appreciation of the freedom he had so recently regained. Freedom to recover. To grow. To conquer once more. "We will give them a trial soon, then." He slapped Aarif on the back, and even Tarek gave a soft growl of eagerness. "Griffen, the women who fought us earlier this day, those wicked creatures who injured my true brother—I want to know more about them."

The shifts in Griffen's posture and expression were subtle but easily detectable to Strada. Hatred. Hunger. Anxiety. The emotions radiated off the man until Strada could scent the tang of each separate feeling. So his human allies, Griffen and his twelve companions with their rudimentary elemental talents and their snake tattoos, had encountered these women before.

"The Sibyls." Griffen's tone was controlled, but hints of rage laced each syllable. "They're part of an ancient world-wide order known as the Dark Crescent Sisterhood, pledged to the Dark Goddess and trained in combat since they were children." His fingers curled, then relaxed. "The Coven had contact with them many times before the downfall of the Legion. They were on the list I provided you when we came to our agreement with their allies in the NYPD's Occult Crimes Unit—but their numbers have been low of late. I don't think they can muster much consistent interference with your business."

Strada remembered the history lesson Griffen had given him after Strada captured him during one of his Coven's midnight rituals. The Legion was a defunct cult that had achieved a basic confederation of many smaller paranormal groups. They had attempted domination of the city, and ultimately worldwide politics. The Legion had failed because its leaders were weak and greedy. They lacked Strada's finesse and simplicity of purpose.

As for Griffen and his capture, it had taken some time—and much money—for them to come to a voluntary and cooperative accord, but Griffen and his Coven were now dedicated, if subordinate, members of Strada's pride. Griffen was telling Strada what he knew of Sibyl Motherhouses and their locations, but Strada cut him off by holding up one hand. "No. I want to know about *them*. The four women who challenged us. I want their names, their strengths and weaknesses. The location of their lair."

Griffen went silent, and he looked perplexed. "Four would be unusual. Sibyls normally fight in groups of three."

"There were four. One had the flavor of earth about her, and one called to the wind and made it obey her." Strada gestured toward the ceiling, sensing the night sky far above. "One commanded fire, and the other seemed to be able to make water do her bidding."

"Water?" Now Griffen sounded amazed, but also relieved. He was smiling again, and his gaze gave off more hate than ever before. "Yes, that makes it much easier. I'll have what you need very soon."

Strada dismissed this, too, with a quick wave of his hand. "Those who dare stand against the Eldest will fall, swift and hard."

Griffen dipped his head in response, *"Culla."*

Would that Tarek would learn such respect.

Deep in the renovated human office space, a telephone rang.

The silent ranks of Created parted like a sea of fur, fangs, rags, and witches with brooms as Griffen moved to the jangling bell and pushed a button on the telephone's black base.

"Panthera Security," Griffen said in a calm, professional tone. Strada took a moment of pleasure in the fact that he and Griffen had established a cover that would be particularly irritating to the enemies who hunted them. *Borrowing tricks,* Griffen called it.

"What the hell was that shit in DUMBO tonight?" The voice that shouted back at him had a European accent, and Strada knew at once that they were dealing with one of their new "employers."

"None of your concern," Griffen responded without any undertone of annoyance. He had explained to Strada about working a position called "customer service" in his life prior to the fall of the Legion, and how that had prepared him for any type of verbal assault.

Swearing poured through the telephone's speaker, followed by "Your people almost killed a freakin' cop!"

Griffen's high cheekbones and square chin settled into a mask of patience. "The man who lost his life was a suspected serial killer. A detective was wounded, but as far as we know, he's still alive."

More swearing. Then, through the telephone, "When he

does croak, you'll have the other forty thousand badges in the boroughs hunting you like dogs."

Aarif's lip twitched at the canine metaphor. Tarek looked bored, staring out the warehouse windows. The Created didn't shift or make a sound.

"Do you have further work for us?" Griffen asked, his muscles remaining infinitely relaxed. "Another contract? If not, our business together is finished."

There was a stunned pause in the noise coming through the telephone speaker, followed by a hastily grumbled, "Soon."

The caller hung up.

Tarek and Aarif stared at Strada, waiting.

Hope flickered in the depths of their eyes.

Tarek was shifting slowly into tiger form, fur washing across his human skin like a beautiful golden wave. Aarif was beginning to flicker, the intoxicating blue of his flame form showing through his eyes and pale cheeks.

Strada couldn't deny them.

He nodded, and that fast, his true brothers were gone, racing from the warehouse, fire form and tiger form moving faster than human eyes could see. Strada had to use every ounce of his self-possession not to join them. He, too, could taste the meat, the fear, the blood their victim would spill.

Griffen sighed. "Strada, if you and your brothers keep eating the people who hire you, the New York City market won't support you for long."

"Point taken." Strada actually managed a smile for his human ally as he surveyed the powerful, quiet mass of the Created Griffen was helping to train. "Fortunately, it will not have to."

(4)

Bela's blood pulsed in her ears as she pressed her hands against the sides of the injured detective's face, growling from the fiery misery of Duncan Sharp's wounds. She did what she could to absorb more of his pain. Not much. Not nearly damned enough.

Camille Fitzgerald ran out of the basement treatment room to send word to the NYPD, leaving Bela with Andy Miles, Dio Allard, and the hastily summoned Mother Keara, fighting to save the detective's life.

Or his soul.

Bela's thoughts pitched against each other, still jumbled from the battle and the hard run back to the brownstone in Manhattan that she had inherited from a group of fellow Sibyls.

"Saving his soul," she muttered to herself. "Right."

Where the hell had that come from?

Stubble scraped Bela's palms as she let her earth energy flow into the detective to ease his torture, as much as she dared, since he was only human—at least for now.

No regular hospital could help him, that much she understood, even if they weren't saying it outright. Something was very, very wrong with this man's wounds. It wouldn't be safe to expose other living creatures to what they were seeing. If they couldn't patch him up right here in her newly refurbished laboratory with its treatment room and full complement of traditional medicines and medical equipment, Duncan Sharp wouldn't make it.

Andy and Dio were struggling to cast the man's broken

arm while Mother Keara battled the supernatural slash wounds to his neck, shoulder, and chest.

Bela made herself look at those wounds.

Deeper now. Extending like living things, trying to eat away his skin and maybe even his bones. The slashes were oozing some sort of foul, bleak energy she had never encountered before, but the chain and ancient coin around the man's neck seemed to be holding it back on at least one side. Bela hated the sight of that energy, and she despised what it was doing to the man she was trying to help.

Enough. She focused her earth energy into blocking the advance of those slashes, just like Mother Keara was trying to do with her fire. *No more death. Not here, not now— not ever again.*

Damnit. She was pulling at her power so hard that the floor was rattling under her toes, but she couldn't see that it was making much difference. Her muscles strained to contain a fraction of the earth's might and muscle, and she damn well would find some way to lend it to this human. It dug at her insides to admit he probably didn't have much of a chance. Camille had taken the man's badge and identification upstairs to notify the NYPD of the detective's situation, via their liaison at the department's low-profile Occult Crimes Unit.

Duncan Sharp's agony surged through Bela's fingertips, and it would have knocked her backward against the yellow cinder-block wall if she hadn't braced her legs against the rush of energy. Goddess, pain like that—it would kill a normal person. It might even kill a Sibyl.

She was dizzy from the force of it, half disoriented for a second, but she fought back, and the detective fought, too. Bela had never sensed such raw, natural power in a human before, and his determination impressed her.

"He's strong," she said, giving him another dose of earth energy, hoping it wouldn't blow him apart.

"He's dying," Mother Keara countered in her crackly

voice. The sound seemed huge in the fifteen-by-fifteen space in the bottom corner of the Manhattan brownstone. "Hold him tight, now—hear me, child!"

Bela increased the pressure in her hands, sending even more earth energy to surround the man's prone form and press him into the hospital bed's bloodied sheets. The old woman jerked the sleeves of her green robes upward as she bent over his bare chest. On the opposite side of the bed, Andy and Dio moved out of her way, slinging wet strips of plaster, their battle leathers smeared with white streaks of the paste.

The deep slashes to Duncan Sharp's neck and shoulder shifted from purple to black. Hair sprouted at the edges of each bloody cut. Orange tiger-like hair. The gluey scent of the plaster and the tang of antiseptic mingled with the smells of ozone and burning flesh as Mother Keara tried cauterizing the slashes again, this time with a directed jet of blue flame from her index finger, as exact as any surgical laser. The eerie light from the controlled fire made her fragile features seem almost translucent, and bits of her gray braids smoked from dozens of tiny sparks.

The tiger fur disappeared, and the slashes stopped expanding wherever the full heat of Mother Keara's fire touched the man's flesh.

The detective's eyelids fluttered. He let out a low moan and jerked against the padded metal cuffs binding him to the rails of the hospital bed. Bela shoved both heels against the green tile floor, refusing to surrender her hold on his face. He fought her, his neck bowing as he tried to free himself from her grip.

His heart stuttered, once, then twice.

"Come on." Bela hit him with another blast of earth power, and another, and another. She wasn't quitting, and neither would he. "Come on, damn you!"

His heartbeat caught like an engine and roared strong again.

"Yes!" Bela's shout echoed in the treatment room. "That's more like it."

Her own heart picked up the same rhythm, almost bursting from the rush of small triumph. How much could he take? Humans weren't cut out to absorb so much elemental energy, but regular painkillers were out. That kind of medication would dull his mind and his instinct to resist death. The infection or poison in those slash wounds might spread faster.

Bela bent forward and pressed her lips against Duncan Sharp's ear, ignoring the stench of fire and blood and lingering dirt and ammonia from the battle. "Keep fighting this," she snarled, hoping to engage the amazing determination she sensed roiling through his essence.

Some part of him seemed to respond to her, and his breathing and heart rate slowed into a more reasonable pattern. The relief helped Bela breathe better, too.

Mother Keara stopped stinging the detective with her fire and dropped into the room's only chair at his beside, limp, her head down like she might be trying to meditate. "Best I can do for now," she mumbled. "I'll be needin' a rest. Some beer. And a little help with this, I think."

The lighting in the lab's treatment room showed the blood and bruises in glaring detail as Andy and Dio went back to fixing Duncan Sharp's arm. Droplets of water rolled down Andy's leather sleeves as she worked, drawn from nearby pipes, faucets, and sprinklers, but also from the ample ambient moisture in the air. Andy's damp red curls were plastered against her freckled cheeks, and she alternated between chewing her lip and glancing at Bela for reassurance as she tried to concentrate on the strips of plaster.

"You can do it," Bela told her as she gently massaged the detective's jaws with her fingertips. "It's just a simple radial fracture."

"Just a simple radio what-the-fuck," Andy shot back.

"Like I've been studying human anatomy my whole damned life, Bela. I'm an ex-cop and a greenhorn Sibyl, not a surgeon."

Bela ignored her bluster and kept working on the detective. Sibyls, even new ones like Andy, had no need for scans to tell them what was broken or how to set it, and Andy was doing just fine. Better, even, than Bela could do, because Andy was a water Sibyl. Healing was her most natural talent outside the management of water, like science for earth Sibyls, communication for fire Sibyls, and archiving and research for air Sibyls.

Every time Andy placed another strip of plaster on the man's arm, she infused both the cast and Duncan Sharp with a dose of water power, soothing and cleansing and absolutely reconstructive. Bela wasn't even sure Andy knew she was doing that. It just flowed out of her, in perfect rhythm and measure.

Whenever Andy gave the nod, Dio flicked her fingers and sent a rush of air to dry a section of the cast. Even with the bursts of wind, Dio's wispy golden hair remained in position, every strand, pulled tight against her head and fixed at her neck by a single leather tie. Very neat. Far too neat for an air Sibyl. Unlike Andy, Dio wasn't making eye contact with Bela at all, but that was nothing new, and nothing Bela could deal with right now.

Duncan Sharp's bouts of pain were just about all she could handle, though they were becoming less and less intense. He seemed to be sleeping now, and the wounds still weren't expanding. Another minute or so, and the cast was finished. As well done as any hospital could have managed—maybe even a little better—but that broken arm was the least of the detective's problems.

Mother Keara was still resting and muttering and meditating as Andy and Dio turned to the treatment room's shiny medical sink and washed their hands. That dark, chilly energy oozed toward them out of Duncan Sharp's slash wounds, but it shattered against the elemental protections on Mother Keara's robes and Andy and Dio's leather battle suits.

Dio glanced at the remnant energy as it dissipated, and pointed it out to Andy.

"Bad shit," Andy diagnosed. "Do we need to reinforce anything to hold that energy, Bela?"

Bela shook her head, not wanting to break her concentration enough to speak.

The metal frame of Duncan Sharp's hospital bed, the cuffs on his wrists and ankles, and the walls of the treatment room were already completely encased in elemental locks—fire, air, earth, and water energy stacked like tightly fitted bars built to contain supernatural forces.

Well, exactly like bars, because once upon a time, the treatment room had been an actual jail cell intended to contain paranormal creatures. When she took over the brownstone, Bela had expanded the area into a reasonable-sized infirmary, put up drywall, improved the plumbing, laid tile, and painted the whole room a festive yellow.

Well, it had seemed festive at the time. Now it seemed like lemons exploding all over neon bananas.

"This place is too flippin' bright, by the way." Andy shook her hands off, not bothering to reach for a towel to dry them. Dry never lasted long for Andy, anyway. "You know that, don't you?"

"Whatever," Bela mumbled, keeping her focus on the places where her fingers connected with Duncan Sharp's face.

"Blue might have been a better choice for a sickroom," Andy continued, straightening up the sink area. "Or brown."

"All earth Sibyls love brown," Dio said to Andy, keeping her face turned away from Bela. "And of course we don't have enough of *that* color around here."

Bela managed not to sigh. Dio was referring to the fact

that Bela had reworked the whole outer laboratory surrounding the treatment room in soft sands and browns, to
modernize it. She had kind of gotten carried away and
painted the whole brownstone in the same shades while she
was at it. She hadn't gotten around to replacing the furniture yet, but she was planning on that, too.

"Dry up!" Mother Keara's sharp Irish command to be
quiet was punctuated by a flicker of flame from both of her
shoulders, followed by a jet of smoke that covered both
Andy and Dio, muting the yellow of the wall behind them
with a thin layer of soot. "Upstairs with the both of you.
Help Camille get ready to call a few more Mothers."

Andy and Dio finished cleaning up from the casting and
took off like two scolded kids. Mothers—especially fire
Sibyl Mothers—tended to have that effect on people.

Mother Keara's sharp eyes followed Dio's retreat until
the outer lab door slammed. She lifted one tired, trembling
hand and pointed a knotty finger at the door. "She's trouble, that one. Maybe there's a reason she kept to herself all
those years and never joined a triad. You should be takin'
her scrawny ass straight back to Greece."

Bela drew a careful, slow breath, then disengaged her fingers from Duncan Sharp's face. She didn't detect any
change in his pulse or his breathing. So far, so good. Figuring she could risk a minute or two away, she turned to better face Mother Keara—and made sure to put a little earthy
rumble into her response. "Dio's mine, old woman. Don't
insult my air Sibyl or my judgment."

Mother Keara rubbed her wrinkled chin as she laughed.
"You *never* do what you're told, do you? If I'd known you
as a baby, I'd have found yer fire. Why yer mother set you
to shakin' rocks and dirt, I'll never understand."

"Me neither." Bela started for the sinks but found she
didn't want to go much farther away from Duncan, in case
his terrible pain came charging back. She hesitated near the

foot of his bed. "I've never been much good at the whole earth-moving trick."

Mother Keara shrugged. "Who needs terrakinesis? Lots of shake, rattle, and roll, for what? Can't rightly use it in a full-pitch battle without tearin' down whole cities."

A little flame issued from Mother Keara's right knee, and she stared at it like she might be divining the future in its red-orange depths. "You're a first-rate terrasentient, great at readin' what the earth has to tell you. That'll be good for our Camille, since she's got a measure of pyrosentience. Readin' objects with fire, that's almost a lost skill at Mother-house Ireland—and it needs developin'."

The tiny flame disappeared, and when Mother Keara looked at Bela, she seemed sad on top of fatigued. "Camille's never been the best at pyrogenesis—fire makin'. She took a lot of guff from her sister Sibyls over it, comin' up."

It was Bela's turn to shrug. "Camille did well enough firing up in DUMBO when we had to have her help. I can live without the smoke and sparks the rest of the time." Though in truth, she missed the crackle of fire energy in the air, and worried a lot about Camille's physical and mental health because of that absence. Fire Sibyls cut off from their inner heat suffered in ways Bela didn't even want to consider.

Mother Keara scratched the side of one braid, setting another bit of her hair on fire and putting it out, all in the same motion. "It's in her, the full measure of fire talent. It's just lost in all her grief and guilt. One day, the right spark, and—" Mother Keara didn't need to find a metaphor. She just opened her palms and let the flames burst upward to char the stone ceiling of the treatment room.

"Bela?" Camille's call from outside the main laboratory door was tenuous, but Bela could tell by her tone that she had important information.

"Go ahead," she said. "And you can come in if you want. He's stable for now."

There was a whisper of footsteps, and Camille came to stand in the door of the treatment room. Framed by the bright yellow walls and door facing, she seemed even more petite and withdrawn than usual, and the absence of smoke and fire on her person was baldly obvious in such close quarters with the heat blazing from Mother Keara's every curve and angle.

Camille's long auburn hair was pulled into a ponytail that hung over her shoulder, and the curling tip of it nearly reached her slender waist. Her nervous aquamarine eyes went from Bela to Mother Keara, then quickly back to Bela again as she dug at the leg of her jeans with chewed, ragged nails. "The Occult Crimes Unit notified One Police Plaza," she said. "I told them to stay clear until we understand whether or not his wounds are contagious, but they wanted an update in no less than fifteen minutes. It's been about that long."

Mother Keara gave no response, and Bela knew the old woman was trying not to intimidate Camille.

Bela moved aside so that Camille could see the sleeping detective and the wicked-looking wounds readily visible on his tanned chest, neck, and shoulder. "We've fought it to a draw for the moment. Meaning he's not dying right this second or changing into anything other than human. Yet."

More of that sickly dark energy slid out of Duncan Sharp's slash wounds, heading for Camille, only to perish against the elemental locks of the cuffs and bed.

Camille drew back a step, watching the foul energy break apart. "What *is* that shit? And what were those things that attacked us in DUMBO?"

"Trouble, no doubt," Mother Keara grumbled as she stood. She hobbled across the room toward Camille and put out her hand for support, though Bela didn't think she really needed it. As Camille took her by the elbow and moved to help her out of the laboratory and back upstairs, Mother Keara looked pointedly at Bela. "If that porcupine of an air Sibyl you're so bent on keepin' is worth her freight, she's upstairs in her archives right now, huntin' answers."

Bela was too tired herself to argue the point or defend Dio again. She let Mother Keara go with Camille to summon more Mothers, and took a seat in the metal chair Mother Keara had vacated. The metal was still hot enough to melt ridges in her leathers along both sides of her ass.

Wonderful.

Bela rubbed her hand across her eyes and refocused on Duncan Sharp's breathing and heartbeat. Still steady and regular. She didn't catch any hint of pain at the moment.

Good.

She made herself get up and go to the sinks. From a too-yellow cabinet overhead—Goddess, what had she been thinking when she bought that paint?—she took down a smooth cotton cloth and dampened it with warm water. She brought the wet cloth back to the detective's bedside and began to dab away the grit, soot, grime, and blood from his stubbled cheeks.

With each gentle swipe, she could see more of his tanned face, from the strong line of his jaw to the corners of his mouth. The guy probably had a drop-dead grin to go with that thick brown hair, which would be curly if he hadn't cut it so short. She imagined Duncan Sharp awake again, fit and well. If that gorgeous face could relax, it might be boyish.

Her own breathing slowed more, falling into rhythm with his as she bathed away what she could of his pain and damage. She glanced at his slash wounds, which were still behaving for the moment, with the ancient coin resting beside them on its golden chain. Bela knew better than to toy with ancient things, so she left the coin where it lay and moved on to bathing the bulging muscles of the detective's shoulders and chest.

He had big, strong hands, which she lifted as far as the metal cuffs would allow, letting them rest on his rock-hard belly at the top of the sheet covering him at the waist. She was careful not to damage the cast Andy and Dio had crafted to support the broken bone in his right forearm.

There.

Now he looked more comfortable.

And, damnit, even more handsome than he had three minutes ago.

Bela stared into his face, so close at the angle she had taken to clean him up, squeezing the rag in her fingers, trying to decide if she was finished.

She couldn't make up her mind.

She couldn't even move.

From over her head, on the main floor of the brownstone, came the distinct and powerful shifting of elemental energy that let Bela know the ancient channels of communication and transportation had been opened. Her living room was probably filling up with Mothers, stepping through the projective mirrors used to connect the brownstone and every Sibyl dwelling to the Motherhouses and each other.

Just what she needed.

A buttload of cranky old women powerful enough to shake, burn, and blow down New York City, all come to monkey with this man's health—and probably with her quad before they departed.

Bela was grateful for their help. It was lovely that they were coming. And kind. And she really wanted to scream now.

She went back to bathing Duncan Sharp's face and neck.

It had been a long day and night on the heels of a damned endless month. She had spent the last four weeks trying to bind together a fighting group that just wouldn't—

or couldn't—mesh yet. They had taken on extra patrols to build experience with each other, but so far the best they could muster was a few semi-competent battles. The rest of the time, they jumped and banged and rattled against each other like popcorn in a hot pan. At least down here on the brownstone's basement floor, with her bedroom, the long, dark, and cool hallway to the lab, the big lab space itself, and the little treatment room contained in the corner, Bela could feel settled and calm, and a little bit at home. Even if she was downtown.

Bela had never thought she'd live in the city. Way too prissy for a Bronx girl. But hey, when your best frenemy gifts you the most killer brownstone in Manhattan, you don't say, *Ew, no, thanks, that's too poof-ass for my blood.*

"You have a temporary breakdown and paint the walls a heinous yellow," she muttered to the sleeping detective as she forced herself to stand up and lower the washrag. "Then you load the place up with an injured detective and a full complement of Sibyl Mothers. Welcome to *my* house, Duncan Sharp."

As if to answer her, the detective opened his eyes.

Oh.

Bela's breath stilled in her throat.

Her quad's growing pains, the Mothers, and even the insane yellow walls faded into distant regions of her mind.

Oh, my.

Gray-blue was all she could see now, as clear and startling as a winter sky at dawn.

Those eyes were . . . beautiful. A little wild. Definitely different. Bela tried to jumpstart her breathing but couldn't pull off even a gasp.

It wasn't just the color. It was the depth—a dark, flickering intensity like shadows on crystal. He had a tired, haunted sadness about him that went beyond battles and wounds. How far would a man have to travel, and how much trouble would he have to know, to get power like that in his gaze?

Duncan Sharp's stare brushed her cheek like fingertips, moving slowly down to her chin, and lower, to her neck. Shock mingled with wonder and other emotions she couldn't begin to identify as he focused on her, seemed to take her in—and grinned.

Bela managed to get a little air, but not much.

Boyish, just like she'd thought. *Charming* and *endearing* would be good words, too. Heat crept across her shoulders and up her neck as she smiled back at him.

"You saved my life," he whispered, so low and deep she felt it all over her body. Even in those four words, she got a taste of raw Southern male.

It took a lot of effort to make her mouth work, but Bela stammered, "We—we're trying, Detective Sharp."

"It's Duncan." The grin faded. He closed his amazing eyes for a second, then opened them long enough to add, "You're so damned gorgeous I'm gonna touch you to make sure you're real."

The padded cuffs holding his good wrist clinked as he reached toward her and ran out of chain. His attention shifted to the cuffs, and he jerked against them again before trying to move his casted arm.

"Careful." Bela rested her palm on the warm skin of his wrist, still feeling the heat of his half-delirious compliment. He had no idea where he was, who she was—he wasn't even asking why he wasn't in a hospital, if he realized he wasn't. He probably wouldn't remember a word of this tomorrow—but she would. "We've got you restrained as a precaution."

There was that grin again, and a devilish sparkle in his winter-gray eyes. "Angel, you can tie me up anytime."

The cuffs clinked again.

Angel.

Yeah. He was delirious, for sure, but that accent was

sweet enough to eat, and those eyes had to be the most beautiful things she had ever seen.

They pinned her, held her totally still as he grabbed the metal arms of his bed and lifted himself, higher, higher, until his lips—his lips—Goddess, he was kissing her, and she was letting him.

So quick.

So *soft*.

Like a daydream, one she should jerk herself out of and come to her senses, but really, she'd rather stay right where she was, with his lips brushing hers, sampling her like she was some sort of exotic wine. Her heart jumped and squeezed like he had her in an endless clench, like he might just break free of his cuffs and pull her down with him, and damn, she'd probably let him do that, too.

"You are real," he whispered against her mouth.

Bela felt enough heat in her face to wonder if Mother Keara was right, that she was secretly a fire Sibyl ready to break out in roaring, rolling flames. When he lowered himself back to his pillow, she couldn't move, couldn't stop looking at him, couldn't stop staring into the endless, intriguing depths of his eyes.

And that's when those beautiful eyes started to change.

It was just a flicker at first.

A quick light-to-dark.

Bela drew back her hand from his wrist as his pulse accelerated. "Duncan?"

He said nothing. The flicker happened again, and she backed off in a hurry, a few feet from the bed.

"Detective Sharp." Bela made herself sound harder, to see if she could get his attention. "Can you hear me?"

Duncan blinked but stared at the yellow wall over Bela's shoulder. He had gray eyes again, then a blink, and—black eyes.

Gray again.

Then black.

Then gray.

"Mother Keara," Bela called, too freaked to add any earth force to her volume as her own heart started thumping hard enough to crack her ribs.

Duncan looked confused. Then upset. Then pissed off.

Then . . .

Then he seemed to go away altogether.

His eyes went night-black and wide, and the angles and lines of his face shifted to the profile of a completely different man. Or creature. Bela was still staring, even though she was backing up fast and raising a hefty shield of earth power between herself and whatever was lying in that hospital bed.

Duncan Sharp, or the blend of positive and negative energies he had become, let out a distinctly inhuman growl.

The fine hairs along the back of Bela's neck prickled.

"The Unrighteous will come," he whispered in a voice that sounded like something straight out of Satan's realm. "They'll kill you," the Lucifer voice said, like he wanted to be sure she heard him.

"Shit." Bela was in the treatment room's doorway now, breathing in fast, jagged gulps. The air seemed colder than it should be. Poisonous green-black energy bubbled out of Duncan's slash wounds, exploding against the elemental locks until the room trembled.

"Mother Keara!" Bela yelled, this time putting some punch in it. "Down here, now!"

Where the hell was her sword?

Had she left it upstairs when they got back?

Shit, shit, shit!

Duncan Sharp lurched upward, rattling against the cuffs on all four limbs. "Run!" he bellowed, and Bela wouldn't have been surprised to see his head start to spin around. "Bug out, soldier, now, now, now!"

She raised both arms and hurled enough earth energy into that treatment room to crush Duncan Sharp to bits of blood and rubble.

It didn't faze him.

He was still coming off the bed.

The chains on the handcuffs strained. A few links bent apart.

Then a wall of earth, fire, air, and water power shoved Bela sideways and exploded into the space, surrounding the flailing man and mashing him flat against his pillows.

He lay there, mouth open, eyes wide and flickering from gray to black.

Bela glanced to her left to see Mother Keara standing next to little Mother Yana from Russia and tall, graceful Mother Anemone from Greece. On Bela's right, Andy was spouting gouts of water as she directed her elemental energies, and Dio and Camille were getting a shower as they held Andy's hands to keep her steady.

The Mothers kept up their steady stream of power until Duncan Sharp, or whatever was trying to act through his battered flesh and bones, gave up and collapsed.

Less than five seconds later, he lapsed into a deep, unconscious sleep, and the poisoned energy from his wounds flickered away into nothing. The gold coin around his neck glittered in the light of the treatment room, looking for all the world like a metallic cap, sealing off whatever was trying to break out of his essence and take over the brownstone.

Bela wasn't certain she was still breathing. She had to push against her own chest to make sure she was still standing there, in her own basement, in her own laboratory.

Yellow. Check.

Sand tones. Check.

Creamy brown background. Check.

Crabby Mothers, wet water Sibyl, paralyzed fire Sibyl, prickly air Sibyl—check, check, check, and check.

"Bet that woke the new neighbor," Andy said as she drew back the last waves of her water power and Dio and Camille turned her loose. "Good evening, Mrs. Knight. How do you like your new place? Oh, never mind the little satanic possession drama in the basement next door. We have everything under total control." She scrubbed a dripping hand across her mouth. "Fuck *me*. Did he just turn into one of those things we fought in DUMBO?"

The older Mothers moved past Bela and the rest of her quad to examine the sleeping patient. Bela's senses told her that his body, at least, was holding its own. Her mind ricocheted between the Duncan who'd woken, spoken to her, and *kissed* her—and the disturbed, different Duncan who had shouted at her and almost torn the handcuffs and bed apart.

Had they already failed him? Was Duncan Sharp transforming into something inhuman? Something they would have to exterminate for everyone's safety? Bela's insides started to ache. She wasn't sure she could do that, not after he'd taken on those demons and fought so hard to live. He had a strength about him, physical and spiritual, that pulled at her.

After a few seconds, Mother Keara stood and pronounced, "He's still human."

Relief brushed Bela like a feather to the heart, and she put her hand on her chest.

Mother Keara conferred briefly with Mother Yana and Mother Anemone.

"This will take some time," Mother Anemone said in her lyrical, breezy voice as she rolled up the delicate sleeves of her blue robes. "We'll have to work in shifts this morning, and likely most of the day and night."

"Go." Mother Yana's tone was distracted as she wove more earth energy into the elemental locks securing Duncan Sharp. "The day vill pass fast enough, and you have patrol again come dark, no?"

"No," Camille said, then, "I mean, yes. We do."

"Ve vill call you vhen ve need you, Andrea, to help vith the healing," Mother Yana told Andy. She held both bony hands over the detective's chest, likely keeping his pulse steady. "Ve vill try not to pull you from your fighting duties, but it may be necessary."

For a moment, Andy looked like she wanted to argue, then seemed to regain her senses. She caught Camille's hand, and the two of them started for the lab door, dripping a trail of water behind them.

Dio shifted her weight, then cut Bela a quick glance. Her stormy eyes were noncommittal, but she managed to mumble, "We made you a sandwich. Well, Andy made you a sandwich." She paused and made a face, because Andy and sandwiches . . . well, Andy liked to be creative, and the results weren't always palatable. "While she was steaming the sprouts and cabbage, I dug through the archives to figure out what the hell we're dealing with. So, eat—if you can swallow rye and sprouts and cabbage at the same time. Go to bed. We'll talk when we go on patrol."

Bela started to thank Dio, but Dio clamped her mouth shut like she'd said too much and took off, moving with an air Sibyl's speed and grace.

Had Dio just tried to be nice?

A tiny throb of pain touched Bela's temples. Headache. That happened when she got too stressed and confused. She rubbed her face just above her eyes and decided that last bit about Dio and niceness had been overly optimistic. Or maybe delusional.

She yawned.

Sleep would definitely be good right about now, sandwich or no.

Bela glanced into the treatment room again, but she couldn't see Duncan Sharp for the swarm of Mothers and curtains of elemental energy blocking her view. Disappointment made her fingers twitch. Even though he had sort of shifted into something weird and screeched at her in a devil voice, she really wanted one more glimpse of his face before she crammed down whatever bizarre sandwich combination Andy had constructed, then crashed.

How sick was that?

My world is FUBAR. Hell, maybe it's just me—I'm *FUBAR.*

Wasn't that the military and cop term for "fucked up beyond all recognition"?

"FUBAR," she said out loud as she started for the door, and the word seemed to bounce against the tables full of shining silver instruments filling the main section of her research space.

(6)

FUBAR.

That sounded like a woman's voice, and Duncan liked it even though it had to be a cooked-brain hallucination. He could use a good woman. A strong woman who could drive away the darkness that hunted him like Satan on safari whenever he tried to dream.

Did women like that even exist—and if they did, why would they consider a banged-up piece of meat like him?

Duncan's muscles screamed and burned as he trudged across the sand, which was more rock and flint than anything else. Two dead. Radios shot to hell. He would have carried Johnston and Simms back with him, but he knew he'd never make it, so he'd recorded the spot on his map, and now he was trying to get home. Such as it was. Bunch of shacks and tents in the middle of nowhere—but they'd go back for Johnston and Simms. A sun as big as five planets hammered him with each step, turning his already tanned skin into some new grade of leather. The cuts on his neck from the IED explosion burned like somebody had poured acid on his face.

Second-degree burns. Almost lost part of my nose and some of my fingers.

"Don't forget the cough for a year, after sucking down all this dust," he mumbled, hating the parched burn in his throat, and the fact that he couldn't stop taking this walk even though he had survived it years ago. "Why does everything always come back to this place?"

"Because we never really left Afghanistan," John Cole said, and Duncan realized his best friend was beside him and matching him step for step, across the endless desert. "Not completely."

Duncan glanced at John, who had short hair instead of long. He was wearing his best dress uniform, ribbons and all, pressed and perfect, just like all his buddies who went home in bags—after the Dover Military Mortuary cleaned them up spotless for that last ride home.

"Can't hide, sinner," John said with a wry smile, putting a little tune to the words.

"Fuck, John." Duncan kept walking, because he always kept walking, because if he stopped, he'd fall down and fry under the merciless Afghan sun, or get chewed to pieces by a nasty bunch of camel spiders. "You're dead."

John was quiet for a few strides, then said, "Technically."

Duncan squinted at the baked brown ground, blinded by the yellow-gray afternoon light. If he was back in camp— and he wondered if he'd ever get back—a screwdriver would be so hot it would scald his palm if he touched it.

But . . . that was then, wasn't it?

That was back in the war, after one of more than a dozen roadside bombs went off and blew two jeeps all to hell.

And this was a dream.

Maybe . . . a new war? One he didn't even understand yet.

Duncan wondered if John's body would be patched up and sent home to Georgia. Would his friend get the fabled flag-draped casket treatment, all these years after they made it out of the damned desert that killed a part of both of them?

He drew another breath of boiling air. "Am I dead, too, John?"

"You're hard to kill." John laughed, staying shoulder to shoulder with Duncan as they walked faster, as if speed would somehow beat the heat. They found a rhythm, a left, right, left, right that suited them. Duncan could almost hear some stiff-dick drill sergeant calling cadence. Sweat coated his face.

He thought he should probably wake up.

Shouldn't John being trying to—he didn't know, find the light or something? Duncan would have asked him, but he knew John wouldn't answer.

A minute, or maybe it was an hour or half a day later, John said, "There *is* a woman, Duncan."

When Duncan turned his head to answer John, his friend was gone.

In his mind's eye, even as he tried to charge through his nightmare desert, Duncan saw the woman. Her dark hair. Her dark eyes. He remembered a sword and leather. A light scent of almonds and berries. The way her lips felt against his ear.

Keep fighting this.

That's what she'd told him, and he'd felt her voice all over his body, like it was inside whatever made him breathe and move.

Duncan kept walking, because that's what he did, and what he knew how to do. "Now that's a woman worth living for," he told the desert, like the desert cared about anything at all.

"He's handsome, isn't he?" Andy moved beside Bela, her footsteps loud and clunky on the Central Park path. Camille was walking to their far right, and Dio was a few paces behind them, in typical broom position in case they had to fight while they were on patrol.

"Duncan Sharp almost changed into . . . something." Bela glanced at Andy, who had her leather face mask on but unzipped. The ends of the zipper gleamed in the moonlight. "He said a bunch of crazy shit, and I thought he was going to eat me."

Andy snickered. "Yeah, but he's drool-level gorgeous."

"Yes, damnit, Andy, he's handsome." Bela rested her palm on the hilt of her sword and wondered what Camille and Dio were thinking. Neither had said a word since they headed into the New York City night.

Did they have a clue that she barely had her mind on tonight's patrol? That where she really wanted to be was back at the brownstone, checking on Duncan Sharp's progress with the Mothers?

Some mortar I am. I can't even unify my own quad, and I'm worrying about a stranger instead of what might be lurking in those trees.

Andy, who hadn't and probably never would master the art of silent movement, definitely had a clue. She kept giving Bela a look like, *cha-cha-cha*. Plus, she kept talking, like she knew Bela needed the distraction. "Mrs. Knight, the new neighbor, came by and asked about all the noise and shaking and shit. I told her we had a water heater malfunction."

The rich smell of dirt and trees and dew-coated grass grew stronger as they moved farther into the park. The creak and whisper of battle leathers mingled with a light breeze, and Bela heard the tap of Camille's sword's leather scabbard against her leg as she drifted in closer.

"Water heater," Camille muttered. "That'll work exactly once."

"Maybe a few times." Andy shrugged. "Could be a lemon of a water heater."

Dio spoke up, the sound of her voice startling Bela. "Mrs. Knight won't stay. Nobody lives next door to Sibyls very long."

"I bet that realty company would love to burn down our brownstone." Andy glanced to her left, into a dark clutch of trees. The leaves shivered as they passed.

Bela's instincts itched, but she couldn't sense anything unusual, at least not anywhere close to them. She let the quad walk a little farther, just to be sure nothing really crazy was happening on the streets.

So far, it was quiet.

Too quiet?

Her instincts itched again. More like a tickle, or a shiver.

One more time, Bela let her earth senses spool away from her, into the fertile ground on every side of them. Here and there, her terrasentience detected humans walking, or sitting, or jogging, or . . . yep, right there behind a big rock, doing what humans liked to do most.

Despite the hitch-and-go in her heartbeat, it seemed like a fairly normal night.

As she started to draw her earth power back to her, it took some willpower not to let her awareness slide back to the brownstone, to the basement, to be sure Duncan was still breathing.

Damn, she needed to get a grip—and keep it.

They reached the south end of the Mall and the Olmsted Flower Bed. Even in evening light, Bela's sensitive Sibyl vision catalogued the vivid pinks and purples and whites of the plants gracing the area as if midday sun were playing off the blooms. Seemed as good a place as any to get more organized. She found a private spot and stopped the quad by holding up her hand.

Dio, Camille, and Andy pulled into formation around her as she unzipped her leather face mask and tucked it into her weapons belt. She studied each unmasked face but found no sign of tension outside the normal angst of patrol and trying to work together. "Anybody got anything?"

Camille shook her head. "No communications through my tattoo."

"Nada in the water around here." Andy dripped and shrugged.

Dio said, "Some idiot kids are smoking weed near the bandstand. I can smell it. But no, nothing supernatural. So, does that mean we're to go over what I found in the archives and see if we can hunt down these assholes?"

Bela nodded, and noticed that Camille and Andy were nodding as well.

Dio unzipped the top of her leather bodysuit, reached inside, and pulled out a folded piece of art paper. "Okay, then. These are the creatures that almost kicked our asses in DUMBO."

Her golden blond hair seemed almost white in the moonlight, and Bela held back a sigh as she tried to focus on what appeared to be pencil drawings. Air Sibyls were supposed to be a study in controlled chaos, but Dio seemed to be dedicated to self-regulation to the point of austerity. Her leathers were so clean Bela wished she could smear double handfuls of dirt all over the elbows, just to make Dio feel more normal to her.

Dio's gray eyes landed first on Bela, then on Camille as she held the sketches toward them. "Rakshasa," she said. "Ancient cat-demons."

"Demons." The word hit Bela hard, and her skin

crawled at the memory of the Legion and their monstrous servants, the Asmodai. Asmodai were nothing but elementally stacked killing machines, soulless and mindless and hungry. Thank the Goddess they were gone from the face of the earth, and no one was busy creating more of them.

The Legion had created other types of demons, but they weren't pure nothing-else-but-evil like the Asmodai. Cursons, for example, were half-breeds, with human mothers and human souls. Cursons could learn to manage their demon essence, and lots of them worked for the Occult Crimes Unit. Some had even married Sibyls. Full-blooded Astaroth demons also worked for the OCU and forged deep bonds with Sibyls. Most Astaroths had been young human children when their Legion masters converted them into supernaturally powerful, intelligent, winged creatures— but the Legion discovered, to their great harm in their final battle with the Dark Crescent Sisterhood, that Astaroths retained their humanity and free will, and most preferred to battle for truth, justice, and peace.

Nobody even thought of Cursons and Astaroths as demons anymore, not really, because demons—demons meant pain and war and loss. Demons meant . . . death.

Don't go there, said the ghostly voices of Nori and Devin, but it was too late.

The faces of her lost fighters rose to haunt Bela, and her belly cramped from the force of the sudden grief. "We haven't had to fight demons for almost three years. Just psychic con artists and pissed-off locals with a splash of elemental talent."

Camille didn't say anything, but her sudden tension grabbed Bela's heart. Camille stood fiddling with the leather face mask she rarely wore; her long auburn curls were tangled from all the time she spent twisting them with one delicate hand while everybody else talked.

Did the faces of the triad sisters Camille lost three years

ago loom in Camille's mind like Nori and Devin haunted Bela's brain? Bela thought they probably did.

And did those dead triad sisters accuse Camille of failing them?

But she was young—and she wasn't a mortar.

Swallowing hard against the tight muscles in her throat, Bela made herself stare at the drawings. Colors and lines from the top page danced through her mind, making no sense.

Demons.

Demons, for the sake of the Goddess. Again.

"Did you say cats, Dio?" Andy sounded like she really didn't want to believe that little detail. "As in 'Here kitty kitty' cats?"

Dio moved the paper closer to Andy. "I said demons. I drew them, hunted through the archives until I found them last night, then dug through even older archives to find all we know about them. Definitely demons."

Bela winced as the *d*-word pierced her chest again. She finally took in the images on the paper—hand-drawn pictures of man-sized tigers just like the ones they had seen in DUMBO, with a nondescript Sibyl sketched in the margin for size comparison. "They're as huge as I remembered," she muttered, staring at the papers with Andy, and her mind went straight back to Duncan.

What kind of determination had it taken for him to fight huge, feral demons with his bare hands? How had he done such a thing?

And now—those scratches. The infection of demon energy. Did that stone-solid determination give him any chance at all to stay alive?

Drawn to the exquisite pictures, Bela reached out carefully, because the creatures seemed so real they might jump off the page and bite her. She traced the tip of one finger across the sketches of heavily muscled chests and arms. Dio had rendered three Rakshasa, one with white fur, one with golden, and one with black, wielding swords as their fanged mouths hung open in silent, terrible roars. Dark stripes marked the edges of powerful arms and legs, and the creatures wore an odd sort of armor that looked like chain mail, except the chain links were actually tiny spikes. The eyes. That's what really set them apart from all the demons Bela had battled in the past. A malicious intelligence gleamed from those golden depths, as if the Rakshasa were using Dio's drawings to project their essence straight into the park. Especially the white one.

Just looking at the white tiger-demon gave Bela shivers. He was strong. Maybe too strong. He felt like their leader to her, and she was almost sure of that. Next time, the bastard might succeed in killing one of them.

The leaves and blooms in the Olmsted garden gave an odd, off-kilter rustle.

Everyone jumped at the sound and movement.

Bela let her earth senses fly across the pavement where they stood and drove her awareness into the ground, letting it spread in all directions. Moments. Barely seconds. The vigor in her body began to drain away as she focused all of her attention on detecting abnormalities in the energies touching the nearby earth, but she still didn't find anything out of the ordinary. Not even anything supernatural.

So why had the plants moved with no breeze—and why did she still have the shivers?

Camille's gaze fixed on the shivering flowers. "It's not me. I can't—it's not—" Her expression tightened as the bushes and blooms fell still again. "I thought I sensed some energy, but now it's gone. Maybe I was mistaken."

"No, you weren't," Bela and Dio said at the same time.

"But I couldn't get a read on it either," Dio admitted. "All I can say is, it didn't come from the Mothers over in the brownstone, and I'm pretty sure it didn't whip down from headquarters in the northeast."

Andy was at full alert, one fist doubled against her wet

leather-clad leg. "I sensed something, too. No idea what. A crawly feeling on my skin, like somebody touched the back of my neck."

"Or like something brushed against the elemental locks on our suits," Dio said, referring to the elemental energy layered through their fighting leathers.

"At random?" Bela asked the question even though her instincts told her otherwise. That had been a targeted touch, subtle and quick. Maybe a testing of strength, or a sampling of their defenses.

As if pulled by a powerful magnet, her eyes returned to the drawings of the Rakshasa. A second or so later, she realized her whole quad was studying the feral demons again.

"Okay, only Tarzan could call these ugly shit-brains kitty cats." Andy flicked her pointer finger against the white tiger-creature. "Was it them that just gave us the jumping creepy heebie-jeebies?"

"Whatever it was, it's gone now." Camille's frown was epic as she slumped, jamming one toe against the pavement. "I'm sorry. I should have been able to catch a signature, a hint, but I'm not that fast."

Bela risked putting her hand over the fire Sibyl's knuckles, almost hoping she'd get burned. "No one is. You can't be perfect, Camille, and even if you are perfect, stuff will still slip past you sometimes."

Camille raised her gaze to meet Bela's, and Bela saw gratitude and relief on the younger woman's face. Warmth rushed through Bela, followed by a small measure of relief. The tiny triumph was almost enough to chase away the case of the creeps she had gotten from the drawings and the odd rustling of the leaves—but not enough to take the sting out of Dio's angry glare.

Bela was sorry she had glanced at the air Sibyl, because all the warmth ran straight back out of her. This was such a damned roller coaster. Up one hill and slam-boom down the next one.

"Dio, you're really talented," Andy said, either oblivious to Dio's sudden rage or all too aware of it. "These drawings are better than photographs, and you did them so fast."

Camille mumbled her agreement, and Bela heard a note of awe in the unnaturally quiet fire Sibyl's voice.

A splash of red spread across Dio's cheeks. She glanced at the ground for a moment, then seemed to compose herself. "Rakshasa have been around since recorded history, mostly in Eastern and Far Eastern areas." Her recitation sounded as perfect and modulated as a PBS special. "They kill without conscience, and everything I read suggests they enjoy murdering and eating humans, especially for personal gain and to increase their own standing in the world."

"Great." Andy, who would never narrate a PBS special, belched so deeply Bela could smell the French roast and three hazelnut creamers from the vat of coffee she'd drunk before they hit the streets. "So, where are they, and how do we kill them?"

Dio kept her focus on her papers. "Rakshasa are rudimentary telepaths. They shapeshift, and they can look like anybody they choose to copy—but only for a few seconds or minutes."

Andy's lips pursed, like she was committing all that to memory. "Sociopathic, shape-shifting, mind-reading kitties. Got it. Now, where are they, and how do we kill them?"

Dio's fingers curled against the edges of her drawing. Bela knew she was sticking to the list of points she had created when she was preparing her research presentation. Dio was like that. Lists, numbers, order. Andy's cut-to-the-chase questions had to rake Dio's nerves worse than demon claws on stone.

"They can take an incorporeal form, too," Dio added. "To travel."

"The blue flames we saw at the end of the DUMBO battle?" Camille stood straighter now, like her interest had been captured. "Three columns, tall and flickering. They moved like the wind."

Dio nodded, making eye contact with Camille as easily as she seemed to avoid it with Bela and Andy. "In flame form, they're impervious to any threat, even water, but they can't do any damage. I think elemental locking could prevent the shape-shifting, and maybe even force them to stay corporeal."

Andy raised both hands to the starry sky like she was beseeching the universe. "Goodie. We'll keep them all solid and furry. But how do we find them and *how do we kill them*?"

"Pierce their hearts with elementally locked metal." Dio's words rushed out like an errant breeze. Her face was turned toward her packet again, but her eyes were closed. "Take their heads, burn the bodies and heads, and disperse the ashes in different directions."

Andy stared at her, mouth slightly open.

Camille's eyes got bigger, which was hard, since her face always seemed to be more eyes than anything else.

"We have to stab them with special metal, behead them, burn them, *and* blow their soot to hell and back?" Andy's fingers flickered against the zipper of her bodysuit. "Shit. Couldn't they just explode into elemental energy like all the other demons we've fought?"

Dio looked at her drawings. "Ashes of the head in one direction, ashes of the body in the other. Otherwise, they'll reconstitute, fully healed and ready to fight. They come back to life in a hurry once they're completely dead—faster and faster each time they die and return."

Bela tried to comprehend the precision and effort it would take to destroy one of the tiger-things, much less a bunch of them, especially in a battle. The headache she had slept off across the day gave a first poke, like it might be trying to come back, and she massaged her forehead with her palm. "We don't have enough Sibyls in New York City to take on a fresh horde of ancient demons with special pain-in-the-ass properties."

Dio shook her head, but none of her hair moved. "They're not a horde. They're a pride—six, maybe eight at the most, if they're sticking true to history. There weren't more than a few dozen to begin with—but they shouldn't be here." She finally looked up, and her gray eyes brushed across Bela's face before settling on Camille again. "Rakshasa haven't walked this earth freely in a millennium or more."

"Did someone summon them?" Camille hugged herself instead of tugging at her hair, which Bela took as a good sign.

"They can't be summoned." Dio flipped through her packet, then set the papers down. "They're nobody's servants—at least not like that. In older days, they chose whom to support in various wars and conflicts in the Middle East based on who gave them the best gifts, and they built their ranks by attacking and infecting humans they thought had good physical or psychic potential. Legend has it that most of the Created didn't survive the conversion, or the demon foot soldiers just went nuts and ate everybody, allies and fellow foot soldiers alike."

"Kind of like the Legion," Andy said, "only stupider."

Bela could have done without that comparison, but she forced herself to stay focused on what Dio was saying. *Building their ranks. Infecting humans.* That didn't sound good. Her thoughts arrowed toward the brownstone and Duncan, with his dark, boiling slash wounds.

"Is there any cure for it when they infect humans?" she asked, aware of Andy's steady gaze. "Can the Created be . . . uncreated?"

"I didn't find anything about that, no." Dio frowned and glanced in the direction of the brownstone as well. "Once bitten or scratched, humans will turn. They won't be as big or powerful as the Rakshasa who made them, but they're very dangerous, and loyal only to those who infected them. I don't think there's a way to reverse the process."

Dio hesitated, and Bela thought she sounded regretful. Andy's expression melted into a frown, and Camille fidgeted with her hair. Bela tried to absorb their reactions to keep her own emotions under control, but she wasn't that successful. She wanted to throw up the remnants of the spinach-avocado-pepperoni sandwich Andy had made her eat before they left. She wanted to go home, go to her room, lock the door, and just . . . stay there alone, for a long, long time.

"A king got ticked off when the Rakshasa backed one of his enemies," Dio said as she folded up her drawings. "This king found a way to trap the original demons forever in some faraway desert." With a Sibyl's unfailing sense of direction, Dio pointed east—probably meaning far, far east. "All of the Created Rakshasa were killed off, and the race faded from history and awareness."

Andy pushed her red curls behind her ears. "Well, some asshole set the granddaddy kitties free."

"We don't know that," Dio countered, but when Andy glared at her, she lifted both hands just like Andy had done a few minutes before. "Okay, fine. Say somebody did let them out. Why are they here? I mean, why are they here in New York City?"

Camille looked thoughtful. "I get it. They could be in Riyadh, or London, or Cairo. Why us—why now?"

Andy's reflective frown made her look more like a police officer than anything else. "Maybe the better question is, who's paying them?"

Bela stared at Andy, still too numb over Duncan Sharp's

fate to grasp Andy's train of thought. "Where did you get that? Dio didn't say anything about money."

"She made it sound like they're the were-tiger branch of the Mafia, with Persian accents and a Dahmer complex." Andy reached to her hip and did a check on her Heckler & Koch P-11 underwater dart pistol. "Eating people for personal gain, to increase their own standing—all of that, right? I say if they're in NYC, it's because somebody met their price."

"That makes sense." Camille let her hair go, and Bela glanced at her, wanting a spark, a bit of smoke—some hint of her elemental powers surging with her thoughts and emotions.

No such luck.

Camille was as still and controlled as an earth Sibyl as she said, "I think they're a lot smarter than demons we've dealt with in the past. If we assume that the Rakshasa escaped containment somewhere and that they're out to rebuild their power in today's world, they'll understand that they need modern knowledge, weapons, and conveniences."

"And modern sources and symbols of power, like money." Bela heard her own voice talking, but she felt thousands of miles away. Half her brain was already deep into biology and equations, because all infections had enemies. Heat, antibiotics, cold, antithetical energy—there had to be some way to stop a demon infection. They couldn't just let Duncan die. Well, worse than die. Go demon, then get slaughtered by the same Sibyl swords and daggers that had saved him in DUMBO.

"We need to take this info to the OCU and let them work it through their federal contacts," she added. "If we check account activity related to criminal groups, maybe we can pick up a pattern of money changing hands that correlates with Rakshasa movements around the city."

The group went silent, and Bela thought she understood the new, deeper stillness.

"Yep," Andy said, putting the angst into words. "The kitties will be roving the streets. Who knows where they'll strike next—or why? And who would be idiot enough to pay Rakshasa demons to come to New York?"

Bela was about to ask Dio to make a new list of criminal elements on the rise when they got back to the brownstone—groups who might be scrambling for some advantage, no matter how dangerous—but all the flowers and bushes in the Olmsted garden started to shake.

Andy drew her dart pistol. "I think we've got company."

Bela's breath jammed in her throat.

This time, when she reached out with her earth senses, a bitter, foul-smelling pressure slammed against her awareness. Her teeth slammed together against the metallic taste of disrupted earth, of unnatural energy.

Just like in DUMBO, only not quite as strong.

"Rakshasa!" Bela's pulse sped to racing as her quad jammed their face masks back into place and scrambled to draw weapons. The tattoo on her right forearm tingled, then ached with the primitive distress signal Camille sent to summon other Sibyl patrols—but they didn't have many in the city right now.

"Oh, no you don't," she growled to the demons, imagining the leader, that white tiger-beast Dio had drawn, coming to kill one—or all—of the women she now called sister Sibyls.

"Behind me," she called to her quad. "Now!"

(8)

Bela spun toward the southwest as she yanked back her earth power and drove it into the ground about five feet in front of the pavement where they were standing. It would be a barrier, enough to make the bastards stumble, but not for long.

Her breath came fast, faster as she zipped her face mask. Immediately sweat poured into the leather across her forehead, just from the effort of holding the barrier.

She ripped her serrated blade free of its ties and scabbard and hoisted the sword over her head. Battle senses told her Camille was two paces back on her right, *shamshir* drawn, though the blade wasn't on fire. Andy had her dart pistol at the ready on Bela's left, two paces back from Camille, and water energy seeped around the quad, adding power to Bela's barrier.

Dio's footsteps told Bela she had moved wide right, and the clink of her throwing daggers sounded loud and cold in the otherwise quiet night. Wind sputtered, then sailed forward, binding water and earth even closer.

The air around them chilled, and the stench of ammonia made Bela's eyes water. She forced more energy into the barrier between them and the approaching demon. Her elbows wobbled from the effort.

Where the hell were the creatures?

Why couldn't she see them?

Come on, Camille. Bela willed the fire Sibyl to find her spark and add the amazing strength of fire to their elemental wall so that Bela could fight with more force. *These are demons, not drunk kids who found Grandma's* Book of Shadows *in the attic.*

Out loud, she said, "You did it in DUMBO, Camille. I know you can. Dig deep!"

Camille let out a low cry of frustration. The wall's energy wavered as she tried so hard to ignite her fire that it yanked against everyone else's power.

Bela almost dropped her sword, but Camille cut off her efforts just in time to keep the protective barrier from shattering.

"Never mind," Dio snarled before Camille could try again. Battle rage pushed the air Sibyl's volume and anger to full throttle. "Just swing that damned sword when the time comes."

Bela's jaw got so tight her eye twitched, but she got control of her power and her blade. Blood thumped so hard in her temples that it cracked against her skull. She stared into the darkness, searching for any sign of supernatural life through the shimmer of their elemental energy.

"There!" Andy called, pointing almost directly back toward the brownstone.

Two tall, thin columns of blue flame danced and flickered across grass and pavement, weaving through plants and bushes and trees.

In front of the flames came a dark, broad shape, plowing forward like a tank on legs. Six foot five, maybe taller. Brown fur. Fangs. And it was wearing some sort of metal mesh armor. Flowers and grass flew in every direction as the demon stormed toward them, ripping up the earth with its claws.

"Get the heart," Bela told Andy. "Camille, if I miss the head—"

The thing slammed into their protective wall, staggered, and slammed into it again.

Bela's brain bashed against her skull from the impact. She struggled to keep her blade raised, to keep her feet on the ground. Beside her, Andy swayed and almost lost her footing. Somewhere in the distance, Dio let out a shriek from the pile-driving force of dark energy trying to smash through their natural barrier.

The Rakshasa's eyes blazed orange-yellow, full of hate and rage. Behind it, the two blue flames flickered but didn't shift into any other form. Bela hoped like hell the elemental barrier would keep those two demons incorporeal. If they made it into cat-monsters, that many would be strong enough to blow through the barrier and eat her before she could get off a good swing of her blade.

The creature let out a howl that burned through Bela's bones. She felt its intent through the earth it touched. Killing. Blood. And . . . pleasing its master.

An image of the white tiger-demon flashed through Bela's mind.

"Get away from my quad." The words wheezed out of her mouth as she swept earth energy under its clawed feet and let the earth shake. The demon danced, but got its balance back fast. She caused another quake, as powerful as she dared without risking setting off a cascade reaction that would open a fault straight down Broadway.

No luck.

The demon had the hang of that trick now.

Bela slammed dirt left and right at the same time to make a pit, but the demon jumped clear of the hole in the ground.

The Rakshasa raised its big paws and hammered against the barrier.

Bela felt each blow like a punch to the chest. Air mashed from her lungs and she stopped stirring the earth around the creature. It was all she could do to keep the base of the energy barrier steady. She was barely tracking Camille and Andy and Dio now, and she couldn't hold her sword up much longer.

Andy fired once. Twice. The darts hit the demon's armor and dropped to the ground.

One of Dio's three-pronged African throwing knives whistled past Bela and dug itself into the thing's forehead.

It howled once, then ignored the knife in its brain, charged toward Dio, and beat on the barrier in front of her. She faced it down, snarl for snarl, and drew back with another knife.

The demon's massive, clawed paw punched through the barrier.

Bela yelped and stumbled from the fracture of her earth energy.

The creature grabbed Dio's leathers, jerked her forward, and twisted the neckline tight around Dio's windpipe. She choked. Tried to kick at the thing. It raised its other paw to slice her with its claws.

A blazing rush of adrenaline drove Bela forward. "Not happening!" She ground her teeth and poured her focus into hoisting her blade. Before the Rakshasa could so much as breathe on Dio's face again, Bela lunged and hacked its arm off at the shoulder. It reeled away and howled, swiping at the space where its ugly paw had been.

Dio shoved the severed arm away from her and bent over, massaging her throat. She still had a knife in her other hand, but her shoulders were shaking too hard for her to throw it.

Water blasted the wounded Rakshasa, knocking it sideways as the columns of blue flames that came with it moved north and south, to either side of the quad.

Camille started toward the demon, *shamshir* at the ready, but Bela called her back. "The barrier! Help me now!"

Her quad pulled in, weapons facing out, as Bela drew on the earth and built a new wall of energy. Andy's water power laced through hers a split second later. Dio's wind energy came next—but still no fire.

"*Damnit!*" Camille shouted from Bela's left. "I—I can't!"

The blue flame columns circled the new protective wall.

"They're testing it." Dio managed to get to her feet. "And here comes that other bastard again."

The Rakshasa Bela had wounded was charging toward them—with two good arms.

Bela glanced at the ground. The beast's severed paw was still bleeding on the grass.

"Fuck me," Andy said. "Guess that's what 'reconstitute' means."

Dio hurled her throwing knife through the barrier and took off one of the demon's cat ears. It kept coming.

A second knife and then a third hit the thing's mesh armor and fell useless in the grass. The blue flame columns flickered on either side of them.

"They're surrounding us," Dio shouted. "Kill it now. Right now!"

Andy and Camille surged forward, and Dio's wind energy wavered in the barrier. Bela dropped her sword and concentrated every bit of her essence on keeping the protection intact. Her chest crushed as she stopped breathing, giving all of herself to the task. She didn't give a shit if the demon ripped off her head, as long as her quad took the bastard down and got out of Central Park alive.

"To hell with this." Andy dropped to one knee and aimed her pistol. Water sprayed down both arms as she fired. The water-encased dart screamed past Bela like a torpedo, the wave surrounding it moving faster and harder with each fraction of a second.

Bela forced the barrier into the Rakshasa's chest, shaping its edges like a spreader.

The metal mesh armor separated, about an inch, only an inch—and Andy's dart plunged through the hole she created, lancing into the Rakshasa's chest.

The creature bellowed and grabbed for the dart, then seemed to freeze where it stood, immobilized. At the same moment, the two blue flames scattered through the air and retreated into the darkness.

Bela let the barrier collapse and fell toward her sword.

Have to cut off its head.

Her knees hit pavement hard enough to make her teeth rattle. Her palms scraped pavement. Her head swam, and her gulps of air didn't seem to fill her lungs.

Have to get my sword before it pulls out that dart, or starts healing, or—

Her fingers closed on the hilt, but she couldn't pick it up, couldn't pick herself up.

Damnit!

The dart fired backward out of the Rakshasa's chest, and the creature flung itself toward her, across where the barrier had been.

Andy shot the thing with the rest of her darts, one, two, three, all in the chest, missing the heart, and it kept coming. Water and wind slammed into its face, and still it was coming. Inches from her now. Leaning down. Reaching to snatch her off the ground.

Its mouth opened.

Fangs parted. Sulfurous spit dripped and sizzled on the pavement in front of Bela.

Goddess, the stink of it! Like a thousand rotten graves.

She retched as light flickered beside her, and she turned her head, hoping to see Camille with a blazing sword.

Instead she saw a man.

The shimmering ghostly outline of a man, golden and indistinct, except she thought he was wearing some kind of uniform.

Bela's heart gave a wild pitch against her ribs. Time contracted, then expanded.

The apparition spread its arms as if to protect her, and when its fingers brushed across the top of her head, energy rushed into her. Cool. Familiar. Almost like her own earth power. Not enough to let her join the fight, but enough to help her lift her head—and her sword.

The Rakshasa hesitated and growled. It swiped its claws at the specter instead of cutting Bela to ribbons.

Bela rammed her blade straight into the thing's chest. The sword tip glanced off hard bone, rattling her arms at the elbows, but she knew she'd hit her target because the demon stopped moving.

At the same second, Camille blasted through the golden phantasm sheltering Bela. It shattered into thousands of pieces of golden light. Camille screamed and swung her *shamshir* at the Rakshasa's neck.

Flesh tore.

Demon bone cracked.

Bela felt impacts as the thing's severed head knocked her sword out of her grip, bounced off her thigh, and tumbled away, taking her blade on a clattering roll across the pavement. She barely managed to pitch herself sideways, out of the way of a spray of black, stinking blood.

Camille screamed again, stuck out her bloody blade, and shot a torrent of flames at the rolling head. It exploded into fire and burned like ignited wax. She swung her sword around and scorched the body of the demon as it twitched on the pavement beside Bela.

The stink of ammonia gave way to the stench of burned leather and flesh and fur—and fried hair. Bela didn't need to feel her face to know that her eyebrows were gone.

Again.

Her face mask was totally singed away, and her face was so hot it was probably blistering.

She opened her mouth to whimper thanks to the Goddess for her life, but grit and pebbles slammed into her cheeks. The night tilted and roared as a fully formed tornado swept the ashes of the demon's body east, digging a furrow through the park's grass as it went. Bela groaned as she rubbed her palms against her stinging face.

The air around her howled all over again. Bela's ears popped like she was landing in a jet. She grabbed the edges of the pavement and glued herself into the ground with what little earth energy she could muster—not fast enough. Another spinning funnel sucked up the remains of the demon's head and rumbled across her back, bouncing her like a basketball and ripping her leathers open as it headed west.

Trees, bushes, buildings . . . she didn't even want to know what kind of damage those twisters were doing to Manhattan.

Pierce it in the heart, take the head, disperse the ashes— okay, okay. I think we're done now.

Bela lifted her own head.

A torrent of water hit her straight in her burning, stinging face. The swirling shower-blast washed her and the ground around her completely clean.

"Oh," Andy said from somewhere nearby. "Um, sorry."

Bela coughed and snorted out water as Camille helped her get to her feet. Bela's knees were shaking. She heard herself swearing. A lot. And the wind was picking up again, with a totally different flavor. It was focused completely on Bela.

This time, Andy said, "Uh-oh."

Bela shook herself free from Camille's grip. "Andy, Camille—wait for me by the stone fence. This might take a second."

"Not." Andy shook her head, sending droplets raining down from her ears and cheeks. She jogged to Bela and took her hand. "If you go down, I'm going with you."

Camille didn't answer, but she didn't head for the fence, either.

The pressure against Bela's face and ears felt a lot like being fired off the Empire State Building by some giant slingshot. Her heart pounded, but more from anxiety than fear or anger. She had so few opportunities with Dio. Would this be a good one or a disaster?

I might as well say yes to joining your quad, she had told Bela after spending two hours trying to kill Bela out in Motherhouse Greece's stone fighting arena. *If I'm not fighting with you, I'll spend all my time thinking about fighting against you. That's not good for me or you or the Sisterhood. And neither is staying here when we're so short on Sibyls.*

Dio's wind blew Andy dry and almost knocked Camille off her feet. Bela had to use a big dose of earth power to stay on her feet against the incredible force Dio was exerting as she stormed forward.

"You saved me." Dio stopped in front of Bela, her blond hair free of its usual clasp and standing almost straight up in the swirling wind. Dio's rage flowed through each word, through the air itself, into the earth, making Bela's teeth rattle. It was all she could do to hold her ground, and if she hadn't been gripping Andy's hand, she might have blown even that simple goal.

Dio's gray eyes snapped like they were full of lightning, and once more, thunder rumbled in the clear night sky. "You—you saved me."

"Yeah, she did," Andy shouted over the rush of air. "Saying thank you might be appropriate!"

"Piss off!" Dio roared, and it sounded like a brand-new tornado touching ground.

Bela took a wider stance and yelled, "I did what I could," knowing Andy and Dio and Camille understood that she wasn't talking about the moment in the fight when she'd kept the Rakshasa from choking Dio.

For a few seconds, stretching from yesterday into eternity, Dio just glared at Bela and let the wind blow.

Bela stood fast, and Andy and Camille gave no ground beside her.

The roar of the air died back enough for Dio's next

words to sound less lethal. "You're good with that sword, and with the saw-toothed blade you used to carry." Tears glistened in the gray depths of her furious eyes. "You're a master. A genius."

Bela dismissed that with a shake of her head. "I'm not a genius at anything, Dio."

"Don't sell yourself short," Andy said, her voice nothing but a grumble against the still-storming wind.

"Bitch," Dio said, the air losing force by the second, and her voice turning ragged, almost overcontrolled. "Why the hell couldn't you have saved my sister?"

Bela felt the lance of pain like a knife thrust in her chest. "I don't know."

Andy wanted to say more, Bela knew. Andy had been there when Devin died, but so out of control with her new water power that she was as much hindrance as help. Bela squeezed Andy's fingers, hoping she understood.

Let it go. Leave it alone.

Water flowed down Andy's arm, splattering against the wind-swept ground as Dio finally released her air assault.

"You were standing there when my sister died." Dio started off loud, but her voice dropped as she spent her venom. Her normally bright eyes had gone completely blank. "Then you let some ass-wiping demon carry her back to Motherhouse Greece. Thanks for that, Bela."

That was too much for Andy, who let go of Bela's hand and slapped Dio with a fistful of water, plastering Dio's hair to her face and shoulders. "Jake Lowell is not just some random stranger. He's special, and he's married to a Sibyl now—and he treated your sister with respect. We didn't have fighters to spare for an honor escort. A lot of good OCU officers didn't even get funerals until after the crisis passed."

Andy's voice wavered on that last sentence, and she sprayed a little more water.

"For the sake of the Goddess, Dio, the Legion was busting our balls all over New York." Bela wiped water off her own cheeks, aware that Dio hadn't been in that fight. "We were getting slaughtered, like we almost got slaughtered tonight."

The words fell into the now-still air. Shame flickered across Dio's beautiful face.

"Bela saved you," Camille said in a cramped tone. "That would be a good thing to remember, how it feels to almost die and get saved by your sister Sibyl. It doesn't always work that way. It can't, not with what we fight on these streets every day."

Bela couldn't even look at Camille, because she knew what she'd see.

A younger version of the woman, deep in the trail section of Van Cortlandt Park, huddled over the burned, dead form of her triad's air Sibyl, killed in a Legion ambush. Camille had beaten back a demon horde almost single-handedly, just to protect the body. It had taken Bela almost an hour to pry Camille's fingers away from the corpse and get them both out of that park.

"Loss never gets any smaller, especially if you feed it," Andy told Dio, or maybe it was Camille—or maybe it was all of them. "And don't tell me *I* don't know how it feels."

Dio's wind energy started to kick up, but Bela contained it without too much effort. Dio wasn't fighting that hard anymore. Bela had a sensation like a shift in the weather as Dio hesitated, then let the air stop moving.

Shouts got their attention, and a group of Sibyls in face masks raced across the grass toward them, fire Sibyl weapon flaming.

Andy waved to them, shouting that the battle was over.

A minute or so later, the lead Sibyl in the approaching triad retrieved Bela's sword from the ground and pressed the hilt into her hand. She thought it was Sheila Gray, the spook-calm earth Sibyl of the East Ranger triad. With the shortage of fighters, they had been pulling north to cover the Bronx more nights than not.

As Bela sheathed her hot, wet blade, she saw the burning sword the group's fire Sibyl was carrying. Short hilt. Massive blade with rune-like etchings of dying people glowing along its length. Yep. It was the East Ranger Group. Maggie Cregan was the only Sibyl in history to fight with an execution sword. It had belonged to an ancestor—one of Ireland's most notorious hang-ladies. Maggie's sword gradually stopped glowing as she absorbed her fire energy, and she pulled off her face mask to reveal her short red hair. Even in the dead of night, her strange pale green eyes burned with a deadly, psychotic light most people would find very, very disturbing. As it was, Bela felt a flash of envy over Maggie's fire power, wishing Camille could access just a fraction of that energy reliably when they needed it.

"Think that was overkill with the tornados?" Camille was asking Dio as she dusted away the burned remains of her own face mask and patted out several smoking holes in her leathers. "Two of them?"

"I broke them up before they took out any buildings," called Karin Maros, the East Ranger triad's friendly air Sibyl. "It's all good."

"You need to shut up." Dio shook her face mask at Camille. "The frigging ashes got dispersed, didn't they?"

"Did you guys see any columns of blue flame?" Andy had her face mask off, and she was turning in circles, her wet hair spraying water as she scanned their little corner of Central Park.

The East Ranger group shook their heads. "Nothing like that," Sheila Gray said as she carefully unzipped her face mask and took it off to reveal her long ink-black hair, pulled into a pristine ponytail. "Just the tornados with ashes in the center."

Bela gave a quick explanation of Rakshasa and the battle, and saw Sheila's face change from interested to worried as she contemplated a new onslaught of demons in New York City. Dio explained about the killing process.

"The Mothers already know," Camille told Maggie. "They're at our place, helping that detective who got sliced down in DUMBO."

"I thought more demons were going to pop out of the air, but the blue fire columns went away." Andy holstered her dart gun, the set of her mouth grim and very officer-like. "I think those fuckers were *playing* with us. Just testing us to see what we've got, how we fight."

"How fast it took help to arrive?" Sheila suggested, and Bela had the uncomfortable sense that she was correct.

"I guess we just got measured." Bela wished she could sit down. Her knees felt like rubber.

"Not good," Andy grumbled, still staring out at the park like she expected the Rakshasa to come back any second. The East Ranger group was studying Andy more than the trees, and Bela knew they couldn't help themselves. The world's only fighting water Sibyl was a great curiosity to anyone who didn't know her. And even lots of people who did.

A few minutes later, Sheila and her triad said their good-byes and headed back to the streets. As they faded from view, Bela leaned against Camille for support.

"Did anybody see a ghost?" She pushed her singed, damp, matted hair out of her face with one trembling hand and used her fingers to confirm that she had no eyebrows. "It looked kind of like a soldier, only made out of golden light, and I drew some energy from it."

By morning, her eyebrows would be close to regrown— but damn, she hated it when her face got fried. The blisters only lasted an hour or two, but they burned like a bitch for the first few minutes.

Andy, Dio, and Camille all stared at her.

"Nooooo," Andy said. "No ghosts, Bela." Then, "Dio, I think you rattled her brain with all that wind. We'd better get her back to the brownstone and call headquarters to ask the West Ranger triad to finish patrol."

"It wasn't my wind that scrambled her good sense." Dio didn't look at Bela as she retrieved her throwing knives and looped them into her belt. "Her brain was mush a long time before I met her."

"The ghost, or the apparition . . . it was there." Bela used her palms to soothe her burning face with earth energy. "The demon saw it, so it had to have energy. That's why I'm still alive."

Camille threaded her arm around Bela's waist and turned her toward home. "I'm—I'm really sorry I couldn't find my fire."

Bela patted Camille's hand. "You beheaded the thing and saved my butt. You have nothing to be sorry about."

"No kidding." Andy got on Bela's other side and helped steady her and keep her torn leathers from falling off as they started out of the park. "That was one hell of a chop. Gross as shit, too."

Dio didn't come to help out and didn't offer Camille any comfort. She walked behind them, the way brooms tended to do. After a few moments, she said, "If you really saw a ghost, maybe it was Duncan Sharp."

Bela stopped walking.

Anger hit her first, a hot wash of it, just before an equally cold wash of dread. She yanked her arms free from Andy and Camille, and gave serious thought to drawing her sword on Dio.

Get a grip, whispered the long-lost voices of Nori and Devin. *She's yours. Your sister Sibyl. He's just a man, and a stranger.*

Bela's lips curled back from her teeth. Battle rage was rising in her again, hot and powerful and demanding, but she couldn't get a fix on what or whom she wanted to attack, or even why. The voices from her past, for being so almighty rational? Dio, for bringing up such a terrible possibility?

Herself, for bringing this quad together?

"Dio, you're a bitch." Andy tried to tug Bela forward with Camille helping, but Bela sank her earth energy into the grass and didn't move. "She's just a bitch, Bela. Don't listen to her."

"Hey, I'm not being a shithead." Dio caught up with them and faced Bela. "Think about it. We just fought one Rakshasa, smaller than the ones we fought in DUMBO— and not as strong as those demons were. Then there's the fact that other Rakshasa seemed to be escorting it, but they didn't stay and help it finish the job." She pointed toward the brownstone. "The creature came from that direction, and Bela, you said you saw a ghost that helped you. A ghost in uniform—maybe like a police officer, or whatever's left of a person's soul after they turn into a cat-demon."

Bela's mind was going slowly numb.

That made a little too much sense to suit her.

"Please don't be right," she whispered, hugging herself. "He seems like a strong man. A good man. I don't want to think of him like—"

The memory of the demon's head hitting her thigh made bile surge up her throat. Her wet skin got clammy, and she was shaking from more than fatigue now.

Andy got busy offering a few more opinions about Dio's lineage for talking so casually about a police officer's death, but Camille's expression turned nervous and she stared at her feet. "Maybe the Mothers couldn't save him," she said, sounding worried and sad.

Andy stopped her recitation. "The Mothers," she repeated. "Oh. God." In the bright moonlight, Bela saw all the color drain out of Andy's face. "How would he have gotten away from them? There's no way, unless—"

"Shit!" Dio's shout was followed by a blast of wind as

she took off toward the brownstone, sweeping past Bela and Andy and Camille like they were statues.

Camille was the next to move, and Bela found herself running, too, breathless again, teeth chattering, and Andy holding tight to her hand.

(9)

Duncan dreamed he was holding off an ugly-ass monster, keeping himself between the beautiful woman he wanted to touch and one of the psychotic cat-bastards who'd killed John.

Rakshasa, John's voice told him, but Duncan couldn't begin to grasp that word.

He had known his angel was in trouble, and he'd gone to her, but he couldn't say how he'd pulled any of that off.

He thought his heart was beating, hard and fast, but his body didn't seem to be all the way in the fight. He felt . . . floaty. Then his whole head seemed to catch fire, and his arms, and his neck and chest. Damn. It was all he could do to stay on his feet. Like the desert. Just like the desert under too much sun to breathe, but this was Central Park, and it was dark, and he was made out of light instead of flesh and blood, and he was wearing a chain around his neck that seemed to weigh about six hundred pounds.

You're losing it, Sharp.

Death was real to him now, a monster like the cat-thing, black and stretching everywhere like a frigid Afghan night. It was with him. Right beside him, and it wanted him.

Was he cashing it in, right this very second?

Was he nothing but a ghost?

The death-monster slid toward him, blocking New York City from his view.

Duncan held back a shout of pain—and she saw him. His angel. She looked up at him with those beautiful dark eyes, and she knew he was there, trying to help her.

That kept him upright. Helped him ignore the death-monster and even shove it back a few feet.

He touched her hair, so soft, and he willed her to be okay, tried to give her a dose of whatever it was she'd been giving him to make him stronger.

Grab that sword, Angel.

Cut that furry fucker before it cuts you.

The monster took a swipe at him.

Missed.

And his angel dragged her blade off the pavement.

Yes!

She lifted it, swung her arm back, and—

The park exploded into fire and wind and water and nothing. Nothing but long, velvety darkness.

Duncan drifted in that nothing space for a while, then he thought he heard women talking.

Sounding distressed—worried, or maybe upset?

Shit. Am I hearing people talk at my own funeral?

Yeah, sure. John Cole laughed at him. *You're a sinner, Duncan, but you'd have to be a* good *sinner to get that many women upset over your sorry ass.*

"Ve're fine," said a craggy, ancient voice with a Russian accent. "He's holding on, but he did not leave this bed. Better, a bit, ve think, but novhere near getting up and joining you in battle."

Duncan tried to shake himself loose from the dark claws of sleep that dug into his mind, his joints, his muscles.

No luck.

He never thought a pair of eyelids could weigh as much as boxcars, but damn, his were heavy. And his arm hurt. And the rest of him hurt, too.

The sleep-claws pierced him all over again, and he didn't hear anything else for a while.

He woke to a little pinch on his arm, like somebody poked him with a needle to take blood. Then a sexy female voice said, "You're alive."

He heard the relief, felt it almost as plainly as his own heartbeat. The air around him seemed calm, but there was a power to it, and he took a deep breath.

Almonds and fresh berries, just a hint of it. Perfect.

"I'm staying here with you now, until you wake up." Soft lips pressed against his forehead, then went away, and he wanted them back. "No way am I going through that bunch of worry again."

A little while later, he heard the hum of machinery and soft, distant singing. Something he recognized. It was a haunting, melancholy tune he'd learned from some old women in the Afghan desert. They had picked it up from Russian soldiers during the invasion years before.

Cossack's lullaby, John reminded him, then translated a verse, to help Duncan call it into his conscious mind.

> I will die from longing, I will wait inconsolably,
> I will pray the whole day long,
> And at night I'll tell fortunes.
> I will think that you are in trouble,
> Far away in a foreign land.

John went quiet.

Duncan could have listened to the woman sing forever. He knew it was her. The same woman who'd just kissed his forehead—the angel who kept drifting through his dreams.

Maybe if he dreamed about her hard enough, he'd make her real.

10

Bela stayed with Duncan the rest of that night, and all the next day and night, too, taking breaks only when the Mothers worked with him. She wasn't sure why she felt so compelled to do that, except that she was positive he had saved her life in Central Park.

How—now that was a question, but she intended to find out. As carefully as possible, she took small blood samples every few hours, some skin samples, and very, very carefully, some scrapings from his slash wounds. She used them to run standard medical tests, but also Sibyl studies to examine his blood history and find out if he had any supernatural heritage, paranormal energy profiles, even species DNA tracers.

"You have a king's will," she told him after yet another study came back with nothing but normal human indicators. She traced the outline of his face, lingering on the rough stubble of his jaw as she gave him a light dose of earth energy to make sure he wasn't hurting. "You win your battles no matter what, no matter how you have to do it, don't you?"

He stirred at her touch, at her words, and she wondered if he could hear her.

In case he could, she gave him a good talking-to about using all that formidable strength to keep fighting his demon infection and wake up.

Early on the third evening, Mother Keara booted Bela out and told her to spend some time with her quad.

By the time she changed clothes and made it up the stairs and into the kitchen, Bela was realizing how tired she was, which wasn't good, with patrol looming again tomorrow night. For a few minutes, she stood in the kitchen next to Andy, feeling the soft buffet of water energy as she crammed down the Gruyère and pine nut sandwich Andy made for her in silence.

Andy glared at the coffeemaker as if her ferocious stare would speed up its brewing.

It didn't.

Bela swallowed the last of the cheese and pumpernickel. The urge to go back to the basement and check on Duncan nearly overwhelmed her, and she looked at the door to the steps at least five times in thirty seconds.

"He's handsome," Andy said, more to the coffeemaker than Bela. "But now I'm thinking it's more than that."

Bela sighed and burped pine nuts. "He's a fighter. That's all. I admire that—plus, I think something else is going on with him, other than the demon infection. An apparition really did save me in Central Park, before Camille beheaded the Rakshasa, and I'm sure it was him."

"Duncan Sharp is wounded. He's sick, and he might die any second." A few droplets trickled down Andy's cheeks and necks as she touched the coffeemaker. The water inside it hissed as it finally started to brew, and Bela knew she'd have to buy a new machine soon. Andy blew one up about every two weeks.

"You think you can heal him," Andy said. "With your dead triad sisters, you never got that chance."

That hit home, and way too hard. Bela rubbed her belly, where the cheese and pine nut paste churned in unpleasant ways. "Ouch."

She was surprised she didn't hear Nori and Devin talking to her, but then, she hadn't heard them much since she started working with Duncan.

Andy banged the top of the coffeemaker, which still wasn't going fast enough to suit her, but her light brown eyes were distant. The green highlights in those eyes were so strong, they could be taken for either color, depending on the lighting.

"Be careful, Bela. That's all I'm saying. Saving this man won't bring Nori and Devin back to you."

The warning came out soft. Way too soft for Andy, and Bela knew why.

"I hear you." She reached out and squeezed Andy's wrist.

Andy nodded and went to get her coffee mug. If she hadn't moved away so quickly, Bela would have hugged her, and Andy probably would have cried.

Three years, and Andy was still hurting as badly as Bela over her losses. Maybe even worse—and definitely more than she usually let on to anyone. It was three years ago that Bela had watched the worst ancient demon in history tear apart her OCU patrol partner, Sal Freeman, who had been the captain of the OCU—and Andy's lover.

Bela had been the one dispatched to tell Andy he was dead. She'd been forced to see Andy's face, to stand there helpless while Andy's soul broke apart from the weight of the grief. After she had knocked Andy out to save New York City from an accidental tidal wave, Bela had carried Andy for miles to get her back to OCU's townhouse headquarters on the Upper East Side, above the reservoir, cradling her like a wounded child.

Later that same day, after everyone else had joined the final battle against the Legion, Bela had gone with Andy into the downstairs conference room and stood beside her when she saw Sal's body. She had held Andy and felt her racking sobs as the medical examiner zipped up what was left of the love of Andy's life and took him away forever. Then, even after she had lost faith in her own ability to protect anyone she loved, Bela had followed Andy into battle, ready to die to avenge Andy's pain.

That was the moment, perhaps, when they both understood that no matter how close Andy was to the Sibyl triad who gave them this brownstone—the women who intro-

duced Andy to the world of the Dark Crescent Sisterhood—
Bela and Andy would one day fight together.

"The living room's quiet again," Andy said as she
brought her giant mug back to fill it up. Her voice was still
weak, and almost whispery. It hurt Bela to hear it. "Mother
Yana and Mother Anemone are upstairs resting in Dio's
room. Dio and Camille have some ideas about how to find
where the Rakshasa are hiding. I'll be there in a second."

Bela almost had to slap herself to make herself leave the
kitchen and let Andy have the time she needed to compose
herself. She didn't want to abandon her closest friend, and,
if she admitted the whole truth, she didn't want to leave the
basement door behind, either. But, duty was duty, and they
had cat-demons to kill, so she pushed her way through the
swinging door into the large, two-section living room.

Flat, unmoving air surrounded her, oppressing her almost immediately.

How can it be so damned still in here?

In the back section of the living room, Bela dropped onto
the overstuffed couch beside the huge wooden communications platform that also served as her quad's work table.
She glanced quickly at Camille and Dio. They weren't
wearing leathers, but both of them looked like they were
fighting battles in their own minds. They sat in the matching chairs on the opposite side of the big table, each working on papers in front of them without talking.

How could there be *no* energy in the room with three,
count them, three Sibyls sitting within grabbing distance of
each other? Sibyls who were supposed to be part of the
same fighting quad.

It's like living in a crypt.

She wanted to go back to the basement and take up her
vigil beside Duncan Sharp again. At least down there, she
felt . . . welcome. Bela scrubbed her palms against the knees
of her jeans and tried to relax, letting her earth energy fill

the void and her earth senses reach out with more force and precision.

Nope.

Nothing in the room other than warm bodies and heart-beats. The sets of wind chimes, designed to carry Sibyl communications and react to elemental energy, hung still and silent from the ceiling and doorways. No jingling. No tinkling. Bela couldn't detect even a hint of wind, ash, soot, or smoke, and she needed something, damn it, to keep her mind off Duncan Sharp.

She scooted around on the overstuffed couch and did her best to ignore the odd elemental stillness in the room. No matter what position she cramped herself into, she couldn't get comfortable on the soft cushions. She might as well have tried to balance on a pile of camel-colored marshmallows.

Dio, her nails and hair impeccably clean and neat as always, had a map of Manhattan on the table in front of her. Her khaki slacks and white blouse were pressed to perfection, and even the map she was working on had no smudges or errant lines. The dozen projective mirrors hanging at intervals on the walls behind her seemed to magnify her freaky neatness, just like they highlighted the absence of smoke and fire in the air around Camille.

Camille, dressed in jeans and a cream-colored tunic, had a map, too. She was using her pencil to add a few dots in the center. Bela watched her work, shifting on her stack of pillows again.

This place, this whole brownstone, it just wasn't right.

Her quad was more jeans and sandwiches than silk and caviar. Maybe that was part of the problem. As soon as possible, she was junking this fluffy high-end crap for some leather furniture, metal accents, hardwood floors—yeah. Attractive, durable, and easy to clean.

Andy banged through the swinging kitchen door on Bela's left gripping a notebook, a folder, a pen, and a coffee mug that rivaled the size of a small beer keg. She dripped water from both elbows. Droplets splattered on her torn, damp jeans, her hole-ravaged NYC T-shirt, and the plush carpet.

Bela let out a breath at the fresh rush of elemental power and normalcy Andy brought with her, then thought better of the hardwood idea. With the world's only fighting water Sibyl in the house, she should probably go with tile. Hardwood would never last.

Andy put down her massive mug, folder, and writing utensils on the gigantic oak platform before she flopped into the last of the matching chairs arranged in a circle around the big table. She rubbed both hands across her freckled cheeks. "Do we have a search plan yet?"

Dio slid her map forward. "Camille's talked to all the triads in the city, and nobody's sensed any of that sour-feeling Rakshasa energy outright." She had outlined most of Manhattan, then sketched grid lines over the lower portion of the borough. There were question marks on parts of the Bronx and Brooklyn, and one mark on the east side of Staten Island. Dio pointed to the symbols. "Some disturbances in normal patterns were picked up here, here, and here outside of Manhattan, but the elemental energy in this borough is the most stirred up and dense."

Andy took a big swig of coffee, then made a note and asked, "Isn't it always that way?"

"Yes, but this is more than usual." Camille tugged at her hair, then stopped herself, pushed her own map aside, and used Dio's to show Andy and Bela the biggest trouble spots. "Almost like somebody's trying to keep up some shields against paranormal energy, broader and more organized than the Vodoun mambos and Wiccans and Pagans can pull off. Sheila's Rangers tracked the flame-form Rakshasa who ran away from our fight, and they lost the scent and feel of them right around here, in Midtown West."

Dio's heaviest grid lines covered Times Square, Midtown East, Midtown West, Chelsea, Murray Hill, and Gramercy. "The shielding comes and goes through here, the hottest areas. I think if we concentrate on these sections, we'll find something."

"The OCU has doubled patrols in those sectors day and night." Andy pushed her mug away from her on the table, and Bela realized she'd already slammed down half its contents. "The OCU also has contacts digging through financial records, like you suggested. If we can't find the kitties right away, maybe we can hunt down whoever is paying them. I got a copy of the file on the woman who got murdered the night we rescued Duncan Sharp." She pushed her folder forward and flipped it open to reveal photographs and police reports.

Bela leaned toward the table, and her stomach lurched at the top photo—a naked woman lying on a blood-streaked floor, neck and remaining leg twisted into impossible positions.

"Not much of her left." Camille's voice was thinner and squeakier than usual. "It looks like she's been half eaten."

"Duncan Sharp thought John Cole did this, but now we all know it was probably the Rakshasa." Dio's tone was measured. Thoughtful. Bela realized the air Sibyl was looking past the photo rather than directly at it, and for the briefest moment, the air in the brownstone stirred. Wind chimes clanged softly, but only a few of them, as if the air had flowed in a straight, targeted line.

Southeast.

Toward where the murder Dio was talking about had occurred.

Bela kept her gaze steady but used her terrasentience to track the gust, feeling the wind move over the floor of the brownstone, out the door, down the steps, then dissipate in the traffic on Fifth Avenue. Bela's ability to track or sense anything that touched earth, even at some distance, far ex-

ceeded that of most Sibyls—kind of a compensation for a
weaker terrakinetic ability. She couldn't shake the world,
but by the Goddess, she could find just about anything lost
or hiding in it, so long as it had contact with elements of
earth in some form or other.

And this gust of wind speeding across the ground, it was
definitely interesting.

Did Dio have a gift with ventsentience? Could she track
or sense things using the air as her primary investigative
tool? And if she did have that skill—more unusual for air
Sibyls—did she even know it?

Thunder rumbled in the distance, out of season and
strange enough to capture Bela's attention. She carefully
pulled her awareness back from the rock and sand in the
asphalt and concrete, from the small particles of dirt scattered on the floor.

"The tech geeks over at the OCU are checking for similar crimes worldwide," Andy was saying. "Maybe we can
get some sort of pattern that will allow us to track the Rakshasa migration into New York City."

"What's her name?" Camille's question slipped through
the air like a sigh, her voice was so soft.

Bela looked up from her own musings too fast, and before she could stop herself, she asked, "What?"

Damnit, that sounded annoyed.

Careful, came the whispered warnings of Nori and
Devin, seemingly from a thousand miles away. The sound
in Bela's mind startled her, but she managed not to react.

Camille reacted, though. She frowned at Bela's sharp
question, then lowered her eyes—but at least she persisted.
"The . . . woman. The victim. She had a name, right?"

Dio came completely back to herself, and the wind
chimes in the brownstone went still. "Katrina Alsace
Drake. She was an heiress who was in the process of liqui-
dating her assets and donating them all to her charity, the
Societal Aid Fund."

Camille looked up. "I've heard of them. They're a serve-the-poor operation. Food, clothing, housing, legal representation for those who can't afford it."

Andy shifted the picture of the brutalized woman to the side, revealing another photo, this one of a pleasant-looking brunette with big, innocent brown eyes and a wide smile. She was dressed in jeans, a T-shirt, and a work apron. No high-society trappings, no surgical alterations to make herself more perfect. Just a person who seemed to be working to fulfill her own ideals.

It was a dumb, empty question, but it rang true to Bela in this instance, so she spoke it aloud. "Who would want to kill her? She looks like everybody's—"

The words died in her throat, but Dio had already pursed her lips.

Katrina Drake looks like everybody's little sister. Bela didn't smack herself in the forehead, but only because her willpower was formidable. *Yeah. Good one, Bela.*

Dio's next words came out in a tense blast. "Drake's net worth was close to fourteen million. She had funds in stocks and real estate, but she weathered the market downturn well."

Camille kept her voice steady, despite her obvious distress at Dio's reaction to Bela's slip-up. "If we assume John Cole wasn't a serial killer, then who hired the Rakshasa to, um, eat the heiress?"

Andy answered, her green-brown eyes leveled on Dio like she was ready to blast her with a wave if that was what it took to keep her calm. "Jeremiah Drake is a possibility. The husband. Katrina was divorcing him. The courthouse database said irreconcilable differences, conflict with his teenage son from a previous marriage, and all that crap—but who knows the real reasons. Infidelity, abuse, vengeance—anything's possible."

Camille pondered this with a twist of her hair. "And he'd have the means."

"Her money." Bela felt a fresh twist in her gut. "Damn, that's cold."

Andy kept staring at Dio as she rattled off the next possibility. "We've got Merin Alsace, Katrina's brother. With the husband cut loose, all of Katrina's money would go to him—or at least that's what we're figuring until we see the will."

"Timing's off, if the divorce wasn't final." Camille was engaged again, and her fear and fragility retreated. Bela thought she caught the faintest whiff of smoke, but she couldn't be sure. "But who knows if the Rakshasa pay attention to calendars? Hiring them doesn't mean you can control them."

Dio leaned back in her chair, still angry and silent over being reminded of her dead sister, but she was chilling out enough to let Andy relax and keep briefing them.

"We've got Reese Patterson for a source—the Alsace family attorney. Good place to start, and given the society photos I found, he likes cheap-looking blondes." Andy gave Dio a meaningful stare.

Dio glared back at Andy, volunteering nothing, and Bela couldn't help thinking about Nori again, and Dio's sister Devin.

Dio's face looked so much like Devin's, and those wide eyes made Bela see Devin's agonized gaze as she died in Bela's arms during a Legion attack on Fordham's campus. It had been so easy to talk to Nori and Devin, and they were always ready to jump up and help the triad. Feelings and facts and laughter and work flowed so easily. Everything, just . . . everything was easier.

And now?

Now it was a struggle not to close her eyes and tell Dio to screw off, get over it, and go put on something sexy to tease the lawyer into spilling everything he knew. Instead, Bela drew in a few centering breaths, then chose her next words carefully. "Dio, are you willing to dress the part and see if you can get the lawyer talking?"

Dio's mouth came open, and her next question tumbled out with a schoolgirl's snarky edge. "What am I, the quad hooker or something?"

A swell of irritation brought Bela's earth energy to the surface, and she fought back a surge that might have been powerful enough to shake furniture. "No, damnit, you're our broom, and maybe our best shot at starting to clean up this mess."

Dio's mouth clamped shut. A few seconds later, she muttered. "Sorry. You're . . . right, I guess."

Camille reached out to her, but Dio didn't take her hand. Camille frowned and let her arm rest against her chair again. "I think these last few years have hardened all of us. Sibyls, I mean. Maybe too much."

"Losses happen," Dio fired off without looking at either of them.

"Any loss is too great," Bela shot back, leaning forward to see Dio's face even though she was trying to keep her expression hidden. "I say we spend every ounce of blood, sweat, and energy we can making sure none of us goes through that pain again."

Dio got so tense so fast that Bela was fairly certain she could bounce a penny between the woman's shoulders and watch it ricochet through the front window. Dio had her head turned toward the kitchen. She snatched her map off the table, and her throat worked as she gripped the paper so roughly the edges tore in her long, trembling fingers.

Camille's eyes widened at Dio's display of emotion, and her muscles tightened like she was ready to jump up and do battle. A tiny, tiny bit of smoke escaped from her shoulders, and she leaned toward the weapons closet, obviously ready for anything.

Bela's nostrils flared at the welcome scent of a fire Sibyl having strong feelings. She waited for Dio to swear or turn

loose a howling blast of wind to tear up everything in the
living area. Camille could burn whatever she wanted. Andy
would put it out. Bela thought about cracking a couple of
the walls. So much the better for redecorating. It would be
good for all of them to lose their tempers for a few minutes,
let out some of the grief. Bela knew she could take it, and
she was pretty sure Dio, Camille, and Andy needed it, too.

Out-of-season thunder tickled her awareness for the second time since she came into the living room, and if she
wasn't much mistaken, Dio winced at the sound.

*Come on, Dio. Tell me off and blow down some doors.
You'll feel better. We'll all feel better.*

Instead, in a quavering voice, Dio asked, "When's Katrina Drake's will supposed to be read? Will the OCU get a
copy?"

Bela felt the question like a sharp chop to her midsection.

"Don't know," Andy said. Too quiet. Too tense.

Straight back to work again. Okay, yeah, they needed to
work. With the Sibyl shortage, they always needed to
work—but right this second, they needed to feel.

Dio's storm-colored eyes met Bela's, flat and stubborn
and already shuttering like she was pulling thick curtains
all around her heart and mind.

Damnit.

Her meaning was very plain. The whole feeling and
bonding thing—that wouldn't be happening today.

Bela didn't hide her frustration. She thought about going
back to the basement again, but realized that would be running and hiding. What was she doing, anyway, allowing
herself to indulge in fantasies about an unconscious man
who didn't really have a prayer of surviving?

He'll have it hard, and then he'll die, just like us, murmured Nori and Devin, and for the first time, Bela wished
they'd shut up and leave her alone.

They were telling her the truth, though. Duncan's
plight—that was the reality of it, and it hurt like hell, just

like Dio's attitude and Camille's broken fire and Andy's broken heart. And screw Andy, too, for being right earlier, that Bela was trying to get some sort of twisted do-over for Nori and Devin, trying to heal up some of that wound by helping Duncan Sharp recover against the odds.

Bela closed her eyes to escape the silent faces of her quad.

She had to let this attraction to Duncan Sharp go. His life would end soon, no matter what she did, and it wouldn't end well. It would just be another bunch of pain on top of pain, and she didn't need that kind of weight on her when she was doing all she could to carry this quad she had been crazy enough to bring together.

When Bela opened her eyes again, Dio seemed to note the tears gathering there. The air Sibyl's cheeks flushed. Her expression ranged from hard to confused, and finally settled on anxious, and maybe a little ashamed. "I didn't mean to be such a bitch about the lawyer thing. About—about anything."

"Thanks," Bela said, then made herself stop talking through clamped teeth. "If you'd rather one of us flirt with the lawyer, we'll figure something out."

"No, I'll do it." Dio leaned forward, put a hand on her hip, and managed a little lift in her voice as she said, "I'll cultivate my curves. They might be dangerous, but they won't be avoided."

"Ha—that was Mae West." Camille faded back into her chair, likely believing the risk for all-out war on the communications platform had passed. "I like Mae West, and I love finding good quotes. Check this one out. 'He who fights with monsters risks becoming one.' " She glanced from Bela to Dio to Andy, then frowned when she seemed to realize none of them recognized her quip. "Nietzsche said that, or something like it. Friedrich Nietzsche. The philosopher? Oh, come on. I know you both studied him just like I did, at your Motherhouses."

"No, Camille." Dio actually smiled. "No, I didn't. Guess

I'm less bookish than the average air Sibyl. You can be the house nerd, okay?"

The tang and twinge of elemental energy passed through the room. Bela was about to get excited, thinking it was from her quad—but all across the brownstone, wind chimes started to tinkle.

A warning.

Bela dug her fingers into the edges of the couch cushions. "Oh, shit. What *now*?"

Andy was bailing out of her chair, swearing and dripping. Dio and Camille had jumped up and taken battle stances near the front section of the living room.

A powerful knock rattled the front door.

Bela's heart shook with the wood. She shoved herself off the couch and ran for the weapons closet.

11

"Friendlies." Camille's voice barely penetrated Bela's haze of fear and determination. "Stop, Bela. It's okay." The fire Sibyl stood up from her ready crouch.

Bela's hand was already on the knob to the closet, and she almost couldn't stop herself from ripping open the door and grabbing her sword anyway. Dio jogged back to her, breathing hard, and a smattering of wind played across the room. Bela couldn't see Andy, but one of the fire sprinklers was dripping. Now there was plenty of elemental energy in the brownstone. *Finally*. When they didn't even need it.

"I seriously need a long fucking nap," Andy muttered, doing what she could to dry up the sprinklers. "A week's worth ought to do it. Camille, please tell me it's not the next-door neighbor again. I don't think I can take another round of nosy little old lady."

"I think it's Creed and Nick," Camille said.

Bela's fingers trembled as she let go of the closet knob and forced herself to settle.

Camille padded to the door, her bare feet pale against the carpet as Bela tried to remember how to breathe. Dio stood herself down by folding her arms and letting out a loud sigh. Andy came into view, moving to stand beside them as Camille opened the door to admit two hulking, dark-headed OCU officers wearing jeans and leather jackets. The two men matched in almost every feature, except one had shorter hair than the other. The Lowell twins, Creed and Nick, as Camille had predicted.

Before the war with the Legion, Bela would have considered killing the half-demon cops on sight, but she was glad to see them now. They had proven themselves loyal to the Sibyls and the OCU, and they were married to Riana and Cynda. Nick Lowell served as the OCU's official liaison to their quad, and he often went on patrols with them.

Three more men entered with Creed and Nick.

Two wore jeans like the twins, along with Giants jackets. They had sandy brown hair and brown eyes—though one of them looked wilder than the other, with his long pony-tail, loud jewelry, and the bits of tribal tattoos visible on his hands and neck. Human, completely, from what Bela could sense, and they had to be brothers. Both were built like football players, but their wary expressions suggested they were either law enforcement or private security.

The man who entered last had coal-colored hair and a face straight out of some Italian painting, except for the scowl. And the dark suit. All he needed was sunglasses to look like he stepped off the set of *Men in Black*.

"Wonderful," Andy grumbled, cutting off Nick Lowell's initial attempts at introductions. She stared at the man in the suit, her muscles tensing so visibly Bela grimaced, waiting for the waterworks to start.

"Cops and a fed?" Andy's gaze shifted to Creed Lowell, the one with shorter hair. Creed had once been her OCU partner before her water talents became apparent. "What kind of trouble did you bring us?"

"I'm Jack Blackmore," the man in the suit said, addressing Andy before Creed or Nick could speak. He jerked his thumb toward the brown-haired men in the Giants jackets. "These two are Saul and Calvin Brent, from the NYPD." His gaze shifted to something close to analytical as he studied Andy. "So, you're the one who used to be law enforcement?"

Andy's smile was halfway to dangerous. "Yeah. Now I make tidal waves and get cooler weapons."

"Is he FBI?" Bela asked, knowing Andy disliked government agencies interfering with local police business.

Andy's eyes narrowed, and her cheeks turned hectic beneath her freckles. "I think this one's worse than one of the Flaming Bunch of Idiots. What are you—NSA? Some black-ops group that runs off the radar? Oh, wait. Wait. Let me guess. Regular Army, pretending to be a fed?"

The dark-haired man seemed stunned for a moment, but recovered quickly. "I'm an OCU advisor, and for now, I'm in charge. Acting captain."

Andy, who had no doubt been busy forming her next set of observations and insults, froze in place. Dio and Camille moved instinctively toward her, sensing the same gut-level pain Bela felt rolling off Andy like so many ocean waves.

Bela whipped to face Nick Lowell and saw the confirmation on his face. "Out of my hands," he said, keeping his gaze on Andy.

Nick had partnered with her briefly when she was still OCU, and the two of them had helped bring down the monster who'd killed Sal Freeman. Since then, Nick had been assuming the administrative duties but not the title, because no one felt comfortable replacing Sal.

"One Police Plaza sprang Captain Blackmore on us yesterday, and transferred the Brent brothers to our unit, too." Creed spoke more to Andy than anyone. His deep voice sounded unusually gentle. "They're pretty damned good, from what I can tell on paper. I think they'll be assets against these new creatures."

Andy didn't react at all.

Dio and Camille stood less than an arm's length from her, seemingly unable to take another step, to go to her like sister-Sibyls should and wrap her in their arms. Probably because Andy would have drowned them both if they tried.

Bela really wanted to hit something. Her quad needed a new bunch of stress like they needed a pride of tiger-demons up the ass.

"Where did you come from?" Andy asked Jack Blackmore in an icy voice that would have frightened any sane man.

"Narcotics," one of the Giants fans volunteered. Saul, Bela thought.

His brother Calvin said, "A desk, but I was Bronx Homicide for years."

Bela let a measure of her earth energy slide from her body and willed it to wrap around her quad to steady them. To her great surprise, no one shoved away her elemental touch.

"I come from everywhere." Jack Blackmore sounded suddenly tired and older than he looked. He kept his arms at his sides and held Andy's chilly stare without flinching. "Anywhere the Rakshasa have been. I've been tracking the Unrighteous since the first Gulf War."

Shock stabbed at Bela's awareness, and then a vague sense of dread flooded through her. "What did you just call them?" she asked Blackmore. "What word did you use?"

"Unrighteous." His frown underscored the word, and made it sound even more ominous than Duncan Sharp had done, which was saying a lot. "The Rakshasa have a lot of names, but that's the one that sticks in my mind. It's a translation, the best the language guys could do with an ancient word that meant something like unclean, evil, and unstoppable, all rolled into one."

The Unrighteous will come. That's what Duncan had told her in that terrible, shifting devil voice, right before he tried to attack. *They'll kill you.*

Had that been a threat—or a warning?

Andy was thawing a little. Her posture relaxed enough to calm Dio and Camille, too. Bela slowly reabsorbed the earth energy she had freed, still distracted by the memory of Duncan's—or whoever he had been at that moment— weird shout.

"We were just calling them kitty cats most of the time."

Andy's tone was wary, bordering on sarcastic. "The Unrighteous. That sounds biblical. So what are we into here . . . Captain?"

Blackmore's deep voice dropped an octave. "Pain. Death. Torture. Evil. Pick your poison." He glanced at Creed and Nick, both of whom gestured toward Bela.

"She's in charge," Nick said. "The mortar, remember?"

"Mortar. The boss." Saul Brent gave Bela a nod. His gaze shifted to Camille. "Pestle. Communications expert."

Camille acknowledged him with a tug on her red hair.

Calvin Brent took over. "Dio, you're the broom, cleaning up messes, always the last woman out of a fight. Andy, you're the flow, the wavy lines in the Sibyl tattoo, and you're supposed to be good at healing."

"Mortar, pestle, and broom around a dark crescent moon." Saul Brent held out his right arm and tapped the area where Bela's tattoo was located. "The mark of the Dark Goddess. Do we have it all straight?"

Bela held out her arm for him to see it, as did Camille, Dio, and Andy.

Saul's grin was bright and engaging. "We got a crash course in the Dark Crescent Sisterhood last night. Followed by a crash course in demons."

Creed and Nick looked mildly amused. No doubt the Brent brothers had been astounded to learn about the existence of Curson demon officers in the NYPD—never mind Jake, the youngest Lowell brother, who was a full-blooded Astaroth demon who just happened to be good at holding his human form.

Blackmore ignored this interchange and directed his next comment to Bela. "Rakshasa aren't like constructed demons, and they can't be summoned, as I'm sure your research has already revealed. They're much more powerful." He paused but didn't wait for a response. "My best operative went down in DUMBO. John Cole was the only person on earth who's managed to kill some of those monsters before you managed it, which is why I'm here, to ask for your help."

Bela waited for Blackmore to finish his request. Andy's posture suggested she would rather not hear the rest of it. Camille and Dio seemed wary, but also resigned.

"The OCU and other police units I helped establish around the world tell me that the Dark Crescent Sisterhood might have a chance against these demons," Blackmore said. "You proved that to me when you killed one in Central Park."

"We have a chance against anything that goes bump in the night," Bela told him, searching his too-handsome face for any sign of emotion and finding none at all. "As Sibyls, we're committed to defending the weak from the supernaturally strong, and as long as the Rakshasa threaten New York City, we'll threaten them. We'll work closely with the OCU like we have since we partnered with them to defeat the Legion."

"Thank you." Blackmore sounded relieved, but his dark eyes flickered and grew troubled. He glanced at the Brent brothers, then at Creed and Nick. "We've never had a Rakshasa, Eldest or Created, in custody, so I'm sure we'll learn a lot from Sharp. We're prepared to share whatever we discover from his examination with your Sisterhood."

Bela took a second or two to work this out, then caught the frustration in Nick's expression. Creed was shaking his head, as if he had encouraged Blackmore not to take this course of action.

"Excuse me?" Bela asked as the Brent brothers came to stand beside Blackmore. The three of them looked ready to move past Bela and search the brownstone top to bottom, whether she agreed or not.

Bela heated up all over from a stinging rush of pissed-off, and her palm itched to hold her sword. The men weren't threatening her, not really, but they were acting almighty high-handed, and that wouldn't fly. Even a fractious fighting group would react to that kind of disrespect, and sure enough, Andy was already dripping from both elbows. She tugged Camille with her to take positions on either side of Bela, forming a line between the three police officers and the door to the kitchen and basement. Creed and Nick kept neutral posts near the front door, and Dio was fading back like a good broom, giving herself plenty of room to clean up whatever mess exploded when Bela wouldn't let the bastards pass.

Dio was also inching toward the weapons closet, using her wind energy to obscure her movements.

"Duncan Sharp was wounded by the demons." Blackmore's patient tone just missed condescending. "You've had him for days, and you can't heal him." He glanced at the basement door. Either he'd studied plans at some city office or Creed and Nick had spilled their guts about the brownstone's design.

Bela decided she'd emasculate the twins later. "A fire Sibyl Mother is with the detective now, and two more Mothers are resting up for their shift. He's responding well to treatment so far, and he'll be staying with us until we believe it's safe to release him."

"He'll become a Rakshasa, if he hasn't already." Blackmore was still looking at the door to the kitchen and basement, like he might be weighing his options. "We have a facility in New Jersey that can contain him, but it's best if we move him before the change is complete. I have a van outside with a reinforced elementally treated steel cage that should hold up against full assault for at least an hour. Saul and Calvin will help me with the transport."

Nick was frowning, but Creed's lips were twitching like he wanted to burst out laughing. "Didn't you hear her, Captain?" Creed did laugh for a second. "The Mothers are here. That's Sibyl code for 'You're shit out of luck.'"

"If these four don't kick your ass," Nick said, "the Mothers will."

Bela held up her hand to stop Dio before the air Sibyl ripped open the closet door and started tossing daggers and swords and dart guns to Andy and Camille—through the Lowell twins, if necessary. It wasn't easy, but Bela smiled at Jack Blackmore and used her nicest, most civilized voice to explain reality to the arrogant bastard.

"You're not taking Duncan anywhere."

Blackmore got all stiff and red in the face, and Saul and Calvin looked ready to do whatever he told them to do.

"It's not open for discussion." Blackmore clenched his big hands like he couldn't quite believe anyone would argue with him. "It's the safest option for everyone involved."

"This isn't the army, *Captain*." Andy moved closer to Bela as Camille assumed a subtle but definite battle stance. "This isn't even the NYPD. We'll work with you, but we don't work for you, and we make our own decisions about people in our care, no matter who—or what—they are."

"I suppose 'I told you so' would be a cliché," Creed said.

Nick moved so quickly that he was a blur even to Bela's sharp vision. In less than a fraction of a second, he was standing directly behind the Brent brothers, putting his hands on their shoulders. Big golden hands, reflecting his supernatural Curson essence. When Nick spoke, his voice had a deep, demonic resonance that made everyone in the room stand a little straighter. "Give it up. If you try to force this, they'll leave pieces of you all over Manhattan."

"Working with Sibyls is a diplomatic challenge." Creed maintained his full human form, though he was just as capable as Nick of swapping back and forth between man and huge seven-foot golden glowing Curson demon. "And I did tell you so."

"Fine." Blackmore sounded furious. "What is it you want from me in exchange for Sharp? My parent agency can pay for your time and trouble. We have technology that might interest you, and some weaponry."

Andy doused the captain with a cold blue wave she must have drawn from the nearest sprinkler head. The powerful sheet of water smacked the Brent brothers, too, surprising them enough to make them back off a step—though Dio's sharp blast of wind might have been what made them move. The air in the room swirled, ringing chimes and making lamps jitter on tables as Dio strode forward to back up Andy.

Blackmore didn't give any ground as Dio's very targeted gusts settled back to stillness. He just stood there, open-mouthed, dripping on the carpet.

"I suggest you spend a lot more time with Creed, Nick, and the OCU learning about Sibyls before you come back to *this* house and act like an ass." Bela let a little earth energy creep into her voice, until the air seemed to shake with her words. "We're not ready to give up on Duncan Sharp, and we're quite capable of doing our own examining and containing, if it comes to that."

"Parent agency," Andy grumbled at the captain. "Really? Seriously? Go fuck yourself."

Blackmore eyed Andy, and Bela thought she saw something like amusement or respect warring with the frustration in his gaze. He shed some more water, then managed to make his mouth work enough to ask, "Does Duncan have John's dinar?"

Bela gave him a single nod, wishing Camille would fire up and set the bastard's pants on fire.

"Interesting." Blackmore ran his hand through his hair, wringing out another bunch of drips and drops. "I wonder if that gives him some protection. It's what kept John alive all these years, until DUMBO. But then, this is Duncan we're talking about. He might be using sheer force of will to stay human."

Camille was glaring at the man, but there was no sign of smoke or flames. Andy's water energy was building, and if Blackmore set her off again, Bela had little doubt that she'd drown the jerk, or wash him out the front door and leave him flat on his ass on the sidewalk.

"You were ready to cart him off, cut him up, and kill him a minute ago." Dio's wind swirled around her shoulders. "Now you're talking about him like he's always been your best buddy."

"I've known Duncan Sharp even longer than I knew John Cole." Blackmore's posture changed to more relaxed, maybe a little more human, and the asshole factor in his expression cranked down a few notches. "He was a Ranger in the Gulf War, and he's been a dedicated civilian officer since he retired from active duty. If you think you can save his life, I'll do whatever I can to help you. Especially since I don't seem to have another choice."

"Amazing." Andy released some of her water energy back to the universe, making all the sprinkler heads drizzle. "Fed version 2.0. It can walk, talk, show off, make an ass of itself, *and* suck up before it gets its dick ripped off."

Blackmore's eyebrows lifted, and his hands twitched like he was thinking about guarding his groin.

Nick took that opportunity to head for the brownstone's front door, and Bela appreciated his good sense of timing.

"Run along now, boys." She used her earth energy to gently move the captain and the Brent brothers in the direction Nick took.

As Dio added a hefty blast of wind to the encouragement, Creed opened the door for them and watched them stumble across the threshold. It was a wonder they didn't tumble down the steps and go splat on the sidewalk.

"We'll call you when Duncan starts to wake up," Bela called after the men as Nick started to pull the door shut. "If you don't piss me off again."

12

Strada stood in human form with Griffen near a location Griffen had identified as Sixty-third and Central Park. Strada was wearing jeans and a T-shirt glorifying an oddly dressed traveling minstrel called a "rapper." To match the ensemble, Strada had softened and smoothed his features to give a youthful appearance. It was good practice. He needed many faces and personas to succeed in this strange and fascinating time and place.

They were just inside a stone fence under cover of a few trees, far enough back to peer over the top of the large structure to the row of modern houses and buildings beyond. Rich scents of summer filled the air in the waning light of day, strawberries and leaves, grass and flowers. Strada had learned the common and proper scientific names for each new plant and animal he had encountered since his arrival in the city. Strada enjoyed the reds and greens, the yellows and browns, even the moist blue of a sky that didn't stretch across miles of desert.

The stench of modern vehicles—that he could do without.

"Rush hour." Griffen opened his arms toward the crush of automobiles and people and buses trying to press between yellow cabs. "Nothing like the Upper East Side. Sorry."

"Activity provides cover," Strada said, distracted by the ripe stench of a horse-drawn buggy passing nearby. The horse, sensing him, gave a high-pitched whicker and tried to shy down a side street. "You were right to bring me now."

"I've been here before as a guest, but a different group of Sibyls lived here then." Griffen's fists flexed, and the hatred on his face was unmistakable. "Our *friends*." He snorted. "They were supposed to protect us."

Out on the street, the horse bucked against its harness, refusing to move its buggy forward.

Strada knew the full story of Griffen's past, because he had taken it from the man's mind the night he snatched the man out of a ritual he was performing with his Coven in a boarded-up, defiled modern-day temple. He had plied Griffen for cooperation, first by force and then with promises and rewards. "The loss of your priestess lover to the demon leader of the Legion still hurts you?"

Griffen let out a ragged laugh. "Charlotte Heart's death set me free to find true power. Then the fall of the Legion freed my Coven from servitude to those high-handed bastards. As for the Sibyls, I'll enjoy seeing them get their due. The universe always provides for those who serve it with faith and vigor."

Griffen's intense shifts from anger to sarcasm, joy, then religious fervor puzzled Strada. Strada's eyes followed the route of the horse as it dragged its hansom toward the side street again, fighting its handler until it dashed by on the far sidewalk. Humans had such a trickster's mix of emotions, it was hard to sort them all out no matter how long he spent walking inside human skin and watching the world through human eyes. With people and places in this modern world, nothing was ever quite what it seemed.

Take the brownstone directly across the road, for example. It looked plain. Even innocuous. It was clean enough, with three stories of rock walls, simple white curtains and no pots of flowers adoring its sills. Anyone in the city would feel comfortable climbing its few front steps and using its brass knocker to tap on its thick wooden door— anyone who wouldn't be thrown into the onrushing traffic when they struck the powerful elemental barriers the Sibyls had constructed to protect their lair.

Strada didn't even bother testing the strength of those protections. When he used the full power of his Rakshasa vision, the bright, shimmering light was enough to wound his sensitive eyes. He could taste the earth, the air, the fire, the water, even at this distance, and he detected no weakness in the coverage. From what Tarek and Aarif reported from their failed experiment with the Created in this park a week ago, the Sibyls could construct such a barrier quickly and hold it for some time, though it did cost them energy.

When Strada's pride came in earnest to kill these women, they would have to come in force, and in tiger form. There would be no dividing the barriers or prying past them. They would have to shatter the energy, like he planned to shatter its makers.

"The police officer is still inside," Griffen informed him. "I have sentries watching day and night. The minute he's clear, I'll notify you."

Strada answered with a quick purr, then asked, "Is the NYPD truly so unfailing in the defense of its own?"

"Yes. Our former employer was correct." Griffen leaned out of the trees, as if to get a better glimpse of the traffic. Strada appreciated the human's tact in not mentioning how bits of that employer had been recently discovered in a local river. "If you kill a cop, the rest of his brothers and sisters will hunt you without stopping, and they'll do it forever. Think of them like a pride, only with guns and connections to much, much bigger guns, if they think that's what they need."

Strada had no fear of guns, whatever the size, but vengeance for the sake of one's pride—that he could understand. He had rejoiced in the taste of John Cole's blood, retribution for the true brothers the heinous bastard had stolen from him. He would not challenge the NYPD, for now. The time would come for that, when he and his pride were more prepared, and when disrupting the NYPD's operations would be of use to him.

Strada went back to studying the brownstone, and quickly understood that the protections extended to the other houses beside the Sibyl lair, though one of those dwellings had its own unusual barriers. Opposite, really, of the work the Sibyls had done. The blue house to the right of the brownstone had an undercurrent of quiet, whispering energy, seemingly designed to render it plain and utterly unnoticeable. That might have worked, were it not for the bold designs of the Sibyls.

Given the energy that such protections required, Strada doubted they could extend very far in any direction. The physical cost to the Sibyls would be too high.

"Come with me," he told Griffen, and began walking away from the shield of the trees and the stone fence.

Griffen rushed after him to the sidewalk and then the nearest crosswalk. "Will they sense you?"

"Not in this human shape, if I do not cross the barriers they've established. Stay on my right, and I will spare us that difficulty." Strada waited for the light to change, then crossed the traffic-laden street to the sidewalk at the corner of the block that contained the brownstone.

"We could enter through one of the other houses," Griffen suggested, catching up and remaining at Strada's right hand, as instructed.

"The other dwellings are equally defended." Strada used his powerful sense of smell to track and follow the direction taken by the frightened horse that had tried to flee him. Animals had an unfailing sense of elemental energy, both its presence and its absence. Likely, the creature had attempted to take a path of least resistance.

They walked a short way down a side street, then arrived at a long alleyway that crossed behind the brownstone.

"Yes." Strada nodded. "The protections are designed for their lair, and perhaps to make life easier and safer for their neighbors—but they do not cover the entire block. We can position here, and at the far end, there." He pointed to the opposite entrance to the alley.

Griffen looked excited by this, and he lifted himself to his toes to peer over the metal trash receptacles at the alley mouth. "When Sibyls feel threatened, they call for help. More Sibyls and police officers with the Occult Crimes Unit will respond."

Strada dismissed this concern with a soft snarl. "We will determine how much time it would take reinforcements to arrive, and be certain we finish our business quickly. We will test and study until we know our enemy as well as they know themselves, Griffen. We will plan until we feel certain there are no flaws in our strategy. When we move, we will crush theses females and be gone before their friends even begin to understand their fate." He turned away from the alley and strode back toward Central Park, his mind already shifting back to the renovated warehouse office, and to Tarek and Aarif, who were setting up a meeting with a previous employer who had paid them well for a past service. "Our victory must be absolute and devastating. It will serve as a clear message to the remaining Sibyls and their allies not to interfere in the affairs of the Eldest."

Griffen ran along behind Strada like a well-trained child, up the sidewalk and back across the teeming city street. His deference pleased Strada. The human had so quickly grasped the absolute power of a *culla*. One day he would make a fine Created.

"They'll still interfere because it's their job, their role in our world," Griffen said.

"Yes, but with hesitance and dread, or the haste born of headlong fury. The advantage will always be ours."

For a few moments, they moved in silence, but Griffen

had more on his mind. "Sibyls are well trained and cautious. How will you get them into the alley?"

"The same way I would force any cattle to slaughter." Strada swept back into Central Park, enjoying the warmth of the sun on his human skin. "Herd them."

(13)

Over and over again, she was there when he opened his eyes.

Other people came and went, but she was the constant, and Duncan was glad. He couldn't stay awake long enough to learn her real name, but he recognized the feel of his angel, the smell of her—even the sound of her breathing.

He drew a slow breath, drinking her soft almond scent like wine. "You're perfect."

"If you say so." She was close. Smiling. Her fingers brushed across the back of his hand. The sensation warmed him.

"What are you?" he murmured as his vision blurred and his eyes closed.

"I'm a Sibyl."

Duncan figured he hadn't heard that last part right.

He slept again.

Woke.

She was there, pulling a soft sheet higher to cover his chest and ease his chills.

"You call yourself a Sibyl, whatever that is." His voice was hoarse. A cool glass touched his lips, and he took a sip of water. The pressure of her palm on his chest felt like an anchor, binding him to reality and the world. "I think you're an angel."

She laughed. "You have so got the wrong girl, Duncan Sharp."

Her eyes were so dark they drew him in and covered him as softly and surely as the sheet she adjusted. "I don't think I'm that far off the mark. Angel."

"Stop that," she told him, then let her fingers trail across his forehead. A rich, relaxing energy swept across his body, and once more he drifted away.

The next time he woke, she was gently bathing his face, his forehead, now his cheeks and chin and mouth. The connection between them was a real thing, a bright thing, and he wondered if he could touch it if he tried.

"Rest," she said, and her voice made him want to hear more. His body reacted to her nearness, getting warmer and warmer until he had to sit up and find a way to touch *her.*

"Rest," she said again as he yanked against the cuffs on his wrists.

Her fingertips tingled along his jaw, and that wave of relaxing peace claimed him again.

Angel, his mind whispered.

That had to be what she was.

Or maybe, just maybe, she was a witch.

Don't stop. Can't stop.

Duncan tried to breathe, but he was hauling too much weight to inflate his lungs. The desert tore at him as he ran. Superheated gray rock dust stung his eyes. He tasted burning grit and salt, felt the fire in his chest, his face, his gut.

Don't stop!

Two wounded men, one slung over either shoulder.

He staggered.

Bullets dug into flint on either side of him, sparking, spitting dirt and shrapnel into his thighs.

He had to keep moving—

"No matter how much healin' we do, we can't cure the infection, but we have slowed it to a crawl."

Duncan's Afghanistan flashback flickered into blackness. His muscles twitched from the sensation of running his injured buddies out of a firefight. He could still taste the desert—but that was an Irish voice. Old and crackly. Not hateful, but not friendly, either.

Who was it?

Where was he?

Still hot, like the desert—but the sensation was coming from inside him. From his neck and shoulder. Like his skin was on fire, and that fire was trying to spread, only something was holding it back. It was almost like an icy line had been drawn from his chin to his chest and straight through his back, containing the heat.

The old Irish voice spoke again. "He will die, and as he passes, he'll become of them. But you already know that, don't you, cop?"

"I was hoping it wouldn't come to that," a man said.

Shock made Duncan's insides jump, and his teeth clamped together against the pain in his wounds. He realized he wasn't back in the desert after all. He must have died and gone to hell, because the man who spoke—that was his old commander, Jack Blackmore. Blackjack.

"Duncan Sharp won't give up," Blackjack said. "He won't stop. Not ever. You've never seen him in battle."

"I think I have," said the only voice Duncan really cared about, the one that was rich and smooth and feminine. "For almost two weeks now."

He heard the admiration, and felt embarrassed by it. He didn't deserve admiration for just staying alive.

Her warm fingers brushed against his neck and shoulder on the side that wasn't bandaged, and something like electricity flowed all over his skin. The familiar sensation eased the fiery aches in his body and the sting of his latest round of war memories. Duncan forgot about admiration and embarrassment, and he started thinking about heaven instead of hell.

Then his mind went blank for a while. He didn't know how long. Time had no meaning, if he was even still alive to worry about time.

Your angel is a looker, John Cole told him, the words winding through a seemingly infinite darkness. *The red-head's prettier, but she's probably too delicate for your tastes, if you don't count that sword she likes to carry.*

Duncan ignored John's voice. John was dead. His best friend was gone forever, buried in some flag-covered coffin, in his best dress uniform, with all his ribbons. Somehow Duncan knew that, even if he couldn't remember the details. He only hoped he hadn't killed the bastard himself.

I'm here, Duncan.

Shut up, Duncan thought back to the ghost voice.

Then there was more emptiness, with some shocks and misery and pain, followed by more cool electricity, and the sweet, sweet scent of his angel.

Her name is Bela, John told him.

"Bela," Duncan tried to say, but his voice was just a bunch of croaking.

Hours later, maybe days, Blackjack spoke again. "John always wore that dinar, and it shocked anyone who touched it. Have you tried taking it off Duncan's neck?"

"We'll be doin' no such thing," said the old, crunchy Irish voice. "And neither will you. It dates from the time of the Kushan emperor Huvishka. Probably older'n anything you've ever dealt with—and it's keyed its energy to him." After a pause, she cackled and added, "Old things can have great power, Mr. Blackmore, but I suspect you know that, too."

I'm wearing some zillion-year-old coin? Duncan remembered John putting a chain over his head. He tried to hold on to that image, then faded away from the voices and pain again, farther away this time. Sleeping. Or maybe just not existing. He barely felt the shocks, the strange energies that flowed across his body, wherever he might be. Maybe he was gone for good this time.

Bela whispered to him across the miles. "Are you giving up, Duncan Sharp? Pity. I thought you were a warrior."

Duncan ground his teeth. He thought about carrying two wounded men to safety through a firefight that should have killed them all. He thought about walking back from the IED explosion. Thirty miles. Maybe more.

Keep going.

That was his mantra back then in the desert, when the bullets were flying.

Don't stop. Just keep going.

He imagined himself moving back toward that inviting sound, toward Bela. He wanted to see her face again. He wanted to touch her and see if she was as soft as he imagined.

John Cole laughed at him. *You're out of your league.*

"Fuck you," Duncan mumbled.

Then he opened his eyes.

The edges of his vision seemed cloudy. Indistinct.

But she wasn't.

His angel was right there in front of him, bending down, her dark hair pulled against her head, showing off the intriguing lines of her lightly tanned face. She had high cheekbones, and he noticed that her dark eyes had the slightest tilt. And she was wearing black leather.

Shit.

The scent of almonds and fresh berries filled Duncan's nose, beating back the stink of antiseptic, bleach, and plaster as she leaned closer to his face. Her warm breath brushed his cheeks, his neck as her full lips curled into a smile.

"Fuck you, too," she said, then unlocked a pair of cuffs holding his good hand against the rails of a hospital bed.

Duncan frowned and watched his angel withdraw. His thoughts swam in circles, and he tried to figure out who the hell had hammered spikes through his left arm. And why was his left cheek and shoulder on fire? He tried to sit up, to do something to make the angel come closer again, but a voice he would never forget snarled, "Be still before I bust the other side of your face, Sharp."

Force of habit held Duncan in place as he managed to take in yellow walls and more people. He kept squinting until he made out the big outline of the man who had been his commanding officer in Afghanistan.

"Blackjack," he croaked, then rubbed his throat with numb-feeling fingers.

Blackjack and a small army.

Saul and Calvin Brent were standing near his bed. And the long-haired blonde he had dreamed had tornadoes coming out of her ears in DUMBO—Dio, according to Cole's voice. There was the redhead who looked too fragile to fight anything, except for the scimitar thing he had seen her swinging—and that was Camille, per John's quiet commentary. Then there was the cop-like woman, who wasn't wearing leather anymore, unlike her friends. She had on a wet sweatshirt and jeans, and her name was Andy.

Next to all of them stood a gray-haired old woman with a face like a red howler monkey's, and this one was smoking. Like a human pipe.

Duncan blinked, trying to clear his vision.

When he opened his eyes again, he was face-to-face with Bela. "Angel" tried to come out of his throat.

It sounded like he was choking.

Duncan swore to himself and worked to sit up again, but too much shit was weighing him down. Plastic tubes. A cast on his arm. Handcuffs on that arm—and on both ankles, too. Were his neck and face bandaged on one side? His skin felt tight underneath the tape and gauze, like deep wounds were trying to scab and close.

"Stay down," Blackjack commanded, but Duncan felt the cuffs on his other arm and ankles being unlocked.

He struggled into a sitting position, mostly because he wanted a better look at his angel in that unbelievable leather bodysuit.

"You were always mule-stubborn, Duncan," Saul Brent said.

Cal added, "Dumb, too."

"Jesus Christ, could somebody get a shovel for the male-bonding bullshit?" Andy squeezed the water out of one sweatshirt sleeve. "It's getting a little high and deep in here."

"That's not bullshit you're smelling," said Duncan's angel before she drifted out of his line of sight. "It's testosterone."

The howler monkey with smoke coming from the top of her head snickered. Duncan tried not to look at her, because he had no frame of reference for old women who smoked. Literally.

"You're law enforcement," he rasped in the direction of the wet chick, ignoring Blackjack and Saul and Cal as best he could.

"Yeah. Andy Myles. Nice to meet you." Andy squeezed water out of her other sleeve and didn't seem to care that it splattered all over the hospital room floor. "I used to be a lieutenant in the Occult Crimes Unit—the OCU. Now I'm a Sibyl. So are they." She pointed to the blonde first, then the redhead, and finally his angel. "Her name's Bela Argos, by the way, not Fuck You."

Angel. That's her name to me.

Duncan flexed the fingers at the end of his cast. He had to turn his head to see her, and as he stared at his angel, her cheeks flushed. Not much. Just enough to let him know she noticed him.

Yeah. That was good.

How much morphine was he on, anyway? Because he was beginning to have one hell of a fantasy involving that leather jumpsuit and that zipper. In his teeth. Moving slowly down—

"Sibyls are members of the Dark Crescent Sisterhood," Blackjack's voice snapped Duncan back to reality. "They're working with local law enforcement in New York City and other locations."

"We're an ancient order of female warriors with elemental powers," Andy told him. "Trained in one of four Motherhouses across the globe."

"Rii-iight," Duncan managed to force out of his dry throat, hearing the skepticism in his own voice. Next Blackjack would start in about vampires and werewolves and devils and all that other shit he'd started obsessing over in Afghanistan.

Before he finished having that thought, disturbing images flickered across Duncan's consciousness.

Big cat-men. With huge claws. John Cole, shredded to death—then walking beside him in one of his desert dreams. Had he seen those things? Had they really happened?

John was dead. That much Duncan knew for sure, but—

I'm here, Duncan. Here until we finish off the Rakshasa.

Rakwhatthehell? He'd heard that word before but still couldn't make sense of it. And John's voice—that had been quiet but definite, and it seemed to be coming from the middle of Duncan's brain.

Duncan shook his head, and his bandaged neck blazed with pain. "Dark goddess," he said as he rubbed it again and finally focused on Blackjack's way-too-serious face.

So his angel really was some kind of magic witch-warrior?

Duncan might have laughed if he hadn't been sitting in a bright yellow hospital room with chicks in leather and an old lady with smoke coming off her skin, dealing with a John Cole hallucination bouncing around in his head, and remembering giant cat-creatures. Then there were Saul and Cal, flanking Blackjack like bodyguards, looking just as serious as Blackjack did. Saul and Cal were as down-to-earth as they came. They didn't go for bullshit, and they weren't saying anything to contradict Blackjack.

"Sworn to defend the weak and untrained from the supernaturally strong, like he said." Andy caught Duncan's attention by raising one hand. "Yada yada yada. It's the same old serve-and-protect." The sprinkler over her head drizzled a stream of water onto her fingertips. "With extra tricks."

The water hit her skin . . . and disappeared.

No steam, no streaks, no drips. It was just gone.

Duncan wondered how badly his brain had been injured in DUMBO.

"Neat, huh?" Andy's smile was wistful as she glanced at the sprinkler. "Too bad I can't manage it with larger amounts." Her gaze shifted to her feet and the small puddle spreading beneath her dirty white sneakers. "I can attract it to me from the ground, from pipes, from sinks and sprinklers and bodies of water. I can channel it, but I can't destroy it or completely absorb it. Yet. Give me time."

Duncan looked at Bela. Her dark eyes were calm but concerned, and her expression was unreadable. A dozen memories of her whispering to him and touching his face competed with each other. He wanted time to sort through each image and enjoy it.

When he'd first seen her in DUMBO, she'd had a sword, hadn't she?

A long, down-curving blade with a serrated end, like a *kora,* a kind of sword he'd seen once in Nepal. A kind of sword made to behead things. Duncan felt his insides lurch as pieces snapped into place. Pieces he didn't want to see, didn't want to understand—but the picture couldn't be denied.

"Warriors with elemental powers." Just saying it out loud made him feel batshit crazy. He knew he sounded as sarcastic as the old, smoking Irish woman, but he didn't really care. "What are you trying to pull on me, Blackjack?"

"The Rakshasa cut you with their claws, cop." The old

Irish woman let off a burst of flames from her knuckles as she pointed to the bandaged half of Duncan's neck. "You're infected, and there's nothin' we can do to stop you from changin'."

"You're crazy." Duncan's response was reflex. He didn't usually disrespect his elders, even when they were covered with puffs of smoke. The Sibyls, all four of them, twitched at his insult, and the bolt of shame that struck Duncan's insides felt like a rebuke from his very religious mother back in Georgia.

"Sorry," he said. "The way I was raised, this kind of talk would get you taken to church—or sent to hell. I just don't believe in anything you're telling me."

Tell her you won't turn, John Cole's voice insisted, louder than before. *Tell the old woman I won't let it happen.*

Something tickled, then burned against his chest, heating up the cloth of his hospital gown. Duncan glanced down to see the coin John Cole had placed around his neck during the battle at DUMBO.

Duncan tore his gaze from the coin and stared at the fire-breathing howler monkey, disliking her and liking her all at the same time. She seemed like a real bitch—but he liked the strength of her voice and her attitude. Kind of like an ancient, retired police officer. She probably would have worked Vice, or maybe Narcotics.

"Who are you?" Duncan asked the old woman.

"She's Mother Keara," Bela answered him in that rich, silky voice. He felt the sound of it like a tangible comforting force on his aching skin. "One of the oldest fire Sibyls in the world, and one of the wisest. She knows a lot about fighting ancient demons. All the Mothers do. Several of them have been working to keep you alive, but Mother Keara is the only one staying here full-time."

Tell Mother Keara about me and the coin, Duncan.

Duncan studied Mother Keara. The fire in her eyes. The fire in her soul. He could see the general in her then. The way she would protect her troops at all costs. When her gaze strayed to the Sibyls in the room, he noticed that her eyes flickered in a certain way as she appraised Bela.

This old woman was attached to his angel. Probably protective as hell.

Christ, what are you waiting for? John was starting to sound desperate. *Can't you see the power rolling off her?*

Duncan squinted at the old woman. A strange shifting sensation gripped his mind, as if he were joining his thoughts with someone—no, something—else. Something other and alien, yet also familiar. Compatible. He had a flash of the blood-brother ritual he and John Cole had performed when they were eight. Moon Pies, Coca-Cola, and pocketknives, down in the cornfield. All very solemn and way stupid, but it was the same sensation now. A quick cut, a little burning, then nothing but rightness and relaxing. He swallowed, almost tasting the sweet chocolate and hot, fizzy soft drink they had shared that day so long ago.

John Cole's knowledge and awareness flowed into Duncan's, until they mingled almost seamlessly. Then, slowly, like a distant vista coming into focus through a camera lens, Duncan saw a change in Mother Keara. Or, more specifically, the air around her. A rippling aura of fire and death swelled out from her wrinkled skin and gnarled limbs. Sheets of it, in brilliant reds and greens, then a deeper blue like the hottest of flames. The colors came in layers, then layers on top of layers.

"I won't turn," he said, understanding John's urgency now.

The old woman's dangerous energy flared like a flash-bang, and Duncan winced, seeing spots for a few seconds. She leaned toward him, close enough that the deadly heat of the flames that had to be living in her heart and soul made his breath come short.

"What did you say?" she asked, her voice echoing with the force of a roaring explosion.

Duncan's words deserted him.

This was too horror-movie. He couldn't handle it.

Talk to her, John Cole urged, but Duncan shut him out.

This was still his body. Still his life.

Right?

Not for long, John muttered, and Duncan had the horrible feeling his dead best friend was telling him the complete truth.

"I won't turn," Duncan said again, partly of his own will, and partly because he felt as if John Cole had hold of his tongue, flapping it to make him talk. "Not until I'm just about to die."

Then, drawing off John's knowledge, Duncan reported, "This dinar around my neck was blessed by the priest who trapped the Ruck—ah—Rakshasa over a thousand years ago. John Cole found it in the temple the day the demons were released, and that's why he survived. He gave it to me in DUMBO. As long as I'm wearing it, the Rakshasa can't touch me directly. Its energy will help slow the infection, and John knows how to keep me from changing until the moment before I die."

Mother Keara's sharp green eyes drew down to slits. "Your friend John Cole is dead."

"Maybe his body, but his mind—" Duncan broke off. He wanted to pick the right word to describe the process that had put John Cole's thoughts in his brain, but he wasn't completely certain. He also couldn't look at anyone in the room save for Mother Keara. No way did he want to tell this to anyone, least of all an Irish howler monkey with fire shimmering all around her.

Mother Keara glanced from the coin to Duncan's face, gazing so deeply into his eyes he wondered if she could melt his skull without ever laying a finger on him. Then she smiled and tapped the side of her head, as if she understood that Duncan had something unusual going on his brain.

Transmigration, John told Duncan. *Say it. If I have to take you over and make you say it, I will, but you'll look different and sound different, and they'll chain you to the bed again.*

"Transmigration." Duncan figured they'd take him for a full-blown idiot. "John—well, shit. The John voice in my head says to tell you we're sharing space."

Silence reigned between the yellow walls of the room, which, now that he was studying it more closely, looked more like a giant bricked-in jail cell than a proper hospital area.

Blackjack and the Brent brothers weren't laughing. Bela and her Sibyl friends were all staring at him, and none of them seemed to be breathing. For reasons Duncan couldn't explain, their response made everything real to him. The remnants of his denial fell away like torn cloth, and his gut churned. It was all he could do to keep himself still.

"Mr. Blackmore, you haven't lost your best operative," Mother Keara said, smiling that monkey smile of hers. "You still have John Cole and all that he knows. For a time, at least, he's alive and well in Duncan Sharp's mind."

Blackjack's only question was "How long?"

Duncan couldn't process the words, but he saw all the Sibyls shift their attention to Mother Keara. Their expressions changed. He saw emotions. Lots of them.

He wanted to yell at them to stop, to back off, but he didn't yell at women.

How long?

That's what Blackjack wanted to know, but why? What was he talking about?

"How long they remain on this earth is hard to say." Mother Keara's smile faded. "The universe will be fightin' to set things right soon enough, so they won't be continuin' the partnership forever. Weeks. Perhaps a few months before nature takes her own course. The infection will worsen, and as Duncan Sharp begins to die, John Cole's spirit will depart, along with all the protection it's offerin'."

Her words drifted through Duncan's awareness.

He was starting to get it now.

John had saved him from the Rakshasa, and John's spirit and his magic coin were slowing the infection in his slash wounds. But it couldn't go on forever. Somewhere in the universe, a countdown timer had clicked on, and the numbers were spinning down fast. Sooner or later—sooner, probably—this little ball would end, only Duncan wouldn't be turning into a pumpkin when the clock struck midnight.

He'd be turning into a demon.

The fingers on his good hand pulled into a fist. Deep in his brain, Duncan saw images of the Rakshasa, images that had to be from John's memories. With each picture that flashed through his awareness, Duncan understood a little more. Like how long John had been fighting the nasty cats. So that's why he'd been dreaming of the old war—and of new ones he couldn't quite understand.

Next, John showed him the intent of the Rakshasa, as John understood it. The Rakshasa wanted to regain their former glory, to gather power and wealth. It was their only purpose. Their obsession. They would consolidate allies.

They would avenge themselves on any and all who dared to stand in their way.

Like the Sibyls, John said. *Especially these four, who took them on in DUMBO and battled them to a draw. The demons will track these women without mercy and tear them to pieces.*

"No way in hell," Duncan muttered, and even his bad hand curled.

"Only a few months?" Bela's beautiful voice sounded strained as she spoke to Mother Keara. "Couldn't it be longer?"

Mother Keara's shoulders slumped. "We're doin' what we can to contain that infection, but the demon energy fights back. It'll break through the wards and barriers we've set in his body, and in the end it'll take him. Duncan Sharp will become Rakshasa."

Duncan heard the words, but once more they didn't sink all the way through his numbed understanding.

Blackjack and the Brent brothers stood still, staying silent, conveying frustration and rage in their stony expressions. Bela opened her mouth, but no words came out. Her gaze darted to Duncan, then she closed her eyes and turned away from him, staring out the yellow room's open door.

"We know a lot of stand-up guys who are demons or half demons." Andy dripped water faster and faster, like a broken fountain. "Duncan's one of us. One of the good guys. Why couldn't he learn to control himself after the change?"

Mother Keara's long gray hair rustled against her green robes as she shook her head. "You've been readin' the same scrolls I have, child. Rakshasa are inherently evil, perhaps some of the worst entities known throughout history. When he changes, there won't be any of Duncan Sharp's essence left to guide his actions. Created Rakshasa always go mad."

Duncan wanted to close his eyes like Bela and find some way to stare into the center of his own brain until he found John Cole's spirit.

"Is she telling the truth?" he asked John out loud, not caring how insane he sounded.

Yes. Then, more quietly, *I'm sorry.*

Duncan smashed his good hand against the railing of his bed. The metal snapped sideways. An IV pole went flying, and a needle tore out of his forearm, tape and all. Blood welled and trickled down his fingers, but he waved off Blackjack and Andy.

"Leave it." His mind was fixed on the Rakshasa and how fast he'd have to work to take them down before he died. To Mother Keara he said, "You people have been doing something to help me heal faster, haven't you?"

She met his stare with her bright eyes, fire dancing in the green depths. "Yes."

Duncan nodded, feeling the pull and pain of the bandages against the demon cuts on his neck and shoulder. "Do it more. Do it faster. Seal up these wounds as much as they can be sealed, and get me out of this cast. I want to get back on the streets at full strength."

Her stare continued. She looked impressed, but she said, "You're fully human. The pain would be unbearable."

Duncan felt John's resolve join with his own. "I don't give a shit. I—we—don't have time to waste."

Blackjack didn't argue, but Duncan knew he wouldn't. Jack Blackmore was practical, and above all, he was a man determined to take down his enemies. If the Rakshasa were his targets now, then God help them. Saul and Calvin stayed quiet, too, but Duncan figured he'd be hearing their opinions later, if he survived this speeded-healing shit.

As for his angel and her group of Sibyls, they said nothing, and their expressions remained fixed. Duncan felt a flicker of respect from Dio, the blonde with the wicked stare that even an enemy combatant would fear. The little redhead, Camille, nodded to him, and Andy, arms folded, set her mouth in a straight line.

"Do it." Andy's tone communicated as much as the unhappy determination in his angel's eyes. These women were definitely warriors, just as focused on their purpose as Blackjack and Duncan and John Cole.

Duncan forced his gaze away from Bela.

"Take me to the townhouse," Mother Keara was telling Camille and Dio. "The building north and east of here, where your OCU has its headquarters. We'll be needin' a bigger space like their stone basement to pull this off— and a lot more Mothers. Better I do the organizin' and plannin'—and the transports, too. Yana will get cranky if she's dragged back here by any child less than a century old."

To Bela, she said, "He's safe enough for now with what

we've put in place, for a few weeks I think, but keep a Sibyl with him and don't let him be too active past general movin' about. Get as much as you can from all those medical machines—his blood, his genes, his energy, and that infection. Every bit of information you can find."

Bela nodded, and Mother Keara's attention shifted to Duncan. "We'll send for you when we're ready. It'll take some time, workin' out the details, and settin' the barriers to make sure we don't kill you and what's left of yer friend John straightaway, and everyone else in the bargain. Do what Bela says about the medical tests. We need a good sample of yer body's patterns as you get a little health to you."

Duncan almost swore over the delay, but a phrase from his childhood helped him hold his peace.

Beggars can't be choosers.

No shit.

He kept his mouth shut as Camille and Dio took hold of Mother Keara's elbows.

Bela moved over to them and spoke in low tones, and Duncan thought he caught the words *Cole, investigation,* and . . . *murder.*

Murder.

Duncan felt a shiver of energy and a surge of his focus returning.

Yes. There had been a murder—that's why he'd been chasing John in the first place. A woman had been slashed to death. Damnit. Had the NYPD been on that, or did they think John was the perp and put the case to bed? If the cat-demons did it, he at least needed to find out why, and how the killing tied into the similar murders in other cities—and the detail trail would be cold as hell already.

He had to get himself out of this bed.

Dio frowned, glanced at Duncan, and nodded to Bela. Camille had no reaction at all, but Duncan was beginning to realize that might not be unusual. Camille seemed the type to stay to herself, maybe in her own head, but she also seemed kind in her own fashion, especially as she helped Dio lead Mother Keara out of the yellow room.

Saul and Calvin followed them out, as if the brothers had been assigned to stay with Mother Keara while she was in New York City. That wouldn't surprise Duncan at all. Any sane person would be worried about a woman that powerful tottering unsupervised down the sidewalks of New York City.

That left only Blackjack, Bela, and Andy with Duncan.

Typical to his style, Blackjack ignored the bandages and blood and the upcoming healing ritual that might kill both Duncan and what was left of John Cole. He got straight to the rest of his business. From the iron set of his jaw, Duncan could tell he wouldn't like what he was about to hear.

"If this works, you'll be immediately transferred to the Occult Crimes Unit. You'll work under my supervision, and Saul and Cal will keep a watch on you. Mostly, though, you'll work with Bela's fighting group."

"Quad," Bela corrected. "Most Sibyls fight in triads right now, but one day we'll all be in quads again."

Duncan liked looking at her, liked hearing her talk, and he planned to stay right next to her until the cat-demons were handled. But he didn't like Blackjack's tone, or the way his former commander had slipped right back into giving him orders.

"I'm staying with the Sibyls," Duncan growled at Blackjack. "But it's because I want to do it. If I make it past this big healing thing, I don't need a babysitter, and I'm through taking orders from anybody. Fire me if you want to, but stay out of my face."

Blackjack didn't shoot back because Andy started laughing. "I knew I'd like you, Sharp."

Bela didn't look quite so amused. More worried, and a little annoyed, though Duncan didn't know if her emotion was directed at him or at Blackjack.

Blackjack's expression was a cross between frustrated and confused. "Babysitter," he repeated, like he was trying to work up another argument about the need for supervision.

Duncan was a cop's cop, but with weeks to live and demons probably plotting to attack a woman he intended to protect, Duncan didn't want to discuss rank, assignment, command structure, or any other pointless bullshit. His lips pulled back from his teeth, and the fire in his neck and shoulder burned twice as hot. He was about to give Blackjack a piece of his mind, but John Cole shut down his speech centers somehow. Duncan couldn't find the words he needed. What he could find, he couldn't say. He felt like his tongue had been lashed to the bottom of his mouth.

Calm down, John's voice instructed. *Getting pissed only speeds up the infection. All strong emotions do.*

Wonderful, Duncan shot back at him, but when he looked at Bela and thought about the Rakshasa, what they might do to her, he made his muscles relax.

Blackjack finally came up with something, and when he spoke, his voice was calmer and more authoritative than Duncan expected. "It's either my way or we leave New York City today, and my other friends will monitor your infection until you change. We've never had a captive Rakshasa. The information would be useful."

Bela and Andy both spun to face Blackjack, but Duncan never gave them a chance to speak.

"Other friends? Screw that!" He almost slammed his fist into the bed rail again, and would have if he hadn't already broken the damned thing. "You're playing on old rumors, Blackjack."

"He's playing at something," Bela said, and she sounded dangerous.

"Fucking idiot." Andy's snarl was wicked and backed up by a spray of water from the sprinkler over Blackjack's head. "Don't try to pull this shit again, or I'll wash you into Central Park."

Duncan locked eyes with his now drenched former commander, seeking answers. The heat inside Duncan, all but the pain in his neck and shoulder wounds, ebbed in favor of a creeping, icy cold as he saw the truth in the hard flint of Blackjack's gaze.

What you heard in Kabul after the Valley of the Gods— it wasn't rumors, Duncan. John Cole's voice was serious and apologetic. *It's all true.*

Duncan's mind flipped back in time, to the disaster in the mountains near Kabul, when John, a bunch of priests from the Vatican, and a recon unit had gone into a hidden valley to explore a temple. John was the only one who came back alive, and he was gone just a day after that, AWOL, snuffed out, shipped out—nobody knew. John just disappeared. Vanished. And Blackjack bugged out right behind him on a super-fast, super-silent black helicopter with pilots who wore full body armor and reflective face shields—but not before he tried to persuade Duncan to come with him.

Some weird shit happened in that valley, Sharp, Blackjack had told him. *We have to react. We have to respond.*

Blackjack had talked about plans for a new, secret branch of the special forces. Atypical Sightings Reconnaissance. ASR would be based at Fort Campbell, Kentucky, under control of the 101st Airborne, and they would be forming a civilian branch called the ASI, Atypical Sightings Investigations. ASI would be affiliated with the FBI, to act as liaisons with civilian organizations.

We have to reshape whole sections of law enforcement. We could use men like you, Sharp.

But Duncan couldn't go along with bizarre shit like that. Not then, and he was having a damned hard time going along with it now, too. Yet here he was, about to be reassigned to the local nut squad because of Blackjack. The Occult Crimes Unit. Hell, half the officers in the NYPD didn't take the OCU seriously, but Duncan realized the unit probably had been created after the first Gulf War. That's when the ASI likely helped set it up. New York City's OCU might have been formed by Blackjack himself. That's why he was here now, and why he was acting like he was in charge.

"Let me get this straight." Duncan refused to look at Blackjack, and let himself imagine the bastard buried balls up in a hot pile of sand. "Either I accept your authority and do what you say, or you're taking me to some secret military facility to be an experiment—and die."

"The hell he will." The room seemed to give a little shake as Bela spoke, but Blackjack didn't respond at all, except to keep up his stare.

Which was, of course, Duncan's answer.

Duncan understood that the Sibyls weren't caving to Blackjack's threat, and that Blackjack knew better than to challenge such powerful women directly. That wouldn't stop him from acting on the sly, though. From pulling some midnight raid or broad-daylight snatch off the streets.

John shared the nuclear flare of Duncan's fury, but also helped him contain it. Duncan hated being trapped. Even in uniform, he had refused to be contained, confined, and corralled like Blackjack was trying to do. Bullets and explosions couldn't hold him down—and now this?

He had to find something to say instead of getting more pissed off, because he sensed that John was serious about strong emotions making the demon infection harder to control. Duncan let his gaze drift over Andy, then settle on his angel.

Bela's expression was severe now, and it didn't get any softer when Duncan glared at Blackjack and said, "Military prison versus some concentrated time with good-looking women in leather. Hmm. Now that's a hard choice, Blackjack. Damn, you've gotten mean since you went civilian."

"Oh, for God's sake." Andy let loose another spray of water, then knocked past Blackjack as she headed for the door, setting off trickles from the sinks as she went. "Men. Cops. They're *all* the same. I'm going to headquarters to help the Mothers."

"I'll be watching you, Duncan," Blackjack said before he followed Andy out the door, presumably to go with her.

Bela raised her hands, and Duncan felt a surge of some kind of energy. The yellow room's door slammed shut with so much force Duncan was surprised the wood didn't split down the middle.

The crash helped bring his thoughts back to earth, and for some reason it made him feel better.

"That man," Bela said as she turned to face Duncan, her expression six kinds of pissed off, "is a first-class fuck-wad."

"Yeah." Tension ebbed out of Duncan as he watched her face change colors, and he almost laughed. "Blackjack has a way of making people love him, doesn't he?"

"Ass-hat." Bela took a breath. "Shit-scraper. Dickweed." She was slowing down a little bit. The beginnings of a smile tugged at her lips. "Wait, wait. Prick-nose. I think I like that one best."

Duncan stared at her because he couldn't help it. The pink in her cheeks, the way her dark hair tumbled around her shoulders, wild from the energy she just fired at the door with her hands *and* her mouth—damn. She really was the most beautiful woman he had ever seen, and he was alone with her now, and conscious, and he had to say something charming and brilliant.

He wanted to tell her how pretty she was, and that the vigil she kept at his bedside really made the difference. He wasn't sure he would have made it back this far from the demon attack if she hadn't given him so much time and kindness.

Nobody's shown me that kind of tenderness since I was a kid.

You're amazing.

When I can walk, have dinner with me.

Any of those things might have been right, but nothing came out of his mouth.

This was unbelievable.

He was good with women. He *always* had the perfect line, the right words to let them know they were special.

Until now.

"You're—I—shit." Duncan rubbed his good hand across his chin, as if adjusting his mouth might make the words come out better. What the hell was he trying to do, anyway? Hook up with her? He was infected. Dying—or trying to turn into some freaking demon. Was he out of his mind?

"Er, thanks. For—for saving my ass."

I'm an idiot.

Her expression went from angry to amused, and Duncan figured she was reading him fast and well. He cleared his throat and tried to straighten himself in the hospital bed. When he moved, he felt like some asshole was driving hot needles through both of his arms. He winced, but the pain helped him dredge up a few more thoughts.

"About not wanting a babysitter—I wasn't trying to say I didn't want to be here. With you."

God, this was only getting worse.

He should tell her how it felt to wake up over and over again and feel her gentle hands on his face, hear her voice urging him to fight, to heal.

Hell, he should spill about how many times he'd imagined peeling that leather jumpsuit off her naked body. That would be endearing and charming, right?

He glanced at his right arm. *Maybe I'll just hit myself in the head with this cast.*

Bela walked toward him, her movements graceful and

athletic. Duncan's pulse picked up, and his breathing accelerated.

Steady, John urged from deep in his brain.

Duncan jumped and blinked, and Bela stopped where she was, about five feet away from the edge of his bed.

"Did he just speak to you?" she asked. "Did you hear John Cole's voice?"

Oh, yeah. Dead guys talking in my head. Great icebreaker. Duncan let out a breath and thought about bashing himself with his cast again.

"It's okay. I know something about ghost voices." Bela's smile was more wry than happy, which put Duncan at ease even faster than her words. "I have a few of my own, chattering and haunting, but mine aren't real ghosts. Just memories. With attitudes."

Duncan watched her smile get a little sadder. "How did you know John was talking to me?"

"I can see it here." Bela pointed to her dark eyes. "The color changes. The first time it happened, I thought you were turning into a demon."

The first time it happened . . . Yeah. Duncan kind of remembered that. Just a weird, cloudy image of Bela backing away from him. The sound of her shouts for help echoed across his memory, and shame coiled and rattled like a snake in his gut.

A new reality opened in his awareness, and he didn't like it one bit.

How could—

But it was what it was. Denying it wouldn't help. Fact was fact, and the truth was, he'd spent his life fighting to make sure people like Bela didn't have to worry about attacks from crackpots, murderers, and scum. And now—

Had he become the problem?

"I'm sorry." He heard the gruffness in his own voice, and hoped she didn't take it wrong. "I wouldn't hurt you."

She might have believed him, and she might not have believed him. He couldn't tell, and that made him sick. As soon as he and John took care of the Rakshasa, he'd take himself away from here, then take himself out of this game in one big hurry. A bullet to the head while he set himself on fire—that would probably do the trick. He wouldn't risk even the leftovers of his body in cat-form doing any kind of damage to innocent people.

"You've got a lot to absorb, Duncan." Bela started moving again, and hearing her say his name made him go half soft in the head. His thoughts careened wildly from becoming a monster to becoming everything this woman could ever want. Her eyes touched his face, his neck, his chest, and left trails of heat everywhere they roamed, distracting him until both futures seemed possible.

"I know it must be overwhelming," she said as she reached the side of the bed and put her hand on his forearm, just below where the bandages covered the ends of his slash wounds. Her long fingers looked so smooth against his desert-and-street-weathered hide. When he turned his head upward to see her face, he wanted to press his mouth against her neck and taste all that softness. She was everything female, everything he longed for but had never really let himself appreciate. Not like he should have, not like he would have if he'd known how fast his clock was ticking.

Damn, he was being selfish, even thinking that way. He had to stop.

But he didn't want to.

Bela leaned down until her eyes were level with his, and he could feel the sweet tickle of her breath on his cheeks. His muscles went tight as he tried to hold himself back, but blood pounded all over his body.

"Is John listening right now?" she asked.

"No. He takes a powder whenever you get close to me." Duncan absolutely couldn't stop looking at her, not for any reason. "You're private. You're all mine."

Her dark eyes widened, somehow gentle and unyielding

at the same time. "You'll get through this, Duncan." Bela's voice, her smell, the feel of her, danced through his awareness. "We'll help you. *I'll* help you find a way to save yourself."

"I think I'm beyond salvation," he admitted, and he kissed her.

(15)

Bela couldn't think of anything in the world beyond the firm pressure of Duncan's mouth on hers. Hard, but soft. Hot and electric.

She wasn't surprised.

Of course she wasn't.

Hadn't she wanted this to happen again?

Of course she had.

Complicated. Probably not smart. And she so didn't care. When she wanted a man, she never held back, and this man—damn. She had wanted to know more about him from the moment she found him in DUMBO, and the days she had spent taking care of him only deepened that interest.

He tasted like fresh water, natural and satisfying, and his muscled arm tightened under her fingers. With her free hand, she touched his thick, soft hair, then the rough stubble of his jaw. He didn't try to press or take over. He didn't even lean his powerful body forward. No. He was leaving her in total control, and she was still kissing him, and feeling the flutters in her chest, her neck, her mind, her entire being.

I'm taking advantage of a wounded man in a hospital bed.

The thought should have sobered her, but she kept kissing him, then kissing him and touching him. His arms, his chest, his shoulders. His muscles got tighter and tighter under her palms, her fingertips. His breathing more ragged against her face. His mouth more demanding.

Bela's thoughts tilted and spun, and she just couldn't convince herself to stop.

It wasn't until her mind moved on to the four pairs of handcuffs lying on the counter beside the sink, and all the things they could do with those handcuffs when Duncan felt a little better, that she managed to get a grip enough to pull back.

Her heart was beating so fast she could barely breathe, and the distance between her mouth and his immediately frustrated her. She wanted to kiss him again, but instead she ran her finger across his lips.

Duncan's winter-gray eyes grabbed her and held her as forcefully as any embrace.

Bela's skin got so hot she thought she might be feverish, and parts of her body ached for his hands, his mouth, and more. He let her trace his eyes, his ears, his neck. The muscles of his chest seemed to bulge against her palm.

"I should probably apologize," she whispered, taking her hand away from his face, but keeping her fingers on his arm.

The corner of his sexy mouth twitched. "Why? I kissed you."

A little flood of pleasure and surprise washed through her chest. She thought about unzipping her bodysuit to fan herself, but found enough sanity to delay that urge. "I thought it was the other way around."

Another twitch of that sensual mouth almost made her come undone. "Want to fight about it?"

"No."

That drawl could kill a woman.

Bela kissed him again, making damned sure she moved first this time. She pressed both hands against the sides of his face, and he raised his good arm, resting it carefully across her back, his fingers gripping her waist.

When she turned his mouth loose, he didn't let go of her, and this time she thought his eyes would melt her into a puddle of leather and wishes, right there at the side of his bed. He seemed to be looking into her essence, searching for something way down inside of her, and whatever it was, she wanted to give it to him—or at least let him taste enough of it to want more later.

And there would be a *later*. An *after this*.

He would have a next week, and a week after, and a week after that. She was an earth Sibyl, a trained scientist and researcher, with a specialty in biology and medicine. She would find a way to save this special man. Duncan Sharp wasn't going to die *or* become a Rakshasa.

Bela leaned hard against the edge of his bed and pressed her forehead against his. His eyes were so close to hers that her vision blurred, and she couldn't see anything but a sea of gray-blue. He was still searching, searching—but what was he trying to find?

"Tell me what you need," she murmured as she stroked his jaw.

Duncan let out a breath. Closed his eyes. Opened them. She had a sense that he was struggling to find words, and she felt him give up. She leaned away to better see his face, and caught the frustration and embarrassment.

"Tell me." She brushed her lips against his, ready to give him anything at all.

"Are you—" He broke off, and she could tell that whatever he needed to ask her, it was costing him. Duncan's magnetic eyes filled with pain, the kind that her earth energy couldn't soothe, and his grip on her waist tightened as he struggled to make himself finish. "Are you . . . afraid of me?"

The words came out in a rough whisper, almost a plea, and the devastated look on his handsome face almost broke Bela's heart. This was a man who had spent years—maybe even given his life and soul—protecting people. It must have torn him in half to have to ask that question of anyone.

Tears jumped to her eyes, and her throat tried to squeeze shut when she answered him. "I'm not afraid of you, Duncan."

He turned her loose and lowered his head. "Maybe you should be."

"Not happening." She grabbed his face and made him look at her again. On instinct, she drew earth energy straight through the floor to calm herself and drive away the tears trying to rush down her cheeks. "If I have anything to say about it, there's a lot that won't be happening—and I think I know what you need to help you believe me."

This got his attention, and his gaze dropped to her jumpsuit zipper.

Tiny earthquakes of desire rattled Bela in every important location.

For a few seconds, all she could do was stand there trying to look determined and strong even though her mind was filled with a detailed movie of him pulling that zipper down, reaching inside her leathers, and sliding his big, strong hand across her stone-hard nipple.

His palms would be rough, and his pinch strong enough to make her scream.

Duncan's uninjured fist strangled the bedsheet like he was reading her mind.

Bela couldn't resist a quick glance lower, to where the sheet was lifting away from his hips.

Oh, yeah.

That was one *fabulous* erection.

And she was so damned hot she might have to come out of her leathers, even if it wasn't quite what she intended.

Duncan cleared his throat. "I'm not sure I'm strong enough yet."

Yet.

Sweet Goddess, get out of the way. I'm about to shake down the whole brownstone.

Bela let go of his face and fanned her neck with her hand

as she leaned over to the pile of clothes beside the room's only chair. She grabbed a pair of jeans off the top and stood again to find Duncan still giving her that five-alarms-need-ice-cubes stare.

There wasn't enough earth energy in the world to keep her calm around this man now that he was awake.

"The Brent brothers got this stuff from your apartment." Bela was surprised she got the words out, and she enjoyed his quizzical look when she dropped the jeans on the bed beside him. "Since you yanked out your own IV earlier, and all the cuffs are off, the way I see it, you're fit for duty. If you can get out of that bed, put your pants on, and get upstairs, you're strong enough for what I have in mind."

Duncan looked disappointed for a second, but also relieved. He picked up the jeans with his good hand. "Blackjack probably won't like this."

"Good." Bela felt her face brighten at the possibility of helping Duncan and annoying Jack Blackmore at the same time. Double score. And damn, but she wanted to watch Duncan uncover and put those jeans on, but she mentally slapped herself and made herself turn around and bend over to pick out a T-shirt for him. She selected the black one from the stack Saul and Cal Brent had brought by, even though she knew it would make her drool to watch Duncan wander around in it. "When you went after John Cole, it was because you thought he'd killed Katrina Drake."

"Her, and six other women by my count—but just the one in New York City." Duncan sounded a little surprised by the shift in conversation, but interested, too. "I caught the pattern when I was studying some files in the FBI's serial killer database, hunting down something for another case. I saw a photo and a sketch artist's take on one of the suspects, and I knew it was John right away. So I found him and started tracking his movements."

He had gotten to his feet when she turned around, and she found herself facing his bare back.

Bela almost dropped the T-shirt.

His jeans rested snug against his tapered waist, and muscles rippled all across her visual field as he worked to fasten them. Jagged lines and round marks stood pale against his tanned flesh. Shrapnel scars. A lot of them—old, from what she could tell. Bela was reminded once more that Duncan was a warrior in the truest sense of the word.

That did nothing to cool her off.

At all.

"The Alsace heiress." Bela heard herself talking, but her mind was back to very detailed movies about where and how she'd like to touch him next. "We got her name from our liaisons at the OCU, and a list of suspects who might have set the Rakshasa on her. Any idea why somebody would want her dead?"

"Yeah. That's definitely the question." Duncan muttered something she couldn't make out, and she realized he was having trouble with the snap and zipper on his jeans because his injured arm and hand weren't cooperating. She dropped the T-shirt on the bed, reached around, and moved her arms under his to help.

Duncan went very still as she hugged him from behind, and she laid her cheek against the steel of his back, glorying in the rugged feel of his strength and his scars. Her own fingers didn't want to follow her commands, but she fastened the snap, then slid the zipper slowly, slowly upward.

It wasn't easy, given the bulge trying to shove the fabric out of its way.

When she finished zipping his pants, Bela let her hands slip down to cradle him through the thick fabric.

Damn . . .

His head snapped back, and the groan he let out was so low and husky that she felt it in her bones.

You're an ass, Bela. He said he wasn't strong enough, and you know he's right.

But a split second later, he turned around, his gray-blue eyes blazing like a sunrise.

Bela barely got a breath before Duncan grabbed her by the waist. He pulled her to him fast and hard, and she stumbled against his chest, his bandages, and the cool, metallic dinar. The coin's unusual elemental power buzzed against her throat as his good arm gripped her so firmly, so tightly that he lifted her to her toes. His cast pressed against her back, and she melted into him, winding her arms around his neck as his lips took hers fiercely, desperately, desire driving each thrust of his tongue.

Was the room shaking?

Did she care?

Tongue to tongue, leathers to bare chest, she kissed him back with every ounce of energy she possessed, and yeah, hell yeah, the room was shaking, and no, she absolutely did not care. Bela moaned into the kiss, and Duncan's answering rumble of satisfaction made her whole body vibrate.

When he finally released her lips, she wanted to whimper and beg, but she doubled her fists against his chest and pushed herself back. She was shaking now, but the room had settled down, at least. When she opened her eyes, if she ever did, she'd check to see if there were any cracks in the walls or floor.

"You're, ah, stronger than I thought," she said, her voice not much more than a squeak. "But this isn't happening. Not until the Mothers finish your healing and I know it won't kill you."

"You're already killing me, Angel." Duncan's slow drawl flowed all over her, touching her in places his hands hadn't found. "Every time you talk. Every time you move. Every damned time I look at you." He kissed her forehead, her eyes, then so, so, gently, the corners of her mouth. She thought she might die right there, and be happy anyway.

Angel. *He keeps calling me* Angel.

Is that really how he sees me?

She had never had a man call her by a nickname that didn't irk the shit out of her, but this one didn't bother her at all.

"Just so we're clear," he murmured, "are you telling me no?"

Bela opened her eyes to find that his were nothing but blue-hot fire. He was hard against her belly, still about to tear out of those jeans she had fastened, but he didn't try to kiss her again. She wanted to shove him backward on the bed, mount him, and ride him until the walls fell down. She wanted to scream with passion until she didn't have any screams left, and stare into those gorgeous eyes the entire time.

Her throat worked for a few seconds, not making any sound at all, before she forced out, "I'm telling you not yet."

Duncan seemed to consider this seriously, without any kind of anger. "Okay. I can live with that."

Bela laughed, surprising herself. "That's kind of the point."

For a time after that, he just held her, his face in her hair, his warm breath trickling past her ear. The man might not have earth energy, but he could soothe as well as he could excite. Did everything about him have to be so sexy? She might have a chance at rational thought if he wasn't a walking, drawling poster boy for all-American male.

Later, almost in a trance, Bela pulled away from him, picked up the black T-shirt, and helped Duncan pull it over his casted arm and his bandaged neck and shoulder. She rolled the taut cotton over his firm chest and abs, then moved her hands over the soft fabric until she didn't see any wrinkles—or any ceiling dust from the shake she'd given the basement.

When she finished running her palms across his T-shirt, he shook his head. "I can't believe that was so damned erotic, you putting my clothes *on*."

Bela separated her fingers from the heat of his body and had to count to ten to get her thoughts together. "Come on. Let's go upstairs. We'll be more likely to behave, and Dio and Camille should be back in a few. If Andy's through being pissed and doesn't have to help the other Mothers, she'll be with them, and we can go have a word with the Alsace family lawyer."

Duncan didn't object as she led him out of the treatment room, but he hesitated when he saw the laboratory with its ultramodern machinery. Some of the equipment, like the geno-coder, were technology developed at Motherhouse Russia—things humans had never seen if they didn't have earth Sibyls for friends.

"Looks like a first-class operation." He leaned down and inspected the centrifuge Bela had been using to analyze the many samples of blood she had taken from Duncan. "This an offshoot of some hospital I don't know about? Some sort of super-secret government lab deal?"

Bela took a few minutes to explain about the different types of Sibyls and their specialties, and was pleased at Duncan's questions and level of interest.

When they finally headed out of the lab, she told him, "I'm into medical research, but Riana, the earth Sibyl who owned this place before me, preferred advanced crime scene analysis." Bela pointed to the wall farthest from the door and treatment room. "She left me some of her microscopes, because the Motherhouse gave her some newer models. They're pretty useful."

"I know a little about microscopes," he said as they closed the lab door and headed into the cool hallway. Duncan was walking stiffly, but his balance was good so far. "Did fair in chemistry. I took a few of the Uniformed Service University's classes in biological, chemical, and nuclear weapons. Well, really it was nuclear and radiological weapons, if memory serves."

Bela paused outside her bedroom at the foot of the stairs,

surprised. She made sure to keep her back to the closed door of her room, because she definitely wasn't ready for him to see what was in there. That would be . . . way too much information.

Duncan's expression was distant, and thankfully, he didn't seem to be interested in the secrets behind that closed door. He passed his fingers through his close-cut hair. "I thought about Military Contingency Medicine, but the Gulf War came along. I ended up picking Ranger School."

"Army." She took his uncasted hand in hers. "Aren't Ready for Marines Yet, right?"

Duncan's mouth came open as she squeezed his fingers. "Who told you that bunch of bullshit?"

Bela laughed. "My father was in the Marines before I was born. He had lots of jokes, most of them a lot less tasteful than that."

"Your father was a jarhead. No wonder you know how to swear so good." He whistled low and long, and managed to paste on a very serious expression. "A jarhead. And you let me kiss you? Damn, Angel. I thought you *liked* me."

She punched his good shoulder. "You ready for these stairs?"

"Think so."

She kept hold of his hand and walked up beside him, her arm laced around his for support. He didn't object.

"We have a theory about the Rakshasa," Bela said as they reached the brownstone's small kitchen. *Oh, good. Somebody did the dishes—and nobody left a bra hanging on anything.* "We think the demons came here to make money. Andy believes some organized groups are hiring them—paying them to do their dirty work."

Duncan stopped by the kitchen table, which Bela saw did have a bra on it after all, in the corner, under some mail. A red bra, damn it. It was probably one of Andy's. Luckily, he was too busy catching his breath to notice.

"Then we're dealing with demon hit-kitties?" he asked as Bela let go of him and casually scooted the bra farther under the envelopes. "And some bunch of assholes shelled out the bucks for them to kill Katrina Drake."

"Something like that." She gave up on the bra and pushed open the swinging door to the living room, did another quick underwear check, then let him through. "If we figure out who's fronting the cash, we'll find the conspirators behind Katrina Drake's murder, and we'll be that much closer to finding all the Rakshasa and shutting them down, at least in New York City."

"You know," he said as he stepped into the communications area and his good-looking reflection played back at her from the projective mirrors, "that makes more sense than just about anything since I woke up—except you."

Bela's lips tingled when he looked at her, and her arms ached to be around him. This was definitely not going to be easy, but the tired look on his face after a short walk and a brief haul up a dozen steps let her know that waiting was definitely the right choice. Still, upstairs, downstairs, it really didn't make much difference. She wanted to kiss him, even if her entire quad and half the Sibyl Mothers busted in on them before she finished.

As it was, the knock on the door came with no jingle of wind chimes at all.

Duncan moved immediately, stepping between her and the front of the room.

"Down, boy," Bela told him, moving past him easily and redirecting him toward one of the overstuffed chairs. "Trust me, this is probably nothing."

The mirrors startled Duncan, and he raised his good hand like he thought he ought to be menacing one or two of his reflections. It took him a second to understand, then he shifted his focus back to her. "How do you know it's nothing?"

"Ve haf vays. Now sit down." She gestured to the closet as he ignored her and kept right on standing, looking like he was ready to beat up half the Bronx to make sure she was okay. "If I'm wrong and something eats me, there are swords and daggers in the closet."

(16)

Frankenstein's lab in the basement.

Swords and daggers in the closet.

Weird mirrors all over the walls.

And her father was a Marine.

Yep, and you still think she's the hottest thing in New York City. Duncan glanced from Bela to the front door to the closet and wondered if he could pick up a sword right now if he wanted to. *You're probably in trouble here, Sharp.*

Her father was a Marine? John Cole's voice caught him by surprise, because John's presence had been distant for a while, during—well. While Duncan was getting to know Bela a little better.

"Can it," Duncan muttered to John.

She's telling the truth, John said. *There's nothing dangerous here, other than us.* A second or two later, he added, *You have to learn to trust me. What I know, you'll know. I won't hold anything back or let you get your ass in a jam.*

Duncan sat down, but only because he saw who was at the door when Bela opened it. A tiny woman in a purple warm-up suit. Silk. Pricey. Stylishly cut gray hair, no handbag, very long nose—and she was already looking down it when she introduced herself to Bela as Mrs. Knight, the next-door neighbor.

"Did your water heater blow up again?" Mrs. Knight asked. She looked to be about seventy, but her voice was calm and steady when she spoke.

"Water heater—oh. No, it didn't blow up again." Bela sounded uncomfortable, and Duncan had zero idea what

Mrs. Knight was talking about. "We were . . . moving fur-niture back into place. I'm sorry, did we bang around too much?"

"Everything shook." Mrs. Knight's tone was a shade less than friendly.

So that wasn't my imagination. Duncan saw himself smiling in the mirrors. *The earth really did move when I kissed her.*

Mrs. Knight peered around Bela to check him out.

Duncan gave her a nod.

For some reason, a visit from a pain-in-the-ass neighbor made him feel more relaxed and normal, as if the world hadn't turned upside down and blown itself up.

"We'll be more careful," Bela was saying.

The chimes over her head gave a little ring, and the coin around Duncan's neck went hot in two seconds flat. He grabbed the dinar and pulled it away from his skin. The metal warmed his fingers as the coin buzzed and shook like a cell phone on vibrate.

What the hell—

Something's coming, John told him. *Maybe something bad. The chimes and the coin react to elemental energy.*

That got Duncan's blood pumping. His breathing turned shallow, and his arm and slash wounds burned like a bas-tard. Shoving aside his exhaustion, he pushed himself out of the too-soft, too-cushiony chair and headed toward the closet. The knife John had used to carve on the Rakshasa had been destroyed during the transmigration, but Duncan was willing to bet that Sibyl swords and daggers could cut into anything supernatural.

From the corner of his eye, he saw Bela trying to move Mrs. Knight along. The older lady seemed annoyed—or maybe nervous—and she kept glancing around Bela to get the measure of Duncan again.

Damn, lady. I've got my clothes on. He got hold of the closet door, but the knob wouldn't turn. Locked. *Besides,*

*this is New York City, not Georgia thirty years ago. What's
the big deal if I'm here with Bela?*

He grabbed the handle and was about to see if he had
enough oomph in his good arm to break the closet door
open when he heard Andy Myles say, "You have a nice day,
too, Mrs. Knight, and don't worry, everything will be fine."
Then, as she rumbled into the entryway in her wet jeans
and drippy-looking blouse, "Shit, Bela. What did you do,
make an earthquake while we were gone?"

Bela was still standing by the front door, rubbing her eyes
with her thumb and forefinger, like she might be working
on one hell of a headache.

Camille came in next, quiet, with her head down. She
walked straight over to the chairs without looking at Duncan, and perched on the arm of the seat farthest from him.

Dio was right behind her, lugging a bunch of folders and
papers. When she spied Duncan still holding on to the
closet door, she said, "Whoa, King Kong, it's just us." A
blast of air pushed Duncan's hand away from the handle,
and Dio's gaze narrowed and fixed on the dinar. "Did Bela
say something about elemental energy nearby, or did that
coin give you a warning that we were coming?"

He read the mistrust on Dio's face and in Camille's
frown, and his belly twisted. He wanted to tell them they
didn't have to worry about him, that he'd dial his own
number before he ever let himself do damage to innocent
people. Andy was staring at him, too, and Bela, though at
least Bela didn't look so suspicious.

Hell, he couldn't fault the women for worrying. They
didn't know what he could do, what he might be capable
of—and come to think of it, neither did he. All in all, it
seemed like the best bet for their safety to be honest about
everything, and that would keep his angel out of a bad spot
with her fighting group, too.

"The dinar got hot and buzzed." Duncan lifted the coin

and glanced at the oddly shiny edges. "John said it reacts to elemental energy, like your chimes."

The fire Sibyl slipped off her perch and came toward him.

"May I?" she asked, gesturing toward the dinar. "Just a closer look. It's probably better if I don't touch it."

"Sure." Duncan had a sensation of something squirming around his brain as he held the coin as far from his neck as the chain allowed.

Hot, John muttered.

Duncan frowned.

What was hot? The dinar? But it was normal now. No buzzing, no heat.

The woman, dipshit. Camille. She's hot.

To each his own, John. Duncan realized his frown was deeper, and that he might make the women nervous. He made his face smooth out again and kept his lips in a straight line. *She's not for me.*

Camille leaned forward and held a hand over the dinar. Energy flickered around her shoulders and head. No smoke or fire like the old howler monkey general who had been helping him—but Duncan watched, amazed, as a yellow-orange tendril snaked from Camille's outstretched fingers. It slipped around the coin, then drew tighter and closer, until the colors shimmered across the dinar's worn golden surface.

"It's projective," Camille said. "Weird. I didn't know metal could channel and project energy as well as glass—and it's also like the elemental barriers we create." The tendril let go and retreated back to the fire Sibyl's palm as she straightened herself. "It's got some sort of biological key that locks it to his living signature. I think he could voluntarily give it up, but nobody could take it from him and live."

Duncan figured this kind of examination of objects must be commonplace among Sibyls, but wondered about that assumption when he saw how Dio and Andy were staring at Camille. Bela came over from the door, and she was staring at Camille, too.

"It's the projective aspect that probably repels the Rakshasa—and maybe that's what let his energy appear in the park when we fought the Rakshasa." Camille was still all wrapped up in the dinar, and Duncan had a sense that she'd love to play with the thing for hours, just to see what it could do. "It's magnifying its elemental locks and the energy of the person wielding it. That's pretty impressive."

"What you just did, Camille, that's what's impressive." Bela's tone was slightly awed, but her gaze was shrewd and excited. She reminded Duncan of a commander who'd just realized her whole unit had night vision or some other major battle advantage. "I hope you'll keep working on that. It may turn out to be more useful than any of us can imagine."

Camille blushed at the compliment, and her attention shifted away from the coin. A second or two later, she hurried back to her spot on the chair.

For a few seconds, Dio, Andy, and Bela kept studying her, then Andy broke off and stared at Duncan instead. "The Mothers are all here at headquarters. They're arguing like cats in a tuna barrel about the best way to grow you an arm bone and cook your demon infection." She shook a bunch of droplets off her right hand, then scratched the side of her freckled nose. "Shouldn't you be in bed?"

"Bela and I were talking about Katrina Drake's murder." Duncan left out the kissing parts, deciding that wasn't exactly dishonest or keeping secrets. "Whoever hired the Rakshasa—that trail's getting colder by the minute. I think I can help a little bit, on the light work, until your Mothers are ready for me."

Dio still looked wary of Duncan, but she showed him the folders and papers in her hand. "We picked up some more info at OCU. Creed and Nick, our former liaisons, copied the rest of what they have for us. Let me go upstairs and get dressed. If you're up for a car trip, we can get this show on the road."

"Wait a minute." Andy held up both hands like a traffic cop about to start directing the show. "Are you all transferred officially to the OCU, Sharp? Did Jack Blackmore approve you getting involved with this investigation?"

Duncan felt a little jolt of unease. "Ah, no. I'm not, that I know of, and he didn't."

Andy's smile could have lit up half the city. "Hot damn." She clapped her hands, spraying a mist of water in the air. "Let's go."

"I'll help Dio fix herself up." Camille followed Dio to the staircase near the front door, and Duncan thought she was talking a little louder, maybe, after getting compliments from everybody over how she'd checked out the dinar. "I have some outfits that might work, and some makeup—oh, and a really good pair of heels."

"Rather die, thanks," Dio called over her shoulder to Camille, but she didn't refuse the assistance as she jogged up the steps. "You're a lot smaller than me, anyway. I'd look like toothpaste in a tube in one of your shirts."

"Exactly," Camille said, and she was definitely talking louder. Walking a little straighter, too.

Dio's next comment involved swearing that would have made a convict blush.

Andy's contribution was, "I'll get coffee."

She peeled off, making a beeline for the kitchen, and Bela said, "You're addicted to caffeine, you know that, right?"

"Fuck you very much," floated back from the kitchen.

Okay.

Duncan let himself breathe again.

All of this felt like a normal police operation about to be put into play. He let himself enjoy a few seconds of feeling sort of normal, if you didn't count the cast, the cuts, the dinar around his neck, or the ghost in his head.

From upstairs, he heard Dio say, "Are you *kidding* me, Camille?"

"Thank you for being straightforward with my quad." Bela's voice instantly seized his full attention, and when he turned to face her, she was standing close enough to touch.

The arguing upstairs continued, something about halter tops, hookers, and fifteen-inch heels, but Duncan didn't pay it any mind. He raised his arms and put his hands on Bela's elbows. She felt electric to him whenever he touched her, wherever his hands happened to rest. She was so vibrant and full of power. "Secrets divide, Angel. I wouldn't do that to you."

"I believe you." Her dark eyes held his as she came closer and closer, leaning into him, challenging Duncan's self-control with each fraction of an inch that disappeared between them. "I think you're a good man, Duncan Sharp. I think you're an honorable man."

Her lips brushed against his, sending him to another place where nobody was upstairs fighting about "whore-red lipstick."

"That being said," Bela told him in her sweet, sexy voice, "we have to be clear on one very important point."

"Anything." Duncan waited, his body getting hotter and more ready for her by the second. When she kissed him again, she rubbed her belly against his hard length, and her leather and his jeans seemed like no cover at all.

Damn, he wanted her. Wanted to be inside her. Maybe he was strong enough. Maybe if he asked again, she wouldn't say no.

"If you do change into a demon and threaten my quad, I'll take you out." Bela grabbed hold of his casted arm before he could react, and his good arm, too. "It'll be easy." She lifted his hands toward her full breasts, then slid them across her ribs to her back, let go, and put her arms around him. "I'll ram an elementally locked sword into your heart," she said as she tightened her grip and brought her soft lips toward his a third time. "I'll behead you." She kissed him. "I'll burn you to ashes." She kissed him one more time. "And to finish the job, I'll scatter your remains in the Hudson."

Damn, she was hypnotic. The sound of her, the feel of her, made everything bad in the world leave his mind. He didn't want to let go of her, couldn't stop staring at her, and her threats only turned him on more. She was mother tiger to her quad. He could respect that. Maybe she was secretly one of those cat-demons, and he wasn't sure he cared. When she looked up at him, her dark eyes serious and steaming, Duncan almost groaned.

"Don't forget what I said," Bela told him. Another quick kiss, and she turned him loose. "And you're right about secrets dividing people. I won't be keeping any secrets from my quad or from the Sibyl Mothers. Sibyl fighting units have to function like perfectly fitted machines, and—"

A huge thump and bang obliterated the rest of her words.

Duncan grabbed her and used his body to cover her as splinters and bigger chunks of white painted banister pelted his head and back. He turned, keeping Bela behind him, to see Camille and Dio crash off the stairs and hit the floor slugging it out. One second later, they were trying hard to choke each other to death. The redhead was wearing jeans and a tunic, but Dio was dressed in something that looked like two red handkerchiefs. Really, really little handkerchiefs. The fabric whipped in the wind that was starting to rip wind chimes off the ceiling.

"Angel," Duncan said, doing his best to keep some of the wind off her, "I think your machine has . . . issues."

Bela stayed behind him, and she started banging her head on his back. Slowly. Not too hard. But real steady.

Andy shot out of the kitchen, sloshing coffee everywhere. "What the hell? Oh, for shit's sake."

She slammed her mug down on the gigantic table in front

of the couch, raised both hands, and hit the women with a blast of water as strong as any fire hose. The water's force knocked them apart, and both of them smacked the wall beneath some of the big mirrors.

For a few long seconds, they lay there sputtering and shivering.

Andy looked at the ceiling like she might find God in the ornamental plaster. "And what do you think Mrs. Knight's gonna say about all this noise? Christ on a crutch! She'll call the cops, and I swear we should let them haul you both off. Go change clothes. *Now.* Obviously, this little field trip needs to wait a few days—or longer—until you two children get your shit together."

Dio and Camille looked way pissed.

Dio started to argue, but shut up when Andy hit her in the mouth with another jet of water.

Camille watched that happen to Dio and reverted to her usual silence—but Duncan didn't miss the spark of fury lingering in her odd-colored eyes. That had a little promise to it. Maybe this one was finally starting to find her voice in this set of powerful females.

Dio and Camille scooted up from the wall and took off back upstairs, leaving dark, moist footprints in the carpet as they went.

"Bela, quit banging your head on the hunk and let him sit down before he falls down. He just woke up from some kind of freak-ass coma, for God's sake. Here." Andy passed Bela a pad. "Go change into something comfortable, and make a list of what we need from the hardware store for you to fix the banister."

Andy sat down on the couch, took a drink of coffee, then scooted a notebook to where she was sitting, and started working on her own to-do list.

Bela banged her head on Duncan's back another few seconds, then let out a soft groan, slipped around him, and headed for the swinging door.

"You can fix banisters?" he asked as she retreated. He was intrigued by how many different layers she had, and the thought of her wearing nothing but a tool belt gave him a brand-new hard-on, even though she'd threatened to kill him a little while ago.

"My father was a carpenter." Bela pushed the door open.

Duncan wanted to go after her, carry her down the steps, and lay her out on one of those lab tables. That would be sweet, her naked and gasping, wrapping her legs around his waist . . .

And me having a heart attack, or whatever these slash marks will do to me if I'm "too active." Whatever the hell that means.

"I thought you said your father was a jarhead," he called after Bela, his voice cracking a little after his fantasy of taking her hard and fast on a lab table, never mind the tool belt.

"He was a jarhead *and* a carpenter." The kitchen door swung shut behind her.

"A Marine who was a craftsman? Sorry, Angel. That's just against the laws of nature."

Bela didn't answer, and he heard the soft tread of her shoes on the stairs to the basement. He lifted his broken arm and rubbed the cast, just to have something to do with his hands that wouldn't get him arrested. It was probably a good thing they were waiting a few days to go question that lawyer, Patterson, even if it slowed the investigation down. He needed a little more time to get steady on his feet. And in the brain. And, ah, other places.

"Angel." Andy's snorting laugh startled him, because he'd almost forgotten she was in the room. "I hate to break it to you, Sharp, but Bela Argos would give most angels nightmares, never mind the rest of us heathens."

Her Southern twang made Duncan feel more at home, and less alone. He sat down in the chair opposite the couch. "Don't hear many people this far north use that word, *heathen*. Where are you from?"

She tucked her pencil behind one ear. "Outside Atlanta. I came up here for college. You?"

"I got discharged near here and stayed, because I always wanted to live in New York City. I'm from farther south than you, though. Statesboro."

"Wake up, mama," Andy sang, sounding a lot like a slightly tone-deaf Janis Joplin. "Turn yo' lamp down low. God, I can't remember—wait, wait—it's—I'm goin' to the country, baby do you wanna go." She grinned at him. " 'Statesboro Blues.' The Allman Brothers, right?"

Duncan shook his head. "It's Blind Willie McTell's song. The Allman Brothers just covered it."

Deep in his mind, Duncan heard John whisper, *Can't hide, sinner.* Then a little more of their favorite spiritual. *Where you runnin', sinner, you can't hide.*

It was based on a verse from Revelation in the Bible, if he wasn't mistaken.

"Ten points for Duncan Sharp. The man knows his music." Andy downed another drink of coffee, then got to her feet. "Listen, Sibyls are allowed to date and get married and all that jazz, so I don't care if you're sweet on Bela—as long as you're good to her, and as long as you don't die."

Her tone reminded Duncan of one police officer giving another permission to date her sister, and he treated it with that respect. "Thanks, and I will be good to her, and I'm not planning on croaking unless I have no other choice." He scrubbed his palm across his chin, realizing he needed a shave in a big way. "If I blow any of that, are you going to threaten to kill me, too?"

Andy glanced over her shoulder at the kitchen door, then turned her attention back to Duncan. Her eyes crinkled at the corners when she smiled. "Not yet, Sharp. And don't give me any reason to regret that."

17

Bela watched Duncan take a long, slow sip of the coffee she made. Morning sunlight through the brownstone's single kitchen window played off the high line of his jaw, accenting his natural good looks. His color looked better than it had yesterday, during Dio and Camille's fight, which gave her some relief.

The way he'd been staring at her since she got him up and brought him upstairs for breakfast—like he could eat *her*, with or without butter and the biscuits she was baking for him and her quad—didn't do anything in the relief department.

"This is good." He set the cup down on the room's round table, leaned back, and draped his arm over one of the three empty chairs. Damn, but the man filled out his jeans and black T-shirt to perfection. "I thought anything that smelled that strong would have to be bitter, but it's smooth as can be."

Bela took her own drink of coffee, enjoying the rich, dark scent, powerful flavor, and the warmth on her tongue. "It's Andy's special blend. She grows it on her island. Motherhouse Kérkira, I mean. About fifty acres of it."

"I think I've got this Sibyls stuff straight, all but Andy." Duncan kept his hand on his cup, but his eyes stayed on Bela, making it hard for her to think. "Water Sibyls were extinct before her, right?"

Breathe, Bela.

"Theoretically, yes." She drank another swig of coffee, mostly to keep her sanity and take a break from the gray-blue power of Duncan's gaze. "Since the accident that destroyed Motherhouse Antilla centuries ago. Then Andy got attacked by a Legion flunky with a minor skill with water, and it woke up her latent abilities. Since then, several hundred women of all ages have been discovered or come forward. It's like the universe was waiting—then, boom."

Bela set her cup down too hard, sloshing coffee on her hand and the sleeve of her white cotton robe, and felt like a clumsy sixteen-year-old. Her cheeks colored as she used her napkin to blot up the mess, but Duncan didn't seem to notice. He was studying her face, like he might be searching for the key to the meaning of life or the workings of the universe, and it was almost enough to make her sweat even though her pajamas and robe were lightweight.

Duncan paused long enough to give her robe and pj's another appreciative glance, then turned his attention back to her face. "If Andy's a Mother like the older women who've been helping me, why does she get to fight in a group instead of hiding out in Motherhouse . . . wherever?"

"Kérkira." Bela fought to keep her words together, then finally resorted to slow, even battle breathing, which helped her with her composure. "All Mothers fought, back in their younger days. Andy needs her fighting years, too, and she has a few adepts old enough and skilled enough that they're almost ready to wear the yellow Mother's robes on the island. Mother Anemone from Greece spends time there, and Andy will, too, when she's needed."

"That's got to be a bitch, being pulled between two worlds." Duncan looked toward the coffeemaker when he said this, his voice getting more quiet as he spoke, and Bela's stomach clenched at the pain she sensed, pain from the heart, not his wounds.

He was pulled between two worlds, too—the one he knew before DUMBO, and the one he was learning now.

"I'm sure it's hard." She wanted to reach out and touch his hand, but kept herself in check. Did he want to talk about it, what he was going through—how strange it all felt to him? She waited, but he didn't say anything else, and Bela thought he might be a little embarrassed.

"There aren't any Mothers to train Andy," she said, giving him an out in case he needed one. "All the Mother-houses have taken a turn with her fighting skills, and doing what they could to shore up her elemental control—but we really don't even know the extent of her abilities yet."

"Does she?" Duncan gave the coffeemaker a break, but wrecked Bela all over again with the mix of sadness and curiosity in his beautiful eyes. "Does Andy know all of what she can do?"

Bela gave herself another quick break with her mug of coffee. "I don't think so."

"But you took a risk on her. On all of them." Duncan leaned toward her across the table, making the distance between them so much smaller that she thought she could feel heat from his hands, from his coffee mug—but maybe it was her heat, rising off her arms, her shoulders. Being close to him like this, just talking, it seemed right and crazy and relaxed and tense, all at the same time.

"My quad's a crew of misfits," she admitted.

"Nothing wrong with that. In Saudi, I pulled misfits for most of my unit's assignments. They fight harder because they have something to prove." His tone seemed wry, and Bela realized he must have considered himself a misfit, at least back then, in his Army days.

She finally let herself touch him, just her fingers on his hands, but oddly enough, it helped her relax. This time, when his eyes fixed on hers, she could think just fine. "And just what did you have to prove, Duncan Sharp?"

His response was immediate—almost emphatic. "That I was more than a Georgia redneck in sand-colored fatigues."

She shook her head. "You so don't strike me as a redneck."

"I've been out of the cotton fields a long time." His grin stole a fraction of her composure, never mind the fact that he shifted his hand to stroke her fingers.

Still, her thoughts and words stayed strangely calm and organized, and she was able to follow with, "Did your family farm for a living?"

"Yeah." His grin shifted to something like a smile, distant and thoughtful—and a little sad again. "It killed my father. Literally. He flipped his tractor in a rut when I was ten. Broke his neck."

Bela would have asked Duncan if he'd seen the accident, but his tight expression made the answer to that question all too obvious. He kept moving his fingers across hers, and she hoped the sensation calmed him as much as it comforted her.

"My mother didn't make it long after that," he said. "My dad could be a bastard, but he loved my mother, and she loved him back—fierce, total, like wild animals who mate for life."

His eyes found hers again, unsettling her at deep, primal levels as he kept talking, his voice low but urgent, like he wanted to get the rest out before it slipped back to the vault in his heart, where he kept everything locked away. "When I was fourteen, Mom died of pneumonia, but I think her body was just waiting for a reason, since her heart died with my dad. I lived with John and his folks until I finished high school early, just turned seventeen, and John's dad signed for us to go into the service. The rest—Army, Gulf War, police work—you know all that."

Bela laced her fingers through his to keep their contact, needing it now, like she thought he might. "I think my dad grieved himself to death over my mother, too. He lived just long enough to raise me."

"I'm sorry." Duncan squeezed her knuckles gently, then lifted her hand and kissed the back of it before he lowered it to the table again. "How did she pass?"

Bela frowned, surprised at herself for bringing up something she usually kept buried in her own heart vault. "A Legion ambush. It was the cult's first few attempts at making and using Asmodai. My mother's patrol never knew what hit them. The demons tore them apart."

Duncan kissed her hand again, and his gaze stayed gentle. "Is this where you grew up? This house?"

Bela almost laughed at that. "Are you kidding? No. My dad didn't have that kind of money, and he never would have let the Sisterhood buy us a house. We had a little apartment in the Bronx. My first triad and I, we didn't live together, because I wasn't ready to give it up yet and leave behind most of the memories." She glanced around the kitchen, easily three times the size of the kitchen where she ate breakfast with her father. "When another Sibyl gave me this brownstone, I knew it was time to let the old place go. I brought what was important, gave notice, turned the keys over—and here I am."

Duncan kept up the gentle pressure on her knuckles, and his expression told Bela that he understood how hard that had been for her, that it was one of the many sacrifices she had decided to make to pull her little unit of misfits together. Tears tried to make it to her eyes, so she changed the subject. "We need to get you some clothes when we go out today. Where do you live?"

"I rent a room in Chinatown. Not much to clean out, honestly. Just some shirts and jeans, a few pairs of shoes and socks. I live pretty Zen, I guess." He lifted his bad arm and ran the edge of his cast across his chin. "I've got some shaving cream in the bathroom at the end of the hall, too. I could probably use that."

Bela toyed with his fingers and pinched his thumb. "What, no underwear?"

"Nah. Hardly ever wear it."

This time Duncan's grin made her want to pick up his

fingers and bite them, one at a time. She didn't—but only just.

"My truck's in the lot next door to the building," he added as she made herself turn his hand loose and sit back in her chair. "Can't miss it—huge, with running lights, and it's red."

She stared, and he shrugged. "It's a Georgia thing."

"I'll have Camille pick it up and park it in our garage. We've got some extra spots—but no driving, okay?"

"Not a problem. I usually walk."

Bela glanced at his legs before she could stop herself. Those thighs in those jeans . . . damn. "Better drink up. It's time for your stress test."

Somehow she managed not to pant.

Duncan wrapped his hand around his mug, running his thumb along the rim. "Stress test. Isn't that all about pulse and breathing and metabolism?"

Stop staring at his hand. . . .

Stop imagining that thumb moving like that in other places. . . .

"We'll use Andy's treadmill," she whispered like she hadn't had water in a month or two.

"I can think of better ways to get my heart pounding, Angel."

Bela wished she had ice water instead of coffee to drink, but it gave her enough time to catch her breath again. "Don't make me pull out the handcuffs."

His sexy smile nearly drove her straight nuts.

She thought he was about to come up with something devilish about beds and cuffs and heart-pounding activities, but what he said was, "I could get used to this, Angel."

"Get used to what?" Bela heard the surprise in her own voice.

"Good coffee. Good conversation." Duncan took a drink from his mug without ever breaking eye contact. "View's not bad, either."

* * *

A week went by so fast Bela barely had a chance to register it. She and her quad retrieved Duncan's clothes, his shaving cream, and his big red Ford truck. And damnit, she did start getting used to having coffee with him every morning. And breakfast with her quad. Even all the medical testing took on a routine and rhythm that felt normal and soothing. Blood samples, hair samples, skin samples—and Camille did some experiments on Duncan's ability to communicate with John Cole. Riana came by three times to examine Duncan's dinar, too. She left the coin around his neck but ran it through a modified spectroscope that didn't damage it, and tested its resistance to different chemicals.

Each afternoon, Bela processed the results and the samples, and carried all the findings to the Mothers. Jack Blackmore tried to pin her down and demand access to the information more than once, and he got a minor earthquake for his arrogance. Creed and Nick, however, had free access to Bela's reports. She assumed they shared with Blackmore and the Brent brothers, and that was just fine with her for now. She'd deal with those men when and only when they got a damned clue about how *her* world worked.

Every night, when Bela got home, she and her quad went on patrol.

Every frigging night.

They hadn't found one single hint of the Rakshasa, and neither had any of the triads in action in the boroughs.

What they *had* found was four séance rip-off fistfights, one Vodoun *loa* out of control on the Lower East Side—and oh, yeah, a Japanese street gang burned down a building in the East Village trying to build a bonfire big enough to repel an ugly horned *oni* summoned by another gang. Camille barely got the thing beheaded before it beat Dio to death with its gigantic club.

The hardest part, though, was avoiding unsupervised

time with Duncan outside of their intense but safe coffee sessions. The stronger he looked, the healthier he seemed, the more she wanted to turn their judicious "not yet" into one big, screaming, sweaty "right now."

He's sick, she kept telling herself when they chatted about music and which parts of New York City they liked best and everything else in the world, as if the bandages and cast and constant medical testing didn't remind her of his tenuous health often enough.

He might be dying.

That part, driven home over and over again by Andy, Bela couldn't even tolerate considering. So she kept having coffee with Duncan and learning about his favorite foods and books, and what it was like to be an Army Ranger. She took his blood while she told him about Sibyl training, and she scraped cells off his good arm listening to him describe harvesting cotton and peanuts in way-the-hell-south Georgia, and what a hard-ass his father had been about how it was done—and just about everything else, too. Even sweeter, she got to bitch about her own hard-ass father as she watched Duncan go from limping to walking to running on that damned treadmill in just a few days. This morning, before they left to question Reese Patterson, Duncan had been wearing nothing but a bunch of wires and a pair of silk shorts she could have ripped off him with her teeth.

Is it hot in this room?

Bela fanned herself, then noticed that none of the other five people in Reese Patterson's law office seemed uncomfortable.

She needed to get her mind back in the game—*this* game, not the wicked little sport she kept playing in her mind.

Reese Patterson's office in East Harlem reminded Bela of the fourth-floor library at OCU's townhouse headquarters—paneled walls, hardwood floors, expensive area rugs, a couple of shiny oak tables, and lots of shelves of books.

Judging by the size and color, they were law tomes. The pictures on the walls were hunt prints, of course. If there were kits for law office décor, they all came with hunt prints.

The waiting area had been small, almost cramped, but Patterson's work space was expansive. It didn't have any big windows, which made it darker than she would have liked, and a little stuffy. The whole place smelled like musty books and lemon furniture oil, except for Reese Patterson. He smelled like very expensive cologne, applied in excess, likely not just on his thick neck. His suit was silk, probably Armani, black with gray highlights like his thick hair, but the tailoring made him look like an out-of-shape line-backer. He was leaning against the front of his huge cherry desk, his eyes glued to Dio, who was seated in one of the two chairs closest to the desk, right next to Duncan Sharp.

After another broken banister and three more screaming matches, Dio and Camille had finally agreed on a black patent leather designer skirt—short—with a stylish black halter top and amazing little Italian heels. The outfit turned Dio's already svelte figure into runway tall and gorgeous, and the red beads Camille picked out added just the right splash of wild to undo the man. Bela, Andy, and Camille wore much calmer business slacks and blouses, and they were seated on a leather couch along a side wall, with a full view of the whole scene.

"A couple of detectives came by a couple of weeks back," Patterson said without ever taking his gaze off Dio, "but they weren't nearly as lovely as you are. They were from a numbered precinct, not a special unit. Occult Crimes, huh?"

Dio nodded.

Patterson's face colored a deeper shade of pink at her attention. "You think Katrina's murder had something to do with the occult?"

Duncan shifted the badge hanging around his neck to

cover the bulge of the dinar beneath his black T-shirt. They had introduced themselves with his credentials and let Patterson assume that the Sibyls were police officers, too. Not that he had been inclined to care, once he got a good look at Dio.

"The killing had ritualistic elements," Duncan said. "Similar to some crimes we've been tracking in Miami, Atlanta, Charleston, Washington, and Philadelphia."

Patterson offered Dio a mint from a bowl on his desk. "Somebody landed on the coast, and now they're working their way north?"

"Maybe." Dio selected a pink candy, pulling it slowly from the bowl, then using her teeth to tear the plastic.

Bela glanced at Andy, whose expression said, *Yeah, that moving-up-the-coast thing's got merit.* She made a note on her pad that Bela could read from her vantage point. *Check crime orgs with Miami ties.*

"If Dio does that again with the candy, Patterson might fall off his desk," Camille whispered. She was keeping herself on alert for anything weird or unusual. She had some daggers and a couple of Dio's African throwing knives tucked inside the waist of her jeans, just in case. When Bela looked at her, she shook her head once, and Bela knew that she didn't sense any elemental energy here, either.

Dio folded both hands and leaned forward, making the most of her cleavage. "Did Ms. Drake have any ties to splinter religious groups or cults?"

The red beads around her neck moved up and down on her chest as she spoke, and Patterson was mesmerized. "What, you mean friends into crystals and incense and spells?" he asked Dio's boobs. "Nah. Katrina was a Presbyterian. Went to Central every Sunday—you know, the big Gothic-looking church over on Park Avenue."

"How about her husband or her brother?" Duncan's question was smooth and careful, slipped between Dio leaning back and Dio crossing her legs.

Patterson glanced in Duncan's direction before going right back to appraising Dio. "You know I can't go there. Merin Alsace and Jeremiah Drake are still very much alive, and very much my clients, at least until the will's through probate." He gave Dio a wink. "But no, not that I'm aware of. Just between me and you pretty ladies, and, uh, you, Detective Sharp, Jeremiah and Merin, they're a couple of puss—er, what I'm trying to say is, they're not the murdering types. Don't have the intestinal fortitude for anything violent."

Dio let her foot bob up and down a few times, showing off her bare, tanned calf to perfect effect. "What about hiring other people to do their dirty work?"

"Just don't see it." Patterson's head was bobbing with her leg, but he caught himself and settled back to some semblance of a professional demeanor. "Not those two."

Bela had a sense that Patterson might be a bit of a pervert for blondes, but otherwise he wasn't some slick, smooth legal operator. Kind of basic, just a normal guy. His presence reminded her of how normal Katrina Drake had seemed in her photos.

"Has the will been read yet?" Dio asked.

"Saturday, four o' clock, but it's private. Invitation only. I can see to it that you get copies of all the documents, Ms.—"

"Allard," Dio supplied, with a smile so phony Bela almost laughed out loud. "But you can called me Dio. It's short for Dionysia."

"Dionysia. That's beautiful." The man grinned, making his square face a lot more appealing. "Don't think there will be any problem getting you what you want, since the boys are all about finding out who killed Katrina. And pretty as you are, Dio, I think I've said about all I should for today."

"We'll want to interview Mr. Drake and Mr. Alsace,"

Duncan said as he stood, folding his small notepad and sliding it into his jeans pocket.

"Call me with a date, time, and place, and I'll have them there." Patterson finally gave Duncan the acknowledgment of eye contact. "Like I said, they're willing to give their full cooperation. Both of them are torn up over this, and burying Katrina, that's not enough closure. They want some justice . . ."

Patterson trailed off when his eyes landed on the coin peeking from behind Duncan's badge. The color drained straight out of his cheeks, and his posture shifted from relaxed to tense in the space of two heartbeats.

Dio got to her feet without rushing, but Bela saw worry in the tight lines of her face. Camille came to attention, too, and her palms drifted toward the knives in her waistband.

Bela did what she could to check things out with her earth energy, but they were several stories up, and she had more trouble sensing anything at this height.

"Nothing," Andy said where only Bela and Camille could hear her. "He's freaking out a little, but there's no weird energy."

"Detective, may I ask how you came by that chain and coin you're wearing?" Patterson was obviously trying to keep his voice even, but he wasn't doing such a good job.

Duncan squared his stance so that he was facing the lawyer directly, crowding him back against the desk like he was ready to throw a punch if he needed to. "A friend gave it to me. Why?"

Reese Patterson didn't react to Duncan's semiaggressive move because he was too fixated on the coin. "Was that friend by any chance John Cole?"

At this, Dio twitched, pressing her palms against the sides of her short leather skirt, right where her knives would have been if she was in battle gear. Camille and Andy stood, and Andy's sleeves got damp in a hurry. Bela got up, too, more slowly, trying not to attract attention. Her throat went dry, and she accepted a dagger Camille palmed over to her.

Duncan was the only one of them who completely kept his cool. He eased back from Patterson and gave the man some room, a friendly smile on his face the whole time. "Did you know John?"

"I did." Patterson didn't volunteer more information. He turned to his desk and picked up a sticky pad and a pen, then faced Duncan again. "Could you give me a number to reach him? He hasn't been answering his cell."

Bela had a moment of feeling sorry for the lawyer, just in case he was actually Cole's friend.

"I'm sorry, Mr. Patterson." Duncan's smile faded away completely, and his look of sorrow was genuine and heart-tugging. "John's dead. He was killed in DUMBO nearly a month ago."

Bela hadn't thought Reese Patterson could lose any more color, but she was wrong. He went positively pasty, and his shoulders rounded as he lowered the pad and pen, and his head, too. That kind of surprise and spontaneous unhappiness couldn't be faked to Sibyl senses, not even by a seasoned actor. Bela breathed in at the same time Camille and Andy did, fighting the palpable wave of sadness and confusion that swept across the room.

"That—that was Cole who died?" Patterson's question was barely audible. When he raised his head, his eyes were wide and moist. "I heard about the killing on the news, but I never thought . . . I never imagined . . . do you know who did it?"

"Absolutely," Duncan told him, obviously watching the man for more reaction to his certainty, but there wasn't any. "We've got them in our sights. Just have to root them out of their hiding place, and we'll have that murder all wrapped up."

Patterson took this in, rubbing the back of his neck with one thick-fingered hand. A few moments later, he had hold of himself enough to ask, "Do you know if John Cole had a will?"

Bela's eyebrows shot up, and she saw similar looks on the faces of her sister Sibyls. What the hell would that matter? John Cole was a retired soldier and active federal agent, not some Wall Street billionaire.

"No, I wouldn't have a—" Duncan paused, and Bela saw the telltale flicker of black in his winter-gray eyes as Cole's spirit communicated with him. "Yes, actually, he did have one drawn up." Surprise was evident in Duncan's every word, but he played it off well enough after coughing a few times. "Now that I'm thinking about it, he did mention taking care of that. It's with Bestro and Perman, on Broadway, if memory serves."

Patterson wrote that down, again without explaining his reasons for asking, and Duncan didn't seem inclined to press the issue. His expression had turned angry and uncomfortable, and Bela thought those emotions were probably directed at Cole.

"Thank you." Patterson put down his pad and pen, and offered Duncan his hand.

Duncan shook it as Patterson said, "Let me know when you lock up the assholes who killed John. I want to be sure no one *I* know agrees to defend the bastards." He glanced at Dio. "Sorry for my language, Ms. Allard."

Ms. Allard. Back to respect now, another testament to Patterson's genuine reaction to the news of John Cole's death. Bela would have predicted just about anything from this little interview, except what they got. Few answers, and a lot more questions.

And Duncan Sharp, looking almost as shook up as Reese Patterson.

All of Duncan's energy seemed to be focusing somewhere

else, like his mind had forgotten how to keep everything in his body running like it should.

The minute they closed Patterson's office door behind them and stepped into the building's long hallway, Bela stopped and turned to Duncan. "Are you okay?"

Duncan said nothing as Bela's quad surrounded him. His color was draining away, and he was starting to resemble last week's Duncan instead of this week's healthier version.

"This was a bad idea," Camille said. "We shouldn't have let him do this. That new head of the OCU hasn't even given permission—"

"Oh, fuck Jack Blackmore, Camille." Dio popped Duncan with a spurt of wind, driving his chin up and lifting his face. "Duncan's got weeks to live. Maybe just days. He chooses what risks he takes, not us."

"And sure as hell not that ex-Army jackass who doesn't understand that we aren't his good little soldiers," Andy added.

Weeks to live. That took Bela's breath. *Days . . .*

No.

Too much. She couldn't hear that right now. Couldn't even think it.

Duncan's eyes flickered from gray to black, and he swayed on his feet.

Bela's every fiber flared with alarm, giving her power a quick charge despite their distance from the earth below. She pressed her hands into Duncan's shoulders, holding him up and feeding him a dose of earth energy for strength.

"Something's happening inside him, Bela." Andy sounded distressed now. "Something different. I can sense it. We have to get him back to the brownstone now."

"The townhouse is closer." Camille's voice was stronger than usual, and a tiny whiff of smoke followed her as she jogged down the hallway toward the elevator. "I'll send a signal to the Mothers to be ready."

Dio doubled her wind, using the force to keep Duncan from crashing to the carpeted floor.

"Move." Bela caught one of Duncan's arms as Andy grabbed the one with the cast, just above his elbow. Together, they half walked, half fell toward the elevator Camille was holding.

18

Duncan knew his legs weren't working right. For a few seconds, he stopped hearing, stopped seeing, stopped smelling. The world shifted to gray, then black as he threw every ounce of his energy behind finding John Cole's essence inside his thoughts and getting some damned answers.

"Talk to me," he said to John. "Damn it, you talk to me, or we won't live to see tomorrow."

Some part of his mind was aware of Bela and Andy holding his arms to keep him from falling. Were they in an elevator? No. Stumbling out of one. Dio's air energy lifted part of his weight and Camille knocked open doors and got them out of Reese Patterson's office building.

Late-afternoon sunlight hit his face like a hot fist, and the smell of bus exhaust made him cough.

Let it go, Duncan. John sounded distant. Restrained.

"The hell I will." If Duncan could have ripped the voice straight out of his brain, thrown it on the sidewalk, and shot it three times, he would have done so without hesitation. The muscles in his neck got so tight he wondered if they actually might snap. "All that crap you fed me back at the brownstone—*what I know, you know, Duncan*—that's bullshit!"

"He's not talking to us." Bela's voice drifted to him, seemingly across a desert as wide as any in his Afghanistan memories. "Look at his eyes."

"Camille, help them hold Duncan up," Dio said. "I'm getting the SUV."

More hands on him now, these smaller, on his back, surprisingly strong, and too hot. His shirt smoldered, singing the skin on his shoulders.

John's essence reacted to the touch, shifting backward and forward. Coming. Going. Duncan couldn't think. Couldn't process anything.

A new sort of fire blazed through the covered wounds on Duncan's neck, chest, and shoulder. Christ, it felt like they were rupturing. Starting to bleed. The blood smelled like sugar mixed with ammonia, and the stench made him want to hurl. The dinar on his neck vibrated, seemed to send out energy, some kind of bright, pushing power, but it wasn't enough to touch the pain.

Calm down. John's tone shifted from distant to desperate. *I can't handle everything at once.*

"Quit playing games with me, John. You tell me why you have a will, right fucking now."

An engine revved. Brakes squealed. A car door opened.

Duncan felt himself moving again, but he kept his focus on interrogating the frigging ghost in his head. "You tell me why you made a will here, in New York City—and what the hell does Reese Patterson know about it?"

I always file a will in the city where I'm working. John sounded sincere, and Duncan knew he meant what he said—but Duncan also knew John wasn't telling the whole truth. He was sitting down now. Doors slammed shut, and they lurched forward as horns honked.

"Lies by omission are still lies, and you're lying." Duncan wanted to punch the side of his own head, but he was still sane enough to understand that wouldn't help anything. "Can't hide, sinner. Don't even try to run."

Sensations bounced at Duncan, bits and pieces, nothing intact.

"Is he losing it?" Camille, beside him on a car seat, shoving his shoulder to keep him upright . . .

"Why's he talking about sinners?" Dio, swerving left, hitting her horn . . .

"He's bleeding. Hurry." Bela's hands on his other arm, supporting him . . .

John Cole wasn't answering.

"Can't hide, sinner," Duncan said again, and shoved his knuckles against his temples until he saw stars. Maybe if he looked hard enough, he'd find John right there, in the spots floating across his vision.

"It's a spiritual." That was Andy, from the front seat. "I think Sharp's into music, and maybe John Cole is, too. 'Can't Hide, Sinner' is a song title. Old stuff, blues and gospel—spirituals came before all that, from slaves trying to survive working in the fields. A lot of projects have been launched to catalogue and preserve that kind of music."

"Why did you even make a last will and testament, John?" Duncan wasn't giving up, even if it killed him here and now.

A sigh echoed through his consciousness, passing as fast as the buildings outside the SUV. Evening was coming on, so lights began to mark the rushing landscape, winking and blinking in long strings of white.

Then John said, *Katrina wanted me to.*

"Katrina wanted . . . ? *Un*believable." Duncan let his hands fall to his lap, wondering what the hell he had done, letting John into his head and letting him stay there. The slashes on his neck cracked and bubbled, then became a weeping, itching, cooking misery, but he couldn't do a damned thing about any of that. Air whistled through his teeth as he fought to keep himself conscious and on the job, and sweat broke across his forehead and neck.

"Don't do this now, Duncan." Bela's plea sounded desperate, and it hurt Duncan worse than his wounds to hear her in pain. He couldn't stop, though. No way. After years in law enforcement, Duncan knew what it felt like to have his grimy paws on one of the keys that unlocks a case. This was a piece of a puzzle, and snapping it into place might bring everything into focus.

"What was Katrina Drake to you, John? And you better not start lying again."

She was a friend. If you'll tell Camille to hold the dinar, you won't have to repeat all this later. I think she'll be able to hear me.

Duncan reached out, gently took the fire Sibyl's hand, and moved it to the coin. She didn't struggle against him, and he could see in her eyes that she trusted him, at least enough to try what he needed her to try.

"Translate," he said. "Please? If it doesn't hurt you."

"Wait, Camille," Bela's fingers played across Duncan's good arm, and her earth energy scraped his skin as she reached out to her sister Sibyl to stop her. "We don't know that much about the coin's properties."

"It's okay." That spark flickered in Camille's eyes again, and Duncan felt an answering flicker of relief from John—and his own mind, too. "Since it's projective like the mirrors, I should be able to interact with it."

When Bela didn't respond, Camille's strength seemed to build. "I can handle the dinar. At least let me try."

Bela hesitated, then gave in with a quick, sharp nod.

Camille lifted the coin away from Duncan's neck, and when the gold lost contact with his skin, he groaned from the surge of pain along his wounds. The slashes seemed to be expanding. Creeping up, down, left and right. He was like a battle map, and the demon infection was planting flags everywhere it could.

"Duncan, please." Bela's sweet voice prodded at him again. He knew she was imploring him to protect himself, but he couldn't do that, not at the expense of protecting her and her quad.

"This might be the way we find the demons," he told her, then had to shift his attention back to John's essence in his mind before the bastard got away.

"Let him do this, Bela." Andy was talking like a cop now, respecting Duncan and what he was pursuing. He felt grateful for her support. "He's a police officer, a detective with a lot of experience. He knows what he's doing—and when it has to be done."

Bela's hiss of frustration was intense. "It's hurting him."

"Honey, that infection's way past hurting. It's killing him." Andy's tone was almost apologetic, but firm, too. "We need to know whatever he can tell us, or the Rakshasa will take down a lot more people, starting with us."

This time Bela didn't argue back, but Duncan had a sense of her wordless seething.

Camille's knuckles shoved against Duncan's chest as she held the dinar, and Bela sat beside Duncan, stiff and silent. He knew if he lived through their little SUV ride, he'd owe her an apology for worrying her like this.

"What was Katrina Drake to you?" Duncan demanded of John again as New York City blurred outside the SUV's windows. "And don't give me that *friend* crap."

Camille's hand twitched, and the coin vibrated.

Duncan had a strange image of computers in the old dial-up Internet days, negotiating to find a connection. There was static. Some whistling in his head. A groaning, shuddering vibration shook him from inside out.

Then—

I came here to help her when she reached out for a bodyguard with paranormal experience. John spoke, and Camille spoke at the same time. It was her voice, yet Duncan could hear John's resonance somewhere in her words, or maybe it was just the vibrations from his own mind. *Katrina turned out to be a special, gentle woman, but we were just friends. Nothing else.*

"Fuck me," Andy said, turning to stare into the backseat. "That's just creepy, Camille."

"No shit." Dio must have taken her foot off the gas, because the SUV slowed, then jumped forward again.

Duncan ignored the movement and side chatter as much

as he could, and kept after John. "Are you why Katrina was divorcing her husband?"

No.

Duncan waited, but John-Camille didn't say anything else.

"Damn it, John, you're trying my patience."

Another sigh stirred through his thoughts, as if John felt guilty about saying any of this.

"Go on," Camille urged in just her voice, as if she heard the same sigh. "We need to hear this." She patted Duncan's knee with her free hand, only he had a sense she didn't realize she was touching him at all. She was speaking to John. Trying to reach John—

And once again, John seemed to respond to her touch, and now to her encouragement.

Katrina was divorcing her husband because her stepson was out of control. John was tense. Past frustrated. But this did feel like the truth. *Drugs. Punching holes in the wall. Stealing cars. Walker Drake was a mess, and Jeremiah wouldn't do anything to stop his son from ruling the house. Katrina couldn't take it anymore.*

"How violent was Walker Drake?" That question came from Bela, and Duncan thought it was a good one.

Walker's a punk coward, not a murderer—and he's still just a kid. Just turned seventeen. Duncan felt his fist flex, and knew he didn't do it. John-Camille's voice suggested that John would really like to give the brat a working-over. *That little fuck wouldn't have the first clue how to locate a group of demons, much less bargain with them. The day Katrina died, he and his latest squeeze were five kinds of stoned, and useless to the universe.*

Dio executed a smooth left turn, and from the front seat, Andy asked, "How can you be sure Walker was so clueless about hiring hit-kitties?"

John's husky bark of a laugh sounded odd coming from Camille's mouth. *To find demons without an intermediary,*

Walker would need elemental talent. Trust me, Duncan, you have more elemental talent in your little toenail than Walker or Jeremiah Drake will ever have.

"Stop telling me to trust you, John." Duncan wished he could get hold of the spirit hiding in his mind and shake the shit out of it. "How did Katrina know she'd been targeted by something supernatural?"

This made John pause.

The SUV hit a pothole and banged around. Dio said something unkind about another driver's mother, and a new kind of power surged into Duncan from the spot where Camille had her hand on his leg. It was hot. Burning. Uncomfortable to him, and almost as painful as the wounds bleeding through his bandages onto his T-shirt. He wanted to pull away from Camille, but he didn't have to. Bela's hand joined Camille, and the fiery blast got tempered by Bela's cool, calming energy.

John, however, seemed to respond to the fire.

Katrina had instincts. Not really powers or talents, just . . . hunches that usually turned out to be true, but her religious beliefs drove her to ignore them. Even through Camille's translating voice, Duncan heard a wistful sadness in John's report. *She had some nightmares so vivid she couldn't ignore them, and she called the number the ASI keeps in most major newspapers, buried in the classifieds, advertising security services for people under supernatural threat.*

Duncan's understanding of the case files he'd been working before the murder increased, and a lot of things started coming clear. "A classified ad. That's why you've been moving from city to city. That's how you knew where to go."

Yes. The Rakshasa have been heading up the East Coast. The ads and ad responses were the best way we could figure to keep tabs on them, since they never stayed anywhere very long. Then I started to realize Strada had a pattern about whom he likes to murder. He started taking contracts on females only. Women with some beauty, and some innocence.

"The demon has his preferences," Bela muttered, then shivered.

Duncan shared her revulsion, and hoped he'd get his moment with Strada in the very near future.

Most of the calls we get on the Namast Security line are total horseshit, John-Camille said. *But when ground ops checked Katrina out, she matched Strada's little profile. The type of woman that bastard loves to hunt and kill. So I met with her, and she hired me to protect her a couple of months ago.*

John broke off again, and Duncan experienced rushes of guilt and regret, of self-loathing and rage that weren't his own. With the lurching course of the SUV and the weird partial light of dusk, it was enough to make him carsick, because the feelings were all too familiar. They jerked up memories of the war, of soldiers and buddies he failed. Of missions that went bad, and situations so FUBAR he couldn't do anything to right them.

He thought he got it, and maybe understood why John was holding back. "If you were supposed to be protecting Katrina Drake from the Rakshasa, and you cared about her, then why weren't you with her when they came to kill her?"

Oh, yeah.

That was the million-dollar question.

John's essence snapped backward in Duncan's mind like Duncan had cracked him right in the jaw.

Camille let out a shocked little, "Eeep!" She dropped the dinar against Duncan's chest, then grabbed it again as Duncan's world grayed from the energy it took to seize hold of John's disappearing energy.

Fire energy surged into him, burning his leg. Bela moved

her hand to his other knee, then both hands, and earth energy flowed through him just as strong.

In his mind's eye, he blocked John from disappearing. Forced him back front and center. "I told you, John. Can't hide, sinner. It's time to confess."

John's next emotion was anguish. It was so strong, so total, that Camille gave a little sob as Duncan choked back his own cough of emotion.

I was dropping off the wills, John said, and the words echoed through the SUV in Camille's mingled, sorrowful tones. *Hers and mine.*

"You son of a bitch," Andy growled from the front seat. "You let her die to what, look after some investments? Have a shot at her millions?"

No! It wasn't like that. Anger was the emotion now, and the flames on Camille's fingers were real. Holes smoked in the knee of Duncan's jeans before Bela waved one hand in the air and put them out. *Katrina was sure we were going to die. The wills were her idea. She was freaking out about them, and she wouldn't calm down until I promised to take care of delivering them. Katrina was . . . persuasive. And I was a fucking idiot.*

Camille's breath rattled in her throat, and her voice sounded more than delicate when she prompted John with, "And the day you dropped off the wills?"

The SUV was slowing down. Turning again. The sensation made Duncan's insides spin like he was on a carnival ride, and the glare of taillights and headlights didn't help at all.

Walker had just come staggering home with his snotnosed girlfriend, John said through Camille. Their voices shook. *Katrina didn't want to leave the kids unsupervised. I had the house protected with elemental barriers I made using the dinar as a focal point to draw and arrange energy. I thought they'd hold for the half hour it would take me to*

drop off the wills so Katrina could be at peace. There was
a pause. A sob. Camille's or John's, Duncan didn't know.

*Leaving her there seemed a lot safer than taking her
with me.*

A chasm of grief opened in Duncan's mind and heart. His
head slammed against the seat, and he bit his tongue so
hard the sweet copper of blood surged across his mouth.
The slashes ripped and ran, itching like tiger hair was
springing up to line each one. Ammonia-tainted liquid
oozed through his shirt, thin, dark, and eye-wateringly
awful.

John stopped talking, and Camille dropped the coin like
it was red-hot. The metal burned into Duncan's chest, and
he almost shouted from the recoil in his wounds. For a long
minute, he couldn't get a breath. Like being underwater.
Like drowning. His ribs felt like they were splintering from
the pressure.

"John had to go." Camille said, her soft voice slipping
through Duncan's haze of agony. "Your infection's trying
to break past the barriers the Mothers set to contain it, and
he's doing what he can to slow it down."

"Yeah," Duncan managed, eyes squeezed tight against
the pain. Then he did groan, and kept groaning until bits of
power from three separate pairs of hands chased back
enough of the torture for him to catch a few gulps of air.
Earth. Fire. Water. He felt the elements braid together,
working into him and shoring up the walls of energy the
Mothers had lodged into his flesh.

When his vision cleared, he had his head turned, and he
was looking at Bela, and she was looking at him, her dark
eyes wide with concern. Her fingers rested on his knuckles,
and he was grateful for the contact.

"Don't die," she said, and the pain in her voice nearly
put him under again.

He made himself breathe slower, slower, until he wasn't
sounding like a fish flopping on a beach. With what little

oomph he could muster, he sat up straighter, and that was for her. Anything to keep her from looking at him like that, from sounding like that, ever again.

He shifted his hands to cover hers and hoped she understood. He was trying his best to be a cop. To live up to her belief that he was a good and honorable man. He was trying to save her from dying like him, with demon slashes eating into her skin and bones—but damnit, he wasn't trying to die right now.

He wanted to live. He wanted to have some more time with her. A lot of time, if he could.

Please understand, he thought, and wished some weird, mingled voice would speak the words out loud, because he just couldn't get them out.

Bela broke their eye contact and stared at her knees, but she didn't pull away from him.

Maybe that was something.

It would have to be enough until they could be alone again.

"One hell of an interrogation, Sharp." Andy faced him from the front seat as Dio pulled the SUV to the curb and shut off the engine. She wasn't teasing. She actually sounded like she admired what he'd just done.

That was embarrassing.

"Was that everything?" Andy asked.

Duncan didn't want to, but he poked around in the pile of emotions John had left behind before he retreated into Duncan's cells and molecules. "Yeah. I think."

Camille put her hand on the door handle, but stopped and turned around again. Her eyes, too green to be blue and too blue to be green, showed how unsettled she must be feeling. "Do you believe what John said, Duncan?"

"I don't know what I believe." That was honest, even if it didn't offer her any relief. "But I'm pretty sure he spilled everything."

Camille accepted this and got out of the SUV. So did

Andy. Bela opened her door and slipped off the seat, leaving the door open for Duncan.

Dio was still at the wheel, and her matter-of-fact tenor caught Duncan's attention before he could scoot across the seat and make his exit. "Judging by what you were yelling at John Cole when we left that office building, about him telling you all he knows and being full of bullshit, you were pretty sure he'd spilled everything before."

Streetlights made her blond hair glow almost silver as she studied him through the rearview mirror, without turning around. Her eyes were nearly the same shade as his, but hers had storms and wind and lightning at the center, and something else: a certain cold realism that marked her as the hard-ass in this little fighting group. Duncan met her reflected gaze with no resentment.

"Stay alert, and don't stop watching me, Dio." He was trusting her with this, one hard-ass to another. "Don't make Bela be the one to kill me if John takes me over and goes psycho, or if I screw up and turn demon."

Dio's mouth came open, and her eyes blazed. The one hand she still had on the steering wheel went white along the knuckles. "Fuck you, Sharp."

He leaned toward the front seat, fighting the rising ache in his wounds and the black spots starting to dance at the edges of his vision. "Tell me you'll take me out if I don't—or can't—do it myself."

Dio gaped at him. She didn't give him any response other than a more thorough strangling of the steering wheel.

Way off in the dark evening sky, thunder rumbled against the stars.

Bela was getting antsy outside. She leaned back through the open door, and Duncan said, "It's okay, Angel. I'm coming."

He didn't want to believe he'd made a mistake about Dio. Knowing a soldier's strengths and weaknesses, how they were built and what made them tick, that had always been his special skill, in the Army and on the force, too. Sibyls couldn't be that different, could they? Maybe his instincts were failing him now, at the worst possible time. As Duncan moved his aching body across the seat, he had the sinking feeling that he'd misread Dio, and there was no fixing it now.

"I'm a broom," she said as he pulled himself through the door, her tone brittle and grudging, but also sincere. Then the rest of her answer followed him into the night.

"Don't worry. Brooms always sweep up the mess."

19

Bela was somewhere between pissed off and terrified, and she hated feeling that way. She'd been off balance since DUMBO, and she couldn't seem to get her footing or find the right focus.

Duncan.

The demons.

Her quad.

There was so much competing for her mind and emotions, she felt like she had fault lines fracturing through everything that made her alive and female and a Sibyl.

"This isn't the brownstone," Duncan said as he got out, using the SUV's door to hold himself up with his good arm. He didn't seem like he was pounding on death's door anymore, but his face was white at the eyes and mouth, and his neck was hectic red above his dark, blood-soaked T-shirt and cast. "Damn. It's lit up like a circus on opening night."

Dio came around the SUV, and the five of them stood in silence as Bela squinted in the blaze of the safety lights that made OCU headquarters a five-story glare-fest, complete with black, glittering metal safety fence separating it from the sidewalk. On the other side of the fence, unbearably white stairs wound upward on both sides of the entrance, leading to equally unbearably white columns and a way-too-white front door. Even the American eagle seal over the front door gleamed in the megawatt festival—which was sort of ridiculous, given that two-thirds of the people who came and went from the townhouse—and virtually any creature that might attack it—could see in the dark.

"It is bright, isn't it?" Bela took Duncan's hand and

pulled him away from the SUV so Camille could shut the door behind him. The sidewalks were deserted for the moment, and there wasn't much traffic. Unless they wanted to call for help, they'd need to get him through the front door under their own power. She thought they could handle it, and she knew that Duncan and her quad would rather not make a spectacle of themselves.

"Welcome to Headcase Quarters," she said, leading him forward.

"Excuse me?" He hesitated, pulling back a little. "What— I mean, where are we, exactly?"

"We're north on the Upper East Side, above the Reservoir." Andy got hold of his casted arm above the elbow. "This is where the OCU and the Dark Crescent Sisterhood get it on—figuratively."

"Literally, too." Dio got behind Duncan and Camille, and her wind energy swept past Bela's ears. "Way too literally, sometimes. Couple of years ago, a fire Sibyl torched the conference room getting frisky with her boyfriend."

Camille let out a nervous laugh, but Bela didn't. She was noticing Andy, who had gone pale enough to play the ghost of Lady Macbeth on Broadway. She was squeezing Duncan's arm hard enough to leave marks, and worse yet, her hair and clothes were dry, and there was no sign of a drip of water.

Goody. It's unanimous. Nobody wants to be here. Can we go home now?

"I hate this," Andy said, and Bela knew what she meant. Dio and Camille looked at the ground, but Bela made herself hold Andy's increasingly sad and angry gaze even as she used both arms to steady Duncan. "You don't have to stay long. If the Mothers don't need you, you can go as soon as we get Duncan through the front door."

"Duncan can get himself through the front door, thanks," Duncan said, taking more of his own weight without wobbling so much. "Just give me a little time."

Andy frowned, but she nodded.

Bela couldn't help thinking that it really wasn't fair. Bela, Camille, and Dio could avoid the places where they'd lost their loved ones. Riana, Cynda, and Merilee could stay away from the brownstone. But Andy—Andy had to come to Headcase Quarters all the time. She had to suck it up and just deal with the pain, even sit in the conference room where she had last viewed her lover's body. It was that or stay on a distant island training new water Sibyls, or fight in some other city with some other group. Andy refused to do that. She had never said it outright, but she had let Bela know that the bond between them ran too deep for her to give it up, even if it meant having to face the damned townhouse day in and day out.

Duncan was definitely noticing the change in Andy's demeanor, and he wasn't moving an inch toward the fence. "Okay, what's wrong with this place? Why do you call it Headcase Quarters?"

"It's full of Mothers, for one thing." Dio applied a targeted gust of wind to Duncan's ass, and he took a few steps with Bela, Andy, and Camille steadying him. "But that isn't typical. Oh, and a baby fire Sibyl lives here. She'll burn your nuts off if you aren't careful."

Andy broke out of her trance long enough to snort in Dio's general direction. "You leave my goddess-daughter out of this—and my goddess-son, too. Ethan Lowell is wonderful, and Neala Lowell is perfect in every way."

"A perfect little firebug," Dio grumbled, and Andy hit Dio's slacks with a jet of water that made it look like Dio had peed all over herself.

Dio didn't even blink. She just divided her wind energy between moving Duncan and drying her pants. They were inside the fence now, making progress.

"The townhouse has a dark history." Camille kept her hands ready to push against Duncan's back, but he was doing okay without that assistance so far. "But really, it got its nickname because with Sibyls, OCU officers, friendly demons, and who knows what else wandering around inside, there's always something nuts going on."

Andy, who seemed heartened by thoughts of seeing the children she loved better than life itself, added, "The OCU leases the building from the Lowell brothers. You've met two of them, Creed and Nick—but you were still pretty sick, and you might not remember. They're half-demon officers, and they've been working with your friends Saul and Cal, the new transfers."

"Demons. Half-demons. Baby fire Sibyls." Duncan was walking on his own now, with just a little help from them, and he started up the steps. "I think I'm really beginning to dread this place."

Andy explained about how the three Lowell brothers had married Riana, Cynda, and Merilee, finishing with, "They live on the upper floors of the townhouse now, with Ethan—he's Riana's—and Neala, who's Cynda's. There's a guest floor, too, where visiting officers, Sibyls, and even transient demons can stay."

"Like that bastard Blackmore." Dio used her wind energy to push Duncan and Bela up the last few steps to the landing, with Camille and Andy barely escaping the blast. "Maybe he's some kind of demon we haven't discovered yet."

Duncan squeezed Bela's fingers as he pulled his casted arm free of Andy's grip. When Camille moved past him, he gave her a nod as if to thank her for her help. "Blackjack's an old-school special forces officer," he told Dio as she joined them. "That's all that's wrong with him."

Andy gave a sound that sounded as much like a growl as a grunt. "He's a dickhead."

Duncan laughed, then winced and raised his cast to press against his chest. "Dickhead's always been part of his job description. He can't help himself."

Bela pushed the front door open to reveal the herringbone hardwood floor of the entryway, polished to a shine like the rest of the place. A whiff of pine cleanser, fresh paint, and lingering fire escaped into the air, and Bela tasted and felt the unmistakable weight of the elemental energy of nearby Sibyl Mothers.

A *lot* of them.

Nobody was standing on the other side of the door, though, which was a relief. The only officer in view was a uniformed man at a small desk straight across from the front door, about thirty feet away from her. The desk was located near the foot of the stairs, just in front of the thick, winding wooden banister. The officer glanced up, saw Bela, gave her a little wave, then went back to his telephone and notepad. It was time for patrol, so most Sibyls and the rest of the officers on this shift would already be on the streets. That was good. She didn't want to deal with too many other people—and she didn't have much patience for Duncan defending Jack Blackmore. Just the thought of that man made her wish she'd brought her sword out of the SUV.

She stepped inside and gave Duncan's hand a gentle tug. Duncan crossed the threshold with Dio beside him and Andy and Camille bringing up the rear. They stood in the space, roughly equivalent to the whole main floor of the brownstone. Soft light came from an old-style chandelier, with bulbs that looked like candles glowing inside dozens of frosted glass holders. Headcase Quarters was a repository of oversized rooms, giant light fixtures, antiques, and expensive old rugs. There were tables, bookcases, and reading chairs everywhere, even the entryway.

Bela kept hold of Duncan's hand, and made him look her in the face. "Before I have to deal with Jack Blackmore again, just tell me one thing. If you hadn't agreed to his terms, would he have made good on that threat to take you to New Jersey and turn you into a lab experiment while you suffered and died?"

The pained but friendly expression on Duncan's face lost the friendly part, and Bela saw a little darkness in his eyes when he said, "Yeah, probably."

Dio and Camille gave matching snorts of disgust.

"Fucker just better not get in my way," Andy grumbled as she headed out of the entryway toward the wide hall that led to the conference room, basement, and kitchen. "I'll check to see if the Mothers are in the basement."

She barely got the words out before Mother Yana, Mother Keara, and Mother Anemone came steaming out of the basement door on the right of the wide hall. The Mothers hurried forward, along with—oh, great.

Mother Yana had her she-wolf in tow. The creature was so old her fur was all white and silver, but she walked with the same powerful strides she had since Bela remembered seeing her when she was a kid.

Duncan eyed the approaching wolf, then glanced at Bela.

All she could do was shrug. "Headcase Quarters. You were warned."

The officer at the desk across the room supported her statement by not even bothering to look up.

Bela realized her tone was purposely light, but inside, as her quad greeted the Mothers, she was thinking how everything was happening too fast. Wasn't she supposed to have a little time to prepare for this? Another day, at least?

It's not about you, asshole. Duncan needs help now, not later.

But what if that "help" killed him?

He's dying anyway. Everybody keeps telling me that.

But she wasn't believing it, or feeling any ripples in her instincts that might tell her what Duncan's fate would be. In fact, Bela wasn't feeling anything. Her body had gone strangely numb, like she didn't have any emotions or sensations at all. Her mind and heart were blank as the Mothers and the she-wolf gave them the once-over.

"I see it didn't take long for you to be gettin' yer ass in

trouble," Mother Keara said to Duncan. Her gray hair was loose around her bony shoulders, and her green robes hung on arms like she hadn't been eating enough.

"I had work to do." Duncan's comeback was more truthful than sarcastic, but it made Mother Keara laugh anyway. Sparks banked off her elbows, and smoke curled away from her neck and head.

"Vell, now ve have vork to do, too, thank you." Mother Yana's tone was kind, as was typical for her when she wasn't busy being terrifying. Her thin, gnarled hand rested on the wolf's neck, and Bela realized that both the wolf and Mother Yana had the same yellow glow to their dark eyes.

Mother Anemone pulled her blue robes against her tall frame, letting off the light scent of lilacs and sunshine. "Duncan, are you certain about doing this?"

"It'll take hours," Mother Keara warned before Duncan could say anything. "And it'll hurt like you can't imagine."

"Ve can't make guarantees," Mother Yana added, still stroking her ancient companion. "You might fare better letting nature have her own vay."

Duncan's answer was firm. "I'm certain."

Bela's heart gave a tiny lurch, still muted like everything else, but she wished he hadn't agreed. At the same time, she knew he really didn't have a choice, and neither did she.

"Then when you're ready, Duncan, come with us." Mother Anemone pointed to the basement door. "We have half the living Sibyl Mothers in this townhouse basement, ready to help you."

Mother Keara let off a new round of smoke. "Took us a bit to agree on strategy, but I got me a good feelin' about givin' you back some time, and a lot less pain."

"Andrea, we'll fill you in." Mother Anemone's smile was comforting, even though Bela wasn't much in the mood to be soothed. "I don't think your part will be overly taxing."

The Mothers all looked from Duncan to Bela. Dio, Andy, and Camille responded to the cue by walking away to stand just inside the main hallway to the right, leaving Duncan and Bela alone in the entryway. They milled around chatting, fanning out just enough to block the view of the officer at the desk.

Bela would have found that sweet, but she really didn't want to do this. She was feeling something now, and it wasn't pleasant, and what she really wanted to do was run away. The only problem was, she wanted to take Duncan with her, and that wasn't possible.

"You look nervous." Duncan reached up with his good hand and massaged Bela's arm. The contact gave her warm shivers, but it didn't do anything to stop the panic rising in her belly and chest like some sort of separate life-form. She couldn't say anything. All she could do was nod and wish he would touch her more.

Bela tried to look at Duncan's face, but she couldn't do that, either. How idiotic. She had been staring at him just a minute ago, before. . . .

Before all this became definite.

Her skin turned ultrasensitive, like she was nothing but a giant walking bruise.

"Look at me." Duncan's request was quiet, not demanding at all, but Bela raised her eyes to his as if he had issued a royal command.

Damn.

The wintry gray-blue of his gaze doubled the gallop of her heart and halved her breathing. The bloody T-shirt, the sweat on his face, the holes burned into his jeans—all of those imperfections just made him more perfect.

He let go of her arm, looked away toward the Mothers and her quad, then back again. "I don't want you to stay, Bela. I don't want you here while this is happening."

His words slowly worked through the pound and roar of Bela's pulse and her growing ache for his embrace. Confused, she raised both hands, tempted to either give him a shove or grab him and hang on forever. "You—you can't seriously be asking me to leave, with everything you're facing."

"I am asking." He stared at the ceiling for a moment, his throat moving. Bela had a sense that he was searching for the right words to explain himself, but she didn't want to give him the chance to find them.

"Duncan—"

"It's obvious none of your quad wants to be in this townhouse." His voice was a whisper when he looked at her again. "So y'all go back to the brownstone and do your thing. I'll come straight there as soon as it's over."

Bela shook her head, not able to make any sense out of his request, not until she saw the growing unhappiness in his eyes. His expression was a strange mix of shame and caring, and she slowly realized that Duncan didn't want her exposed to the agony he'd be facing.

He was, first and foremost, a man who defended and protected what he treasured.

Right now, it would seem, that was her.

She was flattered and pissed off, and this time she did give the unbandaged parts of his chest a tap with both palms. "You don't have to shield me from anything. I'm not that fragile."

"Well, maybe *I* am." Duncan leaned toward her, angry now, at least by appearance, but what Bela saw underneath that was fear. "At least where you're concerned."

That caught her so off guard she didn't have a response, except to want to reach for him, but the dampness of his shirt and the streaks of blood on her hands from where she just touched him reminded her that he was the one who needed understanding and support.

He backed off from her and studied the ceiling for another few seconds before he said, "I can handle my own pain, Bela." His eyes found hers again, and the misery she saw broke her heart. "I can't stand it when you hurt."

Bela's lips trembled, and her hands shook. She wanted to

cry. She wanted to make love to this man, right here, right now, in the townhouse hallway—and she still wanted to run away. She was over the edge, and she had no idea how to claw her way back to steady again.

Andy was staring at her from across the hall, and the expression on her face almost crushed Bela on the spot.

I never got this kind of chance, that look said. *Don't you dare let it slip away from you.*

Something inside Bela crumbled into pieces. Maybe it was the panic, or the last bit of resistance to this new complication in her life. Her caution and self-control dropped away in its wake, and she grabbed Duncan and held him tight against her, bloody shirt, cast, and all.

"Don't die," she whispered into his damaged chest, welcoming the weight of his cast and other arm as he wrapped her up, then crushed her against him. "Don't let me go, and don't die."

This can't be it.

But what if she never got the chance to touch him again? *This won't be it.*

But what if this was the last time she even got to see him, or hear his voice, or look into those deep, delicious eyes?

He'd only been in her life about a month—and half that time, he'd barely been conscious. Even so, there was far too much not said, and *way* too much not done between the two of them. She needed weeks and months and years to really get to know him, and she wasn't sure that would be enough.

His lips pressed into her hair, then he moved back and kissed her. Slow. Gentle. Moving his lips against hers like he was drinking in her flavor, her taste, her feel. She had every emotion in the book now. Fear and excitement and worry and joy and grief and pleasure—a kaleidoscope of sensations, and the picture wouldn't stop turning and shifting until Duncan broke away from her, held her at arm's length for a few seconds, then let her go.

"Please go back to the brownstone," he said. "I'll see you there in a little while."

Bela was shaking all over as she watched Duncan stride away from her, then follow after Mother Keara, Mother Anemone, and Mother Yana, with that damned ancient wolf padding along behind him. Andy hung back with Camille and Dio, all three watching Bela with anxious expressions

"I'm fine," she said, but nobody looked like they believed her. That was okay. Bela didn't believe herself, either.

The officer across the room, at a signal from Mother Keara, got on his phone and radio and announced a lockdown on the townhouse until further notice. It was a protocol they had put in place during the war with the Legion, to secure headquarters when something dangerous invaded the building, or when the Sibyls needed to work elemental energy in some way that posed risks for humans.

The OCU and the Sibyls had constructed elementally locked safe rooms on every floor. The officer pressed some buttons and flipped some switches on the elementally shielded electronic control panel on his desk. Automatic door and window locks—traditional and elemental—engaged all through the building except for the back kitchen door. That door remained unlocked for exactly ten minutes, allowing for reinforcements to arrive, if reinforcements were needed. The switches also set red alarm lights to flashing in the pattern that warned humans to do the OCU equivalent of taking cover. Once the officer verified that the lights were flashing in the proper sequence, the officer picked up his jacket, pad, and pen, and jogged down the left-hand hallway to tuck himself into the main floor's designated safe room.

Bela watched the officer go, but she couldn't really get a grip on why he was running away. She couldn't get a handle on herself, either, or what her body was doing. Earth energy drained out of her until she felt no connection to the rich ground, the fertile dirt, the steady rock, or the power of the planet's movement as it turned on its axis. Tears dampened her cheeks as she started toward the front door to leave, as Duncan had asked her to do, then remembered it was bolted until Duncan's healing was finished.

Maybe the library would be a good place to go, upstairs where Merilee lived with her husband, Jake. The open portion of the library was welcoming, and usually pretty empty during peak shift times.

Bela moved toward the stairs but stopped when she saw blood all over her blouse. Her slacks. Her hands. Her mind lurched back to the blood she'd had to scrub off in her shower before—Nori's, and Devin's, and Sal Freeman's. Bela raised her hands and stared at her red-streaked fingers.

What was she doing?

Why was she even here?

Nori and Devin had talked in her head off and on since they were taken from her, so why were they quiet as two ghost mice now?

Because, Bela realized, she couldn't preserve anybody or anything in her life, not really. Not even the precious memories of two sister Sibyls who meant the world to her before she failed them so completely. How could she be a proper mortar for a new fighting group? She couldn't even hold herself together, much less three other women with hearts as damaged as her own.

If death was coming for Duncan, there wasn't a damned thing she could do about it. Bela had already learned that lesson three times over. She couldn't stop it, couldn't mitigate it, couldn't do *anything* except suffer the loss—and she didn't think she could make it through something like that again. Not ever again.

Tears streaming so hard and fast she could barely see, Bela turned toward the front door. Locked. Wait, wait. The stairs. She was going to the library, wasn't she?

Her tears turned into sobs.

Gentle hands took hold of her, blocking her frenetic, pointless moving. Bela slapped at her captors, wanting to get loose, but she didn't know why, or where she'd go, or what she'd do when she got there.

Fire energy tingled along her skin, warming her until it stopped her shaking. The flames burned strength into her muscles and freed the words in her own mind, so she could talk to herself, even move her mouth and throat to take deeper breaths. Air energy brushed her face, then blew into her, lending her focus and purpose until she saw her own. The wind kept swirling through her mind, cleaning up the edges of her perception until the world made sense to her again. Water energy flowed through every part of her, binding all the elemental powers into Bela's consciousness, washing her down, and down, until her awareness found the earth again.

Weak with relief, Bela drew deep on her core power, letting the earth's ageless, timeless energy fill her up until her heartbeat slowed to a semblance of normal. Her breathing started to come more easily, and gradually the space around her started feeling solid and real and familiar.

The women standing in a circle with her, hands on her arms and shoulders, they were more than real, too.

Dio.

Camille.

Andy.

They were all with her, holding her at the brink of the townhouse entryway, crying with her and giving her everything they could to help her center herself again.

"Thank you," she whispered, even before she noticed that all the blood was gone from her hands and arms and clothing. It had been cleaned away by a shower of elemental energy—the most powerful washing machine in the universe. Her mind felt much the same, cleaner and less burdened. She had a sense that she wouldn't be hearing from Nori and Devin again, that her ghost voices just might have been put to rest.

Bela's quad gave her nods and smiles, even Dio, though Dio was quick to say, "We still have issues, you and me, okay, Bela? Just . . . not as many. Today."

Bela took that with a smile. It felt normal. Even welcome.

"I'd better go." Andy let go of Bela's arm and backed away from the group, into the main hallway. "It's been a few minutes, and the other Mothers are probably ready for my help now."

From the other end of the hall, the kitchen door banged open, and Jack Blackmore came storming into view. Behind him were Riana, Cynda, and Merilee in battle leathers, and their husbands Creed, Nick, and Jake, all wearing street clothes like they'd been yanked off patrol when the lock-down order was issued. They must have made it in just under the ten-minute margin. Bela didn't see Riana's son or Cynda's daughter, and she assumed they must be in the nursery that had been added to the fourth-floor library, with one of the fire Sibyl adepts who usually watched them.

Blackmore still looked like a dark, brooding god from some Italian painting, but the first thing out of his mouth was way more asinine than divine. "What the hell were you people thinking, taking Sharp out to question Reese Patterson?" He was yelling, and his face was starting to turn red. "I didn't hear about it, I didn't approve it—Sharp's not even officially transferred yet, and—"

"Oh, hell, no, we're not doing this right now." Andy cut off Blackmore's bluster as she wheeled toward him with both arms raised.

Bela had time to jump back into the entryway with Dio and Camille and say, "Andy . . ."

But it was too late for anything else.

Sprinkler heads exploded off the ceiling like machine-gun fire. Pipes groaned and burst in the walls and ceilings.

The Lowell brothers grabbed their wives, and all three couples dived for the conference room door, getting out of harm's way fast.

Jack Blackmore wasn't so quick on the uptake.

Andy's sudden, furious wave hit him from behind so hard it lifted him straight off his feet. The water swept him forward down the hallway, past the conference room and basement door, past the entryway where Bela and Dio and Camille were hanging on to each other's hands, and into the next hallway.

Cal and Saul Brent had the bad fortune to step out of the safe room to see what was happening.

The wave smacked them with a sound like an old-fashioned principal's paddle, and they disappeared into the same tidal surge.

"Kinda looked like bugs on a windshield, didn't they?" Dio gave the wave some extra wind power, driving it down the far hall like a water-fueled bulldozer.

The wave didn't stop until it exploded out the window at the end of the hallway; blasting through both the physical and the elemental locks and sending chairs, tables, pictures, books, glass, wood, plaster, two guys in Giants jackets, and one dickhead with a big mouth tumbling into the New York night.

When Bela dared to turn her head to check on Andy, Andy was already gone. The basement door banged shut behind her as she headed down to help with Duncan's healing.

Jake Lowell reached Bela's quad first, walking in that dominant yet ethereal way only full-blooded Astaroth demons could manage. He stopped at the entryway, gazed down the hall to the big hole in the wall where Blackmore and the Brent brothers had made their unplanned exit, and rubbed the back of his neck. "Man overboard. Well, men. Guess I better go get them."

He didn't sound like he really wanted to, but his short

blond hair shimmered to a lighter, whiter shade, and a few seconds later, he had golden eyes, translucent skin, a decent set of fangs, some scary-looking claws, and a double set of huge leathery wings. He lifted off, careful to stay below the chandeliers in the hallway, and drifted toward the broken wall.

Bela had seen that transformation dozens of times, and it never failed to amaze her. Jake reminded her of some sort of avenging angel when he used his Astaroth skills, and Bela was willing to bet that Blackmore and his buddies might not feel "rescued" when Jake showed up to snatch them off the ground and drop them on a library balcony for his brothers to retrieve. The library was a designated safe room, and Creed and Nick could phase through elementally locked glass, wood, and metal while shifting in and out of their Curson forms. They'd take care of those idiots until the townhouse got off lockdown.

Creed and Nick were already jogging up the stairs and starting to shimmer with a bright golden light. Creed was saying, "You know they'll be feeling that fall in the morning."

"They'll learn, or they'll keep finding new and interesting ways out of the townhouse." Nick didn't seem too concerned about the men outside, just the structural damage. "I'll call the cleaning crew. And a plumber. And a carpenter."

From behind Bela, Dio snickered. "I'd pay real money to see Jack Blackmore's face when he wakes up with two seven-foot glowing Curson demons playing nursemaid."

Riana was the first of the triad to reach the entryway, her coal-black hair loose and straight against the shoulders of her leathers as she glanced from the damage to Bela. The second she looked into Bela's face, she released a wave of earth energy so powerful it felt like an anchor on Bela, steady and weighty and absolutely unshakeable.

"Did you find any cat-demons while you were out?" Bela knew she sounded lame, but Riana humored her anyway.

"We didn't, and as far as I know, nobody else has. The Brent brothers were working on some financial documents we got from a forensic accountant at the FBI." Riana glanced to her right as a chunk of plaster crashed out of the wave-sized hole at the end of the hall. "But I guess that little analysis will be waiting until tomorrow."

Cynda and Merilee joined them, greeting Dio and Camille with nods and smiles, and Bela with almost matching looks of concerned affection.

"Duncan's downstairs," Riana told her triad, not even needing to ask to be sure she was right. "I hadn't realized he was so important to you, Bela. I'm sorry he's having trouble."

Dio and Camille moved closer to Bela for support again, until their arms touched hers. "Duncan's . . . different," Camille said. "A special, rare kind of guy. I think—I think he's kind of important to all of us, in different ways, Andy included."

"I don't know about *special,*" Dio countered, "but if a man could be a Sibyl, it'd be Duncan Sharp. I wouldn't mind fighting with him, given what I've seen of his resolve so far."

Bela let the rush of surprise charge through her without reacting to it. She'd known that Camille and Andy liked Duncan, but she'd had no idea about Dio. That was amazing praise, coming from any Sibyl, but from Dio, it was astounding.

Riana's triad got quiet, obviously just as surprised as Bela by Dio's compliment.

"It got bad today." Camille's voice was steady and animated as she explained a little more, relating details about the visit to Patterson's office.

Dio filled in what had happened in the SUV with the coin

and Camille's ability to channel John Cole's voice, prompting Cynda to look absolutely stunned.

"You have one powerful pyrosentient gift, Camille." Tiny flames danced along Cynda's shoulder-length red hair and leather bodysuit, keeping a rhythm with her words. "I don't know any other fire Sibyl who could have done that, except maybe old Ona, and she hasn't spoken to anyone in years."

The color in Camille's cheeks rose fast, but she thanked Cynda.

Probably out of politeness, both Camille and Dio left out Bela's meltdown in the entryway after Duncan went downstairs with the Mothers, so Bela reported that part herself.

Cynda's green eyes communicated sadness, but also hope. "I'm sorry. I know that must have been miserable, but I really, really think he'll be okay. Mother Keara's been busting her ass to sort out what needs to be done. She's even been in the archives."

"Yeah. And that's why I've had to replace no fewer than thirty-two books in seven days." Merilee put out her slender, graceful hand to Bela, and her blue eyes were filled with understanding. "Let's go to the kitchen. I'll make coffee, and we'll all wait together."

Bela took Merilee's offered hand, but she asked Cynda, "Since you know more about what the Mothers are planning, how much time do you think they can give him?"

Cynda's fire energy increased, and gray-white smoke rolled off her shoulders to fill the entryway. "It sounds like he only has hours right now, so even a few days would be a victory, wouldn't it?"

Bela tried to absorb that without letting the tears come again, but she had to give up and cry. Dio and Camille stayed close, Merilee squeezed her fingers, and Riana gave her another dose of good old-fashioned earth medicine.

"He doesn't want me here," Bela admitted as Merilee

tugged her into the hallway toward the kitchen. "Duncan asked me to leave so I wouldn't hurt when he's in pain."

"Men are idiots, and you're not going anywhere." Dio moved Bela down the hall with a set of gusts, and Riana kept pace beside her, donating a steady flow of calming earth power. "Besides, the townhouse is locked down tight if you don't count the hole in the wall, and somebody has to pick up what's left of Andy and drive her home when this is over."

Camille walked next to Cynda, keeping her chin up, even though she wasn't putting off sparks or fire. "With a healing at this level, we'll have to pour Andy into her bed and hope she doesn't melt through the mattress and leak all over the ceiling."

(20)

The glare of bright white lights in the cool, dark night couldn't mask the elemental power roiling out of the large townhouse that the Sibyls and the police officer had entered.

Strada stood beside Tarek and Griffen in an alley across from the building, shielded by simple but elegant elemental workings Griffen and the Coven he brought with him had devised. Strada held to his human form, careful to stay clear of the far-reaching and solid energy barriers surrounding the townhouse. He was glad Aarif had kept the Created at the warehouse. Exposing them to this level of elemental activity might have unhinged the weaker specimens.

"How many lairs do these Sibyls have?" Strada asked Griffen, who remained intently focused on the townhouse.

"Most fighting groups have their own homes," he said. "And most major cities have a headquarters like this one, where law enforcement can collaborate with the Dark Crescent Sisterhood away from public scrutiny. Then there are the Motherhouses, four of them, as we've discussed."

Strada studied the layers of elemental protections, impressed by the magnitude. He assumed that these were reinforced daily, unlike the barriers at the brownstone across from Central Park. The Sibyls attended to their elemental locks once every three or four days—sufficient, but not optimal. "I want all Sibyl locations in this city located and marked on our map in the warehouse, Griffen. I will notify my true brothers in other cities to do the same."

Tarek growled, curling his human fists against his sides.

"Why do we waste time on details? We are more powerful than they are, brother, especially with our allies. John Cole is dead. He cannot stop us now. We should act."

"It is never wise to underestimate your enemies, Tarek." Strada appreciated Tarek's strength of will and his wish to chew to the heart of any conflict. He didn't want to tamp down Tarek's bloodlust, but Strada had learned much about restraint and planning during his long years of battling John Cole.

Griffen had his hands in the pockets of his sweatshirt, and his dark, cloudy eyes seemed unfocused as he carefully read the energies slipping free of the townhouse's protections. "There aren't many humans, but the Sibyls are here in force tonight. And many of the demons and half-demons who work with them. I think the Mothers—the old ones—must be here, too. A lot of them. Something's going on."

Behind Strada and Griffen, Griffen's Coven of twelve men reacted to his statement by closing ranks and increasing the energy they were feeding into their elemental shielding. Like Griffen, the men wore jeans and black hooded sweatshirts, a modern semblance of ceremonial garb. Griffen referred to it as "work clothes." Strada preferred the soft silk and muted scent of suits, so he kept his true brothers outfitted in that fashion, though Tarek complained about it often.

Tarek shifted from foot to foot, scraping his leather shoes against the pavement. "Why would the old ones come to this place in such numbers? Are they gathering for an attack on us?"

"The Mothers don't work like that." Griffen kept his gaze on the townhouse. "They stay at the Motherhouses training adepts unless the Sibyls need their help with a problem."

Tarek's snarl made it clear that he was ill-satisfied with this reassurance. "So they've never joined in battle, except when their sanctuaries have been attacked?"

"Well, yes." Griffen drew his attention away from the townhouse and focused on Tarek. "They fought the ancient demon who founded the Legion."

Tarek's lips twitched, and Strada caught a glimpse of fangs trying to emerge between human-form teeth. "Which broke your Legion's ranks evermore. We should kill them all now."

"Attacking a group of Mothers head-on is inadvisable." Griffen's voice remained even, though Strada heard the rising irritation. "Even surprised, one Mother is worth a dozen or more fighting men in combat."

"Old women." Tiger claws extended from the ends of Tarek's human hands. "You have little faith in us, Griffen."

Strada raised his own claw-free hand to stop the discussion. "This night, we'll complete the mission we set for ourselves, and gain an even better measure of our foes."

To Griffen, he said, "Loose your forces and see what havoc you can create—but make certain your Coven's shields hold. I wouldn't choose to lose even one valuable ally."

Griffen dipped his head. *"Culla."*

"And Griffen"—Strada made sure to lace his next words with enough authority to frighten the human—"if officers die tonight, my true brothers and I are prepared for the consequences. It's time our two prides become acquainted, the Rakshasa and the NYPD."

A shadow crossed Griffen's face, but he offered no objections.

He turned, a little more slowly than Strada would have liked, and lifted his arms. Moments later, Griffen engaged with his Coven, murmuring instructions that quickly became the beginnings of an elemental chant.

Strada led Tarek away, to a metal ladder that reached up the side of a building, They both shifted to flame-form and followed the ladder's path to a landing several stories above the Coven, to watch their festivities in safety and obscurity.

Exerting a light counterforce to prevailing winds, Strada positioned himself to look at both the townhouse and the brilliant blue flames comprising his true brother. *Patience will restore our glory, Tarek.*

The flame that was Tarek blazed a brighter blue, then calmed to a more temperate shade. As the chant below them became more steady and rhythmic, magnified by the strength of thirteen voices, Tarek said, *I trust your wisdom, brother. For now.*

(21)

Duncan shouted as his body burned.

His head smashed against the protective mat. Flames sizzled across every corner of his awareness, tearing his mind to shreds even though he knew the fire wasn't eating him alive. Wind hammered into his mouth and face until his skin battered his teeth.

Blind. Blind and deaf. He couldn't smell anything but the damned fire, and burning hair, and burning everything.

The dinar on his chest seemed to be eating its way through muscle and vessel and ribs. His wrists and ankles pulled so hard at tethers held by the Mothers that leather cut toward bone.

Water blasted through him until he sucked it into his lungs. His eyes bulged, seeing nothing. He hacked the water out of his body, then hacked it out again and collapsed to the mat.

The arm . . . make it straighter . . .

A lock there, on the top wound nearest his throat . . .

Is his heart still beating, Andrea?

Hold him. Hold him!

Old women yelled. Old women screeched. Old women chanted and touched him and rearranged his atoms and cells.

John's voice came next. *Killing . . . us . . . killing . . . killing . . .*

The tiny bit of sanity Duncan had left knew the Mothers were trying to save him, but he couldn't hold on to that.

Don't fight, he told himself.

But he had to fight, had to keep going.

But how?

A blue-awful shock hit him low and deep, turning his gut to oatmeal.

The tenor of the Mothers' voices shifted.

What the hell?

Tension.

Then fear.

Then rage.

Another terrible blue shock hit Duncan's brain, scrambling what was left of his thoughts. He snapped into darkness. Snapped back. In and out. In and out.

Duncan Sharp knew only two things.

He was dying—and the Mothers were pissed.

"Did you feel that?" Dio pushed herself away from the round cannonball table that filled half the townhouse kitchen, rattling coffee mugs as she got to her feet.

Bela just stared at Dio.

Was Dio out of her mind?

All Bela could do was feel. Agony. Terror. Horror. The blood-chilling shouts from the basement beat against her mind and heart so hard she barely stayed upright in her seat.

"Steady." Riana had her hands over Bela's, holding Bela's fingers against the table's surface. The large hanging fixture above them swung back and forth, shadowing and brightening Camille's face, and Cynda's, and Merilee's. The elemental workings from the basement grew stronger, and stronger, draining the color away from everyone in the room.

So much power.

Too much power.

Then a rib-cracking surge.

"There!" Dio turned a full circle and let loose a wide tendril of air energy. It shattered against the unrelenting power streaming up through the floor, and she swore and closed her eyes. Her muscles went rigid. Another tendril of wind left her, this time knifing across the Mothers' energy and snaking quickly out of the townhouse.

Merilee stood. "Be careful, Dio. You're draining yourself." To Bela, she said, "I didn't know she was ventsentient."

Bela couldn't answer. Steeped in Duncan's misery, watching Dio fighting the excess energy from the Mothers' healing and the townhouse's barriers and starting to lose—her body went numb and dead to her will.

Dio started to shake, going paler by the second.

Camille shoved herself back from the table and ran to Dio. When she seized Dio's hands, Riana, Merilee, and Cynda instinctively ducked under the table's edge, dragging Bela down with them.

No major wind vortex opened, and no flames burst across the room.

What they got was a major steadying of power all through the kitchen.

Then Camille, in an eerie Dio-like voice, said, "Bela. We need you."

Bela yanked free of Riana's protective grip. Reality tilted and swayed as she pulled herself up, then staggered across a floor that seemed to be rippling and melting at the same time. The joining of Dio's ventsentience to Camille's pyrosentience—was that what was pitching the world sideways?

She didn't think so.

It was something else, maybe something to do with those surges.

Duncan's pain jerked at Bela's soul, but she knew where she had to be. She reached Dio and Camille and didn't even let herself think. She just grabbed hold of their wrists, threw her terrasentience into the mix, and—

The earth bellowed in its turning . . .

The sky howled with cloud-killing wind . . .

Molten fire erupted from the center of the world . . .

Bela's mind and body crushed in on itself. She couldn't breathe or think or sense anything past the blast of images that whirled through her awareness. Time. The planet. The universe. Everything that had touched the earth and air and fire seemed to smash against her mind, all at the same time. Human energy, animals, plants, machines—too much, too much, too much!

"You have to anchor us," Camille whispered, her voice a crackle of fire on a match tip, burning from some distant point in the galaxy. "Something's . . . interfering . . ."

I know, Bela tried to say, but she couldn't spare that much energy and focus.

"Got a fix on it." Dio spoke with the rage of the wind. "Unnatural energy. Perverted. Can't—figure—what—"

Bela's whole body rattled as she tried to contain and direct Camille and Dio's elemental power and fend off interference from the Mothers' healing. She wasn't strong enough. She needed to let them go. This would rip her to pieces.

From the basement, Duncan roared like the Mothers were splitting him open, and Bela felt Dio and Camille react. Then she understood.

Some force or being was deliberately disrupting the healing. Some outside energy was interfering and beginning to distort the Mothers' workings, and if Bela didn't stop it now, right now, Duncan would die. Andy and the Mothers could be hurt or killed from the fallout. They could all be killed.

Bela shrieked with frustration, with desperation, and held tighter to Camille and Dio.

"What are you trying to find?" Merilee demanded again, from somewhere Bela couldn't pinpoint.

As deep and angry as any storm, Dio shouted back, "I don't know!"

Lightning blasted into the backyard. Thunder blistered the sky, and the windows in the kitchen shattered.

Bela saw her own reflection tumble by in slow motion, in a thousand shards of glass. Her consciousness moved through them, rendering them to nothing but bits of soda and lime.

I'm projecting myself with no mirrors. I'm moving through matter, absorbing its energy—I'm changing it.

That wasn't possible, but she was doing it, just like Camille had projected herself through Duncan's dinar and allowed John Cole to project through her. And Dio—Dio was projecting herself through the air in ways Bela had never experienced before.

Energy exchanges made sense to Bela in a whole new way.

Maybe she didn't have to fight the energy boiling through the kitchen. She just had to take it through herself, pull it in and project it outward—changed, broken down to its natural components.

She let her muscles go limp, let her mind go clear, and let every bit of power in the room fly into her. Instead of crushing her skull to powder, it flowed, and she projected her earth energy across every line and pulse she encountered. Her consciousness moved through those bits of energy, like she had moved through the glass shards, and broke them down to components. Just as fast, she sent it back to the earth, the sky, the ocean, and the bits of ambient fire dancing across the air.

"The distortion's coming from the alley," Dio cried, and Bela knew Dio was seeing clearly now, riding her element and letting the wind be her eyes. Leaving her body behind her, Bela followed Dio's wind energy with her own earth power, and saw the darkness shimmering at the edge of the alley, too.

"What is it?" Camille's question was slowed, but Bela

knew Camille was using a tiny, focused line of fire to examine the blackness and try to take its measure.

Dio's consciousness shoved at the distortion. "No idea. Just stop it."

Her wrist shook in Bela's grip, but the wind energy she sent had no effect on the thick, menacing darkness. Camille's laser-like fire broke apart at its edges.

"It's a shield." Bela's voice sounded muffled to her own ears, like she was talking through cotton. Her thoughts worked quickly now, imagining how she'd protect her own quad, by wrapping them in a mortar of earth energy, bottom, top, and sides. If she tried to rise above it, she'd lose connection to the ground and lose strength. From the sides, and she'd lose focus.

There was only one thing to do.

"Wait for my mark," she told Camille and Dio. "Build your focus, and follow me when I strike."

Bela drove her awareness down, down to the ground, and under. Deeper, into the hard-packed layers of sand and silt and rock under New York City. Her mind dived until she sensed water a few feet in front of her. Then she turned, coiling her awareness like a great snake of dirt. Drawing more earth energy to her than she'd ever known she could manage, she hurtled upward through it and struck toward that dark patch of alley.

"Now, Camille!" This time her cry sounded like the devil rattle of a 9.0 quake. "Now, Dio!"

Air and fire laced into Bela's power, ramming her higher and faster.

She didn't have to move earth, any more than Dio had to move wind or Camille had to make fire. They just had to shift their awareness through the elements, and let the elements power them.

Bela's awareness exploded through dirt and asphalt and air, displacing an area of ground as great as all the energy she had used to spring through the earth. The slats of the shield—the whole dark space in the alley—blew apart like she had thrown dynamite in a barrel. Thunder and lightning and rain pelted the ground, washing against men falling and scrambling and running away, their faces obscured by the black hoods of sweatshirts.

"I smell them," Dio growled, steering Bela's consciousness deeper into the alley. "Ammonia. The air stinks of it. Look there, on the fire escape!"

Two Rakshasa, one white, one black, leaned forward against the fire escape's metal guard, bared massive tiger fangs, and roared.

Bela screeched right back at them, reached to snatch her sword from her scabbard—

And sat hard on her ass on the townhouse's kitchen floor.

Dio smacked down beside her, and Camille hit right in front of the sink's double-door cabinet.

The floor beneath them still tingled with the Mothers' energy, but the exchange and flavor seemed completely different now, and natural. Bela sensed Duncan below her, still in pain, but not agony. Still fighting to survive, but winning. He was getting stronger, not weaker.

"Is he okay?" Camille asked.

Bela answered her with a smile and a gasp. She didn't have anything left but that, and the wild, nervous laughter that poured out of her. She put her face in her hands to mute it as Camille and Dio started talking at the same time.

"It was projection—"

"I never thought about elemental sentience that way—"

"We moved through *it* instead of moving it through *us*—"

"—a lot more studying and experimenting. It could be dangerous—"

They chattered and chattered, but then their voices got softer and died away.

Bela lifted her head, still flush with the energy she had touched. She felt like she'd had two easy weeks with good nights' sleeps, a bunch of good meals, and fourteen good workouts. *Oh, yeah, baby.* She felt strong enough to take on a horde of Sumo wrestlers.

Which was sort of apt, because Riana and Cynda and Merilee were staring at them. Behind them, in the doorway of the kitchen, a bunch of Mothers were staring at them, too.

Merilee caught Mother Anemone's elbow, her gaze never leaving Dio for a second. "We need to talk," she muttered to the Mother.

Bela was surprised to see Mother Anemone nod and look a little guilty.

A second or two later, Andy shoved through the crowd, and she stared at them as well. Water ran down the sides of her face in rivulets as she folded her arms, both cheeks blazing mad-Andy red. "Okay, you bitches." She misted a wider spray of droplets with each word, and the water in the sink behind Bela turned on with a clink and a rush. "What the fuck was *that*?"

〈 22 〉

The townhouse basement felt cool and comfortable to Duncan as he stretched out the kinks on his mat. He felt like himself again. Well, mostly, if he didn't focus on the really old fire Sibyl trying to talk to him, the coin around his neck, or the ghost of his best friend, still lurking around in his brain.

John Cole had clamped down tight on the issue of the will, insisting that he'd just done what he had to do to keep Katrina happy, and he wasn't going to discuss it any further. So Duncan was letting it be for now. He'd been asleep for a day, had a good meal, had a good shower, and won a good fight with Blackjack, who had a busted knee and black eye he refused to explain when Duncan asked. The bastard finally agreed that Duncan was still a cop, definitely assigned to the OCU, but classified "on special assignment." No attending shift report, no official duties other than sticking with Bela's quad until the Sibyls said he could work alone. Duncan could live with that. For now.

He was having more trouble living with Mother Keara standing next to him nonstop, stinging him with sparks even when he was trying to do his stretches and relax.

"A few weeks, a month, maybe two—it's hard to say, cop." The one Mother still playing fire-breathing babysitter actually looked sad as she explained what the Sibyls thought after the last round of blood drawing and analyzing skin scrapings. "You'll keep yer health until then, so long as John Cole's spirit keeps helping you out. And when death comes, you won't suffer. The demon-change'll happen fast, and we'll take care of . . . putting you down."

Duncan figured he didn't want to ask how.

"Thank you," he said to Mother Keara.

She pointed to the coin around his neck. "The dinar's key to keeping John Cole close to you, and holding our blood and tissue wards in place. Don't take it off, or you'll hasten the process."

"I won't." Duncan didn't want to hear any more negatives right now. He had other things on his mind. "And I'm feeling fine for now. I want to see Bela."

Mother Keara's braids smoked. "She's busy. Not hurt at all, don't go worryin'. The Rakshasa pulled an attack on the townhouse while we were workin', and she and Dio and Camille drove them off. They saved yer life."

Duncan's jaw tightened.

While he'd been thrashing around on a basement mat getting his insides burned up and smashed by elemental energy, his angel had been upstairs fighting demons?

Not okay.

He stood and faced Mother Keara more directly. "I want to see Bela now, please."

She gave him a blow-off frown and shook a knotty finger at his hip—because she didn't reach any higher. "We've been keeping her away, because you'll be needin' another day or two to be solid on yer feet."

"I try to respect my elders, ma'am, and I'm more grateful to you and the other Mothers than I can say for the extra time you've given me. But I'm not asking you, I'm telling you." Duncan put his hand over the dinar to keep it from swinging down when he leaned toward Mother Keara to be sure she heard him. "I don't have a lot of time left to me, and I want to see Bela. Now. I want to be with Bela as much as I can. Either you send her to me, or I'm going up to find her."

All that came out loud.

And powerful.

It had kind of an echo to it.

The coin tingled beneath Duncan's fingertips, and he let go of it to stare at his skin.

From the center of his brain, John said, *Interesting*, then faded from Duncan's awareness.

From somewhere around Duncan's right elbow, Mother Keara said, "Did yer mother ever make things catch on fire, by any chance?"

Duncan glanced down at the Mother, wondering if she'd gotten overheated during his healing. "Ah, no. Not unless she used matches."

"Hmm." Mother Keara sounded like she didn't believe him, but she accepted his word nonetheless. "All right, then. You wait right here, and I'll let her know you're awake and asking for her."

Duncan watched the Mother totter over to the basement door, tempted to follow her just to be sure she didn't jack around with him. He didn't think she would, though. If she hadn't wanted to go get Bela, she would have just set him on fire for being pushy.

That's what he was liking most about Sibyls so far. What you saw was what you got—only better. And he never had to worry about where he stood, because they'd damned sure tell him.

Duncan touched the dinar around his neck again, and he sensed her.

Bela.

She felt like a cool island oasis in a sea full of sharks.

"Come here, Angel," he murmured, even though he knew she couldn't hear him. "We need to talk about no and not yet—and saying yes."

According to Riana's triad, the search for the Rakshasa had turned up nothing. Again. The Sibyls on patrol had tried tracking the demons and the humans who helped them invade the townhouse's elemental protections, but once more, it was like they vanished from the city's borders as soon as they ran away. They had to have one hell of an elemental shield in place somewhere—something strong, yet subtle enough that the patrols were missing it completely.

Bela sat at the townhouse's kitchen table in her street clothes, because Mother Keara and Jack frigging Blackmore, with his purple eye and sprained knee from falling out of the damned wall on the crest of Andy's wave, had refused to let her and her quad go on the hunt. They didn't think it was safe, not until the Mothers had the opportunity to study what Bela, Camille, and Dio had done to stop the Rakshasa's energy attack during the healing.

Stupid.

But not worth the fight.

If truth be told, Bela didn't want to get that far away from Duncan anyway.

"You know we're not tryin' to shame you or punish you." Mother Keara's crackly voice caught Bela off guard. She hadn't heard the Mother enter the kitchen or come to stand behind her. Mothers could be like that, damned silent and sneaky. "We're only holdin' you back until we know more."

Bela kept her hands on the table in front of her and didn't turn around. "You're holding us back, period. My quad might have been able to track those monsters while the trail was fresh. We touched their energy shield. I think we could recognize it again. I know we could do it, if we work together."

"You don't know any such thing. No one, not one person—are you hearin' me?" Mother Keara stomped around the table where Bela would have to look at her, bringing her fire as she came. Bits of flame danced across Bela's wrists and fingers. "Not a livin' soul on this earth knows what might happen, usin' elemental power like the three of you did. The air Sibyls are crawlin' Motherhouse Greece's archives to find what they can to explain it, to help us understand it."

Bela got to her feet and gazed down at Mother Keara. "*We* understand it."

"Do you now?" Shadows and flames played across Mother Keara's wrinkled cheeks as she spoke, and Bela was reminded fiercely of pictures of Rumpelstiltskin and goblins and other tiny, terrible things. "How long can you use it before it drains you down to nothing—or kills you?"

She'd never come out on top in this argument, but stubbornness and irritation drove Bela to keep going anyway. "It's an exchange. We have to keep the output less than the input, that's all."

"And what damage might that output do if it got away from you? What if the next time it takes yer life—or Dio's, or Camille's?"

"Don't you dare use my caring for my quad against me!" Heat poured into Bela's face. She wanted to say a lot more, but she rubbed her temples instead, pushing back a big headache. "Leave off, old woman. I can't talk to you anymore until I get to go on patrol and burn some energy."

Fire burned a streak across the table separating them, and Mother Keara laughed at her. "You should have been a fire Sibyl."

"And you should have been a sneaky-ass leprechaun, so we're even." Bela let go of her head and steadied herself with the table again. She was relatively certain her temper wouldn't drive her to accidentally open a projective hole in the floor and let Mother Keara fall all the way back to Ireland.

Mother Keara's paper-thin hand rested over Bela's on the table, without burning her at all. "Yer detective's awake," she said, no doubt feeling the upsurge in Bela's earth power as she spoke. "I'm thinkin' he'd like to see you now."

Bela's worries and frustrations fractured and dispersed.

She blinked once at Mother Keara and started for the kitchen door, but the irritating little leprechaun snatched hold of the waistband of her slacks. "He looks good now, but don't be fooled, child. He's got weeks at best—a month or two, no more, before we'll have to kill him in demon form, and he knows that."

Bela tried to pull herself free, but Mother Keara held tight to her pants. "You've got yer issues with being told what to do—but I'm tellin' you this. Watch yer heart. Duncan Sharp's damned good at stealing those."

When Bela turned to extract Mother Keara's fingers from her clothing before she burned holes in the fabric, she saw tears in the old woman's eyes. That nearly made her sob. It was all she could do to get herself loose and keep herself together.

Weeks.

Damnit, I don't accept that.

But weeks . . .

The next few seconds blurred as Bela's thoughts spun down, down toward Duncan, and what time they could have together, and what they'd never have. She couldn't really do this, could she? Go down those basement steps and touch a man she knew she was going to lose. The pain of trying to measure minutes and hours before another soul-killing loss would crush her sanity.

Bela's body moved without conscious drive. She felt the kitchen door with her fingertips, then the basement door. Her elemental focus propelled her forward, and her awareness dwindled to the single point of bright heat that was Duncan, his life energy pulsing into the earth below her. It drummed a rhythm like a heartbeat, and she knew that sound like she knew the shape of dirt and the taste of rock, the scent of sand, the bone-deep rattle of the world in its turning.

Pound, pound, pound.

Death didn't seem real or even possible, with life speaking so loudly.

She moved down the townhouse stairs, her feet, her breathing, and her own heart keeping that cadence. Tiny shocks of pain still echoed through her body, remnants of what Duncan had endured, but he *had* endured. And so had she.

Mother Keara was wrong, at least about some things. Bela understood that now, because she knew she wasn't a misguided fire Sibyl after all. She was of the earth and for the earth, born to its service and living by its grace. She didn't need to move the soil and bend it to her will, because it moved *her*. It powered her, lifted her, drove her. She spoke to it, and it spoke to her, and she knew it like a twin, from its molten core to its shifting dust that touched every living thing that walked its surface. From now on, instead of finding channels in its depths or trying to force them into existence, she would be the channel, and let the earth rise through her.

Duncan's essence was one with the stone beneath his feet, and with the ground beneath the stone. He had been bathed by elemental energy, and he was as purely connected to the earth as anything Bela's mind had ever touched. His presence pulled her like a primal force, away from her friends, her quad, the Mothers, and everything she knew for certain. By going to him now, she was walking away from her past and committing to an uncertain future.

Riding the tide of her deepened terrasentience and the direct rush of earth power it gave her, Bela pushed the gym door open, and heavy boards smashed against the stone wall behind it. Bela stared at the splintered wood. With the right focus and concentration, she could have shoved it straight through the rock, all the way to the next block— though she suspected the energy exchange definitely would have laid her out, or even killed her.

So much to learn now. So much new.

The basement stretched before her, as quiet as a temple chamber. The elemental healing had left the room smelling like fire and wind and rain, like a mountain forest after a hard, thundering storm. The stone walls and floor gave off a cool, earthy energy, but that did nothing to chill the heat rising through Bela's body.

All the exercise equipment was shoved to the walls, leaving the cavernous space empty except for a single blue mat in the center of the floor. Duncan was standing beside the mat in his jeans, bare-chested except for the glittering gold dinar, and he was staring straight at her. Both of his arms looked healed and strong, like the rest of him. No cast. No bandages anywhere. He had the glow and vigor of the recently healed, and she knew he'd still be bursting with the elemental energy he'd received. His slash wounds were closed. The scars curled away from his neck and crossed his shoulder, then swept down to cover the left side of the skin over his heart. Some were pale, some raised, some furrowed. They marked him like the shrapnel from his first war.

As a warrior.

As a survivor.

Bela lost another piece of her heart to him. If she could have bargained with the Goddess to trade some of her own days, months, and years to keep him breathing, she would have done it.

Duncan studied her, not smiling, not frowning. When he spoke, his voice was low, and close to teasing. "I know what you did to help save me, and I'm grateful—but I told you not to stay here, Angel."

Bela almost laughed at that. "You should have realized something by now, Duncan Sharp. I never do what I'm told."

Duncan folded his arms across his scarred, muscular chest. His unbelievable eyes sparked, then burned with a warm gray light. "All right. If that's true, then I'm telling you, don't come over here."

Bela slammed what was left of the basement door behind her, surprised when it thumped into place and didn't snap off its hinges. She walked toward Duncan, taking her time, wanting to mark each detail about him and appreciate every nuance.

Her slacks felt like damp weights on her legs, and her blouse clung to her arms and waist like white cotton binding. They were in her way, holding her back, so she took them off. A few buttons, and a toss. A snap and zipper, and a kick.

She was halfway to the mat.

If Duncan's eyes had been warm before, they were flaming now. He kept his arms crossed, but his muscles bulged like he was holding himself in place. Through the chilled stone tickling her toes and soles and heels, the rage of his desire licked across Bela's senses. The steel of his self-control gripped her mind. He tasted like molten metal to her Sibyl perceptions, unbearably hot and smooth, and completely basic and natural.

She took off her bra, and the basement's cool air stung her nipples. The sensitive flesh tightened until it hurt in just the right way, and Duncan's eyes fixed on the hard tips. Bela let him look, and she kept walking.

Soon enough, he'd touch her, before she burned up from wanting him to do it.

Her panties were thin lace, and wet, and they tore in her earth-powerful fingers when she slid them to her hips. The delicate fabric tumbled to the stone floor, leaving her bare. The basement's chill touched her again, lower and deeper, this time making her gasp—and she let him look, let his breath leave him in a whistle, and she kept walking.

Earthquakes were nothing but a push and a pull, a change in motion that forever shifted a planet, from its core to its surface. Duncan Sharp was her earthquake. When she put her hands on him this time, her life, from its core to its surface, would never look the same again.

Bela stopped, inches away from him. "You don't need a condom," she said. Blunt and honest seemed like the best way to talk to him now. "I decide when I get pregnant, and my elemental energy takes care of any other problems."

The temperature rising from Duncan's taut muscles was a tangible thing. Fire Sibyls smoked and burned from less heat than he was throwing off. His eyes traced a path from her face to her neck, from her breasts to her belly, from her dark curls to her toes, then all the way up again.

She broke out in tiny shivers, delicious and maddening. Her breasts felt heavy and ready for his hands, and she ached for him to take possession of the rest of her curves and secret places. His fingers, his mouth, his passion—she wanted everything. A fine mist of sweat broke all over her exposed skin, doubling the shivers.

Through the earth connecting them, Bela listened to the rhythm of their hearts. Fast. Steady. Not matching, but synchronized, a beat for each silence and a silence for each beat.

Duncan lowered his arms and stared at her, all of her, taking his time like she'd taken hers. His consuming gaze showed his gentleness and strength, his desire, but something else, too: a possessiveness she'd never expected. It caught her off guard. It thrilled her. She was glad she was standing naked in front of him, stripped down to nothing on the outside and the inside, too. She wanted him to take her, to own her. She had never felt anything like that before.

More surprises.

The ache between her legs was almost more than she could stand.

"Now I'm telling you this, and you better listen." He reached out and slid his thumbs over both of her nipples. She shuddered, and the ache to have him inside her doubled. "Don't kiss me. And whatever you do, don't make love to me until you scream. Until you can't move. Until you forget everyone and everything in the world except what I'm doing to you, and how hard, and how deep."

His words rumbled, shifting the earth inside Bela like an unstoppable force as he rubbed her nipples again. She moaned, pulling away, then pushing herself right back into his touch. His gorgeous eyes surrendered to her, then claimed her as he pinched where he'd been rubbing.

She was lost.

That fast.

Spiraling into an existence of pure sensation.

Her palms rested on his chest, and his rough male skin felt like heaven under her fingertips. His scars were a landscape, private, personal, and each dent and ridge spoke to her. Duncan let her explore every crease and turn, every flaw and every perfection, his eyes locked on hers as he kept up his massage, moving the responsive tips of her breasts in slow circles between his thumb and forefinger. She leaned forward and flicked her tongue across his smaller nipples, and he groaned.

Bela pushed up on her toes and kissed him as his hands slid to her waist, and oh, yes, he tasted like water, natural and fresh and sweet. His tongue was hot in her mouth, moving with her each time she breathed, each time she pressed herself closer, wishing she could get all the way inside his skin. His dinar buzzed and hummed between her breasts, but it didn't shock her, not when it was touching him, too. Her bare thighs scrubbed against his jeans, his erection. She moved herself up and down, feeling all of him that she could as he caressed her cheeks, her neck, then gripped her shoulders, keeping her close. He let her catch her breath, but never quite let her pull away. His hands were so big. Barely controlled power. She wanted them on her. She wanted them everywhere, and when they really started moving, she was helpless.

"Touch me," she whispered to him over and over, barely aware that she was talking at all.

Duncan formed her body to his, crushing her sensitive nipples against his chest as his lips kept hers captive. Each brush of his scars sent a shock of a different texture from her toes all the way to her lips. She sighed into his mouth as he rubbed the small of her back. Rough, yet gentle. Strong, but so tender when he cupped her ass and squeezed her tighter.

"I never dreamed I'd meet a woman like you." His deep, husky voice made her throb all over. "Now I can't stop dreaming about you."

He kissed her.

"Every night."

He kissed her again.

"This isn't casual for me. I don't have time left for games, and I'm not playing with you."

He lowered his head to her neck and bit her, and she moaned.

"Tell me yes this time." His teeth scraped across the skin between her neck and shoulder. "I need to hear you say it, Angel."

She was getting dizzy from the sound and feel of him. "Yes." Her fingers found the button of his jeans, struggled with it, and got it loose. "Yes." Goddess, he was biting her again, and it felt so good she couldn't take it. Denim scraped her wrists as she shoved his pants down and left him as bare as she was.

"Damn, Duncan. Yes, I want you. I want you right now!"

He kept his mouth at her throat, biting her soft and biting her rough, walking them forward and stepping out of his jeans. He settled himself against her belly, and Bela felt the damp tip, felt him pulsing. He was ready for her.

Was she *ever* ready for him.

She pushed his face away from her neck and kissed him

as she wrapped one hand around his erection and stroked. "I'm not an angel." Her lips danced over his as she spoke. She stroked him again. "You need to know that."

His cock bucked into her palm and she squeezed, loving the firm weight of him, and his feral growl. His jaw tightened, and his gray eyes hazed from arousal. She knew he had to be hurting for release. She was about to die from her own want. Her heart pounded so hard she didn't know how to keep it from exploding.

"You're everything angels are made of." Duncan took her hand and forced it down, rubbing her sensitive folds with his length and her own fingers.

Bela cried out from the sudden, excruciating pleasure, and he swallowed the sound with his mouth. He used his free hand to hold her upright as he made her pump her own knuckles against her tender center, then dipped his head and caught her nipple in his teeth. Biting. Biting hard.

Taking her, yes.

Possessing her, yes.

This time, Bela's moan came from somewhere deep in her depths. She couldn't stop the sound as he sucked the nub and used his tongue to tease it. Her moan went on and on and on, like the thrust of his wrist as he moved himself and her fingers at the same time, sliding, pushing until she couldn't stand it, and then he bit her other nipple.

Ecstasy swelled in Bela's depths, rising, too hot to be contained. Was she hitting him? Yes. Pounding his shoulder with her fist, but not to make him stop, and he knew it. He was reading every groan and gasp, slowing down and speeding up at exactly the right moments to drive her completely, totally past any sane thought.

Duncan let go of her hand and gripped her ass again, this time lifting her and laying her down in the same motion. Bela felt the soft mat under her shoulders as Duncan spread her legs wide and settled himself between her thighs. He braced his arms on either side of her head, his eyes locked on her eyes, and his face so close to hers that she could nip at his bottom lip.

He let her catch him a couple of times, then moved his belly against her folds as he murmured, "You're so damned beautiful. When I look at you, I can't even breathe."

All Bela could do was groan and fight to gulp air herself. She was trembling and still dizzy, more dizzy. Everything spun in slow, grand circles, like she'd taken some ritual drug that slowed time and enhanced the tiniest sensations.

Words left her, but Duncan didn't give her a chance to talk, anyway. He slid himself down, lower, lower, rubbing her wet center with his abs, his chest, his chin with no mercy at all. His breath was warm and soft. "I want to taste you, Angel."

Bela tried to say *Yes, please, right now,* but the best she could do was a long, ragged sigh of delight. She managed to slip her fingers into his hair, but her hands were shaking too much to get a good grip. Her eyes clamped shut as he forced her thighs farther apart with his big hands, exposing her completely, letting his breath wash over her until the ache made her mind whirl faster.

Duncan pressed his face into the heat between her legs.

She made fists in his hair and pulled, lifting her hips to his mouth. His tongue—ah, damn. Right on the sweet spot. Right in the center. Tasting, just like he promised. Tasting, and tasting, and tasting, then licking, then sending lightning hits of pleasure in every direction as he pulled her softly across his teeth and moved his mouth back and forth.

Bela moaned and bucked, and the basement rippled and moved with her. Sweat coursed down her back now, and her muscles burned from waiting and wanting and needing.

"Not yet," he whispered against her swollen center as he slowed his kisses.

She yanked at his hair as the walls trembled. "Don't tease me much more, Duncan. I'll bring down the house."

"You're not scaring me, even a little bit." Duncan shifted Bela forward and rose to his knees before she could rip out his hair for frustrating her so completely. He pulled her ass onto his thighs, and carefully lifted her legs to his shoulders.

Bela's breath stilled in her chest, and she couldn't make her throat work. She was so wide open to him, so absolutely exposed. When she did start breathing, it came in ragged jerks, and she couldn't stop staring into the magic of his eyes. The coin around his neck gleamed as it swayed on top of his scars.

"That's it, Angel." He rubbed his cock against her ass and ran his fingers down her legs until he caught hold of her hands. "Look at me. Look at us."

He eased her hands up her belly, to her breasts, then made her pinch her own swollen nipples. The shock of touching herself while he watched turned her heartbeat to thunder. Her back arched, and he rocked her shoulders into the mat, releasing her hands. She kept squeezing her breasts, loving the way he stared at her fingers, her nipples, then her face and her mouth.

She felt wanted. Completely appreciated.

He gripped her hips and slid himself slowly, slowly upward, toward where Bela wanted him to be.

"Look at your breasts," he told her, and doing it made the pulsing in her folds a hundred times worse. "Pinch yourself."

She pinched and moaned.

The tip of his erection teased her opening, and she looked at that, too. Her hips were moving under own power now, lifting to meet him.

Duncan's muscles flexed as he slid his length in an inch, then drew himself out.

Bela bared her teeth at him, wishing she could bite a hole in his shoulder.

He did it again, and she bit her own lip and yelled into

her closed mouth. Her face was so hot she wondered if she was glowing. Her hands gripped her breasts, covering them and squeezing at the same time, crushing herself down to stand the ache as he tortured her.

With a satisfied growl, Duncan drove himself inside her, deep, yes, way deep, as far as she could take, and she pinched her own nipples so hard tears rose to her eyes. The scream that left her was pure relief. He held her waist up, trapping her right where he wanted her, her legs on his shoulders, and he waited, waited, letting her savor the stretch, the sweet burn, gazing at her like he'd never stop, and she never wanted him to.

"Watch." His command made her walls clench, and her back arched even tighter as she let out another helpless cry from the intensity.

Duncan moved his hips, unhurried, sliding back and forth inside her so slowly it became a new, perfect torment. Bela stared at the point where they connected, where he moved, and each thrust seemed to open her wider.

Gray fire snapped in his eyes as he plumbed her deeper, pulling her hips against his thighs with each slow, sensual plunge.

He was rocking her, taking her, yes, owning her, and she couldn't stop watching.

The coin on his chest bounced as she rocked. Her back moved on the mat and she pinched her nipples, staring as he pumped deeper, faster, spreading her, pushing her. She clenched and released. Couldn't stop. Didn't want to stop. This couldn't end. Never. Ever.

"Don't scream, Angel."

She tore her gaze away from their sex, and she found his untamed grin—and those eyes.

"You heard me." His thrusts got harder, faster. He pounded her, driving her past what she thought she could take. "I said don't scream."

Everything was throbbing. Everything was clenching.

Bela was nothing but molten heat, core heat. Fault lines opened through her essence as the pleasure claimed her. Her eyes closed and her hands fell away from her breasts. She shook as she reached the top and stumbled over the edge, pulling at the earth, feeling its power rise to meet her when she screamed and screamed and screamed again.

Duncan groaned with her as he spilled himself inside her, rocking back and forth with the floor and walls. She liked taking him, loved the thought of her body drinking in everything he could give her. The coin on his neck hummed and gave off a dark, loamy glow, and Bela realized it was absorbing her earth energy, magnifying it and sending it down again, straight through her, maybe to the center of the world.

Duncan kept thrusting, slower, slower, sending aftershock after aftershock streaming through her spent body until she couldn't stand it. She finally pushed herself up and sank her teeth into his shoulder to make him stop.

He kept himself inside her but let her straighten on the mat beneath him, then covered her with his warm, muscled frame and his kisses.

Sweet, total exhaustion wrapped her up like Duncan's strong arms. Bela's eyelids fluttered as she traced his muscled shoulders with her fingertips. She didn't want to close her eyes. If she did, she might miss hours with him, and she didn't even want to miss minutes.

Duncan's lips found her ear. His breath a tickle deep in her mind, his tone teasing and gentle, he whispered, "Don't sleep, Angel. That's it. Don't you dare go to sleep."

(23)

A few hours later, Duncan woke. John was still there in his head, but distant, and letting him be—so Duncan kissed Bela awake and took her home to the brownstone. They found Andy in the living room, dressed in torn jeans and an NYPD T-shirt. She was sprawled on the overstuffed sofa, snoring and hugging a bag of chips and a sack of chocolate cookies. The entire brownstone smelled like ice cream, fudge, and whipped cream, and bowls and spoons covered the big round table in front of the couch.

Andy woke up long enough to burp and mumble, "Dio's had enough rocky road to kill two grown men. She's locked in her archives, and Camille's downstairs in the lab."

Bela froze mid-step on her way to the kitchen and started swearing.

Andy ignored her and went straight back to sleep.

"I'm taking it that Camille in the lab—that's a problem?" Duncan caught hold of Bela from behind, then tried not to be distracted by the feel of her soft slacks and shapely hips in his hands. "A big hairy problem?"

Bela turned to face him, her dark eyes snapping. "Are you nuts? There's a *fire Sibyl* in my laboratory!"

He tried to pull her to him to settle her down, but she let out another string of curses that would have impressed a prison guard and tried to get away from him. He wasn't ready to let her go, especially with her gaze so wild and the color rising in her cheeks.

Damn.

Just seeing her like that made him hard, much less touching her. "Don't you guys share all your important stuff, Angel? Quad unity and all that?"

Bela smacked his chest with her palms. "There's a fire Sibyl in my lab!"

"I got that part." Duncan wanted to kiss her so badly he could already taste her lips.

"The machines," those beautiful lips were saying. "And—and my papers. The one computer that still works—and oh, shit. My chemical cabinet."

Duncan hated to do it, but he let Bela go and followed her into the kitchen. "Okay, I admit sparks don't mix with a lot of stuff you've got going down there, but Camille's pretty careful, isn't she?"

Bela was already opening the door at the top of the stairs, presumably to march down to the basement and earthquake her fire Sibyl into next year. "Camille doesn't spit smoke and flames like the other fire Sibyls I've met," he said, hoping he was on the right track.

"I really don't know how Camille might be if she gets angry, or too excited." Bela headed down the steps, and Duncan tried to stay close. "When she's scared, her fire energy drops. Could be that other emotions would go the other way."

He caught her in his arms again, right outside the closed door he assumed hid her bedroom from view, and kissed her. When he could stand pulling back for a second, he said, "I vote for assuming Camille's level-headed. She'll be respectful of all your shiny stuff and those microscopes I want to play with when I've got time."

Time.

The word gigged him when he said it, and he wondered if Bela felt the quick, tense jerk of his muscles. Her steady gaze caressed him just like her long, graceful fingers, running across his face and neck like she was taking a brand-new read on him.

Duncan wasn't afraid of dying, or what death would be

like. He wasn't worried about turning demon now that he knew Dio or the Mothers would take care of business when he drew his last breath.

No, what hurt him was knowing that time was short, that he wouldn't have much of it with the beautiful woman he couldn't stop touching and tasting and wanting.

Bela kissed him, her lips gentle and sweet, moving on his mouth like a whisper. When she finished, she told him, "I'm on to you, Duncan Sharp. What you're voting for is a tour of my bedroom, or maybe my bed."

When his lips took hers again, he didn't want to stop. Fast and deep this time, then long and slow. She felt like dreams and hopes and warm perfection in his arms. "Yeah," he managed after a minute or two. "That's my vote."

She rubbed his cock through his jeans, and he ground his teeth to stop the groan.

Who needed a bedroom?

He could take her right here, up against the wall.

"Don't do that again, Angel. I can't take the tease."

Bela kept her hand on his erection, and her wicked-mischief expression said she was considering doing whatever she wanted. Her gaze shifted to the hallway, toward the laboratory where Camille was working.

"In here." She let go of him and grabbed the doorknob beside her. With a twist and push, the door swung open, and Duncan followed her into . . .

An eight-year-old-boy's room?

Bela's cheeks flushed as she reached for the wall switch to shut off the light and hide everything Duncan was trying to absorb.

When he wouldn't let her shut off the light, she started to back them out of the room, but he held her tight, her back to his chest, as he counted ten Knicks posters on the far wall. The other wall had a football Giants schedule and poster for décor, Yankee flags, and a Yankees roster from last year, when they'd made one hell of a pennant run. He noticed a leather tool belt in the corner with a hammer sticking out and saw lying beside it a bunch of figurines along her handcrafted dresser—the 1927 Yankees, he thought—two baseball bats in a chair beside the rumpled full-sized bed, and an ancient pink ball in a cup on her bedside table. An unusual white feather had been tucked behind the pink ball, and the cup had worn, colored drawings painted on it beneath the words *Disney World.*

Duncan bent down and kissed Bela's neck, enjoying the almond scent and the heat playing across her skin.

"Not what you expected," she whispered, obviously embarrassed, though he wasn't really sure why.

"No." He concentrated on nibbling the spot in the hollow beneath her jaw, and got rewarded by her quick sigh. "But I like surprises where you're concerned."

"My father painted those figurines." Her tone was more serious, so Duncan stopped nibbling at her cheek and enjoyed the silk of her hair instead.

"He did a great job, from what I can see."

She held his arms tight, like she was scared he was about to back away from her. "The tool belt's mine."

"Yeah." Damn it, his imagination could see her wearing that thing, and not to run upstairs and fix a banister. His erection strained against his jeans.

"I need tools. Sibyls live here. Sibyls with tempers."

"No argument. It's just that the rest of the brownstone is kind of . . . fluffy, compared to this."

"I'm not friggin' fluffy. At all." Then, "I don't let many people in here, Duncan. I don't let anybody in here."

Duncan kissed Bela's neck again and turned her loose, understanding that she needed a minute to get her bearings, and feeling pleased that she had opened her door to him. His body cooperated, at least for the moment, cooling down enough for him to start wondering about the stuff on her nightstand.

"About the fluffy thing, that's a matter of opinion," he said, then pointed to the cup with the ball and feather. "Is that pink thing a Spaldeen? I heard about those old reject tennis balls from guys in my building after I moved here."

Bela nodded. She started for the nightstand, then stopped, her hand outstretched like she wanted to pick up the cup. "During the week, I had to go to the Motherhouse for training—but on the weekends, when my dad was out on job sites, my friends and I played stickball like fiends, all over the Bronx."

She leaned forward and brushed her fingers across the pink ball as her cheeks turned about the same color. "I kicked ass with a broomstick for a bat, but since I had sword practice Monday through Friday, I guess pounding on Spaldeens and other kids with a stick might have been cheating."

Duncan tried to imagine what it would have been like to run the streets as a Bronx kid, then get yanked away to some Russian castle all week long. "We played baseball in empty fields and lots where I'm from, in Georgia, but I didn't have sword practice on my side."

Bela's attention had shifted to the feather, and when she saw Duncan looking at it, too, she said, "It's an osprey feather. My mother found it on our trip to Disney World when I was eight."

He could tell from her expression that she wanted to share these things with him, and that touched his heart. He wanted to hold her all over again, but for different reasons now. "Were you an only child, Angel?"

"Yes." She lifted the feather, with its splashy brown markings.

Duncan watched the feather's journey to Bela's cheek, and a new and deeper ache for her, more emotional than sexual, opened up inside him. "Me too." He coughed, trying to ease the pressure in his chest, and pointed to the

Knicks posters. "So, what did your mom think about your sports fetish?"

Bela lowered the feather, then tucked it back in its place behind the Spaldeen. "I don't know. She died in a Legion attack during a patrol the night after we got home."

For a moment or two, Duncan didn't know what to say. Talking about people who'd been killed—he was used to that after the war and from being in law enforcement. But to hear Bela say that in such a matter-of-fact way—well, damn. He rubbed his chin. She'd had it hard since that time when she was a little Bronx brat with a broomstick.

"How long did the Sibyls fight the Legion?" he asked, to begin to get a grasp of just how hard.

Bela's hand lingered on the Disney cup, and she wasn't looking at him. "A century, give or take. Good thing Sibyls live a long time, if nothing kills them."

"A hundred years. Jesus. And I thought the Gulf was bad." His gaze traveled from Bela to the figurines on the dresser across from where she was standing. Her father had raised her from eight—her father and the old women at Motherhouse Russia.

Did those Mothers really care about her? Mother Keara seemed to, but she wasn't from Bela's group of Sibyls. Duncan had a sudden image of Bela as a little girl, sitting quiet and off to herself as everyone in the Motherhouse came and went at whatever they did. Nobody was beside her, holding her hand or talking to her. She was just sitting. Sitting and watching.

Why did that feel so true?

"How many Sibyls did you lose in that war?" Duncan heard the soft crack in his voice when he asked the question.

Bela's shrug was anything but casual. It was the same shrug that lonely little girl would have given somebody when they finally noticed her and asked if she was okay. "Motherhouse Greece could give you a count. My mother, my first triad—Dio's sister included—and Camille's first triad. So many more."

When Duncan took her in his arms this time, he felt way more than heat and desire. Those other emotions, those stronger ones, they had been inside him and growing, but now they were just . . . everything.

"What we do isn't like normal police work with wings and magic and fangs." Her head rested on his chest, and one of her hands. He covered her fingers with his. "We're soldiers. We fight wars most of New York City and the rest of the world never even know about, and people die."

She pulled back just enough for him to see her face, which darkened until Duncan felt her sadness like a weight in his own gut. "Lots of good people die. Sometimes I think I'm moving on, and sometimes I can't stop thinking about it."

He ran his thumb along her jaw, brushing away a single tear. "I still dream about the desert all the time, and it's been nearly twenty years."

Bela seemed to consider this, then rested her cheek on his chest again. Duncan held her for a long time, but not long enough, because it could never be long enough.

Time . . .

He didn't want to think about time, but it ticked in his mind anyway, moving forward whether he tracked it or not.

His world had gone crazy, and Bela was the only sane thing around him. He didn't want to hurt her or burden her, God, no. Never that. But she didn't seem like the kind of woman who took on burdens she didn't want.

Should he trust that?

What were the rules when he only had a few weeks to keep breathing?

To hell with rules, anyway.

He kissed her hair, her ear, then stroked her shoulders

and back. "I got one more question. Has your room always looked like this?"

She shifted against his chest, and gave a contented sigh when he held her closer. "I didn't get the last three Knicks posters until a year ago."

"Well, that makes it definite, even if I'm an Atlanta Hawks fan."

She drew back to meet his gaze. "That makes what definite?"

Duncan kept her close. He couldn't have turned her loose, even if ten demons broke down the door. Every detail flared in his mind, from the silk of her hair on his arms to the way her lips tugged into a little smile that seemed happy and right.

"I love you, Angel."

Bela's mouth came open, and her eyes went wide. She didn't pull away from him, even though the more noble part of him thought she should.

He put two fingers against her soft lips. "I know I'm a selfish bastard, to ask if you're willing to deal with more death after what you've been through—but I'll do whatever it takes to make you mine for the time I've got left."

Her expression shifted from shock to distance, then seemed to come back to him completely. She slipped his fingers into her mouth, setting him on fire when she ran her warm, soft tongue over his knuckles.

Once. Twice. Again.

Damn, that was tearing him up.

And she knew it.

He could tell by the spark in her dark, beautiful eyes. She let his fingers slide across her lips, making sure her teeth caught the tips as he pulled them free.

"You don't have to do anything," she whispered. "I'm already yours."

Duncan drew her even tighter against him, and her deep, giving kiss sealed her in his heart forever. She lifted her arms for him to pull her shirt and bra over her head, then took his T-shirt off, and his jeans. Her slacks and underwear slipped past her hips when he pushed them down.

Holding her, bare skin to bare skin, had to be the closest thing to heaven he'd ever reach. Duncan was somewhere past hard and aroused, past needing her, even past wanting her. He'd reached craving and starving, but he refused to rush through a single second of making love to her. His woman. His for as long as he could stay alive to please her.

"You're beautiful, Angel. I never want to stop touching you."

She answered him with a soft purr, and her hands started moving. "I think you're beautiful, too."

His scars, the old ones and the new ones, didn't seem to put her off at all. She touched them without any hesitation, like she was trying to memorize every rip, tear, and jagged line on his body. Her breasts pushed upward between her moving arms, and the dinar hummed as her nipples rubbed across the metal.

When he kissed her, she wrapped her arms around his neck and her legs around his waist, giving herself to him completely.

Duncan eased back until he felt the bed touch the back of his legs, then sat on the edge with his angel in his lap, her legs pressed against his hips, kissing her head, leaning lower to taste her neck. She pushed up her breasts for him to sample, then moaned and ran her nails across his shoulders. There was so much he wanted to say to her, but words wouldn't be enough.

He showed her with his tongue on her nipples. He showed her with his mouth on her breasts, her chest, her shoulders, kissing everywhere he went. He showed her with his fingers sliding into her warm juices, then slipping inside her, making her writhe and cry out and grip the sides of his head as she leaned back against the arm he had around her waist.

Bela's dark hair tumbled around her cheeks, and her eyes squeezed tight as she pushed herself against his hand, her ass rubbing across his erection with each thrust. Duncan waited for her breathing to get short and fast, then eased his fingers out, grasped her hips, and lifted her.

Her eyes came open, nothing but dark fire as she pressed her hands against his face. "Yes." She kissed him as she moved in his grip until he felt her warm center over his sensitive lower head. His heart thumped in time with each word she said.

"Yes. Yes. Yes."

He brought her down hard, and she took him deep, with a low, screaming moan that drove him crazy. He lifted her and brought her down again and again, driving himself inside her hot, tight depths. Her hips ground against his. She leaned toward him, hard nipples ready for biting, and he caught them both with his teeth.

The floor rattled, shaking the bed and making her squeeze him tighter.

God. Almost there. This woman pushed his control.

Bela shoved his shoulders, urging him backward, until his shoulders hit the bed's cotton spread.

Duncan lay back, thrusting even harder, groaning with the sweet perfection of seeing her on top of him. She touched herself everywhere as he moved her up and down, pushing into her, pushing her toward climax.

She rode him like she'd been waiting for him all day, all year, her whole life.

"Nothing sweeter than you, Angel." His voice was just a growl. "Nothing better."

Her nails tracked past the coin, digging across his chest.

Her head tipped back, thrusting her breasts high as her walls clenched. Her whole body pulsed and shook as she screamed, and he was done, he was gone, groaning and spilling himself inside her until there was nothing left at all.

Bela draped herself forward, and he wrapped his arms tight around her.

"Unbelievable," he whispered into her ear, and she shivered, sending shocks through his spent muscles.

Duncan started to pull out, but she whispered, "Stay. Stay forever."

New, sweet heat filled him, and he found her lips, kissing her as the room started shaking all over again, answering the slow, cool flow of her earth energy.

Then the walls *really* shook as something down the hall exploded.

Bela's mouth froze on Duncan's, and she got very still.

From upstairs came Andy's sleepy, irritated, "What the fuck was that?"

From down the hall in the lab, Camille yelled, "Damnit, Bela, all that banging around blew up my hydrazoic acid. It stinks like hell in here now."

Bela pushed herself away from Duncan's mouth long enough to yell, "Later, Camille!"

"Hydrazoic acid." He gazed at his angel as she frowned, rubbing the tight muscles in the small of her back. "Hydrazoic acid?"

Bela glared down at him and gave his hair a yank. "You're the one who wanted to leave a fire Sibyl alone in a laboratory."

Duncan turned his head enough to glance at the tools in the corner. "You could throw that leather belt on and go help her clean the mess. I'd like to see you wearing that thing, all naked and hot—"

She kissed him.

Duncan kissed her back. He tucked her against his chest and cradled her there, adoring every inch of her, and every second she gave him.

"I love you," she whispered, biting his ear hard enough that he felt it in his slowly waking cock. "But you'd look better naked in that tool belt. I'm sure of it."

(24)

The last person Bela wanted to see after three delicious days and nights of making love to Duncan was Jack Blackmore.

What a buzzkill.

Good thing she'd left Andy back at the townhouse to supervise Camille, who was still blowing shit up in the lab every few hours, trying to simulate the projective metal in Duncan's dinar. Bela smoothed her white tunic over her jeans, wondering what would be left of the brownstone when she and Dio and Duncan got back.

Duncan pulled a chair out for her, and she seated herself at a wooden table in an interrogation room on West Thirtieth, in the old Fourteenth Precinct station house the OCU still used to interface with the public. He pulled out a chair for Dio on the opposite side of the table, and Dio sat as Duncan headed out to get Merin Alsace for his interview.

Dio was wearing a dress, short-sleeved and knee-length, with bold camel and burgundy patterns that made her blond hair and gray eyes seem almost electric in the big pane of one-way glass that took up the end of the room. Jack Blackmore glanced at Dio but didn't leer, so Bela decided not to rattle a hole in the floor and stuff him in it. For now.

He dropped a stack of files on the table, then eased his tall, muscular frame into the chair at the head. He was favoring the knee he'd hurt when Andy washed him out of the townhouse, and his right eye was still purple with an interesting green tinge. "Creed and Nick already gave you copies of what we have in these files, and there's nothing new so far."

"We've been all through it," Dio said. "Pretty thorough information. We don't have anything to add yet, either."

"They know you're not with the NYPD, but we weren't specific beyond calling you special liaisons." Blackmore arranged a digital tape recorder the size of a cell phone next to the folders he'd brought. "You can ask questions, but back off if his lawyer objects. We don't need him wondering too much about your official title and capacity."

"Got it." Bela glanced away from Blackmore's bruised face, remembering this place from back before the townhouse had become the center of Sibyl-OCU operations. She'd always thought the refurbished building looked like a castle, with its stone façade and turrets. The Traffic Task Force had its headquarters here, and the OCU used it, too, knowing that nobody paid much attention to the top floor.

The stenciled letters on the double doors leading into the handful of rooms said *Police Annex*. It was nothing but a holding cell, a few desks, an office, a storeroom converted into this interrogation room, and a couple of all-purpose areas crammed with old files and gear. The whole place smelled like dust and old typewriter ink, but the OCU could interview people here without having to reveal Sibyls and demons and whatever else might be slithering through the halls at Headcase Quarters. Officially, the annex was listed as an overflow for Midtown South, and that was enough to answer most questions.

Duncan came in with Reese Patterson, who had on a lightweight gray summer suit tailored to fit his broad proportions. The tall, awkward young man who came in after him had on jeans, and a green T-shirt that read GLOBAL WARMING—NOW *THAT'S* HOT, printed over a picture of the earth on fire. Bela thought he looked about eighteen instead of twenty-seven, just a few years younger than her, like the OCU profile had indicated. He had big brown eyes and a wannabe beard, and standing in between Duncan's muscles and Patterson's bulk, Merin Alsace looked like a kid in serious need of a few protein shakes.

The three men took the table's remaining seats, with Duncan closest to Bela, Patterson at the end, and Alsace next to Dio. Not a typical bare-bones interrogation setup, where a suspect got crammed in the corner farthest from the door, isolated from the light switches and thermostat and exit, just to add to the freak-out. But still probably intimidating, with Blackmore and Duncan looking so police-professional in their black slacks, white shirts, and black ties.

Alsace gave Dio and Bela the once-over but didn't seem too interested in either of them. Patterson, of course, gave Dio a flourish and nod. "Glad to see you again, pretty lady."

Dio smiled at him, and the expression seemed genuine. Bela thought she liked the guy, though not the way Patterson would have preferred.

Merin Alsace wasn't smiling at all. He eyed Reese Patterson like the lawyer was a traitor to the realm, and kept doing it the whole time Blackmore and Patterson discussed the digital recorder. Bela catalogued everything in her mind, from the way Alsace's mouth twitched as he got more annoyed to where his eyes focused when Patterson argued a point with Blackmore on Alsace's behalf. She was no police detective, but all Sibyls learned the basics of questioning subjects, like getting a good fix on their behavioral patterns before the tough questions start.

A few minutes later, Blackjack switched on the digital recorder.

Alsace seemed to be familiar with the routine, because the minute Blackmore pressed the recorder's on button, he faced Blackmore and spoke directly toward the microphone area of the machine. "I've already talked to the police twice, so I'm not sure how this is going to help."

Blackmore's expression remained stern but kind, and Bela realized he was adopting a good-father style designed to put Alsace at ease. "We've read the interviews, Merin, and we appreciate your cooperation so far."

Alsace's irritated posture relaxed a fraction, and Bela awarded a few points to Blackmore in her mind.

"Uh, thanks," Alsace said. "So, is this a follow-up?"

Blackmore nodded toward Patterson at the other end of the table. "I'm sure your attorney explained that we're a special division of the NYPD, and we check into crimes that have unusual elements. What he might have left out is that we investigate illegal activity that appears to involve aspects of the occult."

Bela let her earth senses ease forward toward Alsace, and she felt a whisper of Dio's wind moving, too. He didn't react to Blackmore's mention of the occult, at least not on an elemental level.

Alsace's eyes widened, and he shook his head. "Katrina didn't have anything to do with the supernatural. She was heavy into church."

"Religion doesn't rule out interest in paranormal phenomena." Dio's voice sounded as soft as a breeze, but Alsace's answer came fast and firm.

"It did for my sister. Katrina thought anything outside of strict Christian interpretations was evil."

Okay, that had a lot of emotion. Bela could taste Alsace's forceful feelings, even if she couldn't identify them. Still no elemental energy, though. She made eye contact with Duncan, and gave him a slight shake of her head to let him know.

He acknowledged her communication with a tap of his fingers on the table. His gray eyes shifted colors, back and forth, but whatever John Cole was telling him, Duncan didn't bring it into the interrogation.

"What about you, Merin?" Blackmore picked up the ball

again and ran with it. "Do you have any interest in the supernatural?"

Alsace shifted his weight in his chair, and his tone grew more defensive. "I believe in it, if that's what you mean. I'm Wiccan."

Blackmore's face remained completely neutral, and his tone reflected no judgment when he asked, "How did Katrina feel about that?"

"She hated it." Alsace focused on Blackmore, more or less ignoring everyone else at the table, including his attorney. "Katrina gave me a lot of shit about it when we were younger, but we put that to rest after our parents died."

"Because she was their sole heir?" Duncan's turn now. He was playing hard-ass to Blackmore's nice daddy. The shifting eye color definitely added to the effect. "If it weren't for your sister, you wouldn't even have a trust fund, would you?"

Alsace looked at Reese Patterson, who gave him a nod to continue.

"At first, yeah, that was it." Alsace addressed his answer to Blackmore. "We hadn't talked in about five years when my dad passed. I was living in San Francisco and working for the Climate Change Awareness Foundation—C-CAF."

Blackmore rested one hand on his stack of folders. "But you came home for the funeral. Then you stayed because . . . ?"

Alsace put his own hands on the table, then stared at his fingers. "I stayed in New York City because Katrina told me she'd set up the trust fund and give me an allowance if I did, and if I went to church with her at least once a month."

"You must have resented that," Blackmore relaxed in his seat, seeming even more sympathetic. "I hated it when my mother made me go to Sunday school."

"It wasn't so bad," Alsace said. "I picked up lots of

donors for C-CAF from her congregation, and the people were pretty nice. Katrina and I agreed on a year in the city, but I got used to the place. Even the church." He glanced up at Blackmore, who reassured him with a calm smile. "There's as much going on here as California, in my opinion—with the environmental movement, I mean. And here, I'm closer to D.C. to join marches and help with lobbying."

Bela was still tracking Alsace's reactions, and no elemental energy moved around him at all. She decided to try a question of her own, to see where it took them. "Is global warming your only cause?"

Alsace straightened up, happy to answer this one. "I'm a vegetarian, and I strongly advocate no meat or animal products or by-products. And I belong to two antiwar and disarmament groups." He named them, and then Dio picked up the thread.

"Do you practice your magick alone, or do you belong to a coven?"

Both Duncan and Blackmore frowned at the words *magick* and *coven*, but Bela warned them off with a glare. Patterson, she noted, didn't seem to have a problem with the terms.

"We have a little group," Alsace said, "but it's small. We get together every week or so."

Blackmore acted surprised, or maybe it wasn't an act. "Was Katrina aware of that?"

Alsace shook his head, and Bela saw shame and guilt etch into each line and shadow on his face. She suspected the emotions rose from lying to his sister and shutting her out of his life, not because he thought practicing his beliefs was wrong.

"It would have hurt her." His gaze went back to his hands, which were still folded on the table. "She liked believing she'd brought me to the light, you know? To her faith."

Duncan's eyes shifted colors again, from black to gray. "Would she have cut you off financially if she found out?"

"Not possible," Patterson cut in, managing to look at Duncan instead of Dio. "The trust was irrevocable."

Alsace let out a breath. He sounded more sad than combative when he said, "I got my share, and it's plenty. But I'd rather have my sister. She was—" He let out a breath. "Katrina was a good person."

Bela's senses registered his deep sadness, but nothing past that.

Duncan's shoulders hitched backward, like he, too, might be battling some powerful emotion. Somehow the colors of his eyes were perfectly blended, gray at the center and black around the edges.

"Have you ever crossed into curses or negative spells?" Dio asked her question in the sweetest voice, but Alsace physically recoiled from her, obviously disgusted by what she implied.

"No. That's against everything I believe."

Bela thought about the humans in black sweatshirts who had helped the Rakshasa disrupt Duncan's healing. "Do you know people who do believe in drawing power from perverted rituals?"

"Nobody." Alsace sounded emphatic.

Bela glanced from Duncan to Blackjack, until she was sure they understood that Alsace didn't seem to be hiding any secret store of elemental power. The answers he had given seemed straightforward and unrehearsed, and his clear disgust over the suggestion that he would violate the basic tenets of his Wiccan faith lent him credibility.

Blackmore took the finish, since he was the one who had established the best relationship. "Merin, if you and your group hear of a coven practicing perverted rituals, will you let us know? It could help us find your sister's killer."

"Yeah, absolutely." Alsace took the card Blackmore offered him and tucked it into his jeans pocket. "And—

thanks. For trying to hunt down who murdered Katrina. I wasn't sure anybody still gave a shit."

Blackmore shook Alsace's hand, then turned his focus to making notes on a pad beside the stack of folders.

"We care," Duncan told Alsace, breaking out of the hard-ass role. "And we'll do whatever we can to get Ms. Drake some justice."

He stood to see Patterson and Alsace out of the interrogation room, and Alsace shook Duncan's hand before they left.

About ten seconds after they cleared the room's door, Dio said, "I got nothing."

"Me neither." Bela leaned back in her chair. "If Merin Alsace has elemental talent, it's buried under a shield so skillful even a Mother couldn't detect it."

Dio frowned. "Damn, that was a lot of preparation for ten minutes of talking and no real results."

Blackmore didn't look up from his notepad, but he gave a little chuckle. "Welcome to *my* world, Ms. Allard. And we aren't even finished yet."

According to Blackmore's files, Jeremiah Drake had told the first officers who interviewed him that he and Katrina were divorcing because they'd "grown apart"—nothing more, nothing secret, nothing special.

Bela thought that was a cliché, but there was nothing on record to contradict him. The NYPD hadn't turned up any domestic violence complaints or society newspaper columns whispering about public disagreements or dissention. Every photo the police provided showed two dignified people who appeared to get along peacefully if not well—and no suggestive pictures of either Katrina or Jeremiah with someone else.

When Jeremiah Drake arrived about an hour later, Bela noted the same dignity she had seen in the photos collected by the NYPD. He seemed as different from Merin Alsace as he was from Reese Patterson. Average height, fit, dark hair with gray streaks—older than Katrina by about fifteen years. His slacks and shirt were higher-end but not designer, and when he spoke, he sounded well educated without being conceited.

"You already know I didn't profit from my wife's death," he said by way of introducing himself as he took the seat next to Dio, disregarding the digital tape recorder like he really didn't care if it captured every word he said. He rested his hands beside it, easily avoiding the microphone area. "The NYPD has our financial records—most of what Katrina had went to her charitable foundation."

Duncan opened the folder he had taken from Blackmore and placed on the table in front of him, and he glanced at the page on top. "In your first interview, you told the investigators that you and Mrs. Drake never mingled your finances."

"That's right." Drake's energy matched his words exactly, as far as Bela could tell, and like Alsace, he showed no evidence of elemental talent. "We kept our business interests separate from the outset, since we both came to the marriage with means."

Blackmore took the hard-ass role this time, sounding gruff. "Bet you resented her routing her wealth to that foundation."

"I expected her to do just that, Captain Blackmore." Drake's tone got chilly at the challenge. "We weren't selfish robber barons. Katrina and I understood that we had enough money, and we agreed to give the rest back to society. My will is structured similarly, providing for my son, Walker, but splitting the bulk of the proceeds between my business and the United Way."

Still no hint of elemental energy.

When Bela stole a glance at Duncan, she noticed that his eyes had gone black again, with gray at the centers.

Dio's wind energy stirred the air in the room, and she

asked, "Did you attend church with your wife, Mr. Drake?"

Drake turned his focus to her, and his expression communicated both surprise and offense. "Excuse me?"

"Your religious preferences, sir." Dio kept her tone respectful, but she pushed ahead. "Could you tell us about them?"

Drake gave Reese Patterson a look. The attorney scooted his fingers on the table in a go-ahead motion.

Drake sighed. "I'm not religious. That wasn't something I shared with Katrina."

Bela went after the bottom line. "Have you had any experience with the occult or people who claim to dabble in the supernatural?"

"No. I'm an accountant." Drake looked at Bela like she'd lost her mind. "I put my trust in numbers, computers, and reality. What makes you think Katrina's murder had anything to do with the occult?"

"What do you think motivated the killer?" Duncan asked.

Jeremiah Drake went pale, and his emotions surged across Bela's earth-enhanced awareness. Normal human emotions, no elemental enhancements. "I have no idea what would drive a maniac to do—to do *that* to anyone, Detective."

Duncan paused for a moment, then went back to the file he had opened. "You told the initial investigators that Katrina didn't mention feeling threatened or concerned about her safety. You said you didn't know she had hired a professional bodyguard to look after her."

"John Cole. That was his name, right?" Drake raised his fingers to his chest in a quick, almost unconscious movement before putting his hand back on the table. "The man who wore the gold coin around his neck. He was killed in DUMBO the same night Katrina died."

Duncan gave no response except to keep looking at

Drake, encouraging him by not interrupting him. Bela's eyes rested on Duncan's shirt, where she could see the outline of the dinar underneath it, but Drake didn't seem to notice.

"I met John Cole once," Drake said, "but I thought he was just looking after her at the event she was chairing that night, because of the neighborhood. Do you think he was pursuing the killers?"

"We're pretty sure of that, yes." Blackmore was looking at Duncan's shirt, too, but he seemed to realize that and he stopped.

"Poor man." Drake sounded like he meant it. "I don't know why Katrina didn't tell me she thought she was in danger. We were divorcing, but we were still friends. I would have stayed with her. I would have helped her."

Duncan closed his folder. "Any idea what would scare a woman with firm Christian beliefs badly enough to answer an ad for a bodyguard who specialized in paranormal threats?"

"Paranormal—that's what Cole was advertising?" Genuine surprise from Drake. Still no elemental energy. "I find that hard to believe."

"I know you've been asked this question before," Blackmore said, "but Mr. Drake, can you think of anyone who had a grudge against Katrina? Anyone who would benefit from her death?"

At this, Drake's demeanor changed again.

It was subtle, but enough to make Bela's instincts jangle like Sibyl wind chimes. Dio lifted her chin, obviously picking up the same abnormal tension Bela sensed.

"I'm afraid I can't help you there." Drake's hands almost curled into fists on the table, but he relaxed them just as fast. "My wife had no enemies."

Lie, Bela thought, her pulse picking up.

Jeremiah Drake did know someone who might have

wanted to hurt Katrina, but he clearly didn't want to share that information.

Why?

Duncan chased around the financial issues and divorce proceedings for another half hour, but they didn't make much progress. Drake didn't have any more strong reactions, and he never showed a flicker of elemental power.

This time, when Duncan saw Drake and Reese Patterson out of the Police Annex, Dio cut loose with a yawn. "I'm so glad we don't have to do *this* for a living."

Blackmore packed up his folders and digital recorder without responding to her offhand insult, and Bela decided to make her exit. If the two of them decided to spar, she didn't want to get caught in all the yelling and tornados.

When Bela came out of the interrogation room, Jeremiah Drake was standing next to a teenage boy, talking on a cell phone about a stock transaction. He had a finger in his free ear and a tense expression. The boy, who looked to be sixteen or seventeen, seemed unfazed by Drake's mounting tension, and Bela assumed this would be Walker Drake, Jeremiah's son by a previous marriage. The stepson who'd made Katrina's life miserable.

Walker looked like a younger version of his father—same dark hair and handsome features, but without the calm, dignified bearing. The kid's face was a study in barely controlled insolence. The navy jacket, striped tie, and khaki slacks he was wearing suggested one of Manhattan's higher-end private academies, and the golden emblem stitched across the jacket pocket confirmed this. Walker was wearing his collar open, and the tie had been loosened to hang low on his chest. The look and sarcastic smile he gave Bela made her want to slap him hard enough to spin his head around—and cover up her boobs.

Little shit.

She gave Walker a quick once-over with her elemental power, and as John Cole had insisted in his conversation through Camille, the boy had no traces of elemental energy or power. The OCU could jump through all the hoops required to get permission to question a minor—if they could pull it off, given that medical reports confirmed that Walker and his girlfriend had been basically unconscious from a long night and day of partying when Katrina was killed—but it probably wouldn't be worth the effort. The OCU's forensic accountants had already confirmed that Walker didn't have large sums of money available to hire the Rakshasa, and he hadn't made anything other than penny-ante transactions leading up to the killing, or after.

A few moments later, Walker followed his father out of the annex, and Bela wasn't sorry to see him go.

As the double doors to the annex closed, Bela turned her attention to Duncan, who was speaking to Reese Patterson in low tones a few feet away from the entrance. The lawyer appeared to be trying to convince Duncan of something, but Duncan wasn't buying it.

When Patterson saw Bela coming, he gave up his campaign and offered Bela his hand. She shook it as he asked, "Will I be seeing you again?"

"Probably." She smiled at him. He really was likeable, his fetish for Dio and hot blondes aside.

"I'll look forward to it." Patterson grinned, then made his way through the doors.

Bela watched him go.

When the doors closed and caught, she took Duncan's hand, way past needing a little contact with him. "What did Patterson want from you?"

Duncan kissed her wrist, then picked up her other hand and did the same. He lowered his arms, keeping a firm grip on her fingers. "He wants me to go see John's will, even though he doesn't think it'll help the case."

Bela glanced toward the closed doors, where Patterson had been. "That's . . . strange. What does John want you to do? What's he saying?"

"Not a damned thing. He ran his mouth the entire time we were in session, telling me that Alsace and Drake are a total waste of time, and we were screwing up by pursuing either of them." Duncan let go of her hands. "But about the will, I've got nothing. Just silence. I think maybe he's embarrassed, but I don't know why."

Dio came out of the interrogation room just ahead of Blackmore. She held him up by stretching, then headed to Bela and Duncan, a few paces ahead of Blackmore. "Drake got bothered when we asked him about Katrina's enemies. What do you think that was about, Sharp?"

Blackmore was the one who answered when he joined them, carrying a battered leather briefcase. "No idea, unless he was thinking about how his brat kid fought with her. It's not enough to go on to poke around any deeper, at least on an official level."

His look was meaningful, but Bela and Dio were way ahead of him.

Bela already had the annex doors open, and they headed out with Duncan in tow, ready to do some more investigating—Sibyl style.

25

Exhausted and disappointed.

That about summed up the look on Bela's face when they got back to the brownstone around three that afternoon. Duncan hated seeing that, but all he could do was hold her hand as Dio unlocked the front door, used her wind to blow it open, and stalked inside.

Duncan followed, keeping them a few paces back in case Dio blew over anything important. Andy and Camille were sitting on the couch, and Andy was touching up a big bloody cut on Camille's right cheek.

"Beaker shrapnel," Andy said before Duncan could ask. "It'll be fine by morning. Sibyls heal fast—when they're not working with poisonous gases and radioactive isotopes."

When Bela didn't react, Duncan decided it probably wasn't necessary to bail out the front door and take cover.

"We didn't find shit." Dio dropped into the chair closest to the couch. "We went by Merin Alsace's apartment building, Jeremiah Drake's penthouse, Katrina Drake's main charity office—shit. We even went by where Reese Patterson lives and scared the hell out of two raccoons while we were sneaking around through the dumpsters. Not a shred of elemental energy in any of those places, other than ours."

"No shields, no remnants, nothing." Bela looked so tired that Duncan wanted to pick her up and carry her straight to bed. Because of patrols, Sibyls often slept during the afternoon, and she seemed to be used to that schedule. "The only thing I can think of is to find out where Merin Alsace's coven meets and check those locations, but his aversion to perverted magick seemed pretty real to me."

Dio shook her head, and little gusts of wind made chimes jingle across the living room. "This comes back to Jeremiah Drake. I know it does. He really didn't like the question about Katrina having enemies. I'm going upstairs to see what I can find in newspaper and television archives."

She pushed herself out of the seat and took off, leaving a rush of moving air in her wake.

"She's cranked up," Andy said as Duncan stared after Dio, confused.

What kind of library did Dio have upstairs, anyway? There were a few rooms, but enough for that much paper and digital storage?

Bela massaged his forearm and answered his question like he'd asked it out loud. "Air Sibyls do a little better with elementally shielded computers than most of us, and Motherhouse Greece keeps searchable archives of newspapers and television news reports in a database that we can access."

Duncan took Bela's hand in his and gave her knuckles a quick kiss. "Which newspapers and news shows?"

"All of them, I think." Bela yawned.

Duncan knew that Sibyl science and equipment outstripped standard human technology, but now he realized it was way more than that. The Dark Crescent Sisterhood had ways of tracking history and information he barely could fathom.

From the couch came a loud "Ouch!" from Camille, followed by a burst of flames and the scent of scorched hair—and a big splash of water.

"*Now* you fire up and cook something?" Andy pulled a sprinkler head loose and let it shower Camille for her while she patted a cooked section of her red curls. "My *hair*?"

"Sorry," Camille muttered as she and the couch dripped.

"Come on, Angel." Duncan read Bela's exasperation in

the tight lines around her eyes, and he wrapped his arm around her waist. "Let's get you to bed before you fall asleep on your feet."

She leaned into his hug, then let him lead her toward the kitchen as Andy and Camille argued about whether the ointment Andy had put on Camille's cheek smelled like dirty diapers.

"Just you make sure you let her sleep, Sharp," Andy barked from the couch.

The swinging door closed behind them.

"Or not!" Camille yelled as they headed through the kitchen and down the basement stairs.

When they got to the bedroom, which Duncan now called "the locker room" to make her smack him in the shoulder, Duncan helped Bela out of her jeans and tunic. Her languid movements and closed eyes reminded Duncan of an impressionistic dancer, and he had to keep glancing at the Knicks posters to cool off while he rubbed her shoulders and kissed her head, then pulled back the sheet and blanket for her.

I can do this. . . .

A few seconds later, when he climbed into bed naked and eased over beside her, his resolve to let her rest nearly fell completely apart.

I . . . can . . . do . . . this. . . .

She reached out to him and hugged his neck as he tucked her in beside him, making sure the sheet covered her shoulder. "It feels good, just lying here with you, Duncan."

IcandothisifyougotosleepNOW. . . .

He pressed his lips against the top of her head. "Rest, before I prove I'm not a gentleman."

Bela's soft laugh made his skin tingle. A few moments later, though, her breathing became rhythmic and soft. He kissed her again, closed his own eyes, and—

* * *

And he was standing on the ugly carpet in the hallway outside Reese Patterson's office door.

"What the hell?"

Duncan grabbed his legs to be sure he was dressed, and he found himself in jeans and one of his Army T-shirts, the same clothes he had worn the day before. He had left them draped over the baseball bats in the chair beside Bela's bed.

Now he was wearing them. No Glock. No badge. But he had his watch, which told him it was a quarter to eight, about an hour and a half before Bela and her girls would hit the streets and park on patrol—and he was supposed to be with them.

But he didn't remember putting the clothes or the watch on, much less catching a cab or wandering all the way to East Harlem.

"I don't sleepwalk," he said out loud.

John Cole's voice was cold and flat when he answered. *You didn't. I brought us here.*

Duncan twitched at the sound, then clenched his fists at what John said. "What the hell does that mean?"

I waited for you to fall asleep, then took over.

"Took over?" Duncan's blood boiled huge and fast like water on a gas stove. "You miserable, chickenshit little fuck. If I could get you out of my head, I'd beat the living shit out of you."

He turned to head back to the brownstone, but he stumbled. Almost fell. His feet felt clumsy, like they weren't even his. He had to prop his hand on the wall to keep from busting his ass.

John.

"Asshole," Duncan snarled.

Before he could bash his head against the old paint on the building's wall, Patterson opened his door. He eyed Duncan like people eye drunks staggering by on the sidewalk. "Um, good. You're here. Kinda freaked me out when you called—you didn't sound like yourself."

Duncan let go of the wall and tested his balance, which seemed fair enough at the moment. John seemed to have taken a powder, which was a good thing, because Duncan was close to beating in his own brains to get rid of the bastard.

"I wasn't myself, Mr. Patterson." He tried taking a step. Made it, no problem. That was a relief. "It's a long story."

"Well, come in and let's get this done." Patterson stepped aside for Duncan to enter. "And Detective, this is on me, for Katrina."

"I can pay you," Duncan grumbled as he edged past Patterson into the reception room. He had plenty of money from what he'd banked during the Gulf War and accounts he inherited from his parents and other relatives. Since starting with the NYPD, he'd lived in a small apartment in an old building and spent very little. Most of the time he just worked.

"Appreciate it." Patterson led the way to his main office, then went around his desk and lifted a stack of papers. "But no, this is gratis. I owe her that, and lots more."

He handed the papers to Duncan, who was trying his best not to act too surprised or confused, since Patterson had no idea a ghost had brought Duncan to his door without one clue why.

The papers were thick stock, official-looking, with stamps and seals. It took him just a minute of reading to realize what was happening. "Shit. This is the will. John's will."

Patterson seemed to take his irritation as shock or leftover grief, and he gave Duncan a somber nod. "I picked it up from Bestro and Perman today. Gwen Perman owed me a favor—but I promised them I'd have you sign everything, to make it official and get it off her to-do list."

Duncan was thumbing through all the legalese, barely paying attention, and then he got to sections about assets.

His chest tightened right up, staring at all those numbers,

and he looked up at Patterson. "No. I don't want this. I don't want any of it."

Patterson's big mouth pulled into a frown, and he jabbed one thick pointer finger at the paper on top. "Son, that's four *million* dollars, and it doesn't even count the other assets. Full control of the Societal Aid Fund—it's a lot. Even if you dump the cash, you're still talking millions."

Duncan couldn't speak. He was somewhere between furious and freaked, and John, the stupid bastard, was keeping way quiet.

"Four million dollars changes lives." Patterson raised both arms and swept them around to indicate the entirety of his office. "I was a backstreet ambulance chaser who got lucky with the Drakes, and to tell you the truth, before I met Katrina, that's all I wanted to be. But special women can change people, you know?"

Duncan had to clear his throat to keep his composure. "Oh, yeah. I'm clear on that one."

"Katrina changed me forever." Patterson's expression turned sad. "I owe her everything I am, and that's why I rode you at the interrogation, to come here and see this will. Once I realized you were John Cole's heir—it's about Katrina, you see? It's about her legacy. She passed the baton to John, and he passed it to you. Somebody's got to carry on her good work. I'll do whatever it takes to help you do that, Mr. Sharp."

This was more than Duncan could take. Completely. Four million dollars, a house, a charity organization. What the hell would he do with all that shit?

Leave it to Bela, John said. *The house, and the Societal Aid Fund. The money goes to Sister Marianne at Mercy for the Homeless.*

Duncan stayed still, even though he wanted to start yelling at John.

Leave it to Bela? What the—

But wait a minute.

In a few weeks, he wouldn't be here. And the Dark Crescent Sisterhood probably had plenty of need for houses. He'd be willing to bet they had mad skills when it came to business and making money, too. Katrina Drake's charity would never have to worry about failing, or even being underfunded.

Now you're getting it. John's voice drifted through his thoughts, sounding a little smug.

Fuck off, Duncan shot back, as loudly as he could think it. Then he asked Patterson, "How long does it take to do a will?"

The lawyer shook his head, and his gaze dropped to the bulge of the dinar under Duncan's T-shirt. "Does some kind of insanity go with wearing that coin?"

"Maybe. And I'm going to need access to this money."

"I can cut you a check from the office war chest. You reimburse me when everything gets changed over, okay?" Patterson took out a pad and pen. "We'll add a note about the temporary loan to everything else I'll be drawing up. Okay, Detective Sharp. Your will. Fire away."

In just under an hour, they were finished. Duncan made sure to leave instructions with Patterson about delivering the will to Jack Blackmore at the OCU headquarters after he died. Blackjack could be a goat prick as a commander, but as a man, he was one of the most honest—and kind—people Duncan had ever known. He'd have enough sense to hold off on giving Bela the will until she was ready to deal with it.

Just before nine, he managed to make it to the outer hall of the Mercy for the Homeless business office on Thirty-fourth near Herald Square, but they were closed. He located the right mail slot, and tucked the envelope with the check into the box with Sister Marianne's name on it.

It's what she wanted, John said as Duncan hit the pavement again, heading for the brownstone. *Katrina's foundation needed a shepherd, and the Sisters needed that cash so the mission wouldn't have to close its doors next week. I promised her, and now I've done all I can to keep that promise. Thank you.*

Duncan couldn't find a comeback to that. He resented the hell out of what John had just done to him, but since the moment Duncan made John admit how he'd failed Katrina, John had sounded like a beaten, broken man instead of the cocky bastard Duncan had always known. That last bit, about the Sisters and the foundation—John sounded more like his old self.

To be honest, Duncan didn't know what he'd do, how far he'd go to fix things, if he ever let Bela down. God forbid if he let her down and his mistake got her killed.

Don't think it, John told him. *You never want to be that man, I promise you.*

Duncan cut through a long alley to save time. It was dark, but since John had joined his brain, he could see just fine, light or no light. "Have you taken me over before, John?"

Just once, when you were still unconscious and I was trying to warn the Sibyls that the demons would come for them.

"You scared Bela to death with that shit." Duncan checked his watch and started to jog.

I know. That's one reason why I've tried not to do it again. I know she's it for you, Duncan. I wouldn't do anything to hurt her.

"Don't do it again. If you really need something, convince me."

Silence answered Duncan.

He pulled up short near the end of the alley. "If I can't know for sure Bela and her quad are safe from me—from you—I'll go to the Mothers, eat my gun, and let them finish me off. Swear to God. In a full-on battle of wills, you know who'll win."

A sigh echoed through his mind along with the sense of

John surrendering. *Yeah. I do know, Duncan. Fine. I won't do it again.*

"No matter what?"

No matter what.

Duncan turned to jog toward the sidewalk.

A hand shot out from behind a dumpster and grabbed the dinar around his neck.

Duncan yelled as an electric shock tore from his neck to his heels. He twitched and jumped from the current, but he grabbed the hand holding the coin, locked his grip on the wrist, and forced the hand backward until the coin dropped free.

A yelp of pain turned into a wail as Duncan kept bending the wrist.

A very human-sounding wail.

With a big heave, Duncan jerked a man out of his hiding place behind the blue metal trash bin to Duncan's right, then grabbed him by the fabric of his black hooded sweatshirt.

The hood came away to reveal a fairly normal-looking guy with short blond hair and blue eyes. No special or unusual marks, nothing that stood out. This guy could get lost in an airport in a big hurry, and nobody would notice him unless he pulled an Uzi and started shooting.

Blondie struggled but couldn't get himself loose. When he tried to kick Duncan, Duncan slammed him against the edge of the dumpster hard enough to crack all the bastard's teeth.

"What's your name?" Duncan's question came out in a growl, and the coin around his neck gave a sharp, long, painful buzz. The metal burned into his chest, and John's thoughts blasted forward to join with Duncan's. Duncan's awareness expanded until colors and sounds and smells seemed twice as strong. Then three or four times what they should be.

The air in the alley got colder.

Duncan held on to Blondie, but his attention shifted to the far end of the alley. Nothing visible to his eyes—but he could smell it.

Ammonia. Ammonia and blood.

He turned back to his captive. "Wanna bring your furry buddy over here and have a party?"

Blondie wheezed from the blow against the dumpster, but he choked out, "I—I've got a message. From my *culla*. From Strada."

Duncan shot a look at the Rakshasa blocking one of the alley exits. The creature had dark fur. Not the demon leader Strada, according to John's memories, but one of his brothers.

The sealed wounds along Duncan's neck, chest, and shoulder started a low, slow ache, as if in response to the Rakshasa's presence.

Recognition curled in Duncan's gut.

That's the demon who infected me.

With every fiber of his being, he wanted to crack Blondie over the head, storm down the alley, and kill the demon. Only John's desperate, wordless pleas held him back. Strength and will were one thing, but suicide—it wasn't time for that yet, and the Mothers and Dio weren't here to clean up the changing-into-a-demon mess.

Blondie must have taken his silence for waiting, so he spit out his message. "You're already infected, and no matter what help you're given, you *will* die. Strada thinks you're strong, that you've got a lot of potential. Join us. Come with me now, and we'll let the Sibyls live." Blondie's cold blue eyes narrowed. "We'll let Bela Argos live."

Duncan smashed the bastard against the dumpster two more times, feeding his rage at the Rakshasa into each blow and denting the metal. "What do you know about Bela and the Dark Crescent Sisterhood?"

Blondie's eyes were shut, and his face had twisted into a grimace. His answer came out in a whisper.

"Everything."

Duncan drew back his fist to splatter the asshole's nose all over his knuckles, but the Rakshasa at the end of the alley let out a howl that made his neck and back go stiff.

Two bass, bellowing roars answered the tiger-demon.

Blondie raised his shaking hands, and something hit Duncan in the face.

The night went dark.

Stinking, crawling things wriggled across Duncan's skin. *Energy,* John said. *Bad energy.*

Duncan couldn't help pawing it off his skin with both hands, and the rodent in the black sweatshirt took off like Old Scratch was right on his ass.

The Rakshasa at the end of the alley had all he could handle, too, busting tail to lope away from two giant golden . . . somethings.

"Shit." Duncan finished scrubbing invisible bugs off his face, then weighed running away faster than the demon against using the dumpster lid to fight. "Why'd you leave my Glock at home, John?"

The golden monsters charged him, and Duncan ripped the dumpster lid free. Adrenaline supercharged his shout as he raised the square piece of metal, intending to clock the biggest monster upside its big golden ear.

Right about that time, the monster shifted into Nick Lowell. He had a golden chain around his neck, and his badge, but he didn't have a shirt on. The other monster turned into Creed Lowell, but at least he was dressed.

Duncan thought his brain might be melting, but John's perceptions and his matched up. Definitely Creed and Nick. Duncan kept his dumpster lid ready anyway. He'd seen Rakshasa shape-shift before, in DUMBO, but they'd only held the shapes of his friends for a few seconds.

Nick and Creed slowed, then stopped in front of him, and stayed Nick and Creed.

Then Creed looked at Nick and laughed.

Nick smacked his palms against his bare chest and groaned as he made eye contact with Duncan. "Blow it out your ass, Creed. At least I got my pants this time." He jerked a thumb toward Creed. "Pretty boy here thinks he's superior because he can shift without cooking his clothes. I'm still, ah, working on that trick."

"I see that." Duncan lowered his metal lid as his pulse fell back to some semblance of normal.

"Riana and Cynda picked up a massive elemental surge over here." Creed glanced toward the mouth of the alley in time to wave at three women in battle leathers and a tall guy in jeans. With big white wings. Who was flying. "You okay, Sharp?"

"I'm not okay." Duncan stared at the flying man. "But I'm not injured."

Nick followed Duncan's gaze as he pulled a T-shirt out of his back pocket and yanked it over his head. "That's our brother Jake. He's an Astaroth, but he's invisible to most humans in his demon form. He's harmless unless you piss him off. What the hell are you doing way over here?"

"Too much to explain." *While I'm staring at a flying man-demon thing with big white wings.*

Duncan shut his eyes for a second, trying to stop the subtitles he could see in his mind. He wasn't even sure John was doing that. It was probably him, because he'd had enough of weird shit tonight.

"I need to get back to the brownstone." Duncan opened his eyes and tried to look calm and normal. "Can one of you ride shotgun?" *Because the idiot ghost in my head got me dressed and dragged me out without my Glock.*

"You go with him," Creed told Nick. "I'll stay with Jake and the triad. Meet us over by the Reservoir?"

"Done." Nick pointed to the near exit of the alley as Creed ran back to join the Sibyls . . . and Jake the flying demon. "This way's fastest. It'll take us right down the west wall beside Central Park."

"Sounds good," Duncan said. *As long as there aren't faeries or some shit waiting in the trees.*

They left the alley, walking at a good clip.

To settle his thoughts as John retreated to the back of his consciousness, Duncan asked, "So, how's Blackjack doing with his bum knee and eye?"

"He's, ah, over at Presbyterian, in the burn center—but they're letting him go tomorrow." Nick sounded casual, like that kind of shit happened all the time at Headcase Quarters. "Mother Anemone thinks she can fix the scars."

Duncan gave this new development some thought, then asked, "Mother Keara or your wife?"

Nick sighed. "My daughter. But Mother Keara put her up to it."

A block or so later, Duncan had to laugh. "I'll bet Blackjack thought he knew everything about the supernatural until he met the Sibyls."

"His learning curve with the Dark Crescent Sisterhood has been pretty steep." Nick took the lead as they crossed to the Central Park wall—and Duncan actually felt a twinge of relief when he didn't catch a hint of any faeries. "He'd better get a clue before he loses something the Mothers can't reattach."

Another few blocks went by before Nick said, "I'm surprised Bela and her bunch let you out unsupervised, Duncan."

It was Duncan's turn to sigh. "They didn't."

"Oh." Nick gave Duncan the "You poor bastard" look as they turned onto Sixty-fifth. "That's too bad, Sharp. Your learning curve's gonna be steep, too."

26

When Bela saw Duncan coming up the block with Nick, she almost gave in to the shuddering wash of relief and sat right down on the brownstone's front steps. If Mrs. Knight hadn't been in her face, she might have run to him and kissed him. Then punched him right in the face for letting her wake up without him and panic that something terrible had happened.

"The explosions just have to stop—and the smells. It's terrible." Mrs. Knight ignored the rest of the quad and glared at Bela like she was the one repeatedly detonating beakers in the basement lab, which Mrs. Knight didn't even know about. At least Bela hoped she didn't.

Mrs. Knight's red silk jogging suit made her face look darker in the yellow lights from their porches and the streetlamps. "In Charleston, I never had to deal with this level of disturbance from my neighbors. What are you trying to do, anyway? Fumigate the block?"

"We *have* seen a few cockroaches," Camille said weakly, then noticed Duncan and Nick approaching, and brightened a bit.

Andy and Dio saw them, too, and Andy let off a few rivulets of water as she glared in Duncan's general direction.

Mrs. Knight eyed Duncan and then Nick as they walked up to Bela. "What, no leather pants? You boys can't be going to the same costume party."

Duncan glanced down at his jeans, and Nick touched his T-shirt, like he was trying to be sure the fabric was still there.

Mrs. Knight rolled her eyes and stalked off to her own brownstone, grousing about inconsiderate dolts and what the police would make of those leather jumpsuits and realistic-looking costume swords. Under different circumstances, Bela thought she might like the old witch, if she'd just quit slowing them down when they were trying to get out on patrol.

"That woman's feisty," Nick muttered. "I'd quit pissing her off if I were you. She reminds me of the Mothers."

Bela barely heard Nick, or the greetings he exchanged with Andy, Dio, and Camille before he took off, jogging toward the Reservoir. She grabbed Duncan's hand and led him into the shadows beside some stairs to give them a little cover, then let go of his wrist and faced him, her pulse starting to rise—and not from pleasant sensations. For once, his handsome face and gripping eyes didn't work their magic, and she still wanted to hit him.

He stood a few inches away from her, deadly handsome in his jeans and Army T-shirt, and she imagined she could feel the heat rippling off his muscled arms. Whatever he'd been up to, he didn't seem to be hurt, or—

Or what? Closer to turning into a demon?

Bela's anger flagged. Her quad drew closer, like they could sense the roil of emotion in her belly.

You know it won't be like that. The Mothers said he'll be fine, then when the time comes, he'll go quickly. No lingering, terrible suffering. Their wards will see to that.

But what if she wasn't with him when the moment did arrive? She wouldn't get to say goodbye, or hold him or kiss him one more time.

Tears tried to push toward her eyes. "Where the hell did you go?" The question came out with force, but her voice shook. "And what the hell were you thinking? We're supposed to keep a Sibyl with you at all times."

"Sorry, Angel." His gaze fixed on hers, melting her even more. "It wasn't exactly my call."

She punched him in the shoulder, but not hard. "What does that mean?"

"I'll explain all that later." He got hold of both of her hands before she could hit him again and pressed them to his chest. Then he glanced at Camille, Dio, and Andy. "The important part is, I ran into a Rakshasa and his human helper. Sidekick. Minion. Whatever the hell you want to call him. Blond hair, blue eyes, about shoulder height on me, wearing jeans and a black hooded sweatshirt. They ambushed me in an alley."

Bela's fingers fanned across Duncan's green T-shirt as her heart gave a big skip. "Black sweatshirt with a hood?"

"Shit." Andy's steady drip picked up speed, making dozens of dark circles on the sidewalk. "Like the bastards who tried to pervert the healing."

"Has to be." Camille put her hand on her sword hilt. "*Damnit*. I'm not ready yet."

Dio's wind had kicked up to a fair breeze, and she was scanning the wall along Central Park. "Which alley? If we start there, maybe we can finally track the assholes. The trail will be fresh."

Duncan let go of Bela and grabbed the chain around his neck like it could help him remember the exact spot. "Fifty-seventh and Madison, or real close to that. The bastard jumped me at the end of the alley. Popped out from behind a blue dumpster and grabbed my dinar—shocked me like a live wire, but I got hold of him and bashed the bin with his head a few times. We should be able to find that dented dumpster."

Bela still had her hands on Duncan's chest. She let herself stare at him a few more seconds, then pulled herself together to gear up for the run to Fifty-seventh and Madison. Dio had her hand on her knives, turning south with Andy, when Camille shouted, "Wait!"

The powerful sound shocked Bela, never mind the single tendril of smoke that lifted off Camille's left shoulder.

Camille grabbed Duncan's arm before he could leave the alcove. "The man in the alley, did he touch the coin? Actually put his hand on it?"

"Yeah." Duncan lifted the chain and dinar toward her. "Think you can do something with that?"

Camille hesitated, then took the coin in her fingers, jerking and clenching her teeth against the jolt of that first contact, while she worked out how to interact with it. Duncan stayed still, grimacing, but Bela shuddered from the ripple in her earth energy, and both Dio and Andy reacted with frowns.

The three of them moved in enough to block public view of the area next to the stairs as targeted streams of fire, each little orange lasers, flickered from the tips of Camille's fingers as she handled the worn dinar. Her blue-green eyes focused on it so intently Bela half expected the gold to heat up and flow across Camille's palms. Her expression moved from excited and curious to distant, and finally she smiled.

If Bela hadn't known Camille, she might have backed away from that expression. It reminded her of Mother Yana's ancient wolf, right before she sank her teeth into some smart-ass adept.

"Come here, all of you." Camille's voice didn't have the mingled demon tones of John Cole enhancing it, but her instruction carried the pop and hiss of fire behind it, as sure and terrifying as Mother Keara when she was being fierce.

Fire was . . . speaking through her. Projection. The reverse of the usual energy exchange Sibyls used to fight and manage their powers.

Dio and Andy didn't budge an inch.

Bela couldn't say she blamed them, but she sucked it up and stepped closer to Camille, careful to keep a firm shield of earth energy between her and the dinar—and the fire Sibyl. When she got close enough, she used her own enhanced perceptions to study the coin as it shimmered in the dancing light of Camille's grasp.

"Use your earth energy to touch my fire, like we did the night of the healing." Camille's eerie, flaming tone and the smoke now pouring off her shoulders were enough to make Bela's heart race. "You can't help me follow the trace if you don't sense it, too."

Bela slowed her own breathing and tried to keep her tone neutral. "If our sentient energy gets away from us, it could do even more damage than kinetic energy. You saw that with what happened in the alley outside the townhouse. The Mothers haven't given us the go-ahead to try that again, and I agreed that we wouldn't."

Camille, or the fire inside her, snarled.

A line of fire broke across Duncan's left arm.

Bela used her earth energy to snuff the flames before he even got through wincing. Somehow, he managed not to move, which was probably a good thing, given Camille's sudden possession by her element.

"Since when do you give a shit about permission, Bela?" Camille's voice got louder, with an echo like distant explosions. "Do it. I can control us both if I have to."

Duncan gave Bela a look like, *I'm okay with it if you are,* even though it was his neck on the line. Literally. If Camille blew apart or lost her awareness, he'd get torched first.

"You're asking me to trust you with my life, Camille." Bela heard herself talking, even though she felt pretty sure Camille and Camille's fire wouldn't listen. "And Duncan's, and Dio's and Andy's, too. You're asking me to trust you with the safety of New York City."

"Yes, I am." This time Camille spoke more quietly, like she might be trying to prove she could regulate the deadly energy flowing through her, magnified by her own determination and emotions.

Damnit, fire could be tricky.

Either she did this or she'd lose Camille forever. Maybe not to fire, here, tonight, but later, when Camille couldn't get past Bela's lack of faith in her.

Can't hide, sinner.

Duncan's line, John's line, the words from an old song Bela had never heard before, from a place she had never even visited, rang through her thoughts.

She thought she grasped another layer of the meaning.

This was one of those times when Bela couldn't back away from the choices she had made. She had taken herself to Ireland and chosen Camille over the objections of the Russian Mothers and Mother Keara's warnings. She had nurtured Camille, encouraged her to find herself again— and now here she was.

Camille was ready to fight like a fire Sibyl, and wielding a power that might turn out to be greater than anyone knew what do with.

All Bela had to do was trust her.

With everything.

Bela gathered her earth power until she couldn't hold another ounce. If she was going to do this, she'd try to be sure she was the only one who paid a price if it went wrong. She wouldn't let herself look at Duncan as she joined Camille in front of him and tried to focus on the coin.

Her earth energy rumbled in her mind and heart, shifting again, making new little earthquakes in her awareness. She tried to recall the exact flavor and smell and feel of making herself into an elementally charged equivalent of a projective mirror, but she couldn't quite grab the memory of it.

Instead, she started with sampling the coin, letting her earthy awareness slide forward through Camille's fire. Touching the dinar with her elemental power didn't create one of those gut-shocking ripples she had felt when Camille took hold of the coin, so Bela extended her hand and rested two fingers on its hot golden edge.

Perverted energy slammed against her senses.

Her head snapped back.

Mistake!

But no. No, it wasn't.

She kept her shaking fingers right where they were and made herself breathe through the dark, terrible sensations. The toxic energy—she was reacting to traces of it. Bits of leftover force magnified by Camille's pyrosentience. Bela fed earth energy into Camille's perceptions, and let Camille's power feed her own. She used some of the swell to shield Duncan, but the rest she focused on the dinar.

The traces grew even more obvious, taking on a poisonous dark green color. She thought she could smell them, too. Putrid, like eggs turned black with rot, or meat with mold. It would have made her queasy if Camille's energy hadn't steadied her. Bela had no doubt she would notice where energy like this—and this *specific* energy—had touched earth.

A breeze lifted Bela's hair as Dio joined them. To Bela's wildly enhanced perceptions, she looked like she belonged on Mount Olympus, her blond hair giving off a stark golden light, and her skin turning pale white-olive, like alabaster.

"One for all, all for one," she muttered, the power of air hissing through each word, and Dio touched the coin, too.

Bela roared with the influx of power.

The groaning of the earth ran through her again as thunder and lightning echoed over Central Park. She remembered—yes, yes, this was it, this was how they had done it before at the townhouse. They needed water now, and that would make their elemental sentience stronger than ever.

But Andy held back.

Andy, of all people.

Bela waited as Dio acclimated herself, then seemed to get the pattern of the perverted energy enough to track it through the air.

Andy never joined them.

When Bela let herself acknowledge that Andy wasn't going to participate, she said, "Release together, on my mark."

Dio and Camille nodded.

"Mortar," Bela said. "Pestle."

On "Broom" they let go, and the dinar bounced back to Duncan's chest.

He covered the coin with his palm. "Damn, Angel. That was intense."

Bela touched his fingers, then turned with Dio and Camille to see about Andy, who was still standing right where Bela had left her.

Dio stalked over to the end of the stair railing where Andy waited, wind whistling across the street until the trees in the park started swaying. "What was that about?" Dio got right in Andy's face. "You're a Sibyl and in our quad—but you're following rules because you're a Mother, too?"

"Back off," Andy told her, but she didn't drip or wash Dio into the gutter, as Bela expected. Dio seemed surprised by this, too, and she instantly stopped blowing stuff over in Central Park.

Camille's approach to Andy was gentler. "We can track this energy without you, Andy, but we'd be stronger if we had your input."

"Or dead." Andy looked at Bela instead of Dio or Camille. "You three have been at this since you were babies. I just started learning a few years ago. There's no way I could challenge my water power like that. I'd kill us all."

Dio pursed her lips and looked guilty.

Camille seemed to understand with no issue, but Bela immediately wanted to kick herself. Andy had gotten so smooth with using her water energy that Bela tended to forget what a short time Andy had been a Sibyl. She was the only member of the Dark Crescent Sisterhood not born to her element and trained since childhood, save for the handful of women who had shown up at Motherhouse Kérkira once Andy's talent had manifested.

"I'm sorry." Bela put her hands on Andy's elbows, relieved to feel the dampness on her leathers. "Sometimes I don't do so well, keeping up with three other Sibyls instead of just two. I'll keep working on it, I promise. And I will get better."

"Before or after you lose the scent of that shitty energy from the dinar?" Andy's leathers streaked with a fresh round of water as Bela let her go. Andy fished out her face mask and started zipping it into place. "I'm just saying, since you risked wiping out New York City to get a fix on that stuff, we should go for it. Besides, if the Mothers got a whiff of any of this, they'll be here in, like, a minute."

"Shit," Camille whispered, pulling Dio down the sidewalk a few steps, then stopping to jam her face mask over her long red ponytail. "Let's get out of here."

"Just a sec." Duncan broke away from them and ran toward the brownstone. "I need my badge and Glock."

By the time they stopped running, Bela had broken a sweat and removed her face mask. They all had.

They'd been to Midtown East and Murray Hill, with a quick detour into the Garment District that wound back around to Gramercy and finally into the East Village. Duncan kept up pretty well, staying close beside her as she swapped off tracking duties with Camille and Dio, following the poisonous energy trace as far as they could.

"Merin Alsace's apartment is nearby." Andy pulled her little notebook out of her pocket and checked a page as they pulled up in front of what looked like an apartment building on a corner. "St. Marks and Avenue C. About a block east."

"But the trace turns in here." Dio indicated the newly refurbished building with its clean stone façade and flowerpot gracing every sill. "Give the OCU a call, and find out the owners and residents of record."

Andy phoned in, and a few minutes later, she rattled off a list of names with apartment numbers that Dio scribbled on her own notepad.

Camille studied Dio's list, then read the thirty names aloud. "None of those sound familiar to me."

"Me either." Duncan tipped his head back to check out the low-rise. "Six floors—kinda looks like the Flowerbox Building, but I don't think this place has condos."

Bela frowned as the green, stinking trace energy she was using as her marker began to fade. Too much time had passed, and the trail was degrading. "We've got the list, and the energy's vanishing fast. Let's follow it inside while we can still see where it takes us."

Four floors later, they stood outside the door of apartment 4-9, at the end of a hall nearest the staircase they had used. New brown tile covered the hallway, so fresh the grout still had traces of white, and the scent of fresh paint almost blocked the stench from the poisoned energy. The green tracers approached the apartment door, then seemed to disappear behind it.

Bela had to work not to break into cackles like the old Russian Mothers, she felt so triumphant. Camille gave off small but steady puffs of smoke, while water trickled from the tips of Andy's fingers, and Dio churned the air until two wind-devils scooted down the hall's brown tile.

"Here, damn it." Bela grabbed Duncan's hand and squeezed it. "Right here. We finally tracked one of these bastards. Who is it?"

Dio whipped out her list. "Four-nine's registered to a Samuel Griffen, but you know how long it takes to update these databases. This could be years old."

Camille stepped up to the door, fingers extended, tiny fire-lasers already snaking toward the painted metal. "I'll check out what's inside."

"No, stop!" Bela let go of Duncan and moved between Camille and the door before Camille could lose herself in her fire's energy. "There could be elemental traps. We don't want to spring any and get hurt, or blow the sides off the building."

"Guess we'll do this the old-fashioned way." Andy shoved up the sleeves of her leathers and drew her dart pistol from its holster. She had some sort of silent communication with Duncan, like police officers so often did, and without further prompting, he moved to one side of the door and Andy went to the other.

Duncan drew the Glock he had retrieved from Bela's bedroom. "Do me a favor, Angel, and come over here beside me. Dio and Camille, you two stand with Andy."

Bela drew her sword when Camille did, and Dio put a throwing knife in her left hand, her strongest. They moved in silent unison.

When everyone was in position, Andy leaned out of her stance long enough to knock on the door.

No one answered, but Bela sensed movement.

"Someone's in there," she murmured to Duncan, knowing Andy could hear her, too. "One person, I think."

Andy knocked again, louder and without stopping. She didn't give any announcement of who they were, because officially, they had no sanction. This hadn't been approved by anybody, least of all OCU and the NYPD.

"All right, all right," said a male voice Bela didn't recognize, and Andy eased up on her pounding.

Footsteps came forward and stopped.

Bela assumed that the person on the other side of the door was looking out of his peephole and wondering why he didn't see anything. Andy did a quick lean across the hole's range, then popped back to her position.

Whoever was looking likely saw a flash of red hair and leather.

The door's chains and locks rattled.

Duncan and Andy tensed. Bela tightened her grip on her

sword and kept her knees and elbows loose, ready to spring.

The door swung open, and everyone came out of their battle stances at the same time.

Bela lowered her sword even though Duncan kept his gun leveled on the boy who stood blinking in the hallway's meager lights. His wide, shocked eyes were red-rimmed, and the odor of just-smoked weed seeped out of the apartment.

"That's not the guy who jumped me in the alley." Duncan lowered his Glock to his right. "But you look familiar, kid. Where have I seen you before?"

The boy was wearing jeans this time, and a gray sweatshirt, but there was no mistaking the dark hair and eyes, or the smart-ass expression still lingering on his youthful, slack face.

Maybe it was the sword, but this time he didn't try for a look at Bela's boobs.

"Walker Drake." Bela sheathed her blade. "Looks like we need to have a little chat at the old Fourteenth after all."

27

Duncan knew they really didn't have a choice about explaining some of the situation to Jeremiah Drake. Bela did most of the talking about Sibyls and tracking energy, and she came off beautiful and elegant and articulate, even in slightly soiled battle leathers. It was a pleasure listening to her, even if she was discussing things most people would be confined to hospitals for believing.

Jack Blackmore and Duncan filled in details for Drake and his lawyer while Dio, Camille, and Andy kept watch on Walker in the precinct's little holding cell. Actually, Bela's quad was feeding Walker everything they could find in the precinct vending machines to help the little puke come down from the pot he'd smoked before they located him.

When Bela finished, Duncan was surprised Drake didn't laugh them out of the interrogation room. Reese Patterson hadn't answered calls on his cell or his phone, probably because it was four in the morning, so Drake brought some grumpy-looking old guy in a wrinkled black suit. His name was Donovan Figg. With his major thick glasses and his puckered mouth, the lawyer really looked like he deserved that name.

Figg, who was seated at the end of the table closest to the interrogation room door, leaned back in his chair and stared at Blackjack and Bela. "Let's say we even begin to believe you enough to cooperate with this nonsense, or we humor you because Jeremiah's grateful that you located Walker after he'd been missing half the night. Nothing we do or say here will ever hold up in court. Not once I start telling them about all this madness."

"Exactly." Blackjack, who had blown out of Presbyterian's burn center against medical advice when Duncan called, managed to look convincing despite the thick dressings the Mothers had applied to his blistered right arm and hand after he left the hospital. "So you've got nothing to lose, letting us talk to the boy."

He omitted a detail that Duncan had learned: that the OCU had a set of judges and DAs who knew everything about its operations, and cooperated with warrants, arraignments, and trials by making allowances for paranormal circumstances.

"We really aren't considering Walker a suspect at this point." Duncan, who sat closest to Figg, offered this appeasement because it was the truth. "We think it's a wrongplace, wrong-time situation, but we need to know who came and went from that apartment."

Figg sniffed, then picked his teeth with one fingernail, as if to illustrate how hard he was thinking about all this. "The apartment and who goes in and out—you'll confine your questions to that topic?"

"That, and Walker's supernatural associations." Bela spoke without checking with Blackjack, but Blackjack didn't seem to mind. "If he belongs to any fringe groups, it would help us to have the names of other people involved."

Jeremiah Drake, who was seated across from Duncan, looked very unhappy with this, but he didn't raise any objections.

Drake and Figg conferred in low tones for a few moments, then Figg announced they were in agreement.

"You can question my son." Jeremiah Drake got to his feet and walked to the interrogation room's one-way glass. "But I'm staying in here with him."

Duncan went out to the holding cell and got the boy, who looked a little miserable from all the cakes, cookies, chips, and pretzels Andy and Dio and Camille had been stuffing down his throat. "He won't drink coffee," Andy said like she was apologizing. "It's the best we could do."

Camille said, "Definitely stoned, but coming down. I think he's pretty drunk, too."

Walker Drake staggered a little when he walked, but didn't say a word on the way to the interrogation room, prompting Duncan to wonder if he'd been questioned before, even though his juvie record was clean. There had to be a way to ask that question without crossing Figg's lines in the sand, but Duncan couldn't work it out. Maybe in the flow of the fact-finding, something would come to him.

When they reached the interrogation room, Figg patted a seat beside him that placed Walker directly across the room from his father, who was still standing by the one-way glass. "Right here, young man. The nice officers need to ask you a few questions, but don't answer anything I tell you not to. We'll be done in a few minutes, and we can all get home to bed."

Walker eyed Figg like the lawyer made his comedown nausea worse, and Duncan didn't blame the kid for his spectacular eye roll. He took a seat on the other side of Walker, but scooted his chair so that Walker and Jeremiah had a clear view of each other.

Walker rubbed his cheeks with both hands, then seemed to become aware of his father's presence. His head drooped, and it seemed to take him a few seconds to find his overblown adolescent bravado again.

Blackjack didn't even try to ask the kid a question. Duncan figured that was because any moron could tell nice-daddy and mean-daddy routines wouldn't make a damned bit of difference with Walker. Jeremiah Drake seemed to have both of those bases covered.

Bela jumped right in, calm and direct. "The apartment where we found you, Walker. Who lives there?"

Walker crossed his arms over his chest and gave her a fuck-off smirk. "A friend."

"I see." Bela let that sit for a second, then put her arms on the table and leaned toward the kid. "That friend may have helped kill your stepmother."

Walker's eye twitched, and he frowned as his hands slid from his chest to his thighs. "Nobody I know would do that."

"Someone did." Bela held the boy's gaze, and he didn't seem to be able to look away from her. "Somebody hired some very nasty creatures to tear Katrina apart. We know you fought with her. She got on your nerves—but I don't think you wanted her dead, did you?"

Walker didn't answer. His throat worked, and he held on to his own legs like he was scared of falling out of the chair.

Figg's narrow little eyes turned into thread-wide slits. "Don't answer—"

"No, I didn't want her dead." Walker didn't seem to hear Figg at all. "I just wanted her gone, and she was leaving." The kid shifted his weight, gripping the sides of the chair now, and Duncan wondered if the boy had a case of the spins. "I didn't want her dead."

Bela's voice grew gentler, and her dark eyes softened. "We need to know who uses that apartment, Walker. Who goes in and out of it—and who was there tonight, before we found you?"

The kid glanced at his father. Then at his shoes.

Oh. So that's the problem. Duncan wondered if he should block the boy's view of Jeremiah. *Junior doesn't want Daddy to know whom he's hanging out with, or maybe who's supplying his stash.*

Duncan checked Drake's demeanor and realized Daddy already seemed to have an idea. The cloud that passed over Drake's face transformed him from dapper society guy to raving maniac in about two seconds flat.

"You're *not* seeing that girl again." Drake growled like a

wounded animal. "Ah, God, Walker, tell me you weren't with that piece of trash!"

Figg straightened up in his chair. "Jeremiah—"

Drake's face colored a deeper red. "Answer me, Walker."

The boy let go of his chair and banged both fists on the table. "She's not trash!"

Before Duncan saw it coming, Jeremiah Drake launched himself away from the one-way glass, bashing past Duncan to grab Walker across the table.

"Why?" His face had gone heart-attack scarlet, and he shook the kid hard. "How could you even think about it?"

Walker got pale as he pounded on his father's arms. Figg ducked. Bela and Blackjack were on their feet, but Duncan already had Drake. The bastard fought like hell as Duncan hauled him off the kid and pinned him against the one-way glass.

"You don't understand." Drake was weeping now. He closed his eyes. "You don't know."

"I don't," Duncan agreed. "But you don't get to beat the kid, no matter what it is."

Drake went limp and kept weeping, but Duncan didn't let him go.

"I'm fine!" Walker yelled at Bela when she tried to approach him. "Just—get away from me."

The kid was so furious he was crying even though, Duncan knew, Walker would rather have ripped out his own eyes. He'd been that angry a few times in his younger days, and he knew it hurt like almighty hell.

Bela backed off from the boy and eased back into her chair.

"It's my girlfriend's place." Walker aimed that at his father. "And she's not trash, no matter what that bastard says. Her brother keeps the apartment for her because their mother and father are dead—and he checks on her every day."

"Samuel Griffen?" Bela's question sounded natural despite all the craziness that just happened.

Walker turned his head to look at Bela. "Yeah. Sam. That's him. He came by tonight and took her out for dinner. He does that a lot."

Bela smiled at him, not over the top, but enough to get him to sit again. "What's your girlfriend's name, Walker?"

When the boy wouldn't answer, Jeremiah Drake tensed in Duncan's grip. "She calls herself RK," he said while the kid glared. "Rebecca Kincaid. I didn't even know the little bitch had a brother."

This time, Duncan saw it coming, but he couldn't let go of Drake.

Walker knocked his chair over as he shot up and tried to scramble over the table to get at his father.

Bela shook the table with her earth energy.

The kid caught its edges, wide-eyed, and held on while Bela grabbed his ankle. She kept him from going anywhere until Blackjack got the back of Walker's shirt, righted the chair with his bandaged hand, and stuffed the boy into his seat.

After another few minutes, they had clarified that Rebecca Kincaid was sixteen and trouble, according to Drake, and that Drake believed the girl, who had no real parental supervision, led Walker astray. Duncan was able to let the man go, but he took him into the little room with the one-way glass to keep a physical barrier between him and the boy.

"He's a follower." Drake leaned his forehead against the glass and watched while Bela clarified with Walker that Rebecca Kincaid and her brother, Sam Griffen, were the only people in and out of the apartment with any regularity. "He goes along with what everyone else is doing. This is my fourth time at a police station over him—did you know that?"

"I suspected, but no. He doesn't have a record." Duncan

switched off the sound, and Drake didn't object. Bela was doing fine on the other side of the glass, and everything seemed to be moving along.

"Walker doesn't have a record because Katrina and I made deals with the officers involved, and the courts, for diversion because of his substance abuse issues. We admitted him two different times for alcohol and drug addiction. We had him in psychiatric hospitals three times after that."

Drake lifted his head from the glass, and Duncan saw a man who missed his dead wife, or at least her help with this impossible situation, even if they had been having their issues when she got killed. "Walker won't take the meds, and they don't help anyway. He stays clean a few months, then he goes right back to Rebecca. It's like he's addicted to that girl and her lifestyle as much as anything else, and—and I can't help him. His behavior cost me my marriage. If something he did, someone he knew, got Katrina killed, I don't know how I'm going to deal with that."

Duncan felt for the guy; he couldn't imagine what it would do to his world if he had a kid who'd taken such a big left turn. Still, Drake seemed to be putting a lot on the boy, like Walker was a scapegoat for problems Drake couldn't solve on his own.

Sometimes there weren't any easy answers or any easy-to-pin bad guys.

"Do you have any family Walker could stay with tonight, Mr. Drake? You two are too worked up with each other for me to feel comfortable sending you home together."

"I'll call my brother on Long Island." Drake's sigh was pure exhaustion and hopelessness. "He's helped out before. Not that it matters, in the long run."

28

Bela felt like her arms and legs weighed a few tons after using her terrasentience to track the poisoned energy, never mind the patrol and all that angst and violence during Walker Drake's interview—but she was awake enough to appreciate Duncan's reaction to seeing the communications platform used for the first time. When Camille climbed on the big wooden table in the brownstone's living room and started to dance barefoot, she had to laugh at his bemused expression. Andy and Dio cracked up, too, then Dio took her leave and headed to the archives to see what, if anything, she could find on Rebecca Kincaid and Samuel Griffen.

"Work, work, work," Andy griped at Dio as Dio took the stairs two at a time, but Dio ignored her. To Duncan, Andy said, "The first time I watched this communications thing happen, my entire vocabulary dwindled to 'What the fuck.' Here, sit on the end of the couch and keep your eyes on the projective mirrors. I'll crash on the other end and give you splash if any fire gets away from her."

Bela loosened the zipper on her leathers, then wiped down her sword and put it in the weapons closet. The energy in the room shifted a little more every minute, toward Camille, and Duncan appeared to be fascinated by the energy she stirred up by moving fire in patterns.

Flames broke out in the lead-lined trough that wound around the outside of the table. Duncan leaned back against the couch arm to spare his T-shirt, and Bela skirted the table to stand behind him. She let her earth energy flow across his clothes as she rubbed his big shoulders, deflecting stray sparks.

Each time Camille completed a circuit, the flames along the table flared higher. Chimes in the brownstone rang, one to the next, louder and louder, the sound moving in circles as Camille danced. She twisted, spun, and centered herself in front of the set of smaller mirrors, instead of the big ones they used to talk with the Motherhouses and to transport people and objects.

Andy grinned and scooted forward on the couch. "Watch the smaller glass, Duncan."

The center of the little mirrors flared. Duncan's muscles twitched beneath Bela's hands. "I can feel that in the dinar." He tapped his fingers against the coin. "A little buzz."

Bela kissed the top of his head. "The coin's metal has similar properties to the glass. Camille's been trying to figure out how to make other metals projective—hence all the explosions in my lab."

Duncan relaxed under her moving hands again, watching as light grew inside the glass. It swirled in circles like the sounds through the chimes, keeping time with Camille's dance.

Camille raised her arms.

In one of the mirrors, Cynda's face popped into view, with a backdrop Bela recognized from Headcase Quarters. More fire Sibyls appeared in the other pieces of glass, all key to the New York communications relay.

Duncan's gaze fixed on the active pieces of glass. "That . . . looks like picturephones, or Internet chat with cameras, only clearer."

On the table, Camille whirled, arms over her head, tapping rhythms with her feet. When the channels opened completely, she gave her fellow fire Sibyls all the information they had learned from tonight's hunt and interrogation, leaving out how they had managed to track the poisoned energy in the first place.

"Got it," Cynda said as the other fire Sibyls signed off, letting their glasses go dark. "I'll get the OCU after financial and personal records for Samuel Griffen, and my triad will hunt this Rebecca kid on patrol, like the others—but I think we only have three groups out tonight. It may go slow. Get some sleep. We'll call you when we've got her secured."

A few seconds later, her glass went dark, too.

Duncan reached up and rubbed Bela's wrist. "Why don't you just use cell phones?"

Andy lounged back on her end of the couch, getting the cushions and the floor damp from her wet hair and leathers. "I'm the only one who can pull that off—if I haven't drowned mine recently. The longer I'm a Sibyl, the harder it gets."

Camille finished closing the channels and hopped off the table. "It's like computers. Even with elemental grounding, cell phones are so sensitive that our elemental energy tends to kill them in a few days. Besides, you can't send people and objects through cell phones."

Duncan rolled his shoulders into Bela's massage. "You send people through those mirrors?"

"Not through the mirrors, exactly." Camille unbelted her scabbard and got out her oils to work her blade. Fire Sibyls had to take special care with their weapons, since they were always setting them on fire. "The mirrors are just gateways to channels of energy in the earth. We can put people or things in the channels, and they can travel through the adjoining mirror in seconds, or just a few minutes."

"You could go to Ireland and be back before I got downstairs." Bela kissed the top of Duncan's head again, enjoying his clear, fresh scent. Icy mountain streams, fresh snow—it was perfect.

"A Sibyl could travel like that, fast and often." Camille sat on a chair arm and ran her rag along her curved blade. "It's harder on humans. And we found out with Jake Lowell a few years ago that it strips demons down to their demon form. Not something you need to try, Duncan."

On the couch across from her, Andy started to snore. A steady stream of water dripped from her hand, which was hanging off the cushion. From upstairs in Dio's rooms came the sound of swearing, wind, and big stacks of paper being shifted around. Camille drew a deep breath, then blew a whispery lick of fire against her blade, heating the oil until the whole room smelled like tangy mandarin oranges.

"It's never boring around here, Angel. I'll give you that." Duncan got himself up from the couch and gave Bela a hug. "But what if I don't want to visit Ireland while you go downstairs?"

When he pulled back, his gorgeous gray eyes teased her. Bela took both of his hands and pulled him out of the living room and into the kitchen, kissing him as soon as the door swung shut. Duncan took over then, grabbing her by the waist and lifting her up. He pulled her against his chest and carried her all the way down the stairs to her room. They made love hard and fast, and a few hours later, when Bela woke next to Duncan, she couldn't help slipping her fingers around his delicious length.

He came out of sleep slowly as she kissed him, first on the mouth, then the throat, running her nails across him. Her lips moved lower, sampling the scars on his chest, and his rumble of pleasure woke up her whole body.

By the time she moved her mouth across his waist, he was hard, just like she wanted. His low growls at the touch of her fingertips became a groan when she pressed her lips against the tip of his shaft. When she tasted him, his back arched, and Bela wrapped her whole hand around his cock.

"I won't last long like this." Duncan's hand made a fist in

her hair, tugging it gently, the huskiness in his voice sending tingles all over her body.

His skin burned against her lips, and she drank in his salty taste. Fresh, like the rest of him. Ocean water after a cleansing storm. Delicious. She gripped him tight and brought him deeper into her mouth, moving down, down, until her fingers bumped her lips.

"Bela." This time he barely got the word out. His hips moved, pumping even though she could tell he was trying to hold himself back. She moaned against his sensitive skin, and he pumped harder, and harder still when she trailed her tongue along the vein on the soft underside, squeezing and stroking with her hand.

He shuddered each time she made a sound, each time she flicked her tongue against the shaft, the base, the tip. Her fingers toyed with his sack, and that was all he could take.

He moved away from her, pulling himself free. In the same motion, he slipped his arms around her and lifted her up until her head rested on the pillows. Then he crushed his lips against hers, taking her breath, taking her thoughts, and setting her absolutely on fire.

His hands, everywhere, rubbing and stroking and touching.

His lips so demanding. His tongue against hers, hers against his. He spread her legs with his knee, and she opened to him. Wet. Ready. Yes. Just the way he squeezed her breasts nearly made her explode.

"I need you," she whispered into his next kiss. "I need you now!"

The look he gave said, *I adore you.*

It said, *You're mine now. Mine forever.*

Bela's heart thrummed, so fast. She ached everywhere. She wanted him deep, and she wanted him now, and she wanted him always, always, always.

Duncan's eyes gripped hers as he thrust himself inside her, one stroke, smooth and forceful, filling her up, then swallowing her scream with his mouth. Bela lifted her hips to meet him, over and over, clinging to his neck.

"More," she kept whispering, out of control. Her insides shook. The bed shook. Let everything shake, she didn't give a damn. "More. Please, Duncan. More!"

"I love you." He drove himself deep, his voice a sensual rasp. "Everything. Every bit."

Bela couldn't breathe anymore. Her breasts rubbed back and forth against his chest, and every time his coin touched her, she felt its low, humming vibration. All she could do was rock, rock, rock, taking everything, all of Duncan. Her legs locked against his thighs.

So fast now. So hard.

Bela's consciousness broke free and melted into him, into the earth itself. She moaned, and kept moaning. Heat mingled with chills and blended with shudders and shaking and rocking, more rocking, and she kept right on moaning.

Duncan's lips claimed hers again, and Bela's mind left her completely. She bucked and shoved against him, pleasure shaking her inside to out, and it wouldn't stop, she couldn't stand it, had to stand it, but she couldn't. Duncan moved just right, drawing it out, winding her mind farther into the earth, into the power all around her and inside her, and when he came, she started moaning all over again.

"I love you," she whispered when she could talk. "I love you."

He was still inside her when she fell asleep, still holding her, still kissing her, and she dreamed about making love to him all over again.

Bela opened her eyes, disoriented, thinking she heard something, but not sure.

Duncan pulled his muscled arm away from her belly, and they both sat up. The room was so dark, but then, it had no windows, so she couldn't judge the time except by Sibyl instinct, which told her it was after midday but before night-fall.

Duncan picked up his watch from the floor and squinted at it. "It's about three in the afternoon, I think."

Somebody knocked, and smoke filtered under the door. "Bela?"

"What the—? That's Cynda." Bela yanked the sheet over Duncan's waist and her breasts, then called, "It's okay. You can come in."

Cynda pushed the bedroom door open. The soft light of the basement hallway combined with Bela's acute vision to reveal the depths of Cynda's pallor and the size of her frown. She had her leathers on, and her hand was on her sword hilt. Flames played along Cynda's fingers, every-where she was touching that weapon.

At the same moment, Bela became aware of strange en-ergies in the house. Her quad, angry and upset. Riana and Merilee upstairs—doing what? Containing them? Holding them back?

"What's going on?" Bela blinked against the surge of anxiety ruining the absolute relaxation she'd been enjoying in Duncan's arms. "Did you find Rebecca Kincaid?"

"No." Cynda's flames expanded, covering her shoulders. "We found Reese Patterson. We found him in pieces all over his office."

Duncan went rigid beside Bela, and she turned to him immediately, getting more tense by the second.

"When I disappeared." Anger worked across Duncan's face, and worry, and disbelief. He stared at the ceiling the way he did when he was trying to get John Cole to speak to him. "Before the ambush in the alley."

His voice trailed off, sharpening Bela's anxiety to an acute sense of dread. He wasn't making sense. This whole situation wasn't making sense.

Bela turned back to the door. "Why are you here, Cynda? What does this have to do with Duncan?"

More flames erupted, until fire ringed Cynda's body and a haze of smoke filled the bedroom. "Duncan needs to come with my triad to the townhouse—and I think he knows that." Cynda's frown shifted from determined to uncomfortable. "We don't want to fight with you over this, Bela. Any of you. Please don't make us."

Duncan shoved the sheet off his hips. "Nobody's fighting anybody. I'll come with you." He swung his legs off the bed, grabbed his jeans, and stepped into them.

Fear clawed Bela's insides like she was the one with the demon inside. She scrambled out of the bed, but her mind wouldn't tell her what to do next. She had no idea what was happening, but she didn't want to be separated from Duncan—not like this. She wanted to grab him and push him up against the wall. Make an earth barrier he couldn't cross. As for Cynda—

This time when Bela swung toward the door, fists clenched, Cynda stepped back.

"Close that damned door before I hurt you." Earth energy shook Bela's voice, and shook the room with it. "I mean it!"

A tiny crack opened in the floor tiles, arrowing toward Cynda.

The door slammed.

Smoke from Cynda's fire let Bela know she was still right outside, but at least she and Duncan had a little privacy now. Bela hurried to pull on her own jeans and blouse, but Duncan was already in his T-shirt, getting his badge and gun off the dresser.

"Duncan, wait." Bela left her shirt unbuttoned and grabbed his arm before he could stuff his badge in his pocket. "Stop! What are you doing?"

"The papers your friends and the OCU would have found on Patterson's desk were dated, signed, and time-stamped." Duncan's frown looked enough like Cynda's to really scare Bela about how bad this situation might get.

"John Cole's will would have been there, with me as his beneficiary—and my last will and testament. Patterson wrote it out for me before I got jumped in the alley."

Last will and testament.

That wouldn't register at all.

Duncan needing a will.

Bela couldn't add it all up until he pried his arm out of her fingers, then slipped his hands under her shirt, pressing his palms against her bare waist. "When I disappeared on you, I told you, it wasn't my call. I didn't take myself out of your bed and over to Patterson's office. It was John. I just woke up there."

"John took you over and made you go to the lawyer's office." Bela pressed her cheek into his T-shirt and laced her fingers together behind his back. Squeezing. Wanting to keep him with her even as she started to grasp why he'd have to go with Cynda. "To see his will."

Duncan's embrace felt so warm, so alive and solid and permanent. "If I'd had any sense, I would have put myself in some kind of quarantine right then—but it's been crazy. Everything moved so fast, and truth be told, Angel, I didn't want to be away from you."

Bela held on tighter, breathing him in, her eyes closed as she reached for any argument that might work. "But Patterson was alive if he did your will, right?"

Duncan kissed the top of her head, his hands rubbing her bare back under her shirt. "He was alive when I left, but I don't know if I went back, and neither do you."

She stared at him. "You've been with me every minute."

"We can't know that."

Damn him for being so gentle. It kept her from getting as furious as she needed to get.

"I could have been out wandering while you were sleeping," Duncan said.

"You weren't."

Duncan held her in silence for a few seconds, then gently

pushed her back from him, enough to look her in the eyes. "I want the Mothers to have a go at John, and I don't want you there. And not like last time. I mean nowhere near the townhouse."

Bela's chin dropped. The heat in her chest—anger? Disbelief? She couldn't even tell, but this wasn't happening. "You can't be serious. If something goes wrong and the Mothers drive Cole out of your head, that's it for you." She shook her head. "No. We'll clear this up some other way."

It was getting hard to breathe, but he was talking again, those gray-blue eyes loving and rational, his tone so careful and measured she wanted to knee him in the nuts.

"I'm way past serious, and I know the risks, Angel. Besides, even if I know I wasn't having blank time when Patterson got murdered, nobody else does. My papers are there, my prints. I was probably the last person to see him alive."

Duncan pushed away from her then, with more force than she'd expected.

Bela stumbled backward as his eyes shifted to black, then back to gray again. "Shut up." Duncan put his hand on the dinar. The veins in his temples stood out as his face turned red. "You don't have a say in this, John. I'm going."

Bela launched herself at Duncan, smacking his chest with her fists. "Give John his say! If you ask the Mothers to poke around in your head, they will, and they damn well might kill you!"

Duncan caught her pummeling hands and held them with just enough strength to keep her from hitting him again. "I have to do this."

Bela tried to jerk free. "Why, damnit?" She moved into him hard, using leverage from his grip on her hands to shove them both backward, away from the door.

Duncan shifted his grasp to her shoulders and held them both upright. His fingers dug into her as he turned her around, putting himself closer to the door. "Did you *see* the pictures of what the Rakshasa did to Katrina Drake? And Patterson—what do you think he looked like? John could take me over. He could use me to lead the demons straight to you!"

Bela gasped from pain—her arms, her heart, her throat. She turned raw in his grip, and everything hurt.

Duncan's face went soft and he turned her loose. "I'm—I'm sorry." He stared at his hands for a second, then shut his eyes. The wounds along his neck, shoulder, and chest glowed like they were filling with blood, and the sight of that nearly scared her to death.

"What's happening?" She reached for him, but he backed away from her, toward the door.

"Oh, no, you are not leaving like this." Bela lunged toward Duncan and snatched hold of him again. She kissed him, fierce, possessive. Desperate.

He kissed her back, but she could still feel him leaving her.

No!

She moved her lips to his ear, wishing he'd hug her tighter. "You'd never betray us to the Rakshasa, even if John turns out to be a murdering bastard after all. My whole quad likes you—hell, they like you better than they like me, and they trust you." She kissed his ear. "I trust you, Duncan."

"Yeah, well, I don't. I don't trust John, and the bastard's living in my head." He moved her away from him again, gently this time, and what she saw on his face cut her heart in two. His force of will. His determination. The part of Duncan Sharp that wouldn't stop, no matter what. He was going to do this, and nothing she could say would change his mind.

Bela wrapped her arms around herself, trying not to scream.

"Please do this for me, Angel." His fingers caressed the tips of her elbows, and the pleading in his eyes made the

scream rise higher in Bela's chest. "If the Mothers can dig
around enough to show I didn't kill Patterson—and convince me that John's not some time bomb that'll get you
and your quad killed—I'll be right back."

"I don't want to be away from you," she whispered, the
screams breaking into tears she had to cry. "I'm not ready
to lose you."

Duncan lifted his hands to her cheeks, using his thumbs
to wipe the tears away. He didn't tell her she wouldn't lose
him, because he couldn't. She knew that. Duncan was no
liar, and he didn't hand out false comfort. The pain in his
eyes said he'd never leave her forever, not on purpose. But
as the silence between them expanded, as Bela felt her own
tears on her face, reality nudged harder at her than she'd allowed since she first fought to save his life.

I'm not going to win this one.

She almost choked on the hurt.

Duncan's beautiful eyes consumed her, and she felt the
electric pressure of his fingers, so soft on her cheeks, her
lips. "Promise me you won't come to the townhouse," he
said. "I need that from you, Angel."

This time Bela heard what he didn't say, what she hadn't
let herself understand before when he asked her for the
same concession.

*Don't come to the townhouse, because if I change and
the Mothers have to put me down, I don't want you to feel
it. I don't want you to see it.*

"I promise," she said, too loud, almost shouting, hating
the words, and hating herself for saying them. "But I'm
sending Andy with you. She can heal better than anyone."

Duncan considered this as he took his hands from Bela's
face. "If she's willing, I'd be glad for her help."

He didn't kiss her again before he walked out of the bedroom.

If he had, Bela might have taken back her promise, and
every vow she'd ever made. Cynda Flynn Lowell *damned*

sure wouldn't have lived to walk Duncan up the stairs to her triad, out of the brownstone, and away from Bela—and Bela might not have been coherent enough to speak to her quad when they came rushing into her room.

As it was, Bela was able to accept Camille's hugs and Dio's swearing, and Andy's solemn promise that she'd do whatever it took to bring Duncan back to her.

Bela just wasn't sure she could believe in any of it.

Time.

Bela slid her fingers along the waist of her jeans.

Her entire life had been taken over by a sense that some grand clock was ticking, and she couldn't stop it, couldn't smash the glass, the hands, the gears, and gain any reprieve.

She glanced at the clock hanging near the front door. "It's been hours. They should be back by now."

From behind her, in the brownstone's living area, Camille and Dio didn't answer, but Bela felt a surge of their energies, directed at supporting her.

Camille was sorting through tiny metal charms she'd made in the lab, using her laser-like fire to examine them. Dio was sketching at the big wooden table, drawing ways to take out Cynda and her triad the next time they came face-to-face. She'd come up with a few realistic, bloody scenarios, but Bela wouldn't spend too much time looking at any of them. Riana, Cynda, and Merilee were probably the only women in New York City who could have walked into Bela's home, hurt her like that, and walked out in one piece—save for her own quad and Mother Keara. *Cynda did what she had to do. That's all.*

The front window offered a view of Fifth Avenue and Central Park. Lights from cars, buses, and taxis gleamed against the gray dusk, and the trees behind the stone wall across the street seemed shadowy and ominous.

Was he still alive?

Would she know if he wasn't?

Were the Rakshasa close by?

Could she sense them if they were?

The questions came, endless, relentless, ticking like the clock in her head.

Bela wanted to believe that her Sibyl instincts would tell her if Duncan turned demon, if he died. That her mind would warn her if tiger-demons were sneaking toward the brownstone.

She couldn't know any of that for certain.

Nothing, absolutely nothing, felt certain now.

She didn't even know for sure that the Rakshasa could seek or find locations protected by elemental locks. It was just a suspicion.

Bela squinted at the trees, letting her enhanced vision give her the details. Walkers. Joggers. Bikers. Runners.

Dogs on leashes.

No monsters.

And no Duncan.

The leaves hadn't started to turn yet, but Bela could almost taste the coolness that evening was bringing to the city.

"None of us are that good at healing, but maybe we'd be moral support," Camille said from her usual perch on one of the overstuffed camel-colored chairs. "Are you sure you don't want to go to the townhouse?"

Damnit, of course I want to go.

But she couldn't do that to Duncan. Not after she'd promised.

"I'm sure." Bela dug her teeth into her lip so she wouldn't start crying again.

"He'll be fine." Dio's voice carried a note of authority mingled with irritation, like she refused to even consider another alternative. "He has to be fine. The Mothers will be careful, and Andy's there."

Bela leaned her forehead against the cool window glass to calm herself down, staring at the endless lines of vehicles beginning to clog up in the early-evening rush.

Camille held up a single copper charm. Bela could see it in the window's reflection. "This one's the most similar to the metal in Duncan's dinar, in terms of how it responds to my energy."

"House nerd," Dio muttered, leaning over the table to sketch more bloody murder.

"But now I'm thinking it can't be in the treatment, like how we make the elementally locked bullets and knives for the OCU." Camille turned the charm over in her fingers. "It's got to happen in the forging. Some sort of elemental transformation that happens when the metal's in its liquid form, or maybe cooling, with a glassy surface."

Bela's attention pulled away from the view out the window for a few seconds, and she looked at Camille. "So you'd need to start with basic ingredients and forge from scratch?"

"Exactly. Then I could make each of us a projective coin like the dinar." Camille let the copper charm bounce on the pile of other charms, and Bela felt a tiny tingle in her earth energy when it made contact with the other metals. "I don't think my charms could repel Rakshasa, but it would magnify our elemental sentience. We'd be able to track fainter traces in our elements, even over long distances."

Bela studied Camille's delicate features and the light, controlled fire energy playing in the air around her shoulders. "I can't believe I'm saying this to a fire Sibyl, but you can keep using my lab whenever you want. We'll all help you. Except maybe Andy. One flood, and all those machines would be history."

"No, definitely not Andy." Camille laughed.

Bela glanced at Dio, who swiped a red pencil across her page. "Don't look at me. I wouldn't know a beaker from a burner."

The chimes all across the brownstone gave a faint jingle.

Bela startled, then looked at the door. Her chest tightened. "Please, let this be Andy, bringing Duncan back."

Dio and Camille glanced at the chimes as Bela let her earth energy flow outward to find the source of the energy moving the chimes. Excitement drove her awareness faster than usual, out of the brownstone and over the sidewalk, then farther, across the street and into Central Park, toward the townhouse—

Oh, Goddess.

Bela staggered back from the window and hit her knees.

Dark power.

Like a moving wall of horror.

It rolled over her. Terror. Nightmares. Little-girl fear.

She sucked air and tried to yell.

No sound but the chimes.

Ringing louder. Out of tune. The noise warped and hissed and flattened until the pipes sounded like bones banging in a graveyard wind.

"Unrighteous!" The word choked out of Bela's throat like someone was strangling her, and she couldn't control it. Pain. Pain everywhere in her body. Her head was exploding. Her awareness fractured like glass crushed under heavy boots.

Someone screamed.

Camille?

Dio?

Bela's body went stiff as she fought to drag her earth power back to herself, and her eyes slammed closed. The ground shook from her panic, hard enough to make her teeth clatter together.

"Filthy," her voice rasped. Nails on a chalkboard, even to her own ears. "Scrape it off, please, get it off me!"

But she couldn't escape the creeping sense of putrid mold covering every inch of her.

The ground was poisoned.

The earth was hurting her.

Hands grabbed her shoulders. Cool metal pressed against her chest. Copper. Camille's charm. A fresh blast of air power swept through Bela, and fire, hot and furious, hacking at the deadly earth energy trying to pull her down forever into its suffocating depths.

Bela focused on the copper, on its purity, on how the fire and wind touched it, and touched her. She let it move through her and join with her natural earth power to fend off the horrible, unnatural energy.

The darkness howled at her.

Bela howled right back, and tore herself away from the horrors trying to suck her dry. The stench of ammonia threatened to overwhelm her, but heat blasted into her and wind beat against her face, cleansing her, purging the awful sensations from her consciousness. Thunder roared right above her head, making her ears pop.

Bela's eyes flew open just as the lights in the brownstone exploded into fragments of glass and sizzling, burning filaments. Darkness covered the room as Bela sucked in air and stood, shaking, with Dio and Camille supporting her.

"They're coming," Bela gasped. She pulled Camille's charm off her chest and clenched it in her fist. "Here. Now."

Dio swore and let her go, flinging herself toward the weapons closet. Less than a minute later, they were suited up and armed, but Bela was still shaking as she drew her sword.

"How many?" Camille asked, hefting her *shamshir* over her shoulder, ready to hack anything that came through the front door.

Dio shifted her African throwing knives into one hand and grabbed Bela's free wrist. Bela felt the full strength of air and wind supporting her as she forced herself to reach out with her terrasentience, toward the advancing Rakshasa again.

There.

Still in the park, but closer now. She felt them like a sick, infected wave rolling across the grass. The perverted energy boiling outward from their advance left no question that the typical elemental locks on the brownstone wouldn't repel them. Not with these numbers. Not with this strength.

"Three," she said. "No, five. Seven. Damnit! Ten! At least ten. How could there be ten? Probably more. And humans with them, with elemental talent."

"Death," Dio whispered, tracking the filth by air, just as Bela was following their advance on the ground. "One purpose. Killing."

The white Rakshasa Strada was leading this attack. Bela kept her distance from where the demon's claws tore into the earth, but his intentions were palpable. He was coming to destroy anything that might pose a threat to him or his fellow demons. They would start with the brownstone, but they wouldn't stop until every Sibyl in New York City— every Sibyl in the world—was dead.

"They're going to slaughter us all," Bela and Dio said at the same time as they pulled back from the tracking, and Dio let go of Bela's wrist.

Camille's *shamshir* burst into flames. At the same moment, she let loose a blast of fire energy into the communications system, cracking half the projective mirrors around the platform table and ringing some of the chimes so forcefully the pipes burst into flames, molten metal singing holes in the wood and carpet.

The tattoo on Bela's forearm burned, mortar to pestle to broom, down its wavy connecting lines with an urgency and pain she hadn't felt since the Legion wars. She knew every Sibyl in New York City, maybe even in the world, felt that same burn.

The message would be more than clear.

Help us!

But who could reach them in time?

"Bela." Dio's terrified, furious tone drew her back. "We

can't win. We're going to lose this fight, and we're going to die."

Rage and dread burned through Bela like a wild surge of Camille's power. "No. I won't let it happen."

"Bela—" Dio started, but Bela cut her off with a snarl.

"We can make it to the townhouse." She pushed Dio toward the kitchen door. "Out the back, into the alley— you first, then Camille. I won't let them kill you. Us. *Any* of us."

Camille growled like a rabid animal, and Bela could feel how it ripped at the fire Sibyl to disengage from any battle, even a hopeless one, without a fight.

Dio was already hammering toward the kitchen.

Bela grabbed Camille's elbow and got a defensive burn for her trouble.

"Camille!" She held on anyway, letting her fingers burn as she pulled the fire Sibyl toward the kitchen, her earth-enhanced voice rising above the roar of Camille's expanding flames. "Get out of here! Run, Camille, *run*!"

30

Everything was too bright, even though it was dusk.

Duncan stared out the back window of Riana Lowell's big black Jeep as Andy Myles inched them through the sluggish traffic. He wasn't sure if he was seeing more light because of what the Mothers had done to make sure John couldn't take him over again, or because the light was really there. Blackjack, riding up front in the shotgun seat, looked out the windows like he could see the strange brightness, too.

Behind them on the road, Saul and Calvin Brent were driving Mother Yana, Mother Keara, and Mother Anemone in Bela's SUV. They had come along to explain their findings and thoughts, how they had forced a closer mental bond between Duncan and John—but something was wrong.

Off.

Duncan's gut hurt from it.

John, still furious and flattened from all the Mothers' prodding, stirred in Duncan's brain, then seemed to come to attention.

I feel it, he said.

The world seemed completely ass-backward and fucked up. Maybe it was the End of Days, and nobody had bothered to tell Duncan. He dug his fingers into his jeans, trying to get a fix on what he was sensing, but he had to grab the panic bar above his door as Andy changed lanes too fast. Christ. This woman was going to climb a cab's ass or breed with a city bus and kill them all.

Everything in the streets seemed to get louder.

Too loud!

Duncan reached to cover his ears.

Flames shot out of the coin around his neck, burning the metal into his chest, branding him, melting toward bone until Duncan yelled from the pain and pried it off his skin.

He couldn't think. Couldn't understand.

John screamed. Primal. Out of his mind, like a man shot to pieces. Duncan's slash wounds blazed, tearing his skin as they extended.

"Damn!" Andy stomped the Jeep's brakes so hard Duncan almost snapped his seat belt. His head bounced off the back of Blackjack's headrest. The squeal of tires stabbed at his sensitive hearing as the Jeep bucked to a stop. Air bags burst into deployment as the SUV bashed into the Jeep's back bumper.

No air bag ever touched Andy. She was already out of the vehicle, running like Satan was chasing her, past the stalled traffic, straight down Fifth Avenue.

Blackjack punched at the cloth, then used his pocketknife to slice his way free of the side air bags as Duncan ripped off his own jammed seat belt and got out, his brain swimming from pain and confusion. The moment his feet hit pavement, he glanced back at the SUV. Calvin Brent was crawling out of it. A couple of cars had jammed to a stop behind them. Horns honked. Fists waved out open windows as traffic tried to wedge itself around the fender-bender.

Duncan processed that the SUV's other doors were open and that all the Mothers were gone. He swung his gaze back toward the direction Andy had taken. The old women were moving on, right behind her, flying down the sidewalk like racing teenagers. He doubted most civilians could even see them, they were moving so fast.

Cold dread gripped him.

"Bela."

The stench of cat piss struck him in the face, distant but

strong. His slash wounds ripped another inch in both directions.

"Bela!" Duncan wheeled, grabbed Blackjack by the collar, and shook him so hard his eyeballs must have rattled. "She's in trouble. They're in trouble. Call for backup. Do it now!"

Blackjack tore away from him, yanked out his cell, and started spitting commands.

Duncan was running before any of that registered, following after Andy and the Mothers. He was aware of Blackjack yelling from behind him, and the Brent brothers, too.

Something about his weapon.

His Glock.

Which he didn't have.

The Mothers had taken it from him at the townhouse, and they hadn't given it back.

Screw it.

Bullets didn't kill these demons anyway.

His chest hurt. The slash wounds felt alive.

Duncan's feet hammered against the pavement as he dodged two taxis and a honking Cadillac to reach the sidewalk. It was dark outside, but he could see like it was daytime—and he remembered that John Cole had night vision. That talent was Duncan's now, shared for as long as they stayed alive.

Still . . . here . . . John groaned from the epicenter of Duncan's awareness, and the agony in Duncan's chest and arm and neck eased. *Won't . . . let you down.*

Duncan focused on his legs, his feet, his hands, pumping as hard as he could. The muscles pulled tight across his cooling wounds, aching like a half dozen bayonets were slicing into his throat and pecs. Sidewalk seemed to crumble under his feet as he crushed pavement with each step. Pain made his vision blur, but it didn't slow him down. He used it, fed off it, and ran faster. Andy and the Mothers were close now, half a block ahead, no more. Another few steps, and Duncan's lungs seemed to collapse against his ribs.

Keep moving.

Get to Bela.

That's what he had to do.

Andy and the Mothers turned a sharp right, down a side street next to the brownstone. Duncan followed. The dinar around his neck fried him all over again, but he didn't waste time knocking it away.

Blood spurted through his T-shirt.

The blood was the wrong color, the wrong scent.

Ahead of him, metal clanged against stone. Women shouted. Water splattered into Duncan's face. Fire and wind roared around him. The earth beneath New York City rumbled as his pulse jumped in his throat and the wrong-colored blood flowed stronger, too cool and sticky to be real.

Shit, John muttered from somewhere inside his body. *On it. Just go.*

New fire broke out, this time inside Duncan's neck and shoulder. Like John had taken a damned blowtorch to his veins and arteries. Like he was sealing off the bleed.

Duncan stumbled but kept running.

Andy and the Mothers wheeled into the alley behind the brownstone, and Duncan stayed right behind them.

Another few steps, and he saw them. Bela and Dio and Camille.

Sweet God.

He slowed to get his bearings, find his entry point, but the Mothers and Andy went weapons-hot and blasted into a mass of what had to be twenty Rakshasa closing on the Sibyls in a wide arc.

The cats blocked the path to both alley exits as they swiped with their deadly claws. Drool dripped from open tiger mouths. Feral roars broke beneath the howl of wind, the screeching hiss of fire, and the growl of moving water and earth. The air smelled wet and sulfurous at the same time, barely muting the stench of cat piss and sour animal.

Strada, the big white-furred bastard, towered above the rest of the demons.

Towered over Bela.

Duncan's chest nearly broke apart when he saw her. Her dark hair swirled in the wind as she swung her blade, the jagged tip barely keeping the big white cat at bay as rocks and debris bashed into bricks and fire escapes and dumpsters on all sides.

He barreled toward her as Andy made it to Bela's side. Water burst from pipes and drains, washing into Strada as Andy pumped darts into Strada's chest. The little Russian Mother rose up between Andy and Bela, swinging long hunting daggers at anything not wearing Sibyl leathers. Behind them, at fighting distance, Mother Keara reached Camille, and both of them caught fire like minions escaped from hell. Mother Keara's big Oriental blade took heads and arms and hands, and Camille's *shamshir* opened throats as their primal battle screams rose over the chaos. Dio pulled in behind them with Mother Anemone, both of them drilling demons with deadly throwing knives.

The nearest cats fell back as Duncan slammed himself forward.

Fresh waves of elemental energy struck him and tried to bash him out of the alley.

Some sort of shield.

A wall the Sibyls hadn't made.

Duncan leaned into it, digging his boots into the pavement.

Bad energy. John was back. Surging forward in Duncan's mind. Trying to help. *Like the night you got healed. Find the source and cut it off.*

A dozen men in black sweatshirts backed out of the mass of Rakshasa, their backs toward Duncan, their hands raised and letting off what looked like poisonous green clouds. With John's night vision, Duncan could see the sick clouds of green forming the barrier he couldn't break past.

"The source. Got it right here, John." Duncan forced his way forward. He kept going. And kept going. When he reached the first asshole in a sweatshirt, he snatched hold of the bastard, using his hood to yank him backward.

Draining, miserable energy spiked all through Duncan's body, paralyzing him—but it centered on the dinar, and John's essence was right there, moving through the metal, throwing off the attack.

Duncan roared through his teeth, forcing his arm around Sweatshirt's neck even as the bad energy tried to hammer him backward into the pavement. On the edges of his vision, wounded Rakshasa ripped knives and darts out of their chests. Some fell, looking dead, then regrew limbs, sprang up, and charged toward Bela and the Sibyls again. Wind funnels plowed forward, blasting into the demons, but they stood fast. The earth split at their feet, spitting chunks of asphalt in every direction, but they jumped over the rents and tears like they didn't exist.

A woman screamed, and Duncan hurled everything he was made of against the energy holding him back. His arm moved forward just enough. Contact. Elbow lock. Leverage. He snapped Sweatshirt's neck and threw him down. If the fucker got up, Duncan would tear his damned head right off.

The other men in sweatshirts never turned around, and didn't seem to notice or give a shit that one of them was down. The barrier holding Duncan away from his angel faltered, but only for a second.

Duncan yanked the hood off the next bastard and jerked him backward.

He'd get to Bela, by God.

He'd get to her if he had to do it one inch and one snapped neck at a time.

31

Bela swung her sword and stepped back. Back again. Soon she'd hit the alley wall.

Trapped.

No room to fight.

She threw huge waves of earth energy at the demons, but they fended them off. Neutralized most of it. The same with air, with fire, with water.

"I feel like I'm fighting blind!" Andy's scream lanced into Bela's awareness. "They're pulling my power out of me!"

From somewhere in the center of the teeming mass of demons, a man let out a roar louder than any demon.

Duncan!

Bela's gaze went right to him.

He threw a man in a black sweatshirt away from him.

The man bounced off an alley wall like a broken doll, and Duncan slammed forward through the few remaining humans trying to fight.

He hit trapped walls of earth, wind, water, and fire, Sibyl power, blocked by the demons—and he kept coming. Rocks and dirt and God only knew what else chewed into his cheeks, and Duncan Sharp kept right on coming, toward her, for her, back to her.

Bela's eyes teared against the air's streaming, hot grit.

Strada charged her again.

Bela's battle cry tore through her, earth energy driving her into the air as she jumped high and kicked the demon in the teeth so hard his head turned sideways and he crashed to the pavement.

Dio chunked a knife through the chest of a smaller cat

who had flanked Bela. The Rakshasa fell on her, heavy and immobilized, and Bela shoved it to the ground.

Camille spun around and hacked off its head, fire lacing her shouts of rage as she whirled back to the line of advancing demons. At the same instant, Mother Keara drew back a gnarled hand and blasted the cat corpse with an unbelievable bomb of orange-red flames.

Dio and Mother Anemone blew the pile of ashes into two whistling gouts of wind headed in opposite directions, and a rush of water struck whatever bits of the destroyed cat might remain, washing them straight down the nearest gutter.

Bela screamed, giddy with triumph, and heard her quad and the Mothers screaming, too.

The line of demons pressed forward again, blocking Bela's view of Duncan—and a Rakshasa bellow sliced through across all other sound.

The sound drove against Bela's ears, making her heart stutter. Sweat poured down her neck as she turned to meet it, keeping herself between that sound and her quad.

Her arms throbbed from bashing her sword against flesh and bone over and over again. Her legs ached. Her gut was on fire, but her eyes worked well enough to see Strada back on his feet and coming hard, with nothing but violent death in his blazing golden stare.

Bela snarled at the bastard and hefted her blade. "Come on then, you lousy cat-fucker. We'll see who comes out of this alive!"

(32)

Duncan drove himself through the remnant elemental energy slowing him down. He beat it sideways and shoved it out of his way. He grabbed cat-demons by the backs of their necks and threw them aside like kittens.

Now, his mind told him.

Now, John echoed.

Twenty feet. Fifteen. The muscles in his thighs burned and popped. Wind beat his skin against his bones. Fire singed his hair, his face, his mouth.

He kept his gaze fixed on Bela.

She swung her sword at the white tiger-demon, and the earth shook when it struck him and lodged in his shoulder.

Strada ripped the blade out of his body, then tore the sword's hilt out of Bela's hands and threw it so hard it lodged in a dumpster.

Lightning blasted all around Duncan, blowing holes in the asphalt and rendering another skewered cat to ashes that streamed straight into Duncan's face. He clawed the soot out of his eyes just before a jet of water knocked him back a step.

The white tiger-demon drew back a meaty paw and struck Bela so hard Duncan felt the blow in his own jaw.

She spun and dropped to her knees.

A rage like Duncan had never known burned away every shred of his reason. He let out a roar that started in his mouth and throat but blasted through the dinar, so loud it seemed to stretch across deserts and oceans and time itself, leaving him deaf to the battle, deaf to everything but the ragged sound of Bela's breathing.

For a split second, the Sibyls and the demons hesitated in the pitch of their battle, stunned by the weapons-grade noise.

Duncan tore through the weakened elemental energy gripping his arms and legs and thundered past Andy, Dio, Camille, and the Mothers. He let out another roar, and cat-demons dropped to their knees, covering their ears.

Duncan broke between Strada and Bela, who was still on her knees, struggling to stand.

Duncan pulled her up and swept her behind him.

Strada's hateful golden eyes fixed on Duncan's dinar, and the big demon went still where he stood. All around him, Rakshasa fighters seemed to get confused. Some fell back, breaking the solid line of advance.

"Time to die." Duncan tried to reach for Strada's neck, but John held his arms still.

You can't kill him with your bare hands.

Hot rage charged through Duncan. "The hell you say. I can take him, John."

He's not Created. He's Eldest, and you're wearing the coin. You can't touch him any more than he can touch you—the energy repels.

"Watch me." Duncan struggled against John's control of his arms. He heard the Sibyls forming new ranks beside him, boxing out the cats on his left and right, and giving Bela some cover. Her soft swearing sounded like music to Duncan. If she could curse, she could breathe, and if she could breathe, he could save her—and he would, no matter what John tried to say or do.

What's the only way out of a blind firefight in a dead-end alley?

John's tone was scarily calm.

Duncan stopped fighting John's interference.

He remembered John's riddle from the thousand cranked-up, mutilated versions of Capture the Flag they had played until they starting making war for real.

"Bluff," Duncan said, and control of his arms came back to him.

John supplied the second part of the answer. *Throw your empty gun in the other bastard's face.*

"And run like hell," Duncan finished, his mind completely clear again.

He did a quick check of his hands, his arms, his legs, his feet. All still there. All ready for action.

"Okay, John." He set his jaw and took a hard breath. "You take the point."

Duncan had the sensation of John's awareness moving forward again, not taking over, but as close as he'd get to that now.

Strada's eyes blazed golden, then black as Duncan stepped forward and he had to give ground. All his smaller cats moved back a few steps with him, and Duncan could see, feel, even taste how the coin repelled them.

The effect's never been that strong before, John said.

It was strong, all right. The tigers didn't want to be near it, didn't seem to be able to challenge it, not at all.

"Can you enhance it even more, John? Pull our energy through the dinar like you did my voice?"

He got no answer, but heat blazed through the coin around his neck.

The tiger-demons howled and backed off another few steps.

Duncan's wounds burned and oozed blood, but he shifted his position enough to get an estimate of the size of the shield he and John were creating. About eight feet in all directions.

"Get behind me," he told the Sibyls, hearing a trace of John's voice mingling with his own. The alley wall would protect against attack from the rear. The demons couldn't approach him from the front, not with the coin around his neck. He figured the Sibyls' elemental energy wouldn't penetrate the shield the coin established, and the fact they weren't trying to use any pretty much confirmed that assumption. "Stay close."

Whispers of movement let him know his command had been obeyed. He heard the sound of Bela's rapid breathing, felt the heat of her presence radiate against his back, so vibrant, so *alive,* and that doubled his determination to pull off the bluff John was laying out for him.

"You are no one," Strada growled at Duncan. He sounded like he was trying to convince himself. His gaze stayed locked on the coin hanging around Duncan's neck, and he sniffed the air, tiger nostrils flaring. "I do not know you."

"But you do," Duncan said with John, hearing the echo of his friend's voice even more clearly. "I killed your true brothers in London and St. Petersburg. I slaughtered your true brothers in San Francisco and Mexico City. And soon, very soon, Strada, I'm going to kill the rest of your psychotic family—and you, too."

The white tiger-demon threw back his head and let out an ear-crushing howl of absolute madness. His smaller kitties backed up a few more steps, and a couple of them scattered, fleeing the alley—or Strada. Duncan didn't know or care which.

He kept eye contact with the crazed tiger-demon as more of the bastard's followers deserted him.

Duncan. Get ready to throw your gun.

Duncan put one arm behind his back and gave quick signals, hoping like hell somebody back there, somebody like Andy Myles, had a clue about military hand signals.

Attention. Seven. Wedge formation. North.

"On my mark," he said, knowing that Strada probably heard, but banking on the bastard being too confused and stunned to make sense of it.

"This is a trick." Strada leaned toward him, eyes wide and wild. He butted his big white head against the invisible barrier the coin created. Duncan couldn't see the field of energy, but he knew it was there. "You speak with a dead man's voice. I tore out John Cole's throat myself."

"Did you?" John made Duncan's left eye wink. "Here, kitty, kitty, kitty . . ."

A fresh howl of rage tore out of Strada.

The alley seemed to vibrate, and Duncan understood that the new vibrations weren't coming from the cat's shriek or the Sibyls.

Headlights sliced into the alley. A slightly damaged Jeep with a banged-up SUV right on its ass jumped the distant curb on the side street and barreled straight down the alley toward them, bashing and scattering Rakshasa in every direction.

Brakes squealed, and Duncan caught a glimpse of Blackjack's stony battle face through the tinted windshield.

"Move out!" Duncan shouted, and lunged toward Strada before the cat-demon even finished shrieking.

The coin's energy pounded Duncan with a weight worse than sitting in the hot seat in a G-force simulator. His skin tried to peel off his bones, but before he exploded, he fell backward.

So did Strada and his remaining cat-demons.

By the time Duncan got to his feet, the Sibyls were loaded and the SUV and Jeep were already screeching backward out of the alley. Duncan hauled ass after them. More Sibyls were trying to cram into the alley, but Duncan waved them off and shouted, "Fall back. Get out of here. Fall back!"

His dinar-enhanced voice seemed to carry for miles.

The Sibyls hesitated only a second, then bugged out like a swarm of leather-clad ants, all heading north.

The Jeep slowed as the SUV swerved into traffic behind it, sending dozens of cars spiraling left and right and three of them crashing into the wall at Central Park. The back-seat passenger door popped open, and Duncan hurled himself inside, caught the handle, and slammed the Jeep's door shut as Blackjack gunned the engine and tore off down the pavement.

Bela cried out and grabbed for Duncan.

He wrapped both arms around her, pulled her straight off the Jeep seat, and buried his face in her leather-covered chest. Her heart thumped against his cheek as she held him and kissed his head. She was shaking. Her fists were tight in his hair. And she was alive.

He felt weak with relief, and powerful enough to bash down mountains.

Alive, alive, alive.

Duncan rocked her against him, taking in the sweet scent of leather and almonds and sweat. He was vaguely aware of Blackjack driving the Jeep with Andy next to him. The only thing that truly existed in Duncan's world was the woman in his arms.

For a long few seconds, he kept her all to himself, doing his talking with his mouth on the whisper-soft bare skin just above her zipper. Her lips pressed against his ear, and when she pulled back, she gazed into his eyes like she was reading every word written on his soul.

Her fingers traveled across his chest to the dinar hanging on its chain outside his bloodstained shirt. When she touched it, emotion and sensation jolted him so hard he had to suck air as if he'd taken a gut punch. *Damn. Damn!* He wanted to peel her clothes off and make love to her right there, and he didn't give a damn who saw. The same passion flared in her dark eyes, and he almost came undone.

Bela's hand fell away from the dinar, and she tucked his head under her chin.

"Just hold me," she whispered, and he held her for block after block, listening to the pounding of his pulse in his ears. Duncan couldn't think of anything he'd rather be doing.

". . . headquarters," Blackjack was saying as he drove. "The townhouse seems like the safest place."

Andy went stiff in her seat. Bela sat up straighter in Duncan's lap, and concern forced him to look up at her. It was then he realized that she had a massive bruise on her cheek, so bad her jaw might not work right for a month.

He thought about Strada, and about tearing the cat-demon's head off his big white body. After he ripped off the bastard's legs and arms. One at a time.

"That looks bad, Angel." He touched her chin just below the bruise.

Bela put a hand to her face. "Sibyls heal quickly," she said, but he caught the edge in her tone as her eyes stayed fixed on Andy.

"Hey." Duncan gently turned her to face him. He inclined his head toward the front seat and lowered his voice so Blackjack couldn't hear him. "I don't know what you're worried about, but don't. Whatever might go down at the townhouse, I've got your back—and hers."

Bela's expression softened. She moved her fingers from her own cheek to his. "I've fought beside some of the best warriors in the world, but watching you face down a horde of Rakshasa demons with nothing but your bare hands and a dinar on a chain—that was worth seeing."

Duncan smiled at her. "I've never seen anybody use a sword the way you did. Pretty mean kick you've got, too."

Bela glanced at Andy. "I'd do anything to save them."

Her voice caught, and her chest hitched.

Duncan took Bela's chin in his hand and turned her face back to his so that she could see the truth in his eyes. "Then so would I."

He kissed her then, and settled her head under his chin. As far as he was concerned, he could hold her forever, if he had forever left.

(33)

Bela got out of the Jeep with Duncan, and they stood with Jack Blackmore and Andy on the sidewalk outside the safety fence at Headcase Quarters, waiting for Bela's SUV to arrive. The Brent brothers were probably steering more slowly and carefully through the streets of New York City because they were driving the Mothers.

The night's energy had gone back to a more normal rhythm, and Bela didn't have any sense of the Rakshasa tracking them or following them. They probably didn't have to track, though. If they knew about the brownstone, the demons probably had a fair grasp of where all the Sibyls in New York City lived. She sent out a few tendrils of earth energy, using her terrasentience to be sure they weren't about to be attacked again, and got nothing.

For now.

Bela glanced at Duncan beside her, at the stains on his shirt, and realized his demon wounds were open at the top and bottom, weeping blood into the cotton. Her heart squeezed so hard her knees almost caved.

He saw her looking and took her hand in his before she could touch the slashes. "They got worse when we stopped to join the battle, and when John and I yelled—and when we magnified the dinar's shield to cover all the Sibyls."

Bela let earth energy slip from her fingertips, and the bleeding slowed to almost nothing. "Projective energy," she whispered, relieved and miserable at the same time. "It magnifies demon energy like everything else. Camille told you not to use it."

"I thought she told me not to walk through any mirrors." Duncan's grin let her know he understood—and probably had understood when he chose to do it, to save her life and everyone else's.

Bela rested her palm on Duncan's cheek, fighting the blistering, aching agony of knowing time was slipping away from them even faster now. She wanted to touch him more, all over. She wanted days, weeks, months of making love to him, but she couldn't have that. Not now. Maybe not ever.

"The Mothers cleared me in the Patterson murder," he said. "And they worked things out with John so I'm in control now, for sure. They—"

"I don't need to know." Bela drew her fingers across his face and lips, then let her arm relax against her side as he gave her a confused look. "I never doubted you, Duncan."

She had to turn away from him then, because rage from the battle had gone to war with grief over what was happening to him, and she didn't want him to see her cry. A few yards away, Andy walked away from Jack Blackmore. Her face had gone pale, and she looked tense enough to blow up fire hydrants.

Rage boiled over the sadness inside Bela.

She strode away from Duncan, went to face Andy, put both hands on Andy's shoulders, and looked her straight in the eyes. "We're here to regroup, and then we're leaving. You do *not* have to stay here."

Andy's gaze flickered to the townhouse. "They'll try to make us. Blackmore's already on about it. The Mothers, the OCU—everybody will back him up."

"Screw them all." Bela shook inside, hot all over, then freezing the next second, but outside, she heard herself sounding calmer and more definite. "This ends tonight, because we're going to end it. You and Camille and Dio and me. Are you with me?"

Andy's eyebrows lifted, and her color perked up. "Fuckin' A. Just tell me when."

Thunder whickered in the distance, but the night sky was clear and full of stars. Before Bela could give much thought to it, a quick squeal of brakes announced the arrival of her SUV. Bela and Andy turned toward the sound, and Bela saw her beat-up vehicle lining itself up behind the Jeep on the curb.

The Brent brothers bailed out of the SUV as Dio and Camille helped the Mothers disembark. Calvin Brent looked like he'd been caught in a Mixmaster, with his wind-twisted clothes and blown hair. The taller brother, Saul, had a few holes singed across his black NYPD jacket.

Bela gave Mother Keara a quick glare as the old woman marched up to her, letting off a light fog of smoke. "Was that necessary?"

"I *told* the fool I had to sneeze." Mother Keara rubbed one watering eye. "It's not my fault yer humans are so blessed slow. Those cat-demons make me sniffly."

She stalked off toward the townhouse and sneezed again, scorching the sidewalk. Mother Anemone flowed along behind her, emanating peace and a certain breezy disapproval. Mother Yana hobbled by almost at the same pace, back to needing Camille's support since losing her cane in the battle with the Rakshasa. The ancient Mother's frailness came and went, but Bela didn't question it. When she was that old, she'd hobble whenever she felt like it.

Camille searched Bela's face as she went by, and Andy's. She slowed to a stop. "We'll take care of this, right, Bela?"

Bela gave her arm a squeeze. "Absolutely."

"Let me get her settled." Camille jerked her head back toward Dio, who was still standing with both hands on the SUV's back door, head turned away from Bela. "You handle that one."

Shit.

A big knot tied itself in Bela's stomach.

What now?

Actually, she didn't give a shit.

Bela had had all she could take of Dio's temper, and all she could take of Dio's rejection. That would end tonight, too, one way or another. Her rage drained away into a cool, earthy anger, and she let it fill her until she felt ready.

"Don't follow me," Bela told Andy as she walked away, heading for Dio. "And keep Duncan and Blackmore back, too."

"On it," Andy said, and water energy built at Bela's back as she moved away.

When Bela reached the SUV, Dio didn't raise her head.

Bela looked at the sky and then the earth for strength. She was a mortar, the base of her quad. If she couldn't pull this together—pull *them* together—then nobody could.

"What do you want from me?" Bela asked Dio, sincerely wanting to know. "Am I supposed to apologize for staying alive tonight? Do you regret knifing that cat and saving me?"

Dio's head whipped up, and her stormy eyes went wide with horror. Her mouth trembled, and she wailed, "No!"

Then she burst into tears and put her face in her hands.

Bela stood next to her, experiencing something like shell-shock.

I so don't get what's happening here.

Dio kept crying.

Bela lifted a hand to comfort her, then put it down. Lifted it again.

"Oh, screw this. Screw it all." She grabbed Dio and jerked her into a firm hug, yanking all the earth power she could to protect herself.

The tooth-cracking blast of wind energy didn't make her let go. No way. Not this time. "Help me understand, Dio. *Make* me understand."

Dio gave her another wind blast. "You're—you're invading my personal space."

"I don't give a shit." The power of the earth laced through Bela's words, meeting the air energy pushing toward her with incontrovertible force. "Let me in, Dio."

Dio gasped and went stiff in her grasp. Bela tried to ease up on the energy she was channeling, but it wasn't easy. Dio started to shake, and thunder exploded over Central Park, less than a mile away. Her fists closed on the shoulders of Bela's leathers, and she sobbed again, like her heart was shattering.

Bela cried with her, over a thousand different things, but more than that, she held on, and kept holding on, until the storm eased and Dio released her stranglehold on Bela's arms.

"I almost didn't," Dio whispered, pushing both of her hands against the top of her head.

Bela risked leaning back from her so she could see Dio's face. "You almost didn't what?"

Dio's lips trembled. "I almost didn't save you."

That shell-shocked feeling hit Bela again, and she didn't know what to say.

"The wrong move, or even the right one—it might not have been enough, and that fast"—Dio snapped her fingers next to Bela's ear—"you could have been gone."

"Oh, honey." Bela exhaled, her breath rattling. "I know."

Dio threw her arms around Bela's neck, and a hot whirling hurricane swept around the two of them. "I'm sorry. I'm so sorry."

Bela almost didn't notice the pebbles smashing into her head with concussion force. She hugged Dio back and anchored her legs to keep them both from blowing over. "We don't have to be sorry anymore, okay? We just have to be together as a quad, and help each other."

It took another minute or so, but Dio gradually got herself together, and her wind energy calmed enough that Bela stopped blocking it to save the nearby cars.

"They almost got us," Dio said as she let Bela go and walked a step or two toward the townhouse, running her fingers through her wispy blond hair. She stopped. Turned to Bela again. "I want to go find them *now*. I know I could. I know *we* could."

"We will." Bela linked her arm through Dio's and guided her toward the spot where Andy stood with Duncan and Jack Blackmore. "After we fight it out with the Mothers, the OCU, and the other triads. All of them are going to want to seal us in carbon or some shit, since we're obviously the Rakshasa's targets for now."

"Well, let me go so I can go polish my knives." Dio broke away from her, and her grin made Bela remember all the scenes of murder Dio had so happily been sketching before the demons attacked.

She and Andy and Blackmore headed into the townhouse, and Bela watched them go as she walked toward Duncan, amazed that Blackmore had been standing next to Andy so long without getting drowned or getting anything broken. Andy might be feeling sorry for him, since he was still getting over those burns.

Duncan let Bela walk all the way up to him, and he seemed to be appraising the dozen or so cuts on her face and neck. "That stuff by the SUV with Dio . . . was that a good thing?"

Bela pushed herself up on her toes and kissed his cheek, enjoying the scrape of stubble against her lips. "A very good thing."

Duncan folded her up in his arms and gave her a real kiss, then led her through the gate and up the stairs to the townhouse door.

Before they went inside, Bela stopped, knowing Duncan would stop, too.

Keeping her eyes on the door, she inhaled, trying to calm the sudden racing of her heart. "What you said in the Jeep, that you'd do anything to save my quad . . . did you mean it?"

"Every word."

"Okay." She pushed the door open. "You're about to get a chance to prove it."

(34)

Duncan felt like a big sardine in the conference room full of Sibyls, OCU officers, and Mothers—six or seven from each Motherhouse, except Andy's. He was standing at the head of the room behind a long table, with Blackjack and Bela and her quad. The Mothers massed in robed clumps on the other side, and the Sibyls made a thick wall of black leather between them and the officers. Saul and Calvin Brent hung by the room's big windows, but Duncan didn't see Creed or Nick anywhere, or Riana and her triad.

"We're not staying," Bela told Blackjack. Again. Louder this time.

She almost backed into Duncan when she spoke, and he steadied her with one hand on the small of her back. On his right, Andy kept twitching, and Duncan knew it was just a matter of time before sprinklers started breaking. Dio and Camille had Andy's arms to keep her calm, but that only went so far.

Blackjack blew out a breath. His face turned a little redder as he glanced at Duncan. "Sharp, make her see reason."

Duncan wanted to laugh at Blackjack over that, but he didn't. "I think she's seeing reason just fine."

"Christ, Duncan!" Blackjack reached beet color. "Jeremiah Drake got butchered while we fought those bastards in the alley, and that old lawyer Figg, too. I've got a unit on the way to Alsace's place because everybody you talked to, they're dead—and you know she's next." Blackjack pointed to Bela. Then he pointed to Andy and Dio and

Camille. "They're *all* next. You'd let them put themselves in harm's way?"

"Warriors live in harm's way." Duncan eased Bela to the side so he could deal with Blackjack more directly. "If Bela and her quad want this fight, then I'll have their six. What about you?"

Blackjack raised a finger and pointed it toward Duncan's face. "Sharp, I'll—"

"What, Blackjack? Take my badge?" Duncan pulled his shield out of his pocket and tossed it on the conference table. "Have at it. I'm dead in a few weeks anyway."

Goddess, it hurt to hear him say that.

Bela wanted to snatch the badge back off the table and cram it back where it belonged.

No.

No way.

Seeing Duncan give up his badge so easily made everything too real, too final. The shaking started inside her again, the changing and the rearranging, but she didn't want it, couldn't stand it—no!

Blackjack's mouth opened as he lowered his finger, but for a few seconds he didn't have anything to say. When he got himself focused again, he turned his attention to Bela. "If you're not comfortable staying here, what about the Sibyl safe houses?"

"No!" Bela banged her hand on the table, and it crunched as though she'd hit it with a sledgehammer. Earth energy rumbled into her voice. "Enough of this shit. They came after my family *in our home*. Now we're going after them."

"All of us," Camille said, and half the room jumped because they'd never heard her talk so loud.

"With Dio? I wouldn't advise it." Merilee Alexander Lowell's voice came from the conference room door, and

Bela almost hit her with an earthquake, it startled her so badly.

A quiet pressed over the room. Ranks of officers and Sibyls parted to let Merilee through. Her expression stayed neutral, but Bela saw sadness and worry in her blue eyes.

Dio let go of Andy and stared at Mother Anemone. "You told her?"

In the group of Greek Mothers, Mother Anemone lowered her head. "We agreed I wouldn't lie if asked."

Bela's gut started a slow roll.

Whatever this was, she wasn't going to like it, and they didn't need it. Not now. *Shit!*

By the time Merilee got to the table, all the air Sibyl Mothers looked uncomfortable. When they didn't explain, Merilee rested her palm on the table, halfway to Bela. "Dio's a weather-maker. I didn't know, because I was gone before she and her sister started training. Motherhouse Greece never should have allowed her to join a fighting group, at least not without warning you first."

Bela blinked from the shock.

All the thunder . . .

All the storms in clear skies . . .

Duncan, Camille, and Andy moved out of the way, and Bela turned to face Dio.

Dio's face pinched into misery. She looked away.

"A few air Sibyls do more than move air," Camille murmured to Duncan, sounding awed. "Some have a talent for calling weather, or creating it, but it's dangerous and unstable. They don't train it and try not to breed for it—and weather-makers aren't supposed to fight."

Dio smacked her fist against the conference room wall. "I know how to control myself."

"Your lightning blew out half the windows in this townhouse during Duncan's healing," Merilee's smile was as sad as her eyes. "Control might be an issue—but that's up to Bela. She just needed to know, for everyone's safety."

Bela glanced over her shoulder. Mother Anemone and her fellow Mothers looked unbearably sad. They obviously cared for Dio and hadn't been able to stand seeing her so alone, grieving herself to death over Devin.

They also didn't seem about to make a proclamation that Dio couldn't keep fighting, now that she'd started.

Bela faced Dio again, beginning to let go of the shock.

Dio's clear gray eyes held so much pain Bela wasn't sure she could stand it. Finally. Finally she understood the rest of this puzzle.

"I've never used it in a fight on purpose, Bela." Dio's voice had never sounded so small and vulnerable. "I never would. Please trust me. *Please.*"

And here it is again. Bela couldn't stop gazing into Dio's eyes. *One of my own choices, coming back to bite my ass.*

But this was a choice she didn't think she'd ever regret.

She didn't have to check with Andy and Camille to see what they thought, because she sensed their protective anger as strongly as she felt her own. Duncan had his own energy, like a mountain standing serene in a howling storm, and that buoyed her, too.

"It makes more sense to me now, why you held so tight to your rage over Devin's loss." Bela reached up and touched Dio's soft hair. "The other air Sibyls you trained with, they would have rejected you out of hand once they knew. Your sister was all you had—until now."

Dio closed her eyes.

When she opened them and smiled, it was like the sun coming out.

Bela squeezed her shoulder, then looked at Duncan and the rest of her quad. "We're done here. We've got some demons to kill."

Bela went first, making her way from behind the table into the pin-silent room. The path that Merilee had cleared was still open, and the only thing in Bela's way was Mother Keara. She stood like a stubborn little statue, unmoving but smoking, with green-robed fire Sibyl Mothers on one side and brown-robed earth Sibyl Mothers on the other.

Bela walked toward her, sensing the growing force and energy of her quad behind her.

Mother Keara didn't move.

Bela slowed and stopped a few paces away. "Get out of my way, old woman."

Every Sibyl in the room gasped, and the Mothers present from Russia frowned so deeply they looked like morose, wrinkled-up nesting dolls.

Bela ignored them.

They had never liked her, and she had no use for them, either.

Mother Keara was a different story.

She held Bela's gaze for a moment, then started to laugh.

"Go after that big white bastard," she said. "Killing him would be a game-changer, and you're the only ones who can track him, the four of you."

Mother Keara's own peers started to argue with her, but she set off a firewall tall enough to singe Bela's eyebrows and the ceiling and kept laughing while they tried to quell it and failed. The Russian and Greek Mothers moved away fast. Nobody, least of all wise and cautious Mothers, would be stupid enough to jump into a catfight between a gaggle of ancient Irish fire Sibyls. The whole bunch of them ended up storming out of the conference room, still pitching fireballs and yelling at each other.

Bela felt even stronger now, and as fierce as Mother Keara's column of fire. Duncan's hands settled firm against her waist, and he whispered, "Get us some backup, and I'll come up with some kind of operation plan."

"Who's with us?" Bela asked the Sibyls and the OCU officers in the room.

Every hand shot into the air.

"You can't vote on this!" Blackmore slammed both fists

on the conference table behind them, yelling so loudly Bela's ears rang. "It doesn't work like that!"

"Yes, it does!" Andy yelled right back at him, her voice as mighty and terrible as the yawning roar of a tsunami. "In this unit, it fucking does!"

"Oh, shit," Duncan muttered—and Jack Blackmore was gone again, this time riding Andy's wave out the conference room window, along with some chairs, the blackboard, and three boxes of chalk.

The Brent brothers, at least, had the good sense to jump out of the way.

A lot of the Sibyls laughed, and some of the officers, too. The rest just shook their heads. "Form up in the hall," Bela told them. "Give us five or ten, and we'll have assignments."

As the officers and Sibyls filed out, Bela saw Mother Yana and Mother Anemone at the broken window, gazing out at the ground below with the rest of the air and earth Mothers. "Ve need to talk vith that man." Mother Yana shook her head. "Ve should arrange for him to visit the Motherhouses and spend time vith us so he learns, before he gets himself dead."

"He can go with you to Russia first," Mother Anemone said, a little too brightly.

Merilee met Bela at the conference room door, and before Bela could tell her how many ways to get herself fucked, she said, "Cynda and Riana are in the basement with Nick and Creed. They've got property records for Samuel Griffen—warehouses and storage facilities. I think you should see them."

(35)

Duncan didn't think he'd ever seen a raid like this one—but he'd planned it and Nick Lowell signed off on it, since Blackjack was apparently on his way to Russia through one of those mirror-transport-channel things. Without Blackjack's shenanigans, the whole unit worked together pretty well to pull together intel and details. They decided to move just after dark, so the Sibyls wouldn't be so visible to the public.

Samuel Griffen owned the Garment District warehouse they'd targeted. Recon patrols reported that the building had elemental shields the Sibyls hadn't encountered before, elegant but also simple, more or less hidden in plain sight. Two Rakshasa had been sighted and confirmed on premises, visible through a third-floor window. The smaller kind, not the big bastards, but it was a start.

The place had been polished up to house a business—Panthera Security. Panthera, as in part of the scientific classification for tigers.

Cute, John growled.

The Panthera Security building faced an alley near Times Square. The NYPD had shut down traffic, and plainclothes officers had sealed off the entire block. The Sibyls and the OCU were staging at the far end of the alley.

Duncan had his badge, his Glock—and four women in leather jumpsuits and face masks on his right flank, carrying swords and knives. Three more Sibyls—Riana, Cynda, and Merilee—had his left flank and made up the rest of his part of the raid team. One of them had a freaking bow and arrow, but whatever.

Apparently Sibyls didn't hold grudges long. At least not these two bunches.

My history with Riana's triad is complicated, Bela had explained, and that was good enough for Duncan.

In addition to the Sibyls next to him and six more triads positioned around Panthera—two on the adjoining roofs and four on the ground—Duncan had thirty-six OCU officers at his command. And two Curson demons, flying in with their Astaroth demon brother and three of his winged buddies.

"Not the easiest set of tacticals," he admitted to Bela as she strapped a body armor vest over her leathers, then covered that with a black NYPD raid jacket.

"The demons will take care of themselves." She zipped her jacket, and he wished he could pull off her face mask to see her better. "Worry about the officers."

Duncan gave her a thumbs-up and checked his ranks. OCU SWAT lined both sides of the alley, decked out in boots, black fire-resistant coveralls, and body armor. They all wore black gloves, black face covers, black Kevlar helmets, and night-vision goggles. Their assault rifles had been loaded with elementally locked bullets, and they carried a big payload of flashbangs, too, since the cats didn't seem to like noise. Duncan had them add a few Stingers and tear gas grenades in case the cats had their human helpers armed.

If everything went according to plan, OCU SWAT would shoot straight and do the heart piercing, and the Sibyls would manage beheading, burning, and dispersing.

Duncan's pulse picked up.

"Form up!" he called to his team as he fastened his own vest, careful to leave the dinar on the outside. "Take positions, and get behind your safe lines."

The SWAT officers broke into their assigned teams, four at a time, joining with the Sibyl ground groups, then moving off a few paces to stand behind marks on the pavement—safe lines traced just out of sight of the building's windows. When the Sibyls attacked Panthera's elemental barriers, humans needed to be farther back, so the energy wouldn't kill them.

In minutes, the front and back entrances to Panthera had been covered, with officers close to the door, but also staggered with the Sibyls in a wide arc to prevent escapes. The sky exit had eyes on it, though until the Sibyls broke Panthera's elemental barriers, they couldn't deploy teams to the roof directly.

On Duncan's elementally shielded radio, teams reported.

Ready.

Ready.

Ready.

"Ready," Bela said, her voice sending Duncan's senses into supernova. He really didn't like this next bit, letting her get so far away from him with no cover, but this was what Sibyls did. What Bela did. Duncan had to respect that.

There were no kisses during major police operations, so he gave her a fist bump and said, "Do your thing, Angel."

Bela led her quad into the open, with Riana's triad following. They fanned out, like the triads on the surrounding roofs and, Duncan assumed, at the back of the building.

Duncan stayed inside the mouth of the alley, behind his safe line, wishing he didn't have to.

John's awareness filtered into his to say, *I could shield us with the dinar, but . . .*

"Yeah."

But he'd become a little more demon every minute John made use of that projective energy.

"Not unless we have to, John."

Out on the street, Bela and Riana raised their arms, and the ground shook under Duncan as it gave up its power. New York City rumbled and bumped, then the energy settled into a steady grumble, flowing toward Panthera so hard Duncan thought he could feel it in his teeth. He could smell it, too, rich, fertile, and sweet.

Camille went next, lifting her hands and letting off a torrent of fire. Cynda followed suit, and fire glowed from other key locations. They directed it at Panthera, and flames coated the front of the building, hissing and popping. Smoke drifted overhead, blocking out the city lights, until wind howled down from the cloudy sky to whip the flames and batter at the building's windows. That was nothing—nothing—compared to the waves that hit it. Sheet after sheet of water crashed into the place, somehow joining with the fire and making it stronger.

Pressure built against Duncan's ears. His eyes watered. He kept swallowing, but his throat got drier by the second.

He glanced at the safe line.

What would all this energy feel like on the other side of that line?

Skull-cracking was the only description he could think of.

The building made a deep, low groan, and Duncan's pulse shot to full throttle.

"That didn't sound right," he barked into his radio, but nobody answered him. He tried a few more channels and codes. The thing had gone dead. Duncan jammed it back in his belt—and that sound came again, only deeper this time. Like a foundation cracking, and beginning to shift. Whatever the Sibyls were breaking, he didn't think it was the elemental barriers.

Blood thumped in Duncan's ears, fighting the pressure as he leaned close to the safe line and cupped his hands to his mouth. "Bela, break off!"

All the rumbling and blazing and whistling and splashing covered his command, but Sibyls had sensitive perception. Duncan knew Bela heard him—but she gave him no response. None of the Sibyls in his line of sight so much as twitched.

Shit. John's anxious voice rattled through Duncan's mind. *This is wrong.*

"Break off, damnit!" Duncan forced himself over the safe line. His dinar lifted off his neck, pulling toward Panthera so hard the chain cut into him.

Duncan grabbed the coin and slammed it against his chest.

He got it now. The Sibyls weren't stopping because they couldn't. Panthera's shields were drinking everything they hurled at it—and they couldn't stop the flow and couldn't get away.

"I'm coming, Angel." Duncan tried to take a step toward Bela but lurched forward, towed by the unbelievable elemental magnetism beginning to center on the building. He had to go to one knee and keep his head down to keep from flying forward and smashing into Panthera's front doors.

"John." It was hard to talk. "I need you."

But John was already there, and Duncan's dinar glowed with a hot, painful power. He coughed as his wounds blazed into aches and throbs. Finally he could throw off enough of the energy to move now.

So much noise—

Four steps to get to Bela.

Duncan kept his head down.

Three steps. Two.

He thought his eyeballs might explode.

One step—

"Bela!" He tried to grab her arm, but her energy punched him like a fist, and he staggered backward.

Duncan didn't even get his breath before he launched forward again, this time forcing his way around her until he could see her face.

Her dark eyes streamed with tears, wide and wild and panicked. Tiny red dots formed in the whites and on her cheeks. Her lips had darkened to a pale, terrifying blue.

Not breathing.

Every nerve ending in Duncan's body fired. He shouted into her face, into the wind and fire and water and earth, his thoughts spinning

Live wires—

Can't grab them—

Live wires.

A memory, his and John's, after a blast had taken down poles and lines in the desert. A sergeant going nuts as wires danced and sparked and set everything on fire. *Knock them down, knock them down, get them on the ground!*

Duncan yelled that out loud as he backed away, then hit the deck and rolled himself at Bela's legs. He slammed into her just below the knees and she went down hard. Duncan rolled away and came back again, using his body and legs to knock down Dio and Camille.

Unearthly bellows rose over the energy still flowing, and Duncan looked up in time to see golden glowing Curson demons fall out of the sky. They bowled down Andy and Riana's triad, then lunged for the nearest Sibyl group farther down the street.

Winged demons dove and struck the Sibyls on the roof, then took off toward the other Sibyl teams.

Elemental energy crushed out from Panthera each time it lost a connection with a Sibyl, harder, harder, like a bubble expanding. Hand on his dinar, Duncan could see it, building, moving, and he knew what it meant.

His thoughts broke down to fragments.

"Cover!" he yelled to Nick and Creed and the Astaroths.

"Cover!" He waved his arm at the officers behind safe lines who could see him. He scrambled to his knees and threw himself toward Bela.

With a huge suck inward, Panthera dragged everything not set in cement straight toward its walls—

And exploded.

36

Bela tasted rock dust in her mouth and spit it out.

Why was she underground?

Why couldn't she see anything, hear anything, sense anything?

She moved the earth and rock over her head—ah. Stars. A sky.

Water arced in a fountain to her right, splattering toward her.

She had blood on her face. Still nothing from her ears or her elemental senses. They felt numb.

Something cut into her right hand, something she'd clenched tight in her first. She opened her fingers.

A little piece of copper.

Bela held on to it and sat up. Fell back. Sat up again, so woozy she barely kept her balance. On either side of her, piles of brick and rock and metal and rubble blocked her view.

She remembered rolling on the ground, gasping, retching, trying to breathe. She had crammed her hand in her pocket to get the copper charm to focus herself, make herself stronger, then—

"Oh, Goddess."

She said that, felt the vibration, but she didn't hear it.

Bela slipped the copper charm into her pocket, grabbed the nearest piece of stone, and hauled herself to her feet. Her left arm hung useless and twisted at her side. Broken ribs creaked when she moved. The pain made her scream, and the scream made her spit a mouthful of blood all over the dust at her feet. She closed her eyes and pulled at earth energy to heal what she could—

Nothing.

When she looked around, she saw a jagged, wide field of rubble where Panthera had been, and the street in front of it.

I'm the only one standing.

Red lights flashed—emergency vehicles, trying to reach either end of the devastation.

The building had blown up.

The fucking elemental trap of a building had locked her in place, drained her dry, drained them all dry, numbed her elemental senses completely, and blown up.

Bela didn't hear her own snarl, but she felt it.

If any of the damned building had still been standing, she would have drawn her sword with her good arm and hacked it all the way down to the ground. She'd never experienced a trap like that. Never read about it. Never even imagined it—but she should have.

Projective energy. Drawing it in, sending it out. The trap constructed in the building had taken everything out of her, everything out of all of them, then used their own power to blow them to hell.

And the thought came back.

I'm the only one standing.

She reached out with her senses again, desperate for any hint of Camille, or Dio, or Andy, or Duncan.

Silence.

No heartbeats. No breathing. No life essence anywhere near her.

She had no sense of Riana. Not Cynda. Not Merilee. No Nick, no Creed, no Jake.

They weren't here.

Their life energy just—wasn't.

It was gone.

All of them . . . gone.

I'm the only one standing.

No.

No!

Bela threw her broken body toward the nearest pile of rocks and used her good hand to dig against the jagged stone. Each movement hurt like falling on iron spikes, but damnit, there had to be somebody here, somebody alive other than her. Bela pulled and shifted and clawed rubble until her nails split, until her palm and fingers got so raw each pebble and bit of metal seemed to burn straight through her skin.

Come, on, Camille. Andy? Dio?

Duncan . . .

Bela ripped another bunch of rocks loose and found nothing but bare ground underneath, and the thought came back and this time it wouldn't leave, couldn't leave, because it was true, because nobody she loved was still here, because she couldn't find anything, couldn't sense a single bit of life, and it was too much, too much, too much.

I'm the only one standing.

She screamed so loud and long it drove her to the patch of ground she'd cleared, to her knees, and she puked blood until it came through her nose. She fished the copper charm out of her pocket for comfort, to have something of the earth and Duncan and her quad next to her. Then she leaned forward, holding herself up with her one arm, hacking and choking, her torn, bleeding fist clenched around the copper charm, and she wished she could die. She wished she could hear herself sobbing and screaming and swearing, because at least that would make sense.

When her forehead touched the earth, a shimmer of power flowed into her—enough to stop the choking.

Damnit.

Enough, even, to stop the bleeding from her hand and fingers, and begin to knit her broken ribs.

Damnit.

Enough . . . to let her see a pulse of poisoned green energy, right in front of her eyes.

Bela raised her head and sank back on her haunches, gripping the copper piece. She pulled with her power, and more energy came to her, into her body. Into the copper. It seemed so easy now to use her terrasentience to draw on the earth and turn it outward. Had she ever had difficulty with that?

The Rakshasa energy was so obvious and strong, blasting through the numbness in her mind and heart. She pulled herself to standing again, then staggered across the cleared patch in the debris, toward Panthera.

Oh, yeah. A lot of elemental traces now. Some thin—the new demons? Three thick—the oldest Rakshasa? One of those thickest of all—

Strada.

Bela stared at the trace, at his tracks all across Panthera's ruins. Old ones and new ones. Lighter and darker.

She forced her feet to move toward the darker tracks. A steady stream of them, leading toward Times Square.

She followed them, doing what she could with her power to keep her body going, but really, she didn't care about that, as long as she stayed alive long enough to do what needed to be done. Hunting Strada . . . that made sense. She couldn't help anyone here, because there was no one to help—Goddess, no, she couldn't think about that. No. But she could hunt. With everything Bela was made of, everything she had left inside her, she would *not* let this demon get away to kill more people.

She'd run a sword through that bastard cat's heart, rip off his ugly white head, set him on fire, and blow him to eternity.

After that, she'd let herself think.

After that, she'd let herself truly understand that she'd lost Duncan and her quad and her friends.

After that, the pain could kill her, and she knew it would.

"You took everything away from me." She couldn't hear herself, but talking made her feel more clearheaded and put her crushing grief to the side—at least for a while. "Now it's my turn."

Bela tucked her copper charm inside her leathers so it touched her skin. Then she gripped her sword with her only functional hand and followed Strada's tracks. Her legs kept moving even though her ribs and arms burned as if fire Sibyls had attacked her. Her feet kept falling, one in front of the other, long after she lost all sense of where she was going or how long she'd been walking.

Times Square came and went, just a blur of lights and cars and night crowds and sounds that should have been there but weren't. The three thick traces separated at Avenue of the Americas. Smart move. The fuckers.

Bela tracked Strada north. Rockefeller Center, Radio City Music Hall—bright, happy-looking, so many people. Everything seemed the same, but nothing was. Bela moved and hurt and bled and healed what she could, what she had to.

At St. Patrick's Cathedral, Strada's trail got a lot stronger.

Bela had to let go of her sword hilt on Park Avenue. She ripped at the sleeve of her leathers with her teeth, tearing a strip long enough to bind her broken arm to her weapons belt. Keeping it still eased the agony some. The pain that was left kept her awake.

Her mind chipped and dug back through the day. She tried to avoid seeing faces. Duncan. Andy. Dio. Camille. Oh, sweet universe, why them, all of them and not her? Riana, Cynda, Merilee—her friends, but some of the Sibyls who died tonight, she knew only their names and faces, nothing about their lives. Half the OCU officers, she'd never met. Her thoughts circled through all the painful things, finally landing where she wanted. In the townhouse basement. When she and Duncan had studied the maps and operation plans and all the information Nick, Creed, and

Riana's triad had gathered about Samuel Griffen's properties. One of them was on East Fifty-ninth, near Lexington.
If Strada thought Panthera was the only location compro-
mised, he might take shelter there.

Goddess, she hurt. More earth energy soothed her, but it
lasted for just a minute. Strada's tracks glowed so brightly
now, they hurt her eyes.

Why did the moon seem so dim?

Bela put her hand on the bricks at the mouth of an alley
and bent over, trying not to collapse.

He'd turned in here—but why?

Because he knows.

He knows somebody's following him.

Her lips pulled away from her teeth.

What he doesn't know is who.

Dull traffic sounds made their way into her consciousness, seemingly miles away. Her ears and the rest of her
senses woke up a little. Her Sibyl body was healing itself,
no matter what she wanted.

Bela drew on the earth enough to stand. She slipped her
fingers inside her leathers and retrieved the copper charm.
When she squeezed it tightly and used what little earth
power she had, she could sense people moving nearby, and
plants, and animals. All that life touching the earth, all
around her. And in the alley . . .

Strada was waiting.

Bela's ears buzzed, and her hearing grew more acute. The
strains of a Pink Floyd song drifted to her.

Daddy, what else did you leave for me . . .

Yeah. She could work with that.

Duncan and Andy, they were all about gospel and folk.
Camille liked modern stuff, and Dio had her classical col-
lection. Screw all of that. Give her hard rock. Classic rock.
Pink Floyd was just fine with her.

All in all, you're just a . . .

Vicious, vengeful fury powered Bela's walk into that alley.

. . . another brick in the wall . . .

With each step she took, her mind worked with the copper charm, moving through it, getting the measure of it, understanding it down to the atoms and molecules, and shaping it with her pain. Then she put it in her mouth, to keep it touching her, and settled it between her cheek and gum.

When she found that bastard—

But there he was.

Bela blinked, not trusting her vision, and some of her powerful fury drained out of her.

At the walled end of the alley, at the terminus of the tracks she'd been following, stood a man, not a demon.

Tall and muscular—black eyes, black hair, tanned, expensive gray silk suit. She couldn't tell if the man had Hispanic or Italian heritage, or maybe Native American or Middle Eastern. Whatever it was, it made him easy on the eyes, if you didn't count the poisoned green energy clinging to his skin.

Rakshasa could imitate human form, but only for a few seconds. That's what Dio had told them, Bela remembered. So she gave it a few seconds. Blood dripped down her broken arm, and her good arm, too. She tasted a little in her mouth and spit it out.

The man stayed a man.

Yet the longer she stared at him, the more she could see a hint of white tiger, a suggestion of golden-eyed monster.

"We have a natural human form." Strada's voice was lightly accented and deep in this form, not full of growls and snarls. "We can hold it without limits, unlike shapes we borrow. Does mine please you?"

Hearing the bastard talk jarred Bela out of her shock and brought her back to her purpose. She drew enough earth energy to catch her breath and slow her bleeding again. "You killed them. My quad, my lover—my friends."

Strada laughed, and if Bela hadn't known what he was, if she hadn't been listening with her ever-healing Sibyl hearing, she would have found it natural. Even attractive. "Your loved ones killed themselves, or rather you did, when you attacked my business and my family. The trap I used—old and basic, but very effective."

Bela smiled at him, and she waited until he smiled back.

Then she said, still smiling, "I'm going to kill *you* now, and I'm going to make you suffer."

Strada moved so quickly he seemed to be at the alley's end in one second and standing in front of her the next. His iron-strong hands grabbed both of her elbows, and the pain of his grip on her fractured arm made her hiss and groan.

The demon-man let go of her good arm, grabbed her sword hilt and weapons belt, and ripped them away from her. He threw them against the alley wall.

Bela glared at him as her sword clattered to the ground. "You look like a man, but you still smell like cat piss."

He laughed again and ran a thumb along her cheek. "Such a beautiful creature." With his other hand, he squeezed her broken arm and made her scream. "All the Sibyls, so lovely. So powerful. Could I turn you, I wonder?"

He tried the thumb trick again, and Bela moved her head fast enough to bite him and draw some of his foul-tasting blood, which she spit in his face. He snatched his hand back, pulling at her wounded arm until she let out another shout of pain.

Strada's expression was part angry, part intrigued. "*Now* I understand, my dear. The real question is, if I turned you, could I control you?"

Claws brushed her cheek instead of fingers.

Bela lowered her head, fighting waves of revulsion.

The claws moved to the back of her neck, and the suited man's chest she was staring at shifted slowly to a broad swath of white tiger fur.

She shifted the copper charm to her tongue and reached deep, deep into the ground with her terrasentience.

When Strada squeezed her broken arm again, Bela tore a gout of energy from the center of the earth and spit the charm at the Rakshasa bastard with all the force of a volcano blowing its cone.

His golden demon eyes widened, and his tiger mouth opened.

His paws fell away from Bela and patted his chest, like he couldn't quite believe the blood spreading across his fur.

"Elementally treated copper." Bela smiled as he fell to his knees. "Hurts like a bitch when it pierces your heart, doesn't it?"

She lifted her foot and kicked him over, then limped to the alley wall and picked up her sword. She had to use her teeth to get it out of the sheath, and by the time she got back to Strada, she was so dizzy she could barely keep on her feet.

That was okay. She didn't have to. Not for what she had in mind.

She sank down and straddled the big tiger bastard as best she could, then lifted her sword until the tip rested above his wound. Her own blood dripped down the hilt and blade, adding lighter red to the dark maroon.

"I know you're probably healing, Strada. I know I don't have much time before you can move your arms and legs again—but my sword's made of elementally locked metal, too."

She rammed the blade into his heart, making him twitch and bellow.

Bela waited until he healed enough to look her in the face with his furious golden eyes. She made sure to give him her best smile. "That was for Duncan Sharp. I loved him very much."

Her next blow was for Andy, and the one after that for Dio, and the one after that for Camille.

It wasn't until she started on Riana's triad that her dizziness started to get the best of her. Earth energy wasn't helping much anymore. It was harder to make her thrusts, and she figured she'd just have to let the beheading avenge all the other Sibyls and OCU officers. She blacked out for a second and almost fell off him, but caught herself—apparently in time.

Strada lay absolutely still beneath her, and she pressed the sword blade to his furry white throat.

His hand shot up and grabbed her chin, shoving her so hard she flew backward and slammed into the alley wall, sitting hard on her ass.

Her sword fell out of her hand.

Her head slammed into stone as she tried to breathe.

No air.

Total agony all over her body, pure and blazing and killing.

No earth energy. She couldn't draw any strength at all.

Strada loomed over her, roaring.

He raised his claws—and a big, muscled arm slammed around his neck, jerking him into a choke hold.

Bela knew she was dying, and now she was having visions.

Wonderful visions of Duncan, alive and yelling as the energy from his dinar flared and drove demon and man apart.

Bela's vision darkened, then Duncan's hand cupped her cheek.

"Angel," he said. "You scared the hell out of me."

37

Thank God Bela was alive, but she didn't look good. That arm—and she was bleeding badly from wounds he couldn't even see. He kissed her lips very gently, and her eyelids fluttered.

"Love . . . you . . ." she whispered.

"I love you, too." He thought about picking her up but figured he couldn't get her past Strada before the demon got up again. Duncan had used his dinar and John's help to track Bela here after he fought his way out of the rubble. Her quad was coming, but Creed and Nick and the Astaroths were temporarily out of commission.

Strada snarled, and Duncan knew the demon was on his feet.

He jumped to his feet as well and put himself between Bela and the demon, trapping Strada in the walled end of the alley. His slash wounds burned like somebody had poured scalding water across them, and his chest and neck and arm had hair now, golden orange and black, like Bengal tigers he had seen at the zoo.

Strada gazed at him and growled. "You are turning, Duncan Sharp. More my pride than human now."

"I'll stay alive long enough to kill you—and I'll rip off my own head before I join your pride." God, he hated saying that word, and this demon, even more than the Rakshasa who'd cut him.

"Turn her." Strada pointed to Duncan. "You can still have her, and all of our powers, too. Cut her or bite her, or let me, and we will leave this place together."

Duncan shifted his weight, snatched Bela's sword off the ground, and gave the Rakshasa a come-here gesture with his fingers. "Try to touch her. Just try. I'm begging you."

"The power of your dinar has weakened since last we met." Strada came closer to him and stood about four feet away. "Is it failing as you turn?"

Duncan held Bela's sword and didn't let his expression change. He and John weren't projecting through the coin anymore, because if he used that kind of energy again, he'd go demon pretty much instantly.

But failing as he turned . . . ?

No *idea*, John told him. *If he comes any closer, kill him.*

"Thanks," Duncan muttered.

Sword through the heart, off with the head. He'd have to find a lighter and some wind—

The flash of red lights and the screech of tires sounded like cavalry horns to Duncan as a blue-and-white NYPD squad car spun to a stop at the mouth of the alley. Leather-clad Sibyls bailed out of it, limping and swearing and staggering. Camille had her big, honking sword drawn, and Dio's wind held Andy up, and Andy's dart gun had been mashed all to shit, but here they were.

"Get Bela—" Duncan started to say, but Strada lunged for him.

Duncan drove Bela's sword into the Rakshasa's blood-streaked chest.

Strada's paw swiped at the dinar, grabbed it, and twisted.

The sword pierced the demon's heart, but he yanked Duncan down as he fell, arms and legs and paws locked into position.

Duncan tried to move but couldn't. Not at all. The coin's energy wasn't his anymore, and it wasn't John's.

It belonged to the Rakshasa.

Duncan was just as immobile as Strada—and he was

choking. Spots danced in his eyes. His tongue seemed five sizes too big.

Strada's thoughts jammed through the dinar into his mind, and he heard them like a tiger's roar.

Welcome to death. It only makes you stronger.

(38)

Nightmares blended into dreams as healing water energy splashed through Bela.

"Come on, honey." Andy's voice. "I gotta get you out of here. If I let you go, I'm scared you're not gonna make it."

Andy's voice?

How could that be?

But it was Andy. Bela could feel her gentle touch and smell her crisp ocean scent. She sensed Andy crouched beside her, pouring power into every pounding, aching wound.

Then Dio's voice rang out, strong as the wind. "Camille! Get the demon!"

Bela's eyes flew open in time to see Strada choking Duncan with his own chain, and Camille sailing past her, *shamshir* already swinging toward the demon's head.

Camille brought her blade down, but elemental energy cracked, and the *shamshir* spun out of her grip as she stumbled to the side, fighting for balance.

Duncan's face got darker, and his eyes closed.

Camille spun toward them again, hesitated, then dropped to her knees beside Duncan and the Rakshasa. Tiny lasers of firelight broke across her fingers.

Bela tried to scream at her, tried to tell her not to do it, but she had no strength to make a sound. Dio did yell, as did Andy, but it was too late.

Camille grabbed the dinar with both hands.

Strada and Duncan and Camille jerked like they'd been hit by lightning.

"Do something!" Andy screeched at Dio, but Dio seemed

frozen in place ten feet from the now-glowing demon and Duncan and Camille.

A second later, they were all golden.

Energy spun around the three of them like a swirling sandstorm, natural and perverted, dark and light, and shades in between. For a moment, Bela thought she saw four people instead of three. She blinked against the glare, heart hammering, broken arm throbbing with each frantic beat. The air smelled like hot desert winds and fresh blood.

"Duncan." She tried to push herself toward him, but Andy held her down and kept up the flow of healing energy.

"Be still," Andy said. "I'll be damned if I'm losing more than one of you tonight."

Something like lightning did strike then, only it came from inside the golden storm, not the sky, and it didn't touch Bela at all.

Duncan fell toward the back alley wall and curled into a ball. Breathing. Bela made sure of that.

Camille still knelt beside Strada with the dinar in her hands.

Strada had the chain—but he had turned into a man again.

"Don't let him fool her," Bela whispered to Andy, desperate to be heard. "He'll kill her!"

Strada gazed up at Camille, reverent, disbelieving, like he was seeing his own personal deity in the flesh.

Camille stared down at him, apparently stunned.

Strada pulled the dinar out of Camille's hands, shook out the chain—then slipped the necklace over her head. The coin crackled and sparked, then settled against Camille's leathers like it had found a new home.

Andy's hands pressed harder into Bela's good arm. "Dio!" she yelled again, but Dio was in some other world, staring at the back of the alley.

Strada gently moved Camille away from him and got to

his feet, helping her up as he stood. Then he, too, stared at the back of the alley, to the tight, shaking heap that was Duncan.

"Can't hide, sinner," Strada said, then turned and rocketed out of the ally, leaving no trace of energy that Bela could see.

Camille started toward Duncan, but Dio's wind knocked her back before she could take a second step.

"Don't." Dio sounded like she had a knife in her chest. "He's—he's gone."

Gone? Bela shook her head, staring from Dio to Duncan. How? She'd just gotten him back! How could he be gone if she could see him moving?

Camille eased away from Dio, putting herself at an angle where she could cut off any approach to Bela and Andy. Her fingers rested on the dinar, like she was ready to fend off a Rakshasa.

Dio had her throwing knife in one hand and Camille's *shamshir* in the other, and she was crying.

Bela tried to pull away from Andy but failed. "What are you doing, Dio?"

"Hold her," Dio said to Andy, and Andy did.

"Dio, you leave him alone!" Bela managed the yell, but her voice cracked to pieces and she was sobbing before she finished.

Duncan got to his feet, and Bela knew a totally new pain, one that tore her insides so completely she didn't know how she'd ever piece herself together again.

Duncan wasn't a man anymore.

He had orange fur with black stripes, and fangs, and claws. Still the same beautiful eyes, but the gray glow had a demon fervor, and she sensed his lust to kill.

"Don't let her watch." Dio choked on her own words as she lifted her throwing knife.

Andy tried to block Bela's view with her hand. "Close your eyes, honey. Please."

"Leave him alone!" With a lunatic burst of strength, Bela shoved Andy away from her and tried to stand, but couldn't.

Duncan turned toward her, and the feral look in his eyes went soft. Almost sad. He made a rumbling sound in his tiger's throat, and Bela could have sworn he was trying to say her name.

Dio raised her throwing knife. Aimed.

And didn't throw it.

All Bela could do was cry, and look at him, and want to see something different.

Duncan let out a strangled roar, then took off out of the alley.

"Ah, damnit!" Dio started after him. "Damn me!"

Andy ran toward her, but Camille powered forward and leaped in front of both of them.

The fire that exploded from her hands and arms and head, from her entire being, made an inferno that completely sealed the exit to the alley. Roaring curtains of flame shot over the tops of the alley walls, and sparks rained around her like a fountain made of orange, sparkling lights. The dinar on her chest glowed a violent white-yellow as it channeled her pyrosentience.

"*Enough!*" The fire echo in Camille's voice made Andy and Dio slam their hands over their ears. "*We're going home now!*"

Bela stared at all that fire, so grateful to Camille that she wanted to kiss her. Her sobs alternated with bursts of laughter. It would take all of her earth energy, all of Dio's wind power, and all of Andy's water to even make a dent in those flames. And he'd gotten away. Duncan was gone. Rakshasa. Demon. Lost to her—

But free, and alive, and that *did* matter, somewhere deep inside.

Dio raised both hands. She slowly sheathed her throwing knife, then carefully, very carefully, placed Camille's *shamshir* on the alley pavement in front of Camille. "I'm fine with going home," she said as she stood, tears still streaming down her pale face. "Really."

"Fuck me." Andy stared up at the flames for a few more seconds, then turned and limped toward Bela. "Give me a hand, Dio. We're out of here."

39

Bela stared out the window at the leaves of Central Park, studying the fall shades of yellow and red and orange, and thinking about Duncan. That was nothing new. She thought about him every day, and she had for three months. She rubbed her healed arm without much thought, not because it ached, but because it helped her remember.

Sometimes she thought she looked out the window so much because she hoped she'd see him, hidden away in those trees, looking back at her.

That wouldn't happen. And if it did, he'd probably be coming to kill her.

A ghostly blond shadow flickered past the glass, and Bela knew it was Dio, creeping down from her archives to go to the kitchen. She'd eat fast, then disappear upstairs again. The only time Bela ever saw her was on patrol, and then she didn't talk.

Andy and Camille had gone to Headcase Quarters to take the report for their next patrol, and with just Bela and Dio in the house, the silence could get maddening. It was time for that to end.

Bela broke away from her vigil, walked across their gorgeous new water-resistant tile floor, stationed herself outside the kitchen, and waited.

In a few minutes, Dio pushed through the swinging door, head down—and Bela caught her by the shoulders.

Dio yelped and let off a blast of wind as she looked up.

Bela deflected the wind and didn't hit back with her earth energy.

Dio tried to twist away, but Bela wouldn't turn her loose.

"We can't keep living in the same house without ever being in the same space except when we're on patrol."

Dio got a little paler, though Bela wasn't even sure how that could be possible. When she spoke, her voice sounded like Camille's used to, just a whisper, hardly enough to hear. "Do you want me to leave?"

The question made Bela's heart twist. "No. Of course I don't."

"That sounded definite." Dio seemed surprised but also relieved.

Bela risked letting her go but held her gaze. "I was never angry with you for going after Duncan. You've been angry with yourself. I'm just not completely sure why. Do you hate yourself for trying to kill him, or because you didn't?"

Tears welled in Dio's clear gray eyes, but she didn't answer.

"Don't keep shutting me out, Dio." Bela leaned toward her, just enough to invade her space on purpose. "I'll have to hug you and freak you out."

Dio looked briefly horrified, then sank down on the new leather sofa in front of the communications platform.

Bela took the leather chair across from her and let her have a moment.

A breeze drifted through the redecorated brownstone, carrying the scent of new furniture and grout, of paint and washed linens. To Bela, the whole place smelled like starting over—if Dio would let that happen.

"I let him down. I let you all down." Dio's eyes went to the ceiling, and the chimes tinkled softly from her distress. "He made me promise to do it because he said I was the hard-ass of this group, but in the end, I couldn't."

Bela had to close her eyes against the sweet quake of pain that created. When she thought she could speak without sobbing, she said, "That sounds like Duncan. And I'm not surprised you agreed to try."

Dio focused on Bela, really looked at her, maybe for the first time since Duncan had run out of the alley. "Why?"

"Because you're stronger than the rest of us." Bela rubbed her palm against the soft leather of the chair's arm. "I've always known that, and Duncan must have known it, too."

"I'm not. I—no, Bela." Dio shook her head. "I move the air around and draw pretty pictures, and sometimes I make thunder and lightning I'm not allowed to use. That's not strength."

Bela didn't argue with her. Truth never needed defending. In time, Dio would grasp the reality of her own nature, and Bela could wait for that.

Dio's eyes turned almost luminescent, from emotion and reflections of light and colors from the projective mirrors. "Do you hate me for trying to kill him?"

"For trying to protect me from my own heart? No. And I'll never hate you, for any reason." Bela scooted forward in her chair and squeezed Dio's hand. "We did our best that night. I made a terrible bunch of mistakes, leading you all into an elemental trap that got us blown up. When my senses were so numbed, I thought everyone was dead—it's a miracle everybody walked out of that rubble."

Dio captured her fingers, and her next question seemed infinitely harder to answer. "Are you going to make it, Bela?"

Bela's breath hitched. She tried to smile but didn't quite get there. "I'm trying" was the best she could do.

Chimes rang loud through the brownstone, pushed by a strong burst of outside energy.

Bad memories drove Bela to her feet, but not faster than Dio.

The front door banged open and Andy came in, jeans dripping on the easy-to-dry tile. Camille came next, her golden dinar glittering in the afternoon sunlight.

They stared at Dio and Bela, then both of them smiled

and walked over to the table. Camille sat in the chair next to Bela's, and Andy perched on the other end of the couch from Dio.

It seemed halfway normal, the four of them about to talk about the report, and Bela had five whole seconds of respite from her endless inner grief.

"Still no Rakshasa activity." Andy spread herself out on her favorite end of the couch and grabbed a towel off the stack Bela kept there for her. "They've pulled out of New York City, or hidden themselves so completely we can't find them."

"No luck on finding Samuel Griffen, or Rebecca Kincaid—or Walker Drake." Camille frowned. "Nick and Creed are fairly certain, based on bank transactions and phone records, that Rebecca hired the Rakshasa to take out Katrina and Jeremiah, and anybody else she thought might keep her away from Walker."

"She's sixteen." Dio let go an air-stirring breath. "What will we do with her if we catch her?"

"Hello?" Andy mopped her face with her towel. "This little girl hired her brother's coven and an army of demons to murder an entire family so she could have her boyfriend. I think we can file that under 'will be tried as an adult.'"

Camille fished a leather bag from her jeans pocket as she shook her head. "We may not get to take her to court. The way they disappeared, I'm not convinced that all of them are completely human."

"Rakshasa?" Bela was starting to wish she'd brought a notepad. She made a mental note to move a supply of pads and pens to the other end of the couch.

"Or something powerful enough to fool Rakshasa," Camille said, digging in the little bag.

Everyone shivered at that, Bela most of all.

"Is Jack Blackmore back yet?" she asked to change the subject.

"Still in Russia," Camille said. "Can you believe that? I figured Mother Yana would have fed him to the wolves."

Dio shrugged. "Maybe he's teachable."

"I sincerely doubt that." Andy threw her towel on the communications platform. "Let's see if he survives Mother-house Ireland."

Camille finished rooting in her bag and held her closed fist over the communications table. "Since we're all to-gether again—and all talking instead of avoiding each other—I have presents." She laid out six pieces of metal on the smooth wood, charms in the shape of crescent moons like their tattoos, each with its own delicate chain. "I fin-ished these last night. Pick the one that speaks to you."

Bela went straight for the copper moon and relished the pure, powerful feel of it when she slipped it into her fingers. She fastened the chain around her neck, and the special metal buzzed against her chest.

"Feel that?" Camille grinned. "It's keying to you. It'll work best for you now, always."

Dio's silver piece glittered at her throat, looking like it had always been there, and like it always should be. Andy had picked out a different shade of silver, darker, almost like iron, and it seemed perfect around her neck, too.

Camille scooped up the rest of the metal crescents and slid them back into her leather bag. "The rest I'm keeping for now. If other triads want to try them, they'll have to get an okay from the Motherhouses. I don't want an earful from Mother Keara about 'changin' the ahrder of the uni-verse' and shit."

Andy snickered.

Dio rubbed her chin like she was thinking. "Can you say *shit* with a Irish accent? 'Shite,' or something?"

Bela pressed her charm into her chest, drawing a taste of earth energy through it until her fingers tingled. With a sigh, she stared at the living room wall—and froze.

"Hey, guys. Check out the wall." She pointed. "Do any of you sense that energy?"

One at a time, Andy, Dio, and Camille used their charms, Camille's being the dinar, to sample the water, air, and fire energy coming from the next-door neighbor's house.

"Mrs. Knight." Andy said her name slow and drawn out, like an accusation. "I think we better go have a conversation with her, right now."

"I was wondering when you'd work it out." Mrs. Knight, who told them her first name was Karalynn, had a nice smile when she wasn't all lit up about something. "If we're good at anything, it's shielding. Have to be, or we wouldn't be alive—or in charge of our own lives."

They sat on the floor in Mrs. Knight's living room, which had no furniture at all.

"Who is *we*?" Bela asked, fascinated. "*What* is *we*? Yours isn't an energy we recognize. We never would have seen it if we didn't have some new technology that makes trace elemental energy more obvious."

Mrs. Knight pursed her lips, deepening the lines on her face. She pulled at the hem of her blue silk jogging pants and sighed. "Please understand. My hesitance isn't because I don't like Sibyls or don't think you do good work. It's because we're so vulnerable."

Bela didn't press, and neither did anyone else. Camille even looked a little guilty, since it had been her charms that led them over here.

Mrs. Knight seemed to come to some decision. She stopped fiddling with her clothes and met Bela's gaze. "We call ourselves Bengals."

"Bengals?" The word caught Bela off guard and tripped up her self-control. Her nails dug into the carpet, and the earth gave a slow, whispered rumble. "Tigers? Like Rak—"

"No!" Mrs. Knight's finger stabbed toward Bela's face,

her tone hard and emphatic. "Those bastards stole our lives from us. You have no idea what it takes to get away from them, to find a way to think and live and function again. We try to help each other, but anytime we reach out, we risk everything."

Bela slowly came undone, listening to that, trying to grasp it, to understand—and not run to a thousand desperate hopes that would break her heart and break it ten times again.

Camille placed her hand over Bela's and smiled at Mrs. Knight. "Please tell us exactly what Bengals are."

"Don't you know?" Mrs. Knight smiled—and she shifted.

To a thin, tall creature with orange-and-black-striped fur, fangs, and claws. The change was instant. One moment she was human, the next a tiger.

Bela fixed on the color of her fur, fighting back memories and three months of nightmares and standing at her front window, staring into Central Park.

"We call ourselves Bengals, because those of us who can think for ourselves always have this coloring."

Ah, Goddess, help me . . .

Mrs. Knight shifted back to her human form. "My family was attacked in Charleston, South Carolina. My husband died, and my son went mad and ran with the demons, then got killed by some of the other Created. They're bloodthirsty. They have no minds left. No souls."

Bela couldn't form a rational question, but Andy asked one for her. "Why do you still have your mind? What makes the difference?"

"We don't know, any of us." Mrs. Knight's pensive expression shifted toward sad. "Maybe it's a genetic thing, or a random but regular fluke."

"If you'll allow it, we could run tests to try to find out," Camille said. "Maybe even—"

"Find a cure?" Mrs. Knight sat back, stretching her arms out behind her. "I'm not sure I want that anymore—though

I'll let you do your medical tests. I just want peace, and I want to help others like me. I bring them in here and keep them long enough to set up shelter for them. And yes, I picked this place because you're next door. A lot of us are starting to do that. So, shake and burn and flood whatever you want. I have a feeling you'll prove useful to me sooner or later."

Bela couldn't take it anymore. The words burst out of her before she could do anything to stop herself. "Did he come here? After he turned? Did Duncan stay here with you?"

"If he did, I wouldn't tell you." Mrs. Knight's face suddenly reminded Bela of one of the earth Sibyl Mothers. "Our secrecy is absolute. I'll reveal myself, but I'll die before I out another Bengal."

"Please." The plea came from Dio, and she sounded so miserable that Mrs. Knight softened a little.

"Another group of Bengals reached out to your Duncan—and that's all I know," she said. "He could have gone anywhere, and he may never come back here. Sometimes it takes years to regain enough self-control to risk seeing people from your past. For some, it's never possible."

Dio reached for Bela and gave her knee a squeeze.

Bela had a vague awareness of Andy and Camille offering her smiles, gentle touches. Encouragement? Support?

She had no idea. She couldn't process a single word.

Mrs. Knight went on for a minute or two about how Bengals usually stayed in other cities from where they changed, to cut ties and make fresh starts away from prying eyes and lives they could never have back again. Bela tried to keep listening, but she couldn't do it. Some time later, she realized everyone was still talking, but she couldn't hear them anymore, and she couldn't stay in the room anymore, and she couldn't even stay inside without her head exploding. She did her best to make some polite excuse, but she had no clue what she said before she got up and slipped out Mrs. Knight's front door.

Outdoors.

Thank the universe. She could breathe.

The night air stung her nose, but it didn't clear her thoughts. She needed earth, and more of it than she could touch through asphalt.

Bela ran across Fifth Avenue without waiting for the light, and she kept running, into Central Park and off the sidewalks, until she could feel grass and dirt and take off her shoes and dig her toes deep, deep, and try not to burst out of her own skin.

Time got away from her again, and she didn't know how long she had been standing there when Camille, Dio, and Andy arrived. They were wearing their leathers and weapons, and carrying hers, which they placed on the ground at her feet.

"Get changed," Dio told her, "and let's do this."

Bela searched each face, Dio's, Camille's, and especially Andy's, and she saw the same resolve. They meant to do this, and once and for all bring her—and maybe all of them—some peace.

She stripped out of her street clothes and stepped into her leathers, then belted on her sword and put her shoes back on her feet. The copper charm at her throat tingled against her skin when she touched it, pressing it close. Then she released it and took Andy's hand. Dio took her other hand, and Camille joined them in a circle.

"You start," she told Bela. "It's your hunt, and you know what you're looking for. We'll help you find it."

Bela's heart beat so hard she couldn't hear herself think, so she stopped trying and reached for her power instead. Down, into the earth, into what made sense, and what always waited to whisper its secrets to her. She touched it, found the energy, and opened herself to it completely.

The earth roared into her and burst outward, showing

her energy, showing her New York City and Central Park in ways she'd never seen them before. Heartbeats and breathing, heat and light—so much activity, everywhere! Traces of every type of life. She moved her awareness outward in all directions, until she came to Mrs. Knight's brownstone.

Yes. That was it. The new energy signature she had picked up through the walls, a muted gold, just a wisp of energy, brighter in some places, darker in others.

Bengal.

Fire energy laced into Bela's earth power, and Bela formed an image of Duncan in her mind, as a man and as a tiger. For the first time, it didn't shred her soul to think about him like that.

Bengal.

Duncan as a tiger, as a man, as both.

Bela took her awareness back to their own brownstone and sorted through old and new energy traces until she found his. It was strongest in her bedroom, and when she touched it, she had no doubt it was Duncan's energy.

Air power added fuel to her senses, and she held both the Bengal trace and Duncan's earth "scent" in her mind as she moved back to Central Park, to her quad.

Sweet Goddess! There had to be a thousand golden filaments of energy, obvious to her now, crisscrossing every field and byway, many of them heading to or from Mrs. Knight's brownstone.

But of course there were.

Mrs. Knight's place functioned as a way station, a stop on an underground circuit that ferried Bengals into hiding.

Bela moved through the park in various places, sampling the strands of energy one at a time, finding nothing that set any of them apart from the next one.

Water energy spilled into her terrasentient power for the first time, and Bela almost let go of Andy's hand to slow the influx of awareness. Her brain seemed to widen in her head, and for a few painful seconds Bela felt like she could track anything and everything on the face of the planet.

Have to focus.

I'm a mortar. I can do this. I can take in whatever my quad has to offer, and I can hold it all.

She forced the image of a stone bowl into her mind, the bowl she had spent so many hours holding at Motherhouse Russia, when she learned to meditate.

I'm the mortar. I can hold it. I'm the mortar. . . .

At the park wall, very near the exit closest to their brownstone, Bela saw the thin golden strand she sought. The one that smelled like Duncan, and tasted like him, and smelled like him when she let her awareness sink through it.

He'd been in the park. He'd been near her home, maybe looking at her even as she searched for him—and he'd been there many times.

Bela's heart flooded with emotions, too many to name, and too much to process while still keeping her focus, so she pushed it out of the bowl.

I'm the mortar.

She picked up the brightest strand, followed it across the earth, into the city—

Somewhere around Broadway and Amsterdam, she ran into two giant glowing golden blobs of energy that could only be Nick and Creed Lowell.

And with them—

Bela's eyes came open, and the power of all the elements charged through her, echoing in one word so loud even the trees in Central Park leaned away from her voice.

"Duncan!"

40

"Strada's been here." Duncan sniffed at the alley wall, using his tiger nose and tiger senses, but keeping his human form. "It's recent, but it's weird."

"How so?" Creed examined the spot in his Curson form, so his own elemental instincts would be enhanced, then swapped back to his human form.

"It's the smell." Duncan took another whiff. "We have good samples from the warehouse ruins of him and his two brothers. This is definitely Strada—but it's also . . . not Strada."

Nick Lowell's big Curson hand chipped off a piece of the brick into an evidence bag. "What else do you smell?"

"Don't know, but it's familiar." Duncan thought about the golden circle of power Camille Fitzgerald had created three months ago, to save his life. All that energy moving between his body, his mind, his dinar, Camille, and Strada—but just for a moment, Duncan had thought there had been a fourth person in that circle.

John Cole.

He'd had a face, a shape, an energy signature—and a scent. This scent.

John?

Duncan had assumed that John's spirit had moved on, crossed over, or whatever ghosts did when they got set free—but then, after the golden circle, when Strada was standing there in the form of a human man, he'd said something he couldn't have known to say. He'd come up with something that John Cole would have jabbed Duncan with at exactly that moment.

Can't hide, sinner.

Duncan was about to ask Nick and Creed to let him take another whiff of the tracking sample Nick was carrying when he sensed her.

Every muscle in his body tightened.

Bela.

She was coming like an earthquake, shaking the city behind her. She was coming like a woman who'd had her heart broken and intended to do a little breaking of her own. She was coming, mad enough to shatter stone, and the only thing he could feel was joy. Then grief. Then more joy.

Bela.

"We might have a problem," he said to Nick and Creed, but they felt her before he finished his sentence.

Nick shifted to full Curson and with complete demon resonance growled, "Fuck."

"We don't want to get in the middle of this, Sharp." Creed started his shift. "We won't let her kill you, but—"

"Don't you touch her," Duncan snarled. "If she wants to kill me, then I'm just a dead Bengal. All I want from you is a promise that you won't let me hurt her."

"That won't happen." Creed took his demon form—and just in time.

The alley walls rattled.

Bits of brick and dust and mortar rained like gunfire on the fire escapes and dumpsters. A howling windstorm moved into the space, pitching Nick and Creed away from Duncan. A bomb blast of fire drove them toward the far alley wall, and a roaring, snarling tidal wave of puddle water and sewage splattered them against the bricks.

Duncan saw her standing at the mouth of the alley, an angry goddess in leather, with three more standing behind her, ready for battle.

Wound one, wound them all. It was always that way with women, and a hundred times more with Sibyls.

God, she was incredible.

Bela walked into the alley alone, her dark hair whipping in Dio's remnant breeze. All she had to do was look at Creed and Nick, and the big Cursons hulked off to a respectable distance, taking their sewer stink with them. One turned to guard the alley's other entrance, and the other kept an inconspicuous eye on Duncan.

"So beautiful," he said out loud when she came to a stop in front of him and crossed her arms over her leather-clad chest. Close. Close enough to touch.

Duncan fought to hold himself in human form as he stared at Bela. From the second he'd gained the barest control of himself, alone at the landfill where he'd hidden himself after he changed, he'd wanted to see her again, up close and in person. Just not yet. Not until he'd learned enough from Creed and Nick and had himself better managed.

"I know what you are now." Her dark eyes took him in, exploring him with no mercy at all. "I'm not afraid of you. I can take care of myself, Duncan."

"I've known that since I met you." He wanted to kiss her. He wanted to kiss her until he couldn't remember his own name.

She touched a pendant at her neck, a crescent moon that looked like it was made out of copper. "Camille made me my own charm, like the dinar she's wearing. It helps with terrasentience, and magnifies my other powers."

"I see that." He glanced at the debris in the alley, and deduced that her whole quad had charms like that now. *Look out, world.*

One corner of her mouth twitched. "Think you could take it off me?"

"I wouldn't try."

"Why, Duncan?" The question came out soft, and he knew she was asking why he'd kept himself hidden from her. "Why did you go to Creed and Nick instead of coming to me? I've stood by you since the moment I met you. I would have stood by you through every bit of this, too."

He closed his eyes, but there was no way to fend off the pain in her voice. He'd have done anything to soothe it, to make it go away. Anything short of injuring her in other ways. "Creed and Nick can teach me self-control. They know what it's like to be dangerous to people they care about—so I knew they'd keep my secret, even from their wives, until I was absolutely safe." He made himself look at Bela again, and withstand the wounded look on her face. "I can't take chances with you. I'm still in love with you, Angel. I'd die if I hurt you."

Bela seized his T-shirt in both fists and drove him back against the alley wall as she kissed him, her lips soft and warm and wet. The pulsing heat of her body and the almond-woman-musk smell of her made him want to roar. He grabbed hold of her and didn't want to let her go, ever.

Her nails dug into the sides of his face as she broke the kiss and pressed her forehead to his. "I love you. I'm not whole without you, and my family's not complete. Come home, Duncan. We're all safer together than apart."

Duncan's animal instincts tore through him, and before he could get a grip on himself, he spun her around, trapping her against the bricks. His kiss was too hard, too wild, but she took it, and she moaned, and she kissed him back, and when they finished, he had more fur than skin.

He held up one clawed paw for her wide, dark eyes to see. "I need you to give me time," he growled, trying to manage his voice, but nothing about Bela made him feel controlled. "I need you to believe that one day soon, I'll show up at your door, ready to do everything I can to make this work." He shoved his paw into the bricks beside her head and lowered his face to hers.

She closed her eyes.

"When I ask to come in, will you leave me out in the cold?"

Her eyes came open, and her lips found his. She bit him, then shoved him away from her with some of that new earth force her charm had given her. If he hadn't used his demon strength, he might have made a Duncan-sized hole in the alley wall.

When she walked up to him and rested her palm against his chest, right where John's coin used to be, what she said was, "I don't know, Duncan. You'll have to knock and find out."

Then she left without looking back, and that did break his heart.

Snow fell in Central Park, turning the whole park silent and white.

The brownstone glowed in the cold darkness, looking warmer than Duncan could imagine.

Was that Bela, standing in the window?

The thought of her made Duncan's heart surge.

God, he'd done this so often since he'd changed, stand here and wish for a glimpse of her. He had wanted to see her, hold her, touch her—he'd imagined every moment of it, over and over again. Hell, most nights he would have given up his still all-too-human soul just to hear her voice. Each time it had tortured him worse, but he'd made himself use that agony and go back to his training sessions with Creed and Nick, and with the other Bengals he'd met. He'd kept working until no amount of rage or pain or emotion could force him into his tiger form or make him lose control of the demon essence now mingled with his own.

But tonight . . .

Duncan shook his head. Closed his eyes. Tried to gather his nerve. Wondered where the hell it had gone, then found it again.

When he stepped out of Central Park and started across Fifth Avenue, he thought maybe he'd misplaced his mind, too, because for a minute he felt like he was walking in the desert again.

Or . . . out of it.

After all these years, maybe he was finally leaving his desert behind.

When Duncan climbed the steps to the brownstone, his chest felt so tight, he wasn't sure he could breathe.

In the window next door, the neighbor, Mrs. Knight, was watching him, but she just nodded and made a motion like, *Hurry up already, idiot. It's cold outside.*

Then she disappeared from view.

"Yeah," Duncan said to himself, wondering what the hell that was about before he went back to not breathing.

It was just a door. All he had to do was knock. Just knock.

And hope like hell she answered.

Then hope like hell she didn't shove him so hard he knocked down the wall in front of Central Park.

Duncan straightened himself into a semblance of military posture, lifted his hand, and knocked.

Before his knuckles could hit the wood a second time, the door opened, and she was there.

Bela was standing right in front of him.

Every animal part of Duncan screamed to break through his skin, but he held himself in check, and knew he could do it now. He knew he was ready.

But Bela—

She looked like a vision in her jeans and white sweater, with her dark hair spilling loose down her shoulders.

Duncan wanted to ask her—

Beg her—

John Cole was long gone from his head, but Duncan knew he was the captive spirit now, completely at the mercy of this woman he'd love for the rest of what would likely be an unnaturally long life.

He couldn't speak at all.

He had no words.

"You should know that the strangest Sibyl fighting group in New York City lives here," Bela said. "If you throw in with us, you may get way more trouble than you bargained for."

The vise around Duncan's throat loosened enough to let in a little air. "That's fine. I'm all about trouble. I can be trouble myself—so whatever you do, Angel, don't let me in."

Bela's smile started slow and small, but it spread to fill her whole face.

Duncan felt that smile in his chest and his heart, in his mind and his soul, and the gentled tiger in his mind let out a roar of untamed joy.

Then Bela stepped aside to let him in, and she was already kissing him before he could get the door closed.

❨ acknowledgments ❩

As always, my thanks go first to my readers. I hope you enjoyed Bela's tale as much as I enjoyed writing it. Bela and her entire fighting group call to me in special ways, and I intend for their stories to rock their world—and yours.

Thanks, Chey, for not letting my opening get off track, and for always thinking I can do it. Thanks to my family, for letting me vanish and get this written. And to the people I work with—*now* do you believe I'm not just working there to research a book? I put it in the dedication and everything!

To my editor, Kate Collins, thank you very much for being patient. I've never tried to write a book during a natural disaster before, and if you'd been irritable, I think my hair would have fallen out somewhere between the five-degree temps, endless carbon monoxide alarms, and the month with no power. Kelli, thank you for paying attention to all the tiny details and making sure everything gets where it's supposed to go.

And Nancy—you're in Italy right now, so I hate you. No, seriously. More chocolate. More chocolate!

Read on for an excerpt from
CAPTIVE SOUL
by Anna Windsor

Whatever was following Camille, she didn't think it was happy. Sibyls could sense states and traits, and fire Sibyls were particularly adept at judging emotional energy. The strange part was, she didn't pick up much negative feeling from the thing. It seemed . . . intent. Almost overly focused on its mission—which appeared to be following her.

Well, that's nothing new in my life, is it?

Camille had spent more hours than she cared to count sneaking through Motherhouse Ireland to dodge other adepts hunting for her, or hiding out in one of the castle's hidden rooms to avoid angry Mothers who wanted to teach her a lesson. She could hold her own in any battle, but when everybody wanted to pick a fight at the same time, she had learned it was best to minimize opportunities.

Not exactly what she was doing now, out alone in Central Park, almost daring something to give her grief.

Camille walked faster, purposeful, not panicked. She wasn't prey, so she didn't intend to look like prey. She tugged the zipper on her battle leathers as high as it would go. The bodysuit was designed and treated to deflect elemental energy, but it didn't shield her from a fresh round of shivers. She thought about pulling on the leather face mask she had stuffed in her pocket. Thought about it, but didn't do it. The stupid thing made her feel like she was suffocating.

Camille's fingers flexed. The worn ivory hilt of her Indian *shamshir* felt cool as she brushed her palm against it, though these days she usually called the weapon by its Americanized name—scimitar—because she heard that so often from her quad. Her mother had given her the weapon before she died, and she had taught Camille how to take a head with a single strike. Scimitars had a curved edge made for hacking, and Camille liked the fact that nobody expected a small woman to draw such a long, deadly blade, much less swing it like the Grim Reaper.

Everyone except her quad underestimated her strength—physical, emotional, and otherwise. Since she sucked at making fire, enemy misperceptions about her abilities were her greatest advantage in any type of fight.

Her heat rate picked up to a steady *beat-beat-beat*.

Would she be taking a head tonight?

Camille moved quietly around a copse of trees and bushes, letting the thing behind her gain a few steps. If this needed to come to blows, it was better that she pick the moment and the location. Yes. This little clearing would do. Shielded from view, plenty of moonlight, enough room to swing, but not enough room for too many surprises.

Her mouth felt dry when she tried to swallow. Her quad would be so pissed if she got herself beaten to death or eaten tonight. They'd have no idea why she was out without them, or what she was doing—or that she was doing it for them, to make up for that big mistake.

Let's get this over with.

As soon as Camille heard the rustle of brush near the clearing she had picked, she ripped her scimitar from its sheath, spun toward the noise, and pulled the blade back for a strike.

The thing in the bushes went totally still.

Camille blinked at the spot where all sound had stopped. She had expected the creature to run or fight, not just stand there and wait for her to hack it to death. What the hell was that about?

It occurred to her to kill the thing first and figure it out later, but what if this creature was friend, not foe? Just because something had powers didn't make it evil. Sibyls worked with all manner of supernatural practitioners, and even some kinds of man-made demons. Most natural demons—and the man-made kind, too—were nothing but soulless murderers. The Asmodai the crazy Legion cult used to create, for example.

Camille's insides clenched.

No.

Don't think about Asmodai.

Brainless elemental golems. Strong as hell, targeted on one victim, bent on killing no matter what got in their way.

She'd lost one of her first fighting group to an Asmodai. She would never forget its towering bulk, its blank, hateful face, or the fire pouring out of its mouth and nose and eyes.

Let it go. Now.

No time to dwell on Asmodai, because some demons were a lot more complex, and a lot more human. Cursons, half-breeds, with human mothers and human souls, were Sibyl allies now, and so were full-blooded Astaroth demons. Most of those had been human children when they got converted into demons, so they still had human intelligence and emotions. Hell, Cursons and Astaroths had even married Sibyls. And then there was Duncan Sharp, Bela's husband, a half-human, half-Rakshasa creature called a Bengal. Even their next-door neighbor Mrs. Knight was half demon, a Bengal like Duncan.

So maybe this thing in the bushes was more like Cursons and Astaroths and Bengals—something new to Sibyls and paranormal police officers of NYPD's Occult Crimes Unit, but friendly and a little shy. She still didn't sense any malice from it. It was hard to behead something that gave off the energy of a distracted kitten.

She could almost see it, a man-like outline in the deep shadows under the trees, but even her sensitive Sibyl vision couldn't make out details. Weird. Was it doing something to throw off her perceptions?

"Show yourself," she demanded. She didn't make any

threats, because Camille never made a threat she didn't plan to back up in full.

The thing refused to move, but its energy . . . it was—what? Amused?

That pissed her off enough to begin drawing fire power into her essence, intending to use her pyrosentient talents to send the energy back out, to channel it so she could use it to explore Tall, Dark, and Shady Silence over there.

"You're out past your bedtime, beautiful," the thing said to her in a startlingly human voice. "And that's one hell of a pocketknife."

Camille's grip on her scimitar loosened, and she almost dropped it.

My big mistake.

She needed to get hold of herself, but she barely managed a complete breath. It took all she had to keep hold of her blade. She knew she was overreacting, because if this was the Rakshasa she had been looking for, it would have attacked already.

This was something else. It had to be—but that voice. So raw and low.

So familiar and enticing.

She was losing it.

Even though she'd been searching night after night, she had to admit she'd never expected to actually find what she was looking for, much less have it find her and not try to tear her to pieces.

If it is him, he's a deadly demon, and I can't forget that no matter how many new tricks he's learned. Not this time.

But why would he play with her? Rakshasa weren't prone to dicking around. They killed. Then they ate what they killed. Pretty simple formula.

"Step out of the shadows and let me see you." Her voice still had some authority even though she felt like the tree leaves over her head were rustling through her chest and belly instead. Thank the Goddess for small favors, and for scimitars. One look and she'd know if this thing was her demon or something else entirely. "Come out now."

"No," it said, and its tone suggested it didn't think Camille could force the issue.

Moonlight spilled into the clearing. Camille knew she was lit up like a silvery neon sign, but the thing in the bushes stayed dark and inscrutable. The sense she had of it now wasn't demon at all. It was human. Completely.

Yet not.

The confusion that had gripped her a year ago, the same confusion that led her to make that big mistake, seized her again.

Kill it, she told herself. *Don't take a chance. Chop it into pieces, and if it turns out to be a good guy, apologize to its kin and make peace with them later.*

If it even had any kin.

"Who are you?" she whispered, and now her voice was shaking like the rest of her. She tightened her arms to make sure her weapon stayed in ready position. "What are you?"

The thing in the bushes didn't answer immediately, and the rush of emotion it put off went by too quickly to read.

Then the dinar resting against Camille's chest grew faintly warm.

"You know who I am," it said, and that intense voice curled across her body like she wasn't even wearing her battle leathers. She felt the sound *everywhere*.